PIRATES & PREJUDICE

PIRATES & PREJUDICE

A Clockwork Vampire #4

K.H. KOEHLER

The Monster Factory

Pirates & Prejudice

A Clockwork Vampire #4

K.H. Koehler

CONTENTS

I	2
II	18
III	30
IV	49
V	63
VI	73
VII	86
VIII	98
IX	112

CONTENTS

X	123
XI	134
XII	150
XIII	166
XIV	185
XV	197
XVI	210
XVII	223
XVIII	233
XIX	249
XX	262
XXI	275

XXII	286
XXIII	307
XXIV	317
XXV	335
XXVI	346
XXVII	358
XXVIII	372

ABOUT THE AUTHOR

Copyright © 2021 by K.H. Koehler

All rights reserved. No part of this publication may be reproduced, stored or transmitted in any form or by any means, electronic, mechanical, photocopying, recording, scanning, or otherwise without written permission from the publisher. It is illegal to copy this book, post it to a website, or distribute it by any other means without permission.

This novel is entirely a work of fiction. The names, characters and incidents portrayed in it are the work of the author's imagination. Any resemblance to actual persons, living or dead, events or localities is entirely coincidental.

Paperback ISBN: 979-8-8692-7382-6

Ebook ISBN: 979-8-8692-7383-3

Cover art and interior design by KH Koehler Design

https://khkoehler.net

No part of this book was created using artificial intelligence.

Her heart did whisper that he had done it for her.
— Jane Austen, *Pride and Prejudice*

| i |

The Abraxas, 0700 hours

"Sir, we are being hailed," the ensign announced.

The Chief Navigator of the *Abraxas*, a third-generation werewolf named Finley, stepped away from his station to approach the communications port. "All right, ensign. Let's see what we got."

The young ensign leaned back and adjusted the monitor so CN Finley could see the extremely problematic feed. Static-y snow practically obliterated the image of the incoming Hummingbird, the light, ship-to-ground transport favored by gyros all over the world—those giant floating mini-worlds generally utilized by the vamps because they could rotate against the rising sun. Finley hoped they weren't about to take on shady foreign vamps. This gyro had more than enough of its own.

However, when he adjusted the magnification on his goggles, Finley saw it was sleeker and more elongated than the Hummingbirds he was familiar with.

"Sir?" said the ensign, but Finley barely heard him.

He was glaring at the indecipherable symbols on the sides of the vessel, trying to place its Court, but he didn't recognize the markings.

"Sir, the craft is still hailing us."

Finley turned to Henderson. "I see that, ensign. Keep your skin on."

The ensign, a young man named Mack—short for Macintyre, if Finley wasn't mistaken—grunted in response. It was one of Finley's popular jokes. Even though they weren't part of the same pack—or, indeed, the same species (Mack being a wereleopard and Finley belonging to the Silver Crescent Pack of werewolves)—Finley thought it was both funny and apropos. His own mom used to say it: *Keep your skin on, Martin. Dinna's comin'.*

Martin Finley enjoyed taking a casual approach to leading his men. He liked to think they were more than merely the crew that kept Lord Emmerdale's gyro suspended in the atmosphere above Earth; the ten crewmembers on the navigational deck were also a family of sorts, all of them having some sort of military background.

Despite a nibble of concern, he kept a quirky smile on his lips. Finley's easygoing nature had served him well in the trenches of Kyiv during the Russian Invasion, and now that he was enjoying his retirement, he liked to believe it made him something of a father figure to his ensigns—those brave men and women serving under him. Leaning over Mack's shoulder, he pressed the communications button and spoke into the speaker in a strong but friendly voice, "Attention, friend. We see you. But as you probably already know, we cannot allow docking measures to commence without a show of identity and a boarding pass..."

Finley's voice slowly trailed off when he realized what was happening. Mack saw it, too, and so did every other crewmember who was a shapeshifter or other type of Supe and had enhanced vision. The wave effect in the atmosphere and then the brightness as the bogie Hummingbird fired upon them.

Mack swallowed so hard his throat clicked. "Ch-chief...what in the hell's name is th—?"

He never finished his sentence as the *Abraxas* was hit so hard with an unidentifiable warhead that it ripped a sizeable hole in the side of the ship. That, in turn, generated a vacuum so powerful that most of the crew were ripped in half as they were suctioned out through the virtually indestructible glass viewing screen and into the upper atmosphere. Finley grabbed Mack's hand as he was torn away. But, microseconds later, he realized all he held was the man's arm, ragged and bloodily wrenched from the shoulder socket.

Quickly releasing the grotesque appendage, Finley tried to howl out a warning, but only a belch of blood filled his mouth as all of the fluids in his body were extracted by the atmospheric vacuum. After that, he then felt a dull, almost unimportant tugging sensation and dared to look down. His upper half was flying through the air, a whirl of wind and clouds and viscera all around him. It was creating a strangely fascinating pink storm that almost obstructed his vision as he and his men were blown out into a massive freefall.

Thankfully, most of him burned up long before he hit the ground.

***

The Queen's Gambit, one week later

Edwin McGillicuddy grimaced at the grotesque sight unfolding before him. "Did a bloody massacre take place here?"

The banquet hall had been done up in shades of pink and glaring fuchsia décor, with pink and white lilies as centerpieces, white and red balloons, hot-pink tablecloths on all of the banquet tables, and an unholy glitter-beaded white curtain that ran the whole length of the back wall. Someone had even affixed pink carnations to the glitter wall like a spotted pox. The room looked like an ill-conceived prom concept, and it was definitely *not* what he ordered when he commissioned the event.

He turned to glare at the event planner, a small, thin, nervous-looking human chap, and said, "What in the actual fark?"

The man swallowed nervously at Edwin's reaction. "My Lord...I apologize! We couldn't order the sunflowers you requested...something about a shortage."

"Right. That's fine. But how did you go from sunflowers to *this?*" With a sweep of his arm, Edwin indicated the huge, pink travesty of the room. The more he looked at it, the worse it got.

Another swallow by the event planner. "Since we couldn't order up what you requested, my staff and I...well, we began to improvise, and then..."

Edwin glared contemptuously at the man. Most of these types of companies were accustomed to dealing with Vampire Lords with short tempers and hungry appetites. His lot loved to throw fetes, but they also enjoyed tearing their caterers apart if things were not to their taste, and though he would never go that far—Eliza, after all, would annihilate him—he was endeavoring to emulate that type of Vampire Lord. It was all part of the Plan, as Eliza called it.

Edwin cut him off with a swipe of his hand. "Redo it. All of it. I want yellow, not pink. And get rid of that bloody beaded wall. Do you understand?"

The man shuddered, and Edwin could almost see what he was thinking. He did not sign up for this job to cater a fete being thrown by the Devil McGillicuddy (as the other Courts called him) and once he got back to his home office, heads would roll. "I think I...I can get some yellow roses. Do you like yellow roses, sir?"

"Aye. That's fine. Anything but this wreck. Now remove yourself from my sight."

"It will be done, sir!" Turning, the caterer darted off.

Edwin turned back to the room. He was more sad than angry. It was ugly and most certainly *not* Eliza. It did not reflect what he wanted for her secret birthday fete. However, he knew from experience (and their near decade of marriage) that Eliza did not sweat the small details. If he had invited her up to the ballroom right now, she would just smile at this horror and tell him it was lovely and perfect. Eliza was infuriatingly easy to please.

But there were two issues with that. Number one, he had a reputation to uphold. He had to be a little cruel because it was what his Congress expected of their Lord. Anything else and they might mutiny. Or worse, challenge his rule—and he did not want more blood on his hands than he already had. And, number two (and more importantly), he did not want Eliza "settling." She deserved what she wanted. What she loved. God knew she'd earned it after the various levels of hell on Earth she had been through.

Edwin pressed his hands together, wondering if it was enough. If what he did would *ever* be enough...

"You're fretting," came a mechanized voice from behind him. "I can tell."

Edwin did not turn to face the creature approaching him, but the little hairs still stood up on the back of his neck as his new Enforcer approached. Tommy Quinn, in his altered form, stood almost eight feet tall, weighed half a ton, and made the floor faintly vibrate wherever he went. Everyone on board the *Queen's Gambit* was just a little bit wary of the man—if one could call him that.

"We have no bloodlink. Don't be daft, mate," Edwin told the man.

Tommy clanked to a halt beside him. "Nothing so supernatural. You have tells, vampire. *Human* ones."

"Ah." Edwin stopped squeezing his hands together. Glancing over, he noted that Tommy looked sad and contemplative. He usually did anyway, but it seemed especially profound today. Perhaps something—maybe even this party—had set him off. He wouldn't know, of course. Tommy was a very private man even for being his current Enforcer, and, unlike his past relationship with Cesar, his former Enforcer, Edwin did not have that level of intimacy. They were only mates...and maybe not even that. He didn't know how Tommy felt about him, frankly.

When they first met, Edwin was the green new Lord of the *Queen's Gambit*—formerly the *Marie Antoinette*—and Tommy was little more than a wild animal locked in a cage. Back then, he was a ghoul who couldn't be trusted not to attack anything that moved. That first year was the hardest for him. During that time, Edwin tried to salvage what he could of what made Tommy who he was. Cesar's short-sided efforts to make the man his Heir had transformed him into a mindless eating machine, and, truthfully, Edwin had never heard of a ghoul recovering. Every specialist he consulted told him it was hopeless, that the humane thing was to send Tommy to his well-earned rest.

But Edwin hated the idea of giving up on him—on anybody, really—so he persevered, talking to Tommy every single day and feeding the creature synthetic blood until he recognized a spark of something that had once been human. Or at least aware. It took a whole year before Tommy could speak a few halting words, and another before he could be trusted to be let out of his cage for a short period of interaction (always chaperoned). They began to make progress, but by that time, the inevitable had begun, and decay had started to eat through Tommy's barely functional body.

"I don't know anymore," Edwin said in defeat one day while he was in private conversation with Eliza. "Maybe I should end him? Maybe all of this was a mistake?"

"Do you believe that?" Eliza asked, lying in bed beside him in her quarters.

He clenched her hand. "I just don't know, lovey."

Eliza thought about that for a full minute before nodding. "I've read about a doctor from Tsing Hua University, a flesh mechanic who has done extensive body modifications on soldiers wounded in battle." She looked at him in the way she had that said she knew exactly what she was talking about. "Perhaps we need to approach Tommy the same way we would a wounded soldier. As a high-ranking Lord, head of the first Congress in five hundred years, you could invite her aboard. I doubt she'd pass up the opportunity."

Edwin dutifully looked the good doctor up—Dr. Veronica Vu—and invited her aboard the *Queen's Gambit* to examine Tommy and offer her evaluation. Surprisingly, her diagnosis was more optimistic than he'd expected. Dr. Vu was just as knowledgeable and progressive as Eliza said, and she announced that she was willing to try to replace the parts of Tommy that had degraded, but during the first operation, she quickly discovered the extent of his condition and decided not to proceed. She said it was a case of "chasing the problem around" (her exact words). It would do them no good to replace an arm or leg when Tommy was doomed to continue to decay in other places. In her opinion, he needed a full-body transplant.

That worried Edwin. He wondered if he could trust her, or if the good doctor simply wanted to play Frankenstein. But after talking to Eliza about it, he decided that Vu was likely the only one in the whole world with a handle on Tommy's condition. Maybe he should trust her. In the end, he told her to proceed.

Most of Tommy had become what Vu called "hospital garbage." His injuries, his half-turned state, and the cancer he had been battling prior to meeting Cesar had taken their toll. She decided his brain and cerebro spinal nervous system—what she appropriately called "the tree of life," because that was what it resembled—were the only things worth saving. They were the only things that made Tommy who he was.

It took days, but she successfully transplanted his brain and nervous system into what she called a "Colossus," a large, solid mechanical man of her own design that she had been perfecting for years. It took multiple surgeries and months of recover, but at the end of it, she had successfully connected every nerve to every sensor in the Colossus's body so Tommy had full control of his new form.

Edwin had no idea how Tommy would feel about what had been done to him once he regained consciousness. He expected the man—a man he barely knew, if he was being honest—to rage at the long laundry lists of insults committed against his person. But he was strangely taciturn on awakening. Perhaps he thought he was in hell—or Purgatory, at least—but Edwin couldn't know because Tommy rarely spoke.

Tommy's Colossus body made him look like a metal titan. His head was oval and only vaguely man-shaped, with two lighted slits for eyes and a crude cutout for a mouth. No eyebrows or hair, and only the impression of a nose. His hands were large, his fingers well-formed and capable of almost everything a human was. It wasn't long before Tommy requested clothes to cover his metal body—a large, draping cowl that covered everything but his long, incredibly capable arms and his head.

Edwin, already feeling guilty about Tommy's lot in life, indulged him. He was willing to give Tommy anything he asked, but Tommy didn't request more than that. He seemed resigned to his fate as this metal creature with the brain and central nervous system of a man—a former FBI agent who had dedicated most of his life to protecting humans until it was snuffed out by none other than Lord Foxley.

"There must be something I can do for you, mate," Edwin insisted one day. He was almost to the point of pleading. There had to be some way to make Tommy's life easier.

Tommy seemed to sense this and thought about that long and hard before answering. "I would like some form of employment, sir. I would like to apply as your Enforcer."

By that time, Edwin had been without an Enforcer for years and had practically given up on ever finding someone to replace Cesar, whom Foxley had tricked into a contract for two hundred years of service. Edwin had interviewed for the position, but the only ones who applied were Supes he didn't know who had shady histories. The shady part didn't bother him—he was pretty shady himself—but an Enforcer was someone a Lord had to trust to have their back in a firefight when the chips were down. Not one candidate was someone Edwin trusted.

Edwin, intrigued, asked, "What qualifies you for the position, mate?"

"When I was alive, I was a law officer with the DEA for years. I have the training to take care of my superior. I certainly have the physical power now." Tommy clenched the fingers of his huge hands to prove it.

"But Enforcers usually have a relationship with their Vampire Lords. They're normally intimate."

Tommy nodded in acknowledgment. "True. Still...I thought you were far from a traditionalist, Lord Edwin. Does it matter if we have no romantic entanglement?" Tommy sounded sincere and met Edwin's eyes evenly. "You need someone to have your back. I don't care if I live or die, so if I die performing that service, we both win."

It was a grim way to approach the position, but Edwin could appreciate Tommy's honesty and practicality. His logic echoed Edwin's own chaotic nature, and he felt they might work well together. On impulse, Edwin said, "Fine. You're hired, mate. You begin tomorrow."

That was four years ago. And, since then, Tommy had proven to be worth his weight in gold, which was considerable! No one within or without Edwin's Congress had even breathed a challenge his way. They were too afraid of what Tommy was capable of.

"Eliza's birthday celebration is not going to plan," Edwin pointed out with a sigh, pointing to the hideous decor. "I mean, the whole situation is cocked up to start with. I'm throwing a birthday fete in my wife's honor, and I can't even acknowledge her or make her the guest of honor, but still..."

It was all so bloody depressing, and not for the first time, Edwin cursed his fate. This ship. This Congress. All of the things that had come to him were like gifts he hadn't asked for. He'd only ever wanted *Eliza*...

Tommy swiveled his head at different angles to take in the room. "Nothing ever goes off without a hitch, my Lord. By now, you should be used to that. However...Lady Eliza will appreciate the work you've put into this." His eyes zeroed in on the lilies floating in glass tureens. "The flowers are very pretty."

"Do you know where she is at present? I've been trying to keep her away from this part of the ship all day. I think she suspects, though. She always knows when I'm up to something." He had started fiddling with his hands again and shoved them deep into his jacket pockets.

It took Tommy a moment to respond. But when he did, he said, "Chrysanthemums."

"Steady on?" Sometimes, Edwin suspected that things didn't quite add up in Tommy's brain pan.

After a second, Tommy sort of shook himself like a giant Etch A Sketch, then glanced back over. "I believe she is with Dr. Vu. They are actively working on your little issue." Tommy tapped his breastplate with one finger to emphasize his point, though this body was almost entirely empty of organs.

He absently touched his clockwork heart, the device that kept him alive and functional, and that, in turn, reminded me to glance at his pocket watch. Bloody hell! It was almost four o'clock!

Turning to Tommy, Edwin patted his metal shoulder. "Take care of the decor issue, willya, mate? I need to pick my son up from school!"

***

The *Queen's Gambit*—formerly the *Marie Antoinette*—was by no means the largest gyro in the world. Comparatively, it was a compact ship with limited staff and no real commerce to speak of, unlike other gyros, who often hosted corporations, news and television studios, restaurant chains, vacation resorts, and other high cash-flow businesses. The former (and now deceased) owner of the ship, Lord Summersfield, had designed it to be what the other Courts called a "Black Box." Only a limited number of people were allowed on and off the ship, and only important staff, crew, and, of course, the members of the Congress, actually lived aboard her.

Edwin, as the *Gambit's* new Lord, had kept that tradition alive. Not to honor the wanker he had helped to kill, but only because it was safer for Eliza. And for their son, Oliver.

The gyro didn't have buildings, streets, and grand miniature cities the way the larger ones did. It did have a hundred floors going from top to bottom, with each one serving the needs of the crew and staff in some way, and all of them connected via lifts that could go up, down, or in almost any other direction. There were living quarters, work offices, a gigantic mess hall and cafeteria, several floors dedicated to schools and workshops, the navigational and engineering decks, an entertainment level, and, near the bottom, the science and computer labs. In a way, it was a bit like a city, only layered on top of one another like a birthday cake.

Standing in the white-walled, antiseptic science lab, Eliza leaned down and looked into the electron microscope. The artificial cells in the Petri dish, color-coded blue to show they were active, injectable microcomputers, were rapidly dividing and overwhelming the organic vampire ones, which were dyed red. The resulting purple collective was fascinating to watch for the time it lasted—approximately two and a half minutes. Then the red cells began to rapidly reproduce as if they were fighting a war and swarmed everything in the dish.

She tried not to let it depress her. Failure was part of progress. "They're lasting longer now," she told Dr. Vu.

"By ten seconds. That isn't much."

Straightening up, Eliza gave the doctor a sympathetic smile. "Ten minutes longer than last time. That's terrific progress!"

Dr. Vu sighed. She was a small woman of Asian heritage, barely larger than a child, and her intellect was staggering. But what made Vu truly stand out was her vision and creativity. She had single-handedly created programmable microcomputers that could be injected into the bloodstream and told to do virtually any task. They didn't always succeed, and then sometimes they did but the results didn't last (as in this case), but in only four years, she had trained the computers to remain alive in vampire blood for a whole two and a half minutes—no small feat, seeing how vampire cells were themselves extremely *vampiric*. They seemed to have a mind all their own and a will that could not be bent, never mind broken. Yet.

Eliza was strictly a layperson where this science was concerned. Still, she found it fascinating. And its future applications made this work worth their time. Still, she could see the toll the seemingly countless failures had taken on the woman.

Reaching out, Eliza rubbed her friend's shoulder. "You'll do it! These vampire cells aren't invincible."

"I'm not so sure about that." Vu indicated the collection of test tubes in the racks before her. "Despite studying vamps for thousands of years, we humans don't actually understand how they work. How they are alive after their own deaths. Even after all of this research, I can't make heads or tails of what makes Lord Edwin tick...no pun intended."

Eliza smiled despite the worry nibbling at the edges of her confidence in their work. When they first undertook this little experiment, she was sure Dr. Vu would quickly come up with a solution for her own little problem—her latent vampirism. Dr. Vu had literally built Tommy from the ground up! But as things turned out, she (whatever she technically was) wasn't something the flesh mechanic could figure out so easily. Not that anyone could. Because what Dr. Vu said was true; no one truly understood how vampires worked. It was likely something as much alchemical as biomechanical that kept vampires alive. They, as puny humans, just hadn't figured out what that was yet.

Eliza glanced again into the microscope. The cells were now all angry red as the vampire blood swarmed and transformed the microcomputers, obliterating them and their programming. Vampirism had won once again.

Eight years ago, Summersfield made her his Heir against her will. He had forced her transformation into a vampire. But, somehow, her body had rejected the vampire virus. Dr. Vu—indeed, no doctor—could explain how or why. Perhaps it was because she was pregnant with Ollie at the time. Perhaps her body had insulted itself against the threat of vampirism for no other reason than because an unalive person cannot carry a child to term, and her body was so determined to give life to Ollie that it caused her human DNA to swarm her vampire DNA and put it to sleep.

But Eliza was no fool. Just because her condition was in remission didn't mean it was gone. She had to work at not fretting over that too much. Long ago, she'd accepted Edwin's proposal to be Bride, his eventual Heir, and she would have been at peace with such a transformation, but the idea of being a part of Summersfield, the creature that had terrorized her for years and murdered and raped countless Poppets, frightened her to her core.

To be a part of his legacy...to be like him...no, she would sooner die.

"So, how have you been feeling?" Dr. Vu asked, rousing her from the waking nightmare that perpetually haunted the edges of her thoughts.

"I'm fine. I'm great." She adjusted the magnification on the microscope.

"Do you still see shadows?"

"Not anymore. I haven't seen any in months." There was no point in burdening Dr. Vu with her fears—or the way she occasionally saw a dark manlike form out of the corner of her eyes when no one was standing there. And she was, in fact, physically sound, at least according to her doctors. "You can check my stats, if you like."

Dr. Vu smiled. "That won't be necessary. I trust your assessment of yourself, Lady Eliza."

One of the most useful new inventions they had aboard the ship was NEWTON, a vast neural network that could be utilized either by tablet or thought alone via a chip implanted behind the ear. Through it, any member of Edwin's Congress could speak to each other, draw up figures or stats, or accomplish virtually any other task that required instant communication. And NEWTON was incredibly intuitive. For instance, a virtual alarm she had set for late in the afternoon now told her:

—Lady Eliza, it is now 3:45 in the afternoon. School will be finished in approximately fifteen minutes. Shall I contact Lord Edwin?—

—Thank you, NEWTON. That won't be necessary. I will let him know. —

—Yes, my Lady. — NEWTON politely acquiesced.

She started mind-texting Edwin about the time when he interrupted her thoughts.

—At the school now, love. All taken care of. —

She let out a pleased sigh. —Thanks, husband. I would have handled it, if you're busy… —

Edwin harrumphed. —I'm never busy for Ollie! —

Even though he had a full schedule as the sitting Lord of the *Queen's Gambit*, Edwin always took the time to take Ollie out at least several times a week. Sometimes, they went to the manmade park in the center of the ship, to the matinee to see the classic gangster movies that Edwin loved, the arcade where they took turns playing skee-ball, or they visited the tiny shops in the Bazaar that sold essentials to the crew. Edwin was an incredibly attentive father to their son. And since he was Lord, essentially captain and king of the ship, no one questioned why he should take such an interest in a small child.

She only wished they could do some outings together as a family, but they had to stick to the Plan.

—Since you have Ollie, I think I'll spend a bit more time in the science lab— she told him. —But tell Ollie he's welcome to come down when you guys are finished. I love you, husband. —

—You more, wife!—

He must have sensed a little regret in her mind text because he added, —And happy birthday! I'm looking forward to having you all to myself tonight! —

She laughed textually. —Is that before or after the surprise birthday party? —

—Erm...um...—

Suddenly, she felt bad. She had ruined his surprise for her.

—I'm kidding— she added. —I'm looking forward to just a quiet evening with you!—

He brightened considerably. —Tonight, I'm all yours! — And then he was gone.

Eliza turned to Dr. Vu. "That was a close one. I almost ruined Edwin's surprise. Shall we try another sample?" She indicated the collection of test tubes.

Dr. Vu smiled graciously. "I appreciate the offer of help, but you'll do no such thing tonight, Lady Eliza. Tonight, you'll go home for a nice nap, then prepare yourself for your little birthday dinner and leave the complicated matter for tomorrow!"

| ii |

Edwin had never attended a proper school, so he found it a singularly amazing experience to visit one now. It never got old. The smells of chalk and disinfectant, the siren song of the session bell, the slamming of doors, books stacked against lockers, and the screaming children racing up and down the hallways of the Learning Center (as Eliza had christened it). It was delightful!

He wasn't without an education, of course. In the early 1800s, he received a tutorage as part of Foxley's Inheritance. Foxley refused to have an unlearned Heir and Enforcer, and Edwin had been a surprisingly apt pupil who loved to read once he'd learned how. Still, Foxley had hired Oxford educators for private tutoring sessions. As a result, Edwin had never had this experience. He wondered what it would have been like to be born in the modern era, to have gone to school with his mates, to have had recess and lunch with them, and to sit in class listening to a lecture. He wondered if Ollie enjoyed it. He never talked very much about it to Edwin.

He sat in a chair in the hallway of the facility and watched the children come and go, most of them palling around with their mates. One even shushed by on his hoverboard, displacing papers lying in the hallway. The bell had already rung by the time Edwin arrived, but Ollie was still in class, taking an important end-of-the-semester final.

Most of the teachers noticed him right away and nodded as they passed. Some looked like they wanted to approach him—most likely to thank him for the thousandth time for establishing the center so the employees of the gyro had a place to educate their children instead of sending them to Earth to go to school, but, truthfully, none of this was his doing.

It was all Eliza. She hadn't liked the idea that their crew and staff lived most of the year on the gyro while their families were grounded and living apart. Hence, she'd had much of the ship renovated so the employees could live on board year-round and their children could go to school here. She believed families belonged together, and, so far, it had worked out splendidly.

Theirs was a small school full of a very mixed assortment of children—humans, shifters, and Fae—and they were of all ages and levels of education, much like how military base schools operated. The classes were small, and there were perhaps twenty educators in total, but they taught everything from math, history, and science, to shop, gymnastics, and even mechanics. In the evenings, the facility was turned over to the adult Poppets so they could grow their almost nonexistent education. Eliza hoped they could one day go off and be productive members of society on Earth as she had done—the Poppet Higher Learning Project, another pet project of Eliza's.

"Ah, Lord Edwin," said Ollie's teacher as she cut through the crowd of pushing, noisy youths. Ms. Stafford was a tall, leggy redhead, quite attractive and nothing like the nasty old kiddy diddlers that Edwin remembered from his private education. She was steering Ollie forward with a hand on his shoulder. "Sorry to keep you waiting."

"Quite all right." Edwin stood up and beamed a smile down on his son—though Ollie didn't know that, of course.

Ollie looked up at him, not smiling and standing at rigid attention like a little soldier. He had his dad's wintry complexion but his mother's curling black hair, bright eyes, and astute bearing. He didn't look much like Edwin at the moment, and for that, Edwin was grateful. His eyes, the same fierce sapphire as his mother's, were always moving, taking in the world in a way that made Edwin question what it was he was seeing. He wished they could have long, meaningful conversations, but Ollie had been non-verbal since the age of two. They had taught him to communicate in Sign, and he did so fluently. But, even so, he never seemed to have a lot to say.

"I wanted to show this to you personally," Ms. Stafford said, handing over a square metal box with hinges. "I'm hoping to speak to you or Ollie's mother in a private session sometimes."

That didn't sound good. Edwin took the box, looking at it nervously. "All good?"

"Very good!" Ms. Stafford smiled broadly. "Open the box."

Edwin did so, and some internal device inside projected a grainy, black-and-white image in the middle of the hallway. It looked like a pair of rabbits rooting around a collection of greenery that seemed to belong to the large, carefully cultivated park on the central floor of the gyro. The rabbits nibbled plants and jumped in and out of holes.

"Oliver made the device. Filmed the footage and turned it into a holographic display for his science project," Ms. Stafford proudly proclaimed. "We'll go into more details in private, but I would like to discuss putting your ward in our gifted students' program. I feel Ollie has unique talents that the world can benefit from."

Edwin was impressed. He'd known that Ollie was mechanically minded, not unlike his mother, but he'd had no idea he was so advanced. The device was crude, true, but Edwin certainly would not have known how to create something like this at his age—or any age. Ollie was turning into an artificer before their very eyes!

"That's ace. Good job, mate!" Edwin said and tried to give Ollie a high-five—more of a low-five, considering the boy was only eight and the top of his head barely reached Edwin's chin.

Ollie quickly signed, No one does that anymore!

"Well, excuse me for being ancient," Edwin quipped.

Ms. Stafford laughed nervously. She, like almost every other member of his Congress, didn't know that Ollie was his biological son. Everyone thought this was just an eccentricity on the part of their Lord and not an unusual one. Most Lord would have naturally taken an interest in the strange little boy who was the son of one of their Poppets. Probably not a few worried that Edwin was grooming the child to be his future Heir. But since Ollie was Eliza's son, and Eliza was Edwin's Poppet—in name, anyway—Ollie wasn't technically human under the civil liberty laws of the United States. Truthfully, no one could do anything to intervene in the situation even if they wanted to. Ollie was, in the eyes of the law anyway, one of Edwin's Poppets, his property. He could do what he wanted with the boy.

"I guess I'll let you two get on now!" He could feel Ms. Stafford's concern for his son—the worry that Edwin was up to no good. But that, too, worked to his advantage. The more wary his people were of him, the better for Eliza and Oliver.

"Thank you, Ms. Stafford. That will be all," he said by way of a dismissal.

Ms. Stafford nodded her head to Edwin. "My Lord."

Once they were alone, Ollie signed that he needed to get his backpack from his locker.

"Go on, then, mate!" Edwin encouraged him and waited while Ollie went to retrieve his things. He didn't appear brimming with his usual energy, and as a result, Edwin started to worry. He hoped Ollie wasn't being bullied.

Ollie was two years old when he and Eliza realized that something was wrong—though Eliza said she suspected much sooner. Ollie had always been a suspiciously quiet infant, but, at first, they thought it had to do with him being a preterm baby. He'd been a paltry four and a half pounds at the time of his birth, a dangerously low birth weight that meant weeks in an infant intensive care unit. He couldn't even go home with Eliza until he was nearly three months old.

Eliza did everything she could to help him thrive, feeding him, rocking him for hours, and walking the floor endlessly. But as Oliver grew from infant to toddler, even his occasional fussing and crying stopped.

Edwin witnessed the toll it took on his wife. Eliza went from a state of being constantly alert and waiting for the other shoe to drop to subtlety crying herself to sleep at night—when she slept at all. She was convinced Ollie was ill or that the business with Summersfield had affected him in some way. He recalled Eliza all red-faced and virtually shaking when she admitted she was terrified that some part of *him* had attached itself to their son. After all, she had been pregnant with Ollie when Summersfield tried to make her his Heir.

"He's not...I mean, our beautiful little boy can't somehow be Summersfield Heir, can he?" she asked him one night, huddling the small, strangely cool bundle that was Ollie against her shoulder. "Can an infant even *be* an Heir?"

Edwin wanted to tell her no, that Ollie was *their* son, that he was made of their stuff—his and Eliza's—but he just didn't know enough about these things, and he didn't want to dismiss Eliza's concerns. She would see right through him anyway. So, he told her that whatever was wrong with their son, if anything was, they would get through it together as a family.

And they did. Other than being non-verbal and rather overly serious at times, Ollie was like every other kid. He liked hoverboarding and playing video games. He didn't have a lot of friends, but he rolled his eyes when he was told to go to bed. Ollie's doctors said he was perfectly normal and healthy, though Dr. Vu, one of the few who knew the unusual circumstances of Ollie's birth, couldn't make heads or tails of Ollie's genetic structure. She said whatever he was made of went beyond human, Poppet, or vampire. She didn't even have a name for his phenotype. But he was a seemingly healthy little boy and very smart, and that was all they needed to concentrate on for the moment.

While Ollie was digging his pack out of his locker, Edwin spotted a girl his age waving to him. She was tall, with dark skin and eyes, her hair carefully styled in long box braids. From down the hall, she cleverly signed to Ollie, *I'll see you in English tomorrow.*

Ollie signed back, *Bring the book!* Then he turned, slammed the locker, and hurried back to Edwin, his pack jouncing on his shoulder.

"Did you teach your friend sign?" Edwin asked hopefully as Ollie joined him. Ollie never seemed to have many mates.

Ollie shrugged, which meant he didn't want to discuss it. This was part of his "private life," which Edwin took pains to respect.

He wanted to ask so many questions, to be close to his son, but he just couldn't risk it. Early on, he and Eliza made the joint decision not to tell Ollie the truth. They told him that the Lord of the ship was just his good friend. Edwin couldn't risk someone finding out. He knew—didn't suspect, but *knew*—that someone might one day use Ollie against him, or hurt Ollie to get back at him. He had made too many enemies over the two-hundred-plus years of his existence.

Today, though, he couldn't help but smile a little as they exited the school on their way to the lifts that would take them up to the commerce levels of the ship. Wait till he told Eliza their son had finally made a little friend!

***

"Tommy, I need to speak to you for a moment."

Tommy, heading down a corridor toward a lift, stopped when he heard the familiar voice behind him. He turned, a process that took him several movements to complete and which often made people feel uncomfortable, and was pleased to see it was Edwin's navigator standing in the doorway of the communications lab, signaling to him.

"Hello, Narissa," he said. He always endeavored to keep his voice even and non-threatening with everyone aboard the ship, though he knew it was unnecessary with Narissa. The fierce warrior Fae wasn't afraid of much. A Mechi such as he was probably did not even make her list of concerns. "What can I help you with?"

Narissa looked both ways before saying. "It's delicate. Come inside."

Tommy chugged forward, ducking under the rounded lintel of the door so they were both snugged inside the old Navigational Deck. The walls were covered in reel-to-reel computers, binary relays, communications stations, and the huge sonar amplifier that took up more than half a wall. A stack of obsolete equipment was simply stacked against the far wall. The *Queen's Gambit* only used the equipment here when other means of plot coursing failed. Normally, Narissa spent most of her time on the new Navigation Deck full of shiny bright digital course-setting equipment, most of it controlled by NEWTON, so Tommy found it odd that she should be hanging out in this old dust bin.

"Come look at this. We saw something on the sonic field in New Nav. I didn't believe it, and NETWON kept getting in my way, so I went to take a look at it through some sonar eyes to confirm it." She indicated a large, old screen with a crack running through it. Like most of the equipment here, the device still worked, but it was ancient and pitted with rust spots. All of it was incompatible with NEWTON.

Back when Edwin first took control of the ship, the engineers gave him the option of tearing this old deck out, but he'd opted to keep it intact, antiques and all. Tommy thought sometimes that their Lord ran a bit too sentimental and for his own good, but then, sometimes, it paid off.

Tommy had to squat down to see what was on the screen—a sonic blip about ten thousand parsecs from their current position and much farther up than any gyro had any business being. He squinted—mentally, anyway.

"Is that a ship?" He was not an expert in the field of navigation, but he knew that no gyro should be hanging that far up in the thermosphere. Most gyros, and their aircraft, navigated the lower stratosphere. Some of the larger gyros, like the *Gypsy Queen*, went as far up as the upper stratosphere—about thirty miles above the surface of the Earth—but even the really big ones could not maintain that altitude for long. They weren't built for it. But no craft on Earth not designed for deep space travel could drift through the thermosphere, almost fifty miles up—what was sometimes referred to as "dead man's land." It ran the risk of burning up and its equipment failing.

"Yep. A gyro. A big crippled gyro."

Tommy grunted. The old sky sonar had captured images of the shattered and listing sphere. His brain jumped around until he fell on the only possible explanation. "That's not…it's not…"

"The *Abraxas*? Aye, I think she is."

They had all seen the news about six months ago, when the *Abraxas*, Lord Emmerdale's gyro, completely blipped out of existence in a matter of minutes. It was front-page news for a while, and because Emmerdale was a high-ranking Vampire Lord, it generated an extensive investigation. Since the ship had vanished above the Atlantic Ocean, several deep dives were conducted to try to recover the crew or fragments of the ship. It was universally thought that the gyro suffered a fatal malfunction of its gyroscope—the device that kept the enormous ship airborne—and it had fallen into the sea. But not a sliver of the ship was recovered.

Now they knew why.

The *Abraxas* hadn't fallen at all. It was still stationary but derelict and drifting like a giant shattered egg toward the exosphere, the edge of outer space. Another glance at the sonar indicated the ship was also being orbited by the scrambled debris of itself, creating a sonic shield, which explained why no one had detected it yet. It was deflecting most modern means of detection and was essentially "invisible."

"That's…not very good, is it?" Tommy said, indicating the read-out ticket in Narissa's hands. His voice sounded quivery even to himself.

"Not at all," Narissa said, ripping off the ticket and holding it up to examine it. "According to this, if the *Abraxas* hits the exosphere, it'll start to burn big time. Then it *will* fall and sink, burning debris and all." She narrowed her weird alien eyes. "And the worst part is that she's not above the Atlantic any longer. If she falls in the next week or so, New Jersey is going to be in for a really bad time of it."

Tommy grunted. "I need to speak to Lord Edwin immediately."

***

"What do you think, mate?" Edwin asked, looking over the collection of stickpins in the vendor's glass display case. The wares in the shop were attractive but not overly expensive—pretty manmade gemstones and bits of cut glass set in bracelets, pendants, and rings, the kinds of mid-range gifts that the working class aboard his gyro favored.

Ollie considered the collection carefully before pointing to his choice: a pin with a large metal sunflower on it in shades of brass and gold.

This part of the ship was called the Bazaar, a huge, hangar-like floor that offered numerous open-air shops and kiosks. Groceries, clothing, medical supplies, basic entertainment, and trinkets could be had. At one end of the space was a matinee and arcade, and at the other a small indoor park with numerous walkways, an arbor, some food carts, a beautifully designed fountain, and even a daily puppet show. More extensive needs or eclectic desires needed to be ordered online and delivered up or otherwise purchased in the city down below. That was always an option, but Edwin didn't feel comfortable taking Ollie down to New York. There were too many people out there who didn't care for his kind very much, and he wasn't fool enough not to think they wouldn't make a target of Ollie if they saw them together.

Sometimes, though, he wondered if he and Eliza were doing Ollie a disservice by sheltering him within this floating fortress. What if Ollie grew up incapable of defending himself? Or, worse, what if he grew up with no social skills or became too introverted?

The idea made Edwin's finger itch, and he had to clench his hand near his hip, where he kept his sidearm Belle in a holster at all times. Bloody hell, he hadn't known that being a dad would come with so much fretting all of the time!

"Perfect!" he said of Ollie's gift. His mum would be getting her sunflower at last—even if it wasn't at her surprise birthday celebration that he knew was no surprise to her. He looked up at the shopkeeper, who was hovering quietly behind the glass display case and ignoring everyone else roaming his shop. After all, the Lord-at-Court of the *Queen's Gambit* was visiting *his* kiosk in the Bazaar, and that was a big deal for any shopkeeper. "Can we have a look at—?"

Before Edwin could finish his statement, the shopkeeper had whipped out the pin and started packaging it up for him in a lovely black velvet jewelry box. He didn't charge Edwin, of course. Everything aboard the *Gambit* was his anyway. But excessive wealth made Edwin uneasy, and even eight years on, he still wasn't used to the differential treatment he received from the members of his Congress, so he asked the shopkeeper to charge it to his account.

"It is an honor to serve you, my Lord," the man said, bowing formally to him.

Outside again, Edwin took Ollie's hand and headed toward the matinee where they were showing some old Edward G. Robinson flicks, but Ollie immediately pulled his hand away, looking insulted. When Edwin turned to glance a question at him, he saw Ollie signing, *I'm not a baby!*

"Sorry, mate. Don't want you getting lost."

Ollie, exasperation twisting his face, signed, *We come here on school trips all the time. I know my way around the Bazaar!*

"I get you, mate. But the world is dangerous," Edwin reasoned.

Ollie shook his head. *Not for me. I can take care of myself. And I don't need you protecting me.*

Edwin was honestly taken aback by Ollie's outburst and held up his hands in an *I give up* gesture. "Right, then. No handholding. Got it. Do you want to see a movie or visit the arcade?"

Ollie shook his head. *I want to go home.*

Edwin felt a stab of disappointment but figured that Ollie was growing up fast. Maybe he didn't want to be seen with grownups anymore. "Right, then. We can visit the lab to collect Mum and then I'll take you home..."

Ollie signed too fast for Edwin to follow.

"I don't understand."

Scowling, Ollie shortened his response to, I don't need a chaperone. And I want you to leave my mum alone!

Edwin, stunned, stood there, looking at the people moving around them in the street outside the shop. He thought he hadn't read Ollie correctly. But then a thought occurred to him. "Ollie," he said in a low, hushed voice, "is someone talking about me? Telling stories?"

Ollie, as his teacher Ms. Stafford had stated, was exceptionally bright. Perhaps Edwin was a fool not to expect this.

His son signed very quickly and with great force. This time, Edwin followed him but barely.

They say you're the Devil...that you like to hurt people...

Edwin snorted in insult. "Who says that? Who says I'm the Devil?"

But before Ollie could answer or they could continue this uncomfortable conversation, a commotion caught Edwin's attention. Seconds later, several people slid hastily out of the way as something moved ponderously in their midst. He soon discovered what it was.

Tommy lumbered out of the crowd, looking worried, if such a thing could be said of a Colossus. He immediately zeroed in on Edwin. "My Lord! It's important I speak to you right away!"

| iii |

The Marie Antoinette, eight years ago

Two days after Eliza killed Summersfield, she and Edwin had a private meeting in her quarters to discuss how they would proceed as the first Congress to exist in half a millennium. Along the way, they came up with the Plan.

Still recovering from her ordeal, Eliza was resting fitfully in a rocking chair by the window. Edwin closed the door to the private room and went to sit on the end of the bed to face his wife.

Neither of them spoke for a long moment while both tried to formulate what they were feeling. Both had been through hell, and a great deal passed between them via their bloodlink. Eliza's trauma at Summersfield's hands, Edwin's many injuries and his guilt at having taken so long to free her—though, if he was being honest with himself, it was really Eliza who'd freed herself. He'd had remarkably little to do with that.

"Don't," she said at last, turning away from the window where the light had been slanting across her unusually pale face. He missed the rosy brown aliveness in her cheeks and wondered if she would ever really recover. Because of Summersfield, she was thin and horribly weak. "I wouldn't have been able to do what I did if you hadn't challenged him, Edwin. You were the...the pin in the grenade, so to speak."

He grunted dismissively. "He wouldn't have done any of it to you if I had made you my Heir more quickly, the way we discussed. If I hadn't hesitated..."

She smiled tiredly and rubbed at her belly—a small but precious swelling that overwhelmed him whenever he looked at it. "And the doctors told me if you had...if you had changed me that night the way we planned...I wouldn't have this now."

He imagined their child growing inside her, utterly terrified of what was to come. It shouldn't be real. This shouldn't be happening. What if it was a monster? What if it hurt Eliza? He had so many questions...

"He isn't like that," she said, reading her husband's concerns in that way she had.

His head bobbed up. "'He?'"

She nodded. "Our boy. Our son, Edwin."

"How do you know it'll be a boy?"

Eliza shrugged. "I just do. Call it a mother's intuition. I feel like I know him already. I know so much about him." She hesitated, then continued in a dreamy voice, "I'd like to call him Oliver. What do you think?"

Edwin watched her, utterly speechless. She seemed so certain of everything. Maybe she was still in shock? Maybe this ordeal with Summersfield had caused her to go mad. He wouldn't have even blamed her.

Interrupting his racing thoughts, she asked, "Oliver. How did you come by that for a middle name anyway?" Her eyes shone in the near dark. "I always thought you made it up. Oliver Twist or something."

He shook his head and then smiled as he remembered. "No, it really is my name. You recall the circumstances of my birth?"

"You were born in a house of prostitution," she provided, but she said it softly, with no judgment. "I assume you were born to one of the girls who didn't want to be named."

He nodded. "Aye. The girls there—there were seven at the time—wouldn't speak of it. They made a sister pact not to reveal whose son I was, afraid the girl's reputation would ruin her work among the clients. The girls were very protective of each other. So, no one admitted to it even after I was born. But, as a result, I had a lot of mums…and a lot of names!"

She smiled at that and even laughed. "A horde of red-haired mums."

He nodded. "And because most of the girls were Irish, I could never tell which was my real mum. I looked like all of them." He thought about that a moment. "Not that it bothered me. It was a small detail—unimportant." His smile grew. "'Edwin' and 'Oliver' were simply the two names that stuck around the longest. I don't know where they got my surname from, but probably from some poster on a wall somewhere."

Her smile slipped a little. "That must have been hard. Not knowing who *he* was."

"Didn't care. I had seven terrific mums, and who gets that?"

"I like your perspective, Edwin." Her smile returned and she rubbed at her belly again. "I want to be like that. I want to be a terrific mum."

"You will be," Edwin told her, absolutely convinced. "But still…there are things we need to discuss. Things that will keep you and Oliver safe."

Eliza nodded. "I know." She sighed as she took control of their conversation. Holding up a finger, she cited, "Number one, no one can know I killed Summersfield. As a Poppet, there is no way I can be the Lady of the *Marie Antoinette*. It just won't work."

She was reading his mind again. Or it was simply her incredibly practical nature.

He nodded—reluctantly. "I wish you could be, love. I would give you this floating pile in a heartbeat to rule."

He didn't want the ship. Or the Congress. Never wanted any of it. He had everything he wanted sitting right in front of him. His wife. His child. What more could top that? He would be the happiest vampire in the world just with that.

Their eyes met and he was surprised by the lack of bitterness in Eliza's. She had been through so much tribulation. She had bloody earned her spot as Lady of the *Marie Antoinette*. Hell, she even had vampire DNA, which should have sealed the deal. There was absolutely nothing stopping her from becoming the sitting Lord, except...

"This." She tapped her belly. "This is too important to let pride get in the way. You know if I make myself public, the High Courts will target me. They'll come for us. And for Oliver. Oliver...the first vampire born, not bitten. You know how they are..."

He nodded slowly and sadly. "Aye."

"I know you don't want this, but you have to be the sitting Lord, Edwin. There is no other way."

"I'm aware."

"And I can't be your wife or your Bride, either."

That caused him to suck in a sharp breath. Something he had not expected. "You can't be serious? Eliza, lovely—"

"I am serious," she interrupted. "Deadly." She took a deep breath as she worked to come to terms with her decision. Then she went on. "I want to be here with you, Edwin. I love you—you know that. And aboard this ship is the safest place for all of us. But we have to play this smart, and we have to make the right decisions going in. We have to have a plan."

She took another deep breath before continuing. "You can't single me out. I can't be your Bride. You understand that, right? You have too many enemies, and if the other vampires put two and two together...if the High Courts become suspicious..." She left it at that.

She knew how treacherous vampire politics were at the best of times. They had to protect their son from both the High Courts as well as the long list of Edwin's enemies. Otherwise, Oliver would be targeted, either as a curiosity or a threat. If they weren't careful, the Courts would take him from them and they would never see him again.

Edwin sat there another long, breathless moment, shuddering to imagine what could happen to his little family if they made any mistakes. But after a moment, he suddenly sprang angrily to his feet. "I think I can manage not acknowledging our child. But, bloody hell, Eliza, I'm not abandoning you! Or Oliver! You're *my* family!"

It took some work on her part to calm him down. But once he was sitting again, this time on the floor by her rocker, his hand in her lap, touching their son, she explained how they would need to conduct themselves while aboard the ship. As always, she was being painfully practical and efficient, having lived in survival mode for so long.

It took all night to work out the small details, but eventually, the Plan was born.

Eliza would be his Poppet, but not his Favorite. Not his wife. Certainly not his Bride. Their son would be his pet project, his little interest—because all Vampire Lords were eccentric and even perverse, and Edwin couldn't afford to act any differently and draw suspicion. All of this could even be used to bolster his dark reputation the Devil McGillicuddy, the gangster vampire, once the most fearsome Enforcer ever created. Edwin was not happy with that part, having lived for two centuries as a glorified boogeyman as Foxley's Enforcer, but he understood the necessity of it.

Eliza's doctors were only aware she was pregnant; they had no idea who the father was—and they wouldn't. Eliza was a scientific curiosity, a one-in-a-hundred-thousand case, but not a miracle—not really. She said there were a few cases in the scientific annuls where a Poppet became pregnant because of a flaw in her biological design. It was usually the result of a tryst with a human staff member who worked on board the gyro. Sometimes, the sitting Lord kept the resulting child as a kind of pet. Thus, they would continue along these lines because what other choice did they have? They couldn't put Oliver under the microscope. She wouldn't *allow* it.

Edwin ground his teeth throughout their talk. He understood her reasoning. Didn't agree with it. But he understood. This was the only way he could truly and completely protect his family from all of the threats that would soon be pressing in on them. But by the time Eliza was finished explaining everything, he was sitting there with his head in her lap. If he'd had the tears to cry, he would have.

"I don't know if I can do this without you," he admitted. It didn't even make him ashamed to admit his doubts. What he was facing was a gigantic responsibility. To be Lord of a Congress, the first to exist in so long that it would automatically put them under the watchful eye of the High Courts. But he also wanted to be a good father to a child that would likely be in constant danger—a child he could not even publicly acknowledge. "I *need* you, Eliza. I don't always make the best decisions. You know that."

She stroked his hair. "You will. Give yourself more credit, Edwin. You've gotten us this far."

He sighed tiredly and ran a hand over his face. "This isn't the life I wanted. I want to be living in the townhouse again with you and Cesar. Or maybe on the coast of the Celtic Sea in a little cabin. I wanted to be writing books and raising our son. I just want you and Oliver. I want to be free, Eliza. That's all."

What a pipe dream, he thought.

"I know," she said, leaning down to kiss his forehead, pushing his wavy auburn hair aside to do so. "It's what I want, too, Edwin, but this isn't the hand we've been dealt. And we have to deal with the reality we're facing whether we want to or not."

"We're never really going to be together, are we?"

"We'll make it work," she told him. "We have to."

"Aye. I get ya."

Silence pressed in, and time, and the weight of a thousand decisions.

"Edwin...I have a request." She was speaking softly now.

"Anything."

"Can we do something about the name of this floating pile? I hate this ship, but I'm determined to make it our home, so help me god."

He snorted a much-needed laugh at that. "We'll rechristen it anything you want, lovey. It's *your* pile...your gambit." He swallowed hard. "I hate all of this, Eliza. I hate that...it feels like you're going away while you'll be right here. That we'll somehow always be together but forever apart."

"I'm not going anywhere, Edwin," she whispered, "except back into the shadows."

***

The Queen's Gambit, now

Over the next eight years, Edwin thought often about their conversation that night. He thought about it now as he stepped into one of the board meeting rooms where the rest of his crew and Congress were waiting for his arrival. They all stood up from their seats and respectfully inclined their heads to their Lord.

He looked them over. His inner circle was comprised of remarkably few people because he trusted remarkably few in his life. Tommy, his Enforcer, stood to the left of him, and Malcolm Whitby, his Dog of War, to the right. Narissa, as navigator of his gyro and a representative of the Fae part of his Congress, was here as well, as was the ship's head doctor, Dr. Veronica Vu. With them was the Captain of the *Queen's Gambit*, Enzokuhle, a short, stocky human man of South African descent that Edwin hired after literally falling over him in a pub in the East End of London. He had been day-drinking himself to death after being dishonorably discharged from the Royal Navy for running an underground railroad for Poppets trying to escape cruel masters. It took Edwin all of five seconds to decide to bring the man on board. So far, he'd had no regrets.

"Welcome and please be seated," he told everyone, using his slightly louder and more melodic Lordly voice. Eliza had helped him practice it over many years.

Narissa had NEWTON summon the holographic visual aide in the middle of the table and showed them the pictures she had taken of the *Abraxas*. While she flicked through the pics, Edwin briefed everyone on what Tommy explained was happening a few thousand parsecs from their current position.

"Didn't someone think to inform the authorities?" Malcolm, always practical, asked.

"We did," Narissa said. "But the *Abraxas* has shifted so high out of American airspace that it's technically no longer in its jurisdiction."

"What about the crew?" Captain Enzo spoke up in his clipped, no-nonsense accent. The harsh lights of the room flashed off the commendations on his brown uniform shirt, his thick round glasses, and on the perfectly slick pate of his head. "Do we know if there are survivors? It's been six months, aye, but someone may have been able to get by..."

"We don't know," Edwin admitted. He checked his notes again. "So far, no one has been able to get pictures of the inside. A few drones were sent in, but they all malfunctioned."

"Why did they malfunction?" Captain Enzo asked, looking intrigued.

Narissa clarified that. "There's a debris field trapped in orbit around the ship, and it's muddling our equipment and colliding with our drones."

"So, we don't know if anyone is alive."

"It's unlikely," Dr. Vu spoke up. "The whole ship has been decompressed from the damage to the hull, so unless someone was able to find a pocket of air or oxygen tanks and survived off them for the past two weeks..." She spread her hands, leaving it at that.

Captain Enzo grunted unhappily. "A derelict ship and no one is willing to find out what happened."

"It's a gyro, so it's technically the High Courts' problem, and the humans know that." Edwin had come prepared for this part and nodded to Narissa, who played with the controls on the visual aid. The image of the *Abraxas* in 3-D was wiped and replaced by the image of a very tall, very thin, and exceedingly ancient creature standing on the table.

Their digital visitor was dressed in long dark robes such as a judge might wear, except they were trimmed heavily in gold and embroidered with what looked like blood diamonds, and he wore a decorative headdress and crest, with a scarlet cap. He was so thin that he looked like a creaking skeleton under the heavy robes. His face was hawkish and severe, hungry, with cheekbones sharp enough to spark a flame and teeth long and nicotine-colored that looked like they belonged on a plague rat. His eyes were the worst, though, and made everyone in the room suck in a deep breath—pitch black with no whites or irises whatsoever. It gave him a particularly alien appearance.

Before anyone could even ask him who he was, he offered in a booming voice, "I am Lord Trasch, the Speaker of the High Courts. Lord Edwin has summoned me here today to explain what will happen in the next few hours."

Everyone in the boardroom sat up straighter and shifted uncomfortably in their seat. Narissa, who had trouble keeping her mouth shut at the best of times, mumbled, "You mean Lord Skeksis" under her breath.

Lord Trasch glared down upon them all, throwing off that unique combination of contempt, indifference, and skin-crawling hunger that only the very oldest and most decrepit members of the High Courts could. For the first time, Edwin was glad Eliza wasn't here. Even though he was a Vampire Lord, he had never met Trasch in the flesh, but he had heard of the creature referred to as the Mind Eater, a vampire so old that he rivaled Foxley in his years. Unlike Foxley, though, Trasch stayed deep in the shadows, always sending agents to do his dirty work for him and manipulating things from afar. There were also rumors that he was psionic and could control both humans and other vampires.

Edwin hoped it was all hyperbole. He said, "What do you mean 'what will happen?' I invited you here as a courtesy, Trasch. You didn't—"

Lord Trasch glared his way, his eyes burning like twin black flames. "You invited me. I am here and speaking. Thus, you will be silent, child."

Edwin stopped speaking but glared back at his guest.

The smallest smile of victory ticked the corner of the ancient creature's mouth. "You have chosen to be a Lord-at-Court, Lord

Edwin. Therefore, you must follow precedent." He paused for dramatics before continuing. "When a Lord comes upon derelict holdings, it is their responsibility to investigate and gather intel, which they then must pass on to the High Courts. You did learn this?"

"Er, well..." It wasn't like there was a how-to manual about how to be a Lord at Court...

Trasch, ignoring him, continued. "Once the High Courts have reviewed the intel and examined the holdings, they will then be put in probate. If there is an Heir—the progeny of the deceased Lord—they will be granted the spoils. If there is no Heir, then those holdings will be awarded to the Lord who found them."

Edwin knew for a fact that Emmerdale had never made any Heirs. The cheap wanker had been too tight with his fortune to share it with anyone, even a Bride. "I don't want Emmerdale's broken gyro," he stated and then noticed Malcolm glaring at him.

He knew what Malcolm would say. The gyro could be salvaged for parts, and even the junk sold at auction for a small fortune. Edwin knew that appealed to Malcolm, who was a true tactician. Anything to expand their Congress's holdings and power. Maybe he shouldn't have run his mouth, but something about this whole thing smelled off to him. He turned back to Trasch, who was watching him with his usual disdain as if Edwin had crawled out of a gutter and was too uppity to stay down where he belonged.

"Regardless," the ancient vampire explained, "it is still among your duties to secure the ship. Doubly so if the ship proves a freefalling danger, which, from all accounts, it does."

Trasch held Edwin's gaze, challenging him to try and wiggle out of his responsibilities. A dereliction of duties would make him look weak, he knew, which is exactly what the High Courts wanted.

"I misspoke," Edwin said after a moment, puffing out his chest a little. "Of course I want the *Abraxas*—for junk. I'll get an exploratory team put together immediately."

Trasch smiled, showing off those ugly, long rodent teeth. "Excellent. I will inform my brethren that you wish to act as a true Lord."

Backhanded insult, that.

"Lord Edwin, we anticipate seeing your report in no more than forty-eight hours."

Before Edwin could say anything more, Trasch cut the transmission.

* * *

Edwin asked Captain Enzo to assemble a competent away team. He trusted the man to know who was best for the mission. In the meantime, he took a lift to the Poppet's quarters on another level of the ship. No one ever questioned his visits; as far as they were concerned, it was a Lord's prerogative to visit his Poppets for blood and sex.

He wasn't even to Eliza's door when it slid open and she poked her head out. "Come on in—quickly."

Edwin nodded and joined her inside.

"Where's Ollie?" he asked, looking around her rooms.

"He's having a playdate with his friend Ariel," Eliza said as she led him into the kitchen to pick up a bottle of wine for her and a bottle of blood substitute for him off the floating serving tray. He had made certain she had the best suite on the ship, and it was outfitted with every possible convenience. Eliza's quarters were a complex split-level, with the living quarters, a full kitchen, and Ollie's room downstairs and, upstairs, her sleeping quarters, an office suite, guest room, and a walk-around catwalk that looked down upon the main family room. All of the rooms were shiny white with marble floors, heavy glass and plush white furnishings, and warm inset lighting. It was more stylish than the townhome they shared once upon a time. Still, he missed their townhome even though its age meant things were always breaking down.

The kitchen, brightly lit and ergonomically designed, had all of its silvery modern appliances snugged into its cabinetry walls, with a long, white marble island drifting down the center. The large industrial refrigerator sported black pencil art on construction paper done by Ollie. Edwin examined the art while Eliza popped the bottle corks on their late-night treat.

The last time he was here, Ollie's art had mostly been influenced by the cartoons and video games he loved. But now he saw Ollie had begun drawing original characters, including a lot of weird beasties and heroes in armor. Edwin wondered if his son was a budding author as he had been. Some were just black shadowy man figures with white eyes.

Edwin shook his head, regret nibbling persistently at his heart. He hated the idea of their little family living apart, of not being here to help Eliza with the small but important things—skinned elbows and birthday parties and getting Ollie off to school. He knew he would have been ace at helping Ollie with his English homework.

"How has he been?" Edwin asked, hoping to gain some insight.

Eliza offered him a teasing smile while she handed him the bottle of blood substitute. "Ollie is Ollie. He is very much your son, Edwin." She laughed at that before grabbing a wine glass to go off the floating tray to go with her bottle of red. The two of them jumped up on the island and sat in companionable silence while they drank their respective drinks.

"I worry about him. And you," Edwin admitted, bumping her shoulder.

She bumped him back. "You gave us a beautiful suite and everything we could ever want aboard this ship. And all I have to do is snap my fingers, and there you are. There's no need to feel guilty, Edwin."

"Still, I'm not here for the day-to-day."

She sipped her wine. "The day-to-day would bore you to tears."

"No," he assured her in a soft, sincere voice. "It wouldn't."

A great swell of love and fear rose up inside of him. For her. For Ollie.

She sensed it. While facing him, she leaned in, bumping his nose before she kissed him. He hoped his breath didn't smell of blood substitute. But if it did, she didn't seem to care. "Okay, I admit, there is one thing I miss."

He leaned into her, tracing the white streak in her curling black hair. "Aye?"

"Our alone times. I hate the fact that we have to plan everything out and sneak around." She kissed him again, which did all kinds of wonderful miracles for his mostly dead body. "We can't be spontaneous like we used to be."

Feeling breathless from her kiss, he admitted, "There is a lot to be said for spontaneity."

Grinning evilly, she set her glass down and took his hand, leading him out of the kitchen and up the curving white steel stairs to her bedroom loft.

Her private rooms sported a divan with cushions, a sheer wall of books, a king-sized, four-poster bed with a white down comforter and red satin sheets and white bridal veils, and black and white landscape pictures of Africa and Asia on the walls. The huge, stained glass portal window of red glass set with small gems of yellow citrine, was full of softened moonlight at the moment.

Edwin glanced around at the familiar surroundings and felt himself relax a little. "The little girl in his school. The one Ollie taught

Sign to," he said as he loosened his tie and the buttons of his jacket. "He seems close to her."

Eliza programmed the sliding door closed and turned. She looked devastatingly sexy in her ruched yellow and white pinstripe day dress, the curling fury of her center-parted afro framing her rosy brown face and saucy smile. For a short time, Eliza had experimented with straightening her hair, but lately, she had simply let it go natural, and these days, it was seductively untamable. He felt it reflected her nature. The stripe of white in her hair only made her that much more alluring. "That's the one. Ariel. She's the daughter of one of your employees."

"Ah," he said while Eliza shuttered the portal windows in the room against any potential peeping Toms. "I'll have to check into which one and give them a promotion."

"So they hang around the ship and Ollie can have his little friend?"

"Er...ah..."

She laughed again when the little blood in his body rushed to his face. He hated it when she saw right through him like that.

"That would be very nice on your part, *my Lord*," Eliza agreed before pulling Edwin by the front of his suit coat and kissing him almost savagely. It had been some days since they'd had any alone time, and he could tell she was exceptionally ravenous tonight.

Her presence enlivened him in a way nothing else could, and he quickly shoved her against the wall and stuck his tongue down her throat. She tasted so sweet—like life and dreams and happily-ever-afters. His Eliza. "You shouldn't talk like that," he said intimately against her lips. He ran a thumb down her soft cheek, following the curve. "You know what it does to me, lovey."

"Yes, *my Lord*," she answered and playfully bit the side of his neck, which did all kinds of things to him just then.

He returned the favor, leaving a light trail of kisses along her neck until he found his favorite spot, and then...ah, she shuddered for him and wound her fingers through the curls of his auburn hair, tilting her head so he could take nourishment from his mark.

When he'd taken his fill and they finally came up for air, Edwin said, her blood still fresh on his lips, "So...I need to tell you what happened during the meeting."

She rolled her eyes. "Later please?"

"It's important."

"It's important you get your pants off, husband."

"Blood hell, woman!" he said as she dragged him to the bed.

She asked for a quick tumble, which Edwin was more than happy to oblige her with. He was feeling the weight of their separation, too. After they'd satisfied each other in every way carnal, they settled down together with him running his tongue and teeth over every part of her until she was begging him to drink from his mark again. Edwin slipped his teeth into her and Eliza arched her back. Their lovemaking was prolonged and wordless.

Afterward, they lay naked and panting on the bed side by side, fingers entwined. Edwin turned his head on the pillow so he could watch Eliza breathe in and out, all of the pretty pink color from their exertion flushing her face, throat, and heaving breasts.

"It *has* been too long," he admitted.

She turned to face him, the fingers of her free hand playing over the mark on her neck. "I think we made up for it."

He gave her a long look. "Are you all right, love?" He meant now, of course, but also in the greater scheme of things.

She sighed and crawled into his arms. "Tell me how the meeting went."

Edwin wrapped his arms around her and gave her the skinny, finishing with, "Narissa insulted that tosser Trasch to his face—

not that I blame her—and I almost ruined everything by being too damned honest." He groaned in shame before telling her the rest of what the Speaker explained he was obligated to do. Finally, he admitted, "I know it's a test, Eliza. The High Courts are going to push me in any number of ways to see if I break. I could feel that old reptile's disdain for me even though he wasn't in the room."

She looked up at him, a strangely confident smile on her lips. "You're stronger than that. You won't break. But I advise you to let Malcolm do some of the talking for you from now on. He's quite learned on Court etiquette and always prioritizes what's best for everyone."

"Aye, you're right."

"When are you boarding the *Abraxas*?"

He glanced at her bedside clock. "Tonight. Or as fast as we can safely get the team put together." Sighing, he rolled away from her and covered his eyes with his forearm. "I wish you could come. But it's decompressed and, according to Narissa, about forty below zero on the inside. Only vampires and Fae—and Tommy—are boarding."

Eliza nodded her understanding. "Dr. Vu will likely want to analyze anything interesting you bring back. And so would I." She shrugged. "I know I'm not educated in these matters..."

He smiled at that. "You are absolutely educated in these matters...and I'd value your input. You know that." He felt his expression turn grim. "I'm so sorry about what happened to your birthday, lovey. I had this whole fete thing planned out before this happened. You weren't supposed to know, and I was going to surprise you and, afterward, we were going to have so much fun tonight. And now..."

"Well, I just had the most amazing gift just now!" And, leaning close, she tickled him under his devilish goatee. "Anyway, you can 'surprise' me with anything you like once you settle this business with the *Abraxas*."

He nodded at that, then turned to dig an envelope out of his pants pocket lying on the floor next to the bed. "I was going to give you this later tonight, but I've decided I want you to have it now."

Eliza took the envelope and turned it over, looking at it excitedly. She started to unpeel the back of it, but Edwin stopped her hand. "Open it later when you're all alone. It's your genetic profile."

Frowning, she said, "I don't understand."

He looked her over, suddenly feeling as nervous as some schoolboy. He'd never really gotten over that—that Eliza had chosen *him*. She could have had anyone. But he was the lucky one. "I know you've always wondered what ethnicity you are—where your ancestors were from." He glanced at the landscapes on the walls. "You haven't said it, of course, but I felt it. So, I asked Dr. Vu to do a genetic workup on your blood. It's extremely detailed—and no, I haven't looked at it. I felt it was...private."

Doubt nibbled at him suddenly. Maybe he should have bought her a more traditional gift, flowers or diamonds. "In hindsight, I guess it sounds like a silly gift."

With a sudden, enthusiastic squeal, Eliza wrapped her arms around his neck and kissed his cheek, then flopped back. "Nooooo! Oh, Edwin..." She leaned back on her pillow, tears in her eyes, and clutched the envelope to her chest like it was a love letter. "This is...oh, my god..."

"Did I do well?" he asked uncertainly.

"Well? This is amazing!" She picked up the envelope and stared at it as if she could see right through the paper at all of the secrets locked inside. She seemed on the verge of crying when he heard a commotion downstairs.

Eliza sat up, her hair all a mess now. "Ollie's back early."

Edwin grunted in acknowledgment and got up to dress. Recalling his son's outburst earlier, he thought it best if he slipped away, perhaps via the parapet outside Eliza's bedroom. It was better than to have the boy catch him here in his mum's bed.

I want you to leave my mum alone!

Whatever *that* meant.

After slipping her chemise back on, Eliza suddenly grabbed his hand. "Thank you, husband."

"You are more than welcome, wife." He smiled and kissed the back of her hand before retreating to the parapet. He sat on the safety rail on the private deck, hidden from view, and listened as Eliza slid back under her covers.

Sometimes, if he closed his eyes and concentrated on their bloodlink, he could briefly see through Eliza's eyes. Ollie, back early from his play date, knocked politely on her bedroom door.

"Did you enjoy yourself, Ollie?" Eliza called as she requested the AI to open the door.

Their son nodded, then threw himself forward, landing straight in the middle of the bed with a puff of bedclothes. Eliza laughed at the display. As serious as their son could be, sometimes he could be just as silly as his dad. After Ollie crawled up to face his mum on the pillow, she put her arms around him, hugged him tight, and rubbed her nose against his. They spent the next few minutes snuggling together as a family, laughing and talking about their day.

Edwin felt the desperate need to join them—to tell Ollie everything. Instead, he dropped off the deck, letting his outstretched wings land him softly on the deck below Eliza's quarters.

iv

There were to be five members on the exploratory team—Edwin, Tommy, Narissa, and two other vampires, all Supes that could withstand the demands of a hostile environment with a minimum of damage while they did a surface sweep.

The vamps were two soldiers named Avery and Lightfoot. Avery was an ex-Navy Seal only thirty years old but still capable, and Lightfoot was an Ongweh'onweh vampire over a hundred years steeped in his power and an ex-mercenary, a popular life path for vamps who, for whatever reason, never became their own Lord. Both worked deck security aboard the ship, and both immediately stepped up to volunteer for the away mission.

In the locker room adjacent to one of the departure bays, the three vamps and one Fae suited up in yellow partial pressure suits for the mission. They came with bubble helmets, but they would not be needing those, as Narissa had confirmed the ship had all the necessary oxygen their unique Supe bodies needed to breathe; they only needed the pressure suits to properly contain the extremely small amount of blood in their bodies.

Dr. Vu gave them a brief lecture as they zipped up.

"No 'snap freezing effect' actually occurs in space, contrary to the science fiction movies you all have no doubt seen," she explained.

"The heat from a human body must be lost through thermal radiation or the evaporation of liquids."

She glanced briefly at her notes. "Also contrary, in zero pressure, the blood 'boils' because the veins will explode due to the flesh expanding to twice its size. Now, the atmospheric pressure aboard the *Abraxas* won't be zero-G because the ship is hanging in the *troposphere*. That's on the edges of outer space. So, though it's unlikely you'll die, there could be considerable discomfort all the same."

Edwin made a face at the good/bad news. "So, don't take the suits off."

She considered that. "From what I understand of vamp anatomy, which isn't a lot, your people have very little blood in your veins in general, which means you could probably sustain the pressure out of a suit for about an hour before your blood started to heat up. The cold shouldn't affect any of you in any way. However..." She worriedly glanced over at Narissa to confirm her body worked the same as the vamps.

Narissa gave her a thumbs up. "Vamps are our first cousins. We pretty much all work the same way, minus the icky blood-drinking."

Avery and Lightfoot glared at her, but Dr. Vu nodded and then handed out oxygen plugs to wear in case the atmosphere was thinner than expected. Supes didn't need a lot of oxygen to operate, but they did need some or they might grow sluggish and shut down.

Of course, none of this was going to affect Tommy, whose Colossus body was naturally pressurized for all environments.

Once everyone was suited up properly, they filed into the departure bay. Avery would be piloting the Hummingbird, and Tommy and Lightfoot would be acting as Edwin's muscle. Narissa had their weapons—modified sonic rifles since they didn't want to be toting around anything thermal in case there were gas or chemic leaks aboard the ship.

Before they boarded the Hummingbird, Edwin stepped into a private storage nook full of unmarked barrels, made certain he was alone, and mind-texted Eliza.

—I'm off now, love. —

He imagined her standing at the painted window in her room, waiting to catch a glimpse of his Hummingbird taking off. — I don't need to tell you to be careful. I have a bad feeling about this, Edwin. I feel...like that ship isn't safe.—

He nodded. —Samesies. Bad feeling. But I have Tommy with me. And Narissa. And she's got some bloody big boomsticks she's currently in love with. I'm as safe as I'll ever be.—

Eliza sighed worriedly nonetheless. —Earlier tonight, Ollie gave me the pin you two picked out. It's beautiful.—

He imagined the big, bright metal sunflower pinned to the front of her bodice. He wished he could see it on her. —Did you open the envelope yet? —

—No. I'll do that after you come back. So, you see, you have to come back so we can open it together and find out what I am. —

He nodded. —I know what you are, Eliza. You're the reason for my whole existence. — Before he got too sentimental, he added, —I *will* come back. Love you, wife.— He kissed two fingers and held them up.

—Love you better, husband. —

Edwin bowed his head, said a brief prayer, crossed himself, and then went out to join his crew.

***

"Look alive, vampire!" Narissa said as Avery set the Hummingbird down in one of the empty cargo bays of the derelict ship. She laughed at her stupid joke in a way that made Edwin wonder if the chit wasn't just a bit touched in the head.

Edwin, sitting in the back with the rest of the crew and white-knuckling the seat, sat up straighter. Truthfully, his mind had wandered. He'd been thinking about Ollie. It had begun to consume him, and he knew that wasn't a good thing when his attention needed to be here and now. Narissa, as much as he hated to admit it, had done him a service.

Narissa, a boomstick balanced on one shoulder, smiled at him knowingly, stretching her mouth from ear to ear in that creepy Fae way. Then she lost it. "Just checking, my Lord. I want you at your best."

Edwin sneered at her condescending nature as Avery hit the key to open the latch to the bay. "Oxygen is steady at present," the ex-Seal, ensconced in the pilot's seat, told them.

Edwin sniffed the atmosphere, finding it staler than usual, but not concerning. The blast of cold that hit them all and would have frozen a human solid in under five minutes felt like a spring breeze on his face.

He climbed out with the others and the whole unit found their land legs again. They were standing in a large, brightly lit, but utterly peopleless hangar. It was obvious the backup power was still juiced for now, though it was anyone's guess what the rest of the ship was like. The silence, aside from their occasional breathing, was surreal and oppressive, like something from a bizarre dream.

Debris lightly littered the space. A few supply barrels were lying on their sides, and some utility boxes were open, their contents scattered about. But other than that, it looked like any other cargo bay on any other gyro, with multiple slots for a variety of Hummingbird models, all of them occupied with a craft. Whatever had happened did so quickly, and no one on board had had a chance to stop it or escape.

That didn't bode well, as far as Edwin was concerned.

Before they'd departed the *Gambit*, Edwin asked Tommy to run lead. He felt the bloke would appreciate the challenge, and now the enormous metal Colossus moved to the forefront of their little party, with Narissa and her gun bringing up the rear and everyone else stationed in the center. All of them were armed with small molecular disruptor handguns—like boomers, but smaller—including Edwin, who also had his blood, which could act as its own weapon if need be.

"Remember the mission. We're here to record," he reminded his people, flipping on his Reliable Body Camera (RBC). "Not to touch or take anything. Try to disturb as little as possible."

Everyone murmured their understanding and checked their RBCs were on and working properly. Tommy then lead the group out of the bay and into one of the pickup stations where a large variety of EV shuttles were waiting—the preferred mode of transport on board most gyros. Normally, the EVs, built like large golf carts and running on solar power, transported guests all over the ship in record time, but Edwin had decided they would go on foot. They still had electric engines, and they were still flammable under the right circumstances.

Lightfoot, who was monitoring their G-force with his accelerometer, said, "Breaches past this point. Oxygen at sixty-four percent. Mask up, folks."

They didn't have "masks," but they did have those oxygen plugs, and everyone who was not synthetic made certain to fit them to their nostrils. Tommy stepped forward, a tablet in his hands. "NEWTON, do you have a hold on the network yet, mate?"

"I do, Mr. Quinn," NEWTON responded in his neutral voice. "But only forty percent of the ship. Damaged sectors unreachable."

"That's fine, mate."

NEWTON prompted the large rollaway bay door up, but before it even squeaked a few inches open, it was forcibly shoved and twisted upward as the cargo bay was immediately de-pressurized. It quickly dropped a hundred degrees, and Edwin felt his face frost over, not that it hurt. It was more itchy than anything else.

The corridor beyond was cavernous and dim. A few lights flickered in the ceiling farther along but added no comfort as the group began their trek through the wounded bowels of the ship. A thin layer of ice made the walls glisten like they were in a cave and their breathing echoed hollowly around them. Edwin, second behind Tommy, said, "What do you think, mate? Should we split up?"

He wondered if they should break themselves down into retcon teams. It could mean putting them in more danger. At the same time, the *Abraxas* was a huge gyro, and it was going to take them *days* to cover it end to end if they stayed in one group. Of course, all of this was in Tommy's wheelhouse—Tommy who was an ex-DEA and who had trained with the FBI and run many successful missions over the years.

Tommy, moving with remarkable agility for his ponderous size and weight, stopped to assess the situation. "I don't detect any life on this level." Despite the superior hearing of all the Supes behind him, Tommy still had better overall detection due to his circuitry. He turned to glance at Edwin. "My Lord, I feel it would be safe to split up into two parties as we canvass floors, but we should meet up at the stairs and check in regularly. No lifts! And, I do not suggest exploring any level without a check-in point."

Edwin nodded. "Right, then. You, Avery, and Lightfoot take the west-facing side as Team Alpha. I'll take the east with Narissa as Beta."

His team showed no objections. But, predictably, as soon as they were alone, going room to room, Narissa had to launch into her typical snark. "I didn't know you loved me so much, vampire," she said as she pushed open an ajar door and cased one more storage room in a seemingly endless line of them.

"I love those pointy ears of yours, chit," Edwin admitted, doing the same while at the same time checking his mini-boomer was operational. "They're at least as sensitive as Tommy's."

Narissa hah-ed at his logic. "Tommy," she mused. "A ghoul in a metal suit of armor." She paused when they discovered a couple of dead, frozen humans curled up in a corner of one of the offices she was looking into. No obvious wounds; they had obviously died of hyperthermia after the ship was hit. "You attract the most interesting people, vampire."

"Shut it and work."

Both teams managed to sweep the first floor of the gyro in record time and then meet at the stairs. There were about fifty crew dead, no survivors. They recorded that, taking pictures or collecting IDs if the corpses wore any, as well as examining some of the damage to the hull, which was mostly cracks—but cracks that had flash-frozen the human workers on this floor. Gravity was also slightly bollocked, and a lot of the normally heavy equipment had been knocked around. Avery found a basketball in one of the cash offices and threw it at the walls, where it bounced round and round for a good long while.

The second and third floors were similarly cocked up. Dead staff, sub-zero temps, and gravity that could change depending on where you were standing as the ship used its remaining power to try and correct for it with minimum capability. Lights flickered on and off sporadically, and sometimes, eerily, whole corridors were lit with red emergency lights for a few seconds. The whole ship rumbled ominously as the engines and, presumably, the gyroscope, tried to correct the issues with the fatally wounded ship—to no avail.

Meeting up on the fifth floor, Edwin observed the team was growing nervous. "You think the gyro's fubared to hell?" Lightfoot asked at one point. "I'm not keen on sitting in this tin can if it falls out of the sky. We'll all just burn up."

Avery blurted out, "I think there are ghosts. I'm pretty sure I saw a ghost."

Lightfoot glared at him. "There are no ghosts. And, anyway, you're a vampire. Why would you be afraid of a ghost?"

"How do you know? Have you *seen* a ghost?"

"No, because they not fucking real, knucklehead!"

"Right, lads, settle down," Edwin said, listening to the energy surges in the ship. Lights flicked on and off, and the ship suddenly shuddered and groaned.

"What the hell *is* that?" Narissa said, her eyes huge and shadowed in her face as she stared at the ceiling, her rifle at the ready.

Edwin knew enough about Foxley's invention, the Micro-Electro-Mechanical System gyroscope—the device that vibrated and emitted its own false gravity to keep the whole gyro in orbit—to answer that. He was no expert, but his master loved to talk about his greatest invention. "It's the gyro. It's trying to put the ship back in orbit. NEWTON?"

"It can do that?"

NEWTON answered for them. "The gyroscope is intuitive. It is trying to correct for damage." A pause wherein NEWTON addressed Lightfoot's more reasonable concern. "The gyro has its own renewable energy source, so unless it is itself severely damaged, it should keep the ship up."

"'Should?'" Narissa asked, her eyes growing freakishly large.

Edwin shrugged just to see the worry grow on her face. He'd been on a ship with a badly damaged gyro—Foxley's ship, in fact—

and he knew it took a *lot* to send a gyro plummeting to Earth like a burning meteor. "We haven't fallen yet, chit."

With several members of the party swearing and looking even more worried, they moved to the next floor, and then the next. More dim, half-frozen corridors. A scattering of bodies. More angry growls from the ship. Edwin couldn't really blame Avery for worrying it was haunted. When they reached the floor where the Poppets were housed, they found it suspiciously empty. No one left alive—and no bodies.

"Didn't Emmerdale have Poppets?" Narissa asked him.

"I thought he did," Edwin answered. They were going slower now. The atmosphere was growing progressively thinner, and they were relying more heavily on their oxygen supply. Maybe he was breathing too fast—breathing too much oxygen, which Dr. Vu warned could be an issue and cause lightheadedness—because the corridor was shifting and "pulsing" uncertainly around him. Near the stairwell, Edwin stumbled for the first time. Thankfully, Tommy was suddenly there to catch his Lord by the shoulder as Team Alpha met up with Team Beta.

After regaining his footing, Edwin shook his head to clear it.

"Are you all right, my Lord?" Tommy asked with concern.

"Right as rain." But he glanced around the empty corridors with concern. "The floor above us should be Emmerdale's quarters and the control center for the gyroscope. I think after we canvas that, we'll call it a day."

"That's half the ship. Do you think this will be enough data to satisfy Trasch?" Tommy asked, glancing at his tablet.

An alien coldness was starting to creep up Edwin's spine. Not for the first time, he felt like they weren't quite alone. Maybe it was Avery's ghosts? "I don't frankly give a fark what Lord Skeksis wants.

This will have to do him," Edwin grumbled, and Narissa snorted in response.

They climbed one more set of stairs to the mid-level—traditionally, the floor where the Lord resided and had his navigational bridge. It was also where the control room housed the gyroscope at the centermost point of the ship. By then, everyone in the group except for Tommy was feeling winded and a little disoriented. The exertion shouldn't have bothered their Supe bodies, but the air was incredibly thin now, the kind of atmosphere that would kill a human in minutes, gravity was squiffy, and small articles were starting to float up off the floor. As they reached the landing, they started to pant and gasp.

The cold was worse now. What had begun as a tickle was now more like icy fingers down their backs. Edwin suspected they were nearing the bridge where, according to the scans of the ship that Narissa and Captain Enzo had taken, the breach had been the worst. He could see particles when he breathed out, and the floor was a solid sheet of ice and hard to traverse even with their moon boots. He was in serious need of a hot cup of tea.

Additionally, the corridors here were darker than the previous ones, with almost no remaining lights. It forced the party to rely on their various levels of night vision and Supe instincts to navigate the labyrinthine twists of corridors. It was so cold that thick sheets of ice clung to the walls and, in one section of the ship, a pipe had burst and then frozen over, creating a glassy waterfall falling from a hole in the ceiling. Fat snowflakes fluttered through the almost black, cavernous corridors from some unknown place on high.

Narissa suddenly weaved uncertainly against a wall, and Edwin reached out and steadied her. "I'm fine!" she insisted, throwing off his touch.

"I think we should go back," Edwin suggested.

"I said I'm fine, vampire!"

They had reached a branch in the corridors with a sign printed in Upyrese, the obsolete language of the high Vampire Courts. One branch was marked "Command Center" and another "Captain's Quarters."

The party would need to split up. "This is it," Tommy announced. "One half hour and we meet back here. Then we're bloody done with this pile."

Tommy and the two vamps headed toward the Command Center while Edwin and Narissa ventured the other way, toward Emmerdale's personal quarters. Edwin didn't anticipate they would find much, but one never knew. Emmerdale had a reputation as a real cockroach, surviving multiple wars and upheavals. If anyone on board this ship was still alive (and possibly tucked away in a hyperbolic chamber), it was him. Maybe if they were able to retrieve the good Lord, they would get some answers.

The corridors here were pitch black, and even with their Supe vision, all Edwin and Narissa could see were dark grey outlines. So, it came as no surprise when Narissa cried out after tripping over something in the corridor.

"NEWTON, can you get some lights on?" Edwin asked the AI.

There was a scramble of static, no answer. Evidently, this was a part of the ship the AI couldn't connect with. "I've got it." Narissa flicked on an old-fashioned hand torch and flashed it around the frozen floor and walls, which looked like someone had splattered the place with shining tar that had frozen to the surface of everything. Snow shot downward fiercely here, some of it blowing in their faces from the vents trying in vain to re-pressurize the wreck of the ship, and that, along with the very narrow beam of light, limited their vision even more.

Edwin pulled his own light out of his equipment bag and flashed it around. "Shite."

"What?"

He stepped forward, centering the light on a lump on the floor farther down the way. It illuminated an amorphous pile of bones and clothes half-buried in a snowdrift. Most of the meat was gone off the body—chewed off ravenously—but he recognized the impeccable fashion sense right away. "I think I just found Emmerdale."

***

Tommy knew they were nearing the gyroscopic center. He could feel the device's pulsing vibrations in his nonexistent teeth.

Phantom limb syndrome again. Some days, he woke from his rest period feeling like he was back in his old body. On those days, he felt everything good and bad he'd felt as a human. Then he would remember what he was—a brain, a spinal cord, and some nerve ganglia trapped inside a suit of armor—and he had to decide if he was going to 1. lose it and go on a killing rampage or 2. get on with things. He always chose two, but the first choice was starting to appeal to him.

He'd been a man once, a real man, but then he'd fallen in love with a vampire—his first mistake. Through a chain of interconnected events, he had come to be this...thing, both accidentally and on purpose. Fate had cocked up his life and even his death well and good.

Why do I continue with this nonsense?

The question haunted him every single day since his activation. And, every day, the answer was the same: What else did he have to do with himself? What else did he have to do with his afterlife? He was facing a future that might stretch on for decades or even centuries—or however long it took before the organic parts of his body failed. The idea was depressing beyond calculation.

At least Lord Edwin had given him a job. It was not a great job, and it was a little bit boring, but working as an Enforcer made him useful. All he had to do was look scary and have Lord Edwin's back, and that was something he could do.

"Stop!" he said to his two companions, elbow bent and fist upraised to halt them dead in the center of the frozen corridor. They had finally come upon the navigational bridge—a large, concave room full of abandoned stations. It sported a huge, blown-out side like an egg with a cracked shell. Snow and ice had poured in through the huge aperture and had filled the room, crystallizing it and all of the equipment. No wonder the network was all janky. Some was swirling into the corridor beyond where they stood.

Snow shushed around them as they took a few tentative steps. Emergency runner lights illuminated the walls and floor, which were coated in thick, frozen grue—a revolting combination of blood and dead human viscera. The two vamps with him grunted at the sight, their hands hovering uncertainly near their sonic guns. Avery, the young one, was checking a meter he carried in his other hand.

"What you got, metalhead?" Lightfoot asked Tommy.

Tommy swiveled his head and glared at the vamp, though it likely didn't show on his face, which never changed expression. "Heard something."

"Like?"

"Not sure. A kind of scrabbling noise."

"It's probably rats," said Avery, coming abreast of them both. "Or ghosts."

"Don't start with that ghost shit again," Lightfoot complained, looking grumpy.

"I don't think it's rats. It's minus fifty degrees eff," Tommy reminded the dead men. "Even the vermin on this ship are dead."

Avery shuddered. "Then it's ghosts."

"There are no fucking ghosts!" Lightfoot hollered.

"I thought you were an Indian. Aren't you supposed to believe in that shit?"

"Stereotype people much, kid?" Lightfoot grumbled.

With a shrug, the younger vamp started ahead of the small party, still looking at his meter. Tommy started to caution him, but the young vampire ignored him. "I think the command center is just around this corner. Let's get this over with and then we can blow this pop sta—"

And that's when the monster fell on top of him from a hole in the ceiling.

| V |

Edwin was crouched over Emmerdale's remains when he heard a door squeal open farther down the corridor. His ears pricked at the sound but he didn't immediately go on high alert. Because gravity was so janky, things moved around more than usual, and an unleveled door wasn't an immediate concern.

The sound still made the little hairs on the back of his neck stand up. He tried to zero in on it, but in the chancy, barely-lit darkness, he couldn't pinpoint its exact location. "Aye, hello?" he asked.

Narissa, hefting her gun and looking frustrated she hadn't had a chance to use it yet, turned in the direction of the noise. She had affixed the magnet plate of her torch to the barrel of her gun, and when she turned, it splashed light all over the gore-infused corridor. "What in the actual...?"

"Hang on, chit, I'll go with you," Edwin insisted, but she didn't listen, stubborn Fae that she was. She started marching down the corridor where one of the lights farther on was blinking on and off in an erratic pattern.

He got up, lurched from lack of oxygen, then started limping after her. He got only a few steps before a healthy distrust of the dark stopped him dead in his tracks. "Narissa!"

"I got this, Lord Edwin!" she harrumphed as she reached the slightly ajar door and used the barrel of the gun to push it fully open. She hefted it into position, but a second later, it sagged in her grip. "Holy hell!"

"What?" He started slowly down the corridor toward her.

She turned and grinned at him evilly. "Nothing. It's empty. But I gotcha!"

In that moment, a big, heavy shadow dropped straight down on top of her, knocking her to the floor and causing Edwin to wheel back away from it. It looked like some kind of big, humanoid spider as it pinned the Fae warrior into the floor, her gun skittering off into the dark. Narissa cried out and tried to lever her body up in an attempt to throw a punch at its face, but it wrapped its unnaturally long, gangly arms around her neck, choking her. It was dark grey and shiny, almost metallic in appearance. When it turned to glance at him, he saw slanted white eyes and a mouth full of jagged teeth.

"Shite!" Edwin didn't think; he simply reacted. He raised his gun, his pulse quickening, and got it into a steady, two-handed position. Too far away; he was likely to hit Narissa. He closed in on it, moving evasively and trying to aim at the same time. Unfortunately, the oxygen had gone to his head and the corridor was listing around him again, making it hard to aim.

The creature hissed a warning. It had a lamprey-like mouth full of dagger-like teeth, and it stretched that mouth wide open as it attempted to attach it to the top of Narissa's head. By then, however, Edwin had reached them and gotten a bead on it.

He clicked the trigger on the sonic rifle.

Dammit. He had no idea what the range was on the unfamiliar, and as he squeezed off his first shot, he realized he might just have doomed Narissa by reacting too quickly and not checking the weapon's power meter. Luckily, the hand boomer was surprisingly accurate, and the short sonic blast was incredibly accurate. It turned the creature's head into a black soup that decorated the walls and floor. Its arms shuddered and released Narissa, who fell back onto the now slick-with-monster-brains floor.

Edwin reached for Narissa and pulled her up by the hand. She immediately started swearing and stomping around, her dragonfly-like wings buzzing with irritation. He could tell she was angry about having been taken unaware so easily.

"What the hell was that *thing*?" she demanded from no one, her voice high and screechy with indignation.

More sounds. He detected clicking noises from overhead in the ceiling where the ductwork ran. The two looked at each other and a telepathic message passed between them as can only happen with soldiers who had served their time. They immediately went back to back, aiming their guns at the ceiling.

"What are you?" Narissa growled between her elongated teeth. Both of them tried to avoid the remains on the floor that were still shuddering like some insect that had been smashed but didn't have the good grace to lie still.

But Edwin knew. "Ice vampire," he said, glancing down at the creature briefly, then back up at the ceiling where he could hear more scrabbling like overgrown rats. He'd seen these guys a time or two. "And there's more of 'em. A whole nest we upset."

"What the fuck is an ice vampire?" Narissa demanded.

He didn't have time to explain. He looked back at the headless and now-dead creature lying crumpled at their feet. "Oh, balls."

"What?" Narissa prompted. *"What?"*

"I think that used to be a Poppet."

Narissa swore violently. "Emmerdale did have Poppets..."

Edwin tried to call up NEWTON to tell the others to abandon the ship immediately, but before he could even curse out the static, another creature dropped down from the ceiling and onto all fours on the floor in front of them.

It moved agilely in the dark. Narissa had barely gotten her gun up to aim before it leaped at her, the long fingers of one hand grabbing the barrel of her gun and dragging it off-center, the fingers of the other digging into her face. She screamed and the gun went off—much too closely and at the wrong angle.

Since the weapon didn't use traditional ammo, the sonic rifle didn't have a normal kickback. In fact, boomers had none—if they were discharged correctly and not in a closed-up space. Thus, the sonic blowback in the narrow corridor still knocked the two of them into a nearby wall, cracking the frozen surface of it like a giant mirror. The collision felt like a hammer blow to the back of Edwin's head. The blast also obliterated the ice vampire, though Narissa continued to scream, a hand over her face, even after they'd slid to the floor. The ice vampire had slashed her across the eyes.

More rumbling above like low throaty thunder as the ice vamps mobilized and began to pour through the hole in the ceiling—all or most of them former Poppets, Edwin reckoned. They hissed and chattered as they filled the narrow space, their icy black bodies moving oily across the floor toward the two of them. Toward their prey...

Blimey, he thought, they were good and blinkered now.

**

The creature that had Avery had pressed his back to its chest, with one long, painfully thin arm around his neck. It jerked his head back far enough that Tommy heard bones crackling alarmingly in the vampire's neck. Before he or Lightfoot could even react, the monster attached its round, toothy mouth to the top of Avery's head.

Lightfoot, moaning in fear in his throat, raised his sonic rifle and fired on the creature, but not fast enough. Avery was still screaming when the monster ripped the whole top half of his skull off in one bite. Then its face, and the rest of Avery's head, exploded into black grue.

Lightfoot, shaken by the fact that he'd just killed his fellow vamp, swore and backed up. But by that time, there were more of the creatures dropping through various holes in the ceiling and surrounding them, all of them chittering with excitement. "Fuck fuck fuck fuck fuck! We have to alert the others, tin man!"

"There's no time." Tommy turned to assist his remaining companion, but his movements, though precise, were much slower than a vampire's or even a human's, and by the time he'd grabbed his rifle off his back and taken a bead on one of the creatures closing in on Lightfoot, it already had him in its vice-like grip and was dragging him back into the mass of shiny black creatures that were creating a solid wall behind them. Lightfoot let off another blast of the gun, but it was a potshot and hit the opposite wall, blasting a hole in it but hitting nothing.

Tommy leveled his gun but then decided he couldn't risk shooting Lightfoot, so he fired on the mass of creatures to either side of him instead, hitting a couple of them and obliterating them, but that didn't stop Lightfoot from going down in a gurgling scream as the creatures dogpiled him.

Letting out a string of curses, Tommy chugged forward, prepared to smash right into the horde of creatures, but he only made it a few feet before he felt his movements slow. Several creatures were clutching his arms and legs, weighing him down even more. They were even trying to bite him with their sharp, lamprey-like teeth, but there was nothing about his synthetic body that was biteable, so they just kept chewing and scratching at his armor. The boomer was useless in such a close space and was more likely to bring the ceiling down on them all. Tommy grunted, threw the weapon aside, and started to fight hand-to-hand as he'd been taught in the academy.

***

"This is bollocks!" Edwin shouted, jumping to his feet. He couldn't risk more blowback from the stupid gun in close quarters, so he threw it aside, bit into his wrist, and then flicked his hand, letting his blood flow. The combination of his weak bloodkinetic powers and the sub-arctic temperature froze the stream of black vampire blood into a kind of long, improvised Japanese tachi sword, which he then used to slash at the encroaching creatures.

As he suspected, the vamps screamed when they encountered his blade, his blood a deadly toxin to them the way it was to almost every other Supe. He lashed out again and again, driving them back and trying to keep his wounded companion behind him and against the wall where she was safe.

But the sword didn't last—it was too brittle for such a barrage of impacts—and each time it connected with one of the creatures, bits of it snapped off until what he gripped was little better than a nub. He threw the improvised weapon aside.

More hissing came from the dark down the corridor, and Edwin felt every hair on his body respond to the noise. More ice vamps were making their way toward them. The problem was, they were black in a black corridor, their bodies shot through with frostbite. He had no idea how many there were or if he was going to be able to hold them off.

He backed up, then reached behind to find and clutch Narissa's arm and guide her to her feet. "Move!" he commanded, pushing her ahead of him and toward the open door of a random bedroom suite a few feet away. He dearly hoped there weren't any ice vamps in that room. If they were, they were both dead in a way they were unlikely to recover from.

Narissa, moaning in pain and clutching her face, stumbled inside the suite with Edwin just behind her. Once they had crossed the threshold, he slammed the door and immediately heard the vamps clawing and even biting at the closed door like a pack of starving dogs.

"Fark off!" he screamed at them. He turned to scan the room. Thankfully, it was empty of all life except for the two of them.

Turning to Narissa, whose hand was still clutching her bleeding face and eyes, he said, "How you doing, chit?"

"Can't see. I'm almost completely blind." She said it carefully and calmly in a soldiery way that impressed him. As a warrior in a highly volatile situation, she was reporting the situation, keeping her emotions in check. She turned her head this way and that. "Where are we?"

"One of those fugly giant bedroom suites vamps love. All red crushed velvet. Maybe Emmerdale's rooms. It's got those horribly painted ceilings. Demons or cupids or some shite."

"Gods, I hate those ceilings. Weapons?"

"Guns are gone. We'll need to improvise."

At a glance, there was a fancy English coat of arms on one wall above a cold fireplace mantel, maybe Emmerdale's family crest—Edwin didn't know and didn't frankly care—but it sported a pair of real crossed bastard swords, so he went to retrieve them, one for himself and the other for Narissa, assuming she could handle the weapon with her injuries.

Meanwhile, the horde of ice vamps chittered irately outside the door. They scraped their long nails over the traditional wood door and even struck it with their bodies. The door creaked and bulged with each impact. It was only a matter of time before they broke through.

* * *

The horde of creatures dragged Tommy down to the floor despite him being impervious to their attacks. They slashed at him with their claws and bit down on his arms and legs, but unless they had a can opener, they weren't getting to his soft parts anytime soon. It was almost a blessing, being this thing.

For a few seconds, Tommy lay very still on the floor, not fighting, curious to see if they had the strength to get through his armor or if any of them were bright enough to find a way to rip him apart. But nothing happened.

Finally, getting angry at being assaulted, Tommy heaved the ones on his arms off him, then sat up. The ones on top of him screeked their long claws over his metal chest plate or slashed at his synthetic face, but though they were fierce, they weren't particularly bright, and singularly, not that strong. They were incapable of holding him down.

Getting ponderously to his feet, he felt them slip off his polished metal body. Tommy then stomped them and kicked their heads in. The creatures flew off into dark corners like rag dolls. He realized after some seconds that he was screaming and swearing at them. Grabbing the sonic pulse rifle on the floor, he casually set the meter to its lowest setting, then leveled the weapon and started pulling the trigger in short, controlled bursts, not really aiming except to keep the barrel away from himself.

The creatures, slithering icily across the floor, were reduced to rags, their bizarre purplish innards splattered across the walls. As they fell, he started marching more confidently down the corridor toward the command center glowing dimly ahead. Despite the loss of Lightfoot and Avery, he was determined to finish the mission, get the black box, fetch his Vampire Lord and Narissa, and get the hell out of Dodge.

He jerked the trigger reflexively, blowing away anything that moved or crawled in the shadows or otherwise stomping anything in his way. By the time he reached the doorway of the center, most or all of the creatures were either dead or too wounded to do much more than crawl away.

"Tossers!" Stopping, he took a deep breath. Under the moans of the dying creatures, he heard the crackle of the neural network trying to connect, NEWTON doing what he can to get them back online.

—Tommy? Tommy, mate, I need you!— Lord Edwin said in his head.

* * *

While the ice vamps screamed to be let in, Edwin busied himself with standing at the door like a sentinel, sword drawn, while in his head, he tried to raise Tommy on the network. Tommy, at this point, was his only hope of escape.

The door, a pretty, carven oak affair that was nice to look at but no barrier at all to those monsters, was buckling, too many bodies pressing against it. He wished Emmerdale, that cheap wanker, had invested in more traditional metal sliding doors.

Finally, the creatures shoved at the door and it cracked fully in half, both parts collapsing to the floor as it was ripped from its hinges. Beyond, the wall of ice vampires eyed him hungrily, a black wall full of white eyes and starbright teeth. They collectively opened their slavering jaws as they prepared to rush him...

Edwin's arm shook but he held the long bastard sword straight out, determined to skewer as many vamps as he could and protect Narissa, who was standing behind him, her own sword drawn.

As one, the horde began to slouch forward...and then, abruptly, erupted into black geysers, their innards painting the fancy red and gold flocked wallpaper of the bed chamber. They screamed as they exploded one after another. More gore, nearly indigo in color, was splashed across the bed several feet away, and some even coated Edwin and Narissa.

Edwin cocked his head to one side, trying to decide what was happening. But even as the ice vamps went down in heaps, he sensed a familiar presence. From behind him marched a metal giant, his gun focused on any of the vamps who were trying to escape. Tommy cut them down expertly and with total prejudice before they could make it two feet into the bedroom.

His Enforcer came to a halt in the doorway and looked at Edwin, the piles of ice vamp bodies mangled around his legs. "Lord Edwin," he said in a perfectly calm voice, "you rang, sir?"

| vi |

The Queen's Gambit, eight years earlier

Edwin, it's time.

He got the mind text from Eliza while he was in yet another dull as farking dirt board meeting. He'd had no idea that being a Lord-at-Court was so damned dull. No wonder most Lords went off their heads eventually. Every day, he had to show up at his offices in the private sector of the ship, dressed in an actual suit, so he could attend to a business he barely understood and had no real interest in—the massive, almost overwhelming, business of running a gyro. Essentially, a mini-world.

As a new Lord, he had advisors to explain things to him, of course, but that didn't offset the sheer frustration of sitting through talks about his stocks, expansion portfolio, the "red" and "black" line funds, and the itinerary of people who wanted on or off the *Queen's Gambit* for whatever reason. And then there was the management of his staff, which was its own little hell on earth.

More recently, he'd begun receiving formal requests from major corporations who wanted to set up office space on his little floating world. It turned out, that was how most Lords financed their gyros, something else he didn't know. They had massive (and massively complicated) contracts with human corporations and governments.

They were figuratively (and sometimes literally) in bed with the most powerful people on Earth. And Edwin, a fresh new Lord in charge of a massive new Congress, received a lot of daily requests. Turned out, one of his duties was to go over the list and approve or reject proposals. He heard the words "money flow" from his underlings a lot—his underlings who didn't much care for the fact that Edwin had chosen to keep his gyro a Black Box.

There was a bone of contention between him and the people who ran his ship for him. For Edwin, it was a huge learning curve since he was more of a hands-on kind of guy. Bureaucracy gave him terrible heartburn.

"My Lord, you realize you can't maintain this ship indefinitely unless you open it up to some form of commerce?" his head lawyer was once again explaining to him. He enunciated each word slowly like Edwin was soft in the head. His name was Emerson, and he was a four-hundred-year-old snake of a vamp that would never become his own Lord. As a result, he sold his services as a counselor to young Lords like Edwin, helping them navigate the twisty politics of Court life—for a hefty sun, of course. The fact that he was a vampire and a lawyer was redundant, as far as Edwin was concerned. Emerson was even shrewder and more cutthroat than fucking Foxley, and he was extremely excited about the idea that Apple wanted to install a whole computer lab on board the *Gambit* so they could study and build on NEWTON. Emerson added that they could likely maintain the ship for centuries with just that one contract.

"I have an Andy Warhol painting," Edwin offered, referring to the portrait the artist had done of him back in the 1960s. It was currently hanging in one of the ballrooms. "That's worth something, aye."

Emerson made a face like he smelled something bad. "Sir, this is not a yard sale."

"Er...um..."

Eliza's mind text came in just then, and Edwin refocused all of his attention on his wife and the fact that as impossible as it might seem, he was about to become a father—the first vampire in history to do so. Standing, he dismissed his people. "Put a pin in that, Emerson. We'll pick this up another time."

"My Lord!" Emerson stated in bemusement, standing. He was a very short, slinky kind of vampire with hair slicked back Mafioso-style, barely larger than a child, but his eyes were the coldest and the deadest that Edwin had ever seen. He looked ready to protest, so Edwin gave the vampire lawyer a look that shrank him back a step. He did not have time for this bollocks. His child was about to be born.

After dismissing his board, Edwin wasted no time taking a lift down to the hospital ward. A nurse was standing by for him when he arrived. Most of his staff and crew knew that Eliza was a Favorite of his even if the two of them weren't particularly open about their relationship. As far as they were concerned, she was his property. The nurse knew he would be waiting. "She's just been taken into Delivery, my Lord," she informed him.

"I want to see her immediately."

She nodded and led him through a warren of corridors until they reached the Delivery Ward, which was small and cozy, with just a few private rooms. Eliza was sitting up on a gurney in one of the examination rooms. She didn't look like she was in any pain, but she was clutching her belly, and he could see her dress was damp from her water having broken.

She looked concerned. Their son, their baby, was only seven and a half months old.

"Edwin!" She reached for him.

Thankfully, the nurse had departed, and no one else was there at the moment. He ran to her and pulled her into his arms. "Lovey, how are you doing?" he whispered, running his hands over her face and hair. "How do you feel?"

"Scared." Her face was piqued and her breathing shallow. "It's too early, Edwin! What if there's something wrong with the baby?"

"Don't put the cart before the horse, love. We don't know that. We'll get through this."

Eliza grunted and lowered her head when another contraction hit her. He felt the shadow of the pain in his own body through their bloodlink.

He looked around the spare, cold room. "Why don't you have a room yet?"

She looked up. "I'm a Poppet. Do you think they're going to spend much time on me?"

Growling, he lifted her into his arms and carried her out to the nurse's station despite her protests. "I want the best private ward you have!" he told the male nurse on duty. The menace in his voice was genuine. "And the best doctor. And I don't want my Poppet left alone for a moment!"

The nurse nodded as he stood, then added, "We don't have any maternity doctors on board at the moment, my Lord, just so you know."

"Then go fetch one!"

Edwin carried her to the biggest, brightest room in the hospital and set her down on the bed. The room had pictures on the walls and a large picture window to allow the carefully UV-filtered sunlight in. By then, Eliza's contractions were coming much closer together. Their baby—whatever it was—was in a big hurry to be born.

He glared at the nurse hovering undecidedly in the doorway. "Get the bleedin' doctor before I rip yer damned head off, chit!"

The nurse scrambled to obey.

Eliza, taking a deep breath to compartmentalize her pain, put her hand on his cheek. "Edwin...don't be a monster."

He sighed. "I have to be. You know that, Eliza."

She nodded, albeit reluctantly. Over the past few months, as their child grew inside her and their lives began to change, they'd discussed this more often. If they wanted to be safe—if they wanted their child to be safe—Edwin would need to play the cold, domineering Vampire Lord. If he didn't, he might face a challenge from within his own Congress. Or, worse, the High Courts would become suspicious and start investigating. Thankfully, he already had a reputation for being the devil, the right-hand to that madman Foxley; he just needed to reinforce the image.

Leaning down, he whispered very close to her ear, "I love you, Eliza. And I am so very proud of you, love. Ignore everything I say today."

She nodded.

Standing up, he started barking orders, shoving the staff around until the delivery doctor arrived, one of the best in the world flown up quick fast from New York City. It only took an hour, but, by then, Eliza's contractions were coming very close together.

As soon as the doctor stepped onto the ward, Edwin grabbed the man by the front of his suit and dragged him close so the man could see the black of Edwin's eyes. "This Poppet is extremely important to me. And so is her child. You make certain they both survive. Your very existence depends on it, Doc. Understand?"

The doctor, looking as pale as the medical jacket he was carrying over one arm, nodded.

Edwin let him go and watched him hurry into the hospital's new, improvised maternity ward. Slumping down into a seat in a private lounge, Edwin began the long wait while doing his damned best to maintain his bloodlink with Eliza. Though they couldn't be together, he felt everything she was feeling, a kind of psychic handhold. He would have preferred to have been right there with her in the delivery room, of course, but they had discussed this, too, and

Eliza was convinced he would not be able to maintain his cover if they were together during the delivery and he witnessed any kind of distress from her.

Two hours later, the doctor emerged. He still looked pale, and his green scrubs were wet. Edwin stood up, dismayed by the shadows in the man's eyes. "We have done everything we can, my Lord. Your Poppet is well and resting in Recovery. The baby, however…"

His voice trailed off and he looked worried as if Edwin might thrash him.

Edwin, his voice small, said, "What's wrong with the baby?"

The doctor shook his head. "He's alive but barely. We have him in a neonatal incubator. My Lord…" He swallowed hard. "We are doing our *very* best, but I would not hold out much hope…"

Ignoring the doctor and his grim tidings, Edwin went in to see Eliza, who was sitting up in bed. She was dressed in a hospital gown, her hair awry and her face red and sweaty. Her eyes were red from crying, and she was snorting tears when she saw him.

"Oh, Edwin." She covered her face briefly. "I don't think he's going to make it. I think Oliver…" She hiccupped before bursting into fresh tears.

He made certain they were alone before gathering her carefully into his arms. He let her cry for a little bit into his chest, saying nothing and simply combing his fingers through her air. Whatever became of their child, he knew she needed this release.

"He's so tiny," Eliza finally admitted. "They don't even think all of his organs are fully developed."

Kissing her hair, Edwin told her, "Don't count Ollie out just yet, love. I mean, he is our son. Do you really think he'll just give up on us?"

She nodded, accepting that. But after a few moments, he wondered if he even meant what he was saying. Oliver was going to change their lives irrevocably—and not necessarily for the better. Because of him, he and Eliza would never really be able to be together. They would need to continue to play this ridiculous game. They would need to live apart. In his selfishness, Edwin wished their son would just cease to be, and that scared the living hell out of him.

What if he was turning into the cold, heartless Lord he was pretending to be? What if he turned into a true Vampire Lord one day with all of the accompanying corruption and cruelty?

And then he had an even more horrifying thought. He wondered if most of the Vampire Lords he had come to despise over the centuries, the Lords that played out their endless games destroying humans and each other, started out exactly this same way...

* * *

Back to the present

What an unholy cockup!

Edwin's not-so-victorious return to the *Queen's Gambit* was met with a particular kind of bedlam. After he, Narissa, and Tommy went through decontamination and the techs were sure their blood —those among them who had it—had been equalized, they released them to Captain Enzo, who debriefed them even as a set of highly-trained EMTs were set loose upon them, checking them over for injuries.

Narissa was taken to the medical ward to see what could be done about her injuries while Tommy was freed to return to his quarters for a period of rest and rebooting. Edwin, however, had no such peace to look forward to. He knew they had to do something about the remaining ice vampires aboard the ship, there were reports to write up for the High Courts and, if possible, he wanted to retrieve Lightfoot and Avery's bodies, though he had little hope for that. He suspected their remains had gone the same way of Emmerdale.

He had lost two men and his head navigator was injured. He had screwed the pooch royally with this one.

As soon as he stepped out of Enzo's war room and into the corridor, he saw Emerson waiting for him in the hallway. The vampire lawyer (that redundancy always made him snort) looked concerned as he slipped snakelike up alongside Edwin and kept pace with him. "My Lord, we need to speak!"

"Why? Shouldn't you be arranging to have the data from the *Abraxas* sent to the High Courts and Lord Trasch?"

"Yes, sir. That's the first thing on my agenda. But we have a bigger problem."

Edwin stopped and turned to face his counselor, his shoulders slumping. "What?" For the first time in too long, he felt the weight of his years. All he wanted to do after that fubar of a mission was see Eliza. He wanted to tell her anything and maybe even cry dryly into her bodice. Or maybe go somewhere and punch a great big hole in a wall first. He hadn't decided on that yet.

"I need you to look over your itinerary."

"Now?"

"It's important. Trust me."

Sighing, Edwin took the clipboard from the vamp. He looked at the two top items, both circled with a red pen. "Shite."

"Precisely."

He flipped the top papers to get a feel for how utterly screwed they were. "Shite!"

"I know."

Even though Lightfoot had been a vampire and had abandoned his people many decades ago, the Ongweh'onweh Nation was requesting that Edwin release his body into their custody. They wanted to give him a ceremonial cremation to help him pass to the next world. The problem was, Edwin didn't have the body, and he didn't know when it would be safe to retrieve it—assuming the ice vamps had not completely consumed it. Even worse, Avery's mother had flown up in a Hummingbird, and the pilot of the ship was requesting a pass to board the *Gambit* so she could speak to Edwin personally.

He worried his bottom lip. Sensing his distress, Emerson offered, "I can tell the Ongweh'onwehs that Lightfoot's body may be contaminated and they will need to wait for it to be processed. And we can bar Mrs. Gleeson from boarding. That's in your power."

Edwin thought about it. "Yes to the first. No to the second."

Emerson looked appalled. "You can't be serious! That woman is going to bury us! This could be a PR nightmare!"

Edwin always thought it was interesting how Emerson used the pronoun "us" in all of their conversations regarding the Congress as if the vampire himself had any dog in this race. "She's upset about her boy dying," Edwin observed. "I don't blame her."

"She is going to accuse you of negligence publically, sir!"

"Aye. I was responsible for keeping her son safe. I failed."

Emerson glared at him in outrage, then sighed as if he could not believe what Edwin was saying. "I strongly advise against this move, sir. It will make you seem weak to the rest of the Congress and, perhaps, even to the High Courts."

He was probably right, even so…

"Admit the ship and have my guards see her to a private suite. I'll talk to her shortly."

His counselor walked away, shaking his head. Edwin didn't want to do this, and it might have unforeseen fallout, sure, but he also knew he had to face the music. He'd made a mistake and his crew had suffered. He owed at least this to Avery's mother, didn't he?

An hour later, Edwin walked into the private suite where they had asked Mrs. Gleeson to wait for him, and there, in that room, he started to feel himself falling apart. Mrs. Gleeson was this thin, eighty-year-old woman, and her presence was a sharp reminder that Avery was so young a vampire that he'd still had a living parent. A family. Still, she had the right to face the man who had gotten her son killed in action.

Mrs. Gleeson stood up, shaking from age and grief. Hysterical, she started to scream at him, telling him how her son had survived Afghanistan, and how he had been attacked by Russian mercenary vampires while on the frontlines of Mariupol, a conflict that ended his military career and began his afterlife on Earth. He'd spent months in a depression before taking the job aboard the *Queen's Gambit*, thinking it was safe, thinking it was a way to heal...only to come to this!

Edwin let her cry and howl and try to grab at the front of his shirt. He told her he was sorry over and over and swore he would compensate her as best he could.

Eventually, he left the old woman weeping on the floor, surrounded by his guards, and locked himself inside his private office. He pulled out a bottle of blood substitute generously laced with gin and started to day drink. Greatly.

"Heavy is the head that wears the crown," he told himself. Heavy, aye. But he'd no idea it could conceivably break his neck.

* * *

"Edwin? Edwin, are you here?" Eliza said, standing in the doorway of his office.

Edwin scraped around on the floor to push himself up, scattering empty bottles, then braced his back against his desk as he came to. He realized he hadn't gotten blackout drunk in decades.

Slowly, he glared up through the filmy haze of his eyes and recognized Eliza's form as it came into soft focus. She was watching him, a look of pain on her face. He'd meant to see her, to talk to her—tell her what was happening. He hadn't. Instead, he'd spent the last—he checked the clock on the wall—four hours hiding away in this room, drinking himself into a blind stupor. A glance at his mind texts showed she'd been texting him endlessly.

"I've been all over this ship looking for you," she sighed.

"Go ahead and take your shot, love. Everyone else is."

She gave him a hard look, her lips pressed together. "Excuse me?"

He tried to push himself up into a more dignified position and failed. "Go ahead and tell me what a pig's ear I made of everything."

"Actually, I was concerned you might be hurt. But thank you for treating me like some nagging wife you need to hide away from."

He hung his head. "Ahh, balls...bog off!" He kicked some bottles and shook his head.

Shaking her head at his childish display, she asked, "I can't talk to you when you're like this. What happened over there?"

He tried to get up, but he was too drunk. He only managed to knock a half-full bottle of blood and gin over. "The ship was crawling with those gobshites...were it not for Tommy boy...uh, it doesn't mind. I'm sorry, lovey..." He pinched his nose. The gin was going straight to his head.

With another heavy sigh, she went to join him on the floor against his desk. "You know you scared the hell out of me. When I heard what happened, that two vamps were down, I thought for sure you were one of them."

He swallowed against the painful lump in his throat. "While we were being attacked, all I could think about was not seeing you again. And Ollie hating me." He ran a hand over his face and hair, which was sticking up. "He really hates me, Eliza. Someone...maybe someone at the school...has been telling him stories about me, and now he's afraid I'm a monster."

"Ollie doesn't hate you," Eliza said with conviction. "He's only a little boy. He doesn't understand the situation."

"Then we should tell him."

She swallowed at that and looked askance at him. "We talked about this, Edwin. We said we wouldn't tell him until he was older. We said we would let him be a child for as long as possible."

"But if we don't tell him, he might figure it out on his own anyway." Edwin tilted his head back and stared at the ceiling. "Do you know his teacher wants to put him in a gifted program?"

Eliza didn't argue, but she did sigh. "Maybe you're right. If we don't get in front of this, tell him..." She searched for the right words, then just blurted out, "Ollie will probably just rewire the whole ship, take us hostage, and make us tell him."

He looked at her. She stared back. Then they both broke out in giggle-laughs at that. It was the first time in a very long time that either one of them had found a spark of humor in anything. Eliza wiggled into his lap and put her arms around his neck. He started kissing her but she waved him away. "You smell like a barfly in an East End tavern."

He laughed at that, too.

Bracing her hands on his chest, she pushed herself back and said, "Let me see if I can feel him out. Maybe we'll take a vacation as a family. Then we'll tell him everything and hope for the best."

Nodding, Edwin said, "I trust you." After thinking a moment, he said, "Or...we could do something even better."

"What's that?"

He smiled wickedly. "What if the three of us ran away somewhere? Left all of this behind? Maybe went aboard?"

She gave him sympathetic eyes when she realized he was being serious. "You're really struggling, aren't you, Edwin?"

He swallowed hard. Of course, it was just a fantasy. "I don't like this, Eliza. I don't like what I'm becoming. What I *have* to become so we can survive." He closed his eyes, then opened them again, trying not to complain like some sad little wanker. "I got people killed today. I got Narissa seriously injured. And for what? To satisfy the High Courts? I should have just told Trasch to go fuck himself."

Eliza sat there a long moment in his lap, her hands on his shoulders, as she considered his words. Then she said, "Do you want to know what I think?"

"Of course I do."

"I think you did exactly the right thing."

"How so?" He closed his eyes and dug his hands into her sides. "How does any of this seem *right*?"

"We're maintaining the Plan."

Edwin started to groan when Dr. Vu pinged him.

—My Lord! You need to come down to the labs immediately. It's important. We've found something!—

| vii |

Oliver was kneeling on the floor of the corridor outside Lord Edwin's office, building a robot, when the Walking Man suddenly appeared. He wasn't unduly concerned about the ghost's appearance, though, because he had seen the Walking Man many times before. He was certain the specter haunted the corridors of the ship. But, right now, Oliver was more concerned that he couldn't get the tumblers that controlled the little five-inch robot working.

School gave them projects and equipment and even labs to work in, but that was all baby stuff. Making the 3-D projector that Ms. Stafford was so impressed with was stupid. It was stupid *old* tech, and Oliver didn't care about that. He cared more about making something like this little robot. He thought he might like to be an artificer when he grew up.

The Walking Man walked up to him and stopped inches away. Oliver could feel him staring down at the top of his head. Oliver knew the Walking Man hated him and almost everyone on board the ship—everyone except the woman Alisa, whoever that was.

Sitting up, Ollie pushed his back against the wall and glared up at the Walking Man. *What do you want?* he signed to him.

The Walking Man didn't answer. He never did with his voice, though he did sign on occasion, which is how Oliver knew he was looking for that woman. Probably he should have been afraid—the Walking Man was tall and pale, and his throat was badly mangled—but there weren't a lot of things that made Oliver afraid. Even when he was a baby, he never ran to his mum's bed when he woke up in the middle of the night and saw the Walking Man standing in a corner of his bedroom. He would just pull the covers up over his head and wait for him to go away.

Oliver's memories were of the Walking Man always being around. He even had a dull recollection of looking up from his crib when he was really small and seeing the Walking Man leering down at him. That used to make him cry until he realized the Walking Man didn't have the power to touch him. He could only look frightening.

What do you want? Oliver repeated the question. *Go away!*

The Walking Man gave him a surly look and made the letters for *Alisa*.

Oliver was used to this. Over the years, the Walking Man had asked to see Alisa countless times. Exasperated, Oliver signed, *I don't know who that is! I said go away!*

He started getting up, ready to swing his pack at the Walking Man if he had to, but the door to Lord Edwin's office opened and Mum stepped out with Lord Edwin right behind her. She walked right through the image of the Walking Man, which, thankfully, made him disappear in a wisp of smoke.

"Ollie, we're going down to the lab. Would you like to come?" Mum asked. She looked at him with some concern as if she could tell he was ready to fight.

"Is everything all right, mate?" Lord Edwin asked, stooping to talk to him.

Oliver glanced up into the tall Vampire Lord's eyes. Lord Edwin always tried to appear friendly, and there was a time when Oliver liked hanging out with him, but since hearing the stories in school of the terrible things he'd done, he'd begun to have his doubts. He'd begun to fear Lord Edwin.

Once, Ariel told him about a scary painting she'd seen in another part of the ship. Together, they made plans to go see it, and, the very next day, during quiet time in study hall, they snuck out of the school library and rode a lift to the floor where no kids were allowed to go, the place where they held fancy banquets.

"It's just this way. My dad mentioned seeing it when he was patrolling the corridors the other day," Ariel said, leading the way. When they got to the ballroom, Ariel pointed it out.

It was a large canvas, at least six feet tall, and all red and yellow as if the painting was full of flames. Lord Edwin was smirking and holding a burning dove in one hand and a pitchfork in the other. It was super ugly and gave Oliver a shiver up his spine, especially the way Lord Edwin was smiling and showing teeth, his blackened eyes full of flames.

"See? I told you," Ariel whispered, looking up at the painting in fear and wonder. "Lord Edwin is the devil."

That was more than a few days ago. But Oliver thought about the painting now. Lord Edwin certainly had spooky eyes, all golden-yellowy, and his hair and beard were a dark mahogany red. He *looked* like a devil. And when he put a hand on Oliver's shoulder, Oliver flinched at the cold seeping into his skin.

Lord Edwin withdrew it, looking worried.

"Are you all right, sweet pea?" Mum asked.

Oliver nodded dutifully, not wanting to upset Mum. He loved her, and he knew it was his duty to protect her. *Especially* from Lord Edwin.

She glanced aside at Lord Edwin, then turned back to him. "I'll walk you to school, sweetie. How about that?"

He shrugged, then nodded. Anything to get away from Lord Edwin.

She reached for him and took his hand. "I'll be back shortly, Edwin!" she told the vampire, who nodded. But as he and Mum started down the corridor to the lift, Oliver threw a dubious glance over his shoulder.

The Vampire Lord was standing in the corridor, watching them walk away, looking concerned. And just behind him hovered the Walking Man, a snarl on his twisted face.

***

While the two of them rode the lift to the Learning Center, Eliza turned to her son. "Are you sure everything is okay, Ollie? There wasn't someone bothering you?"

She couldn't be certain, of course, but she had the distinct feeling that Ollie had been "speaking" to someone when she stepped out of Edwin's office. She even looked both ways to check if someone had been harassing him. But he appeared to be alone. Perhaps he was talking to himself?

Ollie shook his head and made the A-OK sign.

After taking him to class and telling him she loved him, she returned to the lift. Edwin was waiting for her. He said whatever it was Dr. Vu wanted, he wanted her there with him.

"I worry about him," Eliza confessed glumly as she stepped inside the car. "I guess every mother worries about her child, though."

"There's a lot to worry about where Oliver is concerned," Edwin agreed, taking her hand and squeezing her fingers. "We don't even know what he is."

Eliza clenched his hand almost too tightly. "What if...?" She found it hard to articulate. "What if he's like Summersfield?" She had to work to tamp down the low-grade panic always hovering at the edges of her mind. "He was exposed to *Summersfield*'s blood when he was inside me. He could have...absorbed it somehow. Oh, god, Edwin..."

Edwin shook his head vehemently. "Ollie is *not* Summersfield's Heir." He said it forcefully—even angrily. As the lift descended, taking them down to the labs, she could see the hard set of his chin, the way he was clenching his teeth. "I honestly don't think he's anyone's Heir. But if he is—if you are—then the both of you are mine." He turned his head, adding in a low growl, "Remember, I gave you a lot of my blood when we were at Ian's castle. It bonded us."

She bit her lip and nodded, hoping he was right. Despite her showing no obvious vampiric traits, Dr. Vu did say she carried vampire DNA, though she didn't know whose. It was recessive, but there. Eliza had to bite back a small need to cry.

Edwin, sensing her distress, squeezed her hand. "You're mine. Ollie's mine."

She wanted to believe him—had to. Anything else was too horrible to imagine.

"I wonder what Veronica found," she mused as the doors of the lift opened and they immediately let go of each other's hand—they couldn't risk anyone noticing. Edwin stepped out first with Eliza trailing behind like a good little Pleasure Poppet. Together, they headed down the long warren of corridors toward the labs.

The large assortment of privately run laboratories in this wing had always impressed Eliza. Diagnostic, medical, clinical, and research and university labs were located here. Even though the *Gambit* was a Black Box, Edwin had allowed several universities to settle in and use its high-tech equipment. It didn't make actual money, but Edwin didn't care about that. He was progressive for a vampire, and he had always been deeply invested in schools and universities, maybe because he'd never had the chance to attend one. She liked that about him.

They passed several checkpoints before reaching the biological research lab, which was practically Dr. Vu's second home. The students and employees never found it strange that she, Edwin, and Ollie should visit the labs together. Eliza was Ollie's mum, and Ollie was Edwin's special project, so they dismissed it as just another of their Lord's many eccentricities.

Dr. Vu spotted them through the large, floor-to-ceiling windows and signaled to them to join her inside. She was all aflutter since getting several shipments from off the *Abraxas* a few hours earlier. Nothing from the belly of the beast; all the things they had transported to the *Gambit* had been in the cargo bay area. Emerson suggested some of the unclaimed cargo might be valuable.

"I'm glad you two could join me. We've been making some interesting discoveries!"

"It sounded urgent," Eliza said, confused by Dr. Vu's excitement.

Veronica nodded. "I've begun analyzing the blood samples from the creatures that Tommy retrieved, but we haven't been able to make heads or tails of it yet."

"Ice vampires," Edwin supplied.

Dr. Vu immediately latched onto that. "Excuse me, my Lord?"

"The samples that Tommy retrieved. The things that killed Lightfoot and Avery. They're ice vampires." He frowned with deep concern as he continued. "Those creatures were Poppets and crewmembers before they were infected with a virus."

Eliza gave him a surprised look. "How do you know that?"

Edwin never missed a beat. "I've encountered them before."

Dr. Vu's eyes lit up behind her glasses and she virtually danced from foot to foot. "I'd love to hear that story. It could help me figure out what they are and how they got that way."

Edwin nodded. "It's a special kind of virus similar to rabies. It's contracted through saliva, if that helps. You have to be bitten."

Veronica nodded. "One mystery solved. Now, we just have to figure out what the obelisk is."

"The obelisk?" Edwin said.

Veronica returned the look. "Didn't you get my itinerary of items retrieved from the *Abraxas*'s hold?"

Edwin flushed with embarrassment at that.

Eliza didn't want Veronica to know their esteemed Lord had crawled off to get drunk and feel sorry for himself, so she stepped in and said, "We were dealing with other important matters. The families of the dead vampires." After Veronica nodded her understanding, she added, "But tell us about the...obelisk."

"Yes, of course. Follow me."

They moved deeper into the lab and through another two checkpoints until they reached the pressure-locked storage units where Dr. Vu and her assistants kept specimens for study and experimentation. She asked Edwin and Eliza to wear plastic lab suits and masks before going into what she called the "anteroom."

"We discovered it among the cargo in the hold of the ship, but it became obvious pretty quickly that there is no way it belonged aboard the *Abraxas*," Dr. Vu explained, leading them inside a brightly-lid, white-tiled lab that contained nothing but the "obelisk," as she called it.

Edwin took one look at it and said, "Shite."

Eliza came up alongside him and said, "That does not sound good."

"It's not good. It's extremely bad, in fact."

They were all looking at a huge, cylindrical device about ten feet tall and perhaps five feet across. It was shaped somewhat like an upright hyperbaric chamber but made of some kind of shiny dark grey metal alloy that Eliza had never seen before. If there was a seam in it, some way to open it, it was invisible. It looked as impenetrable as a safe.

Eliza swallowed bitter worry. The unit reminded her uncannily of a space-age coffin.

"Can I assume you know what this is, Lord Edwin?" Dr. Vu asked as she danced around Edwin in a way that bothered Eliza just a little. She had never considered herself a jealous woman, and she'd never had reason to question Edwin's fidelity, but there was something overly excited about Veronica when she was in Edwin's presence.

Edwin nodded and took a step toward the unit, his eyes affixed to it. He didn't touch it but he did look on it with great trepidation. "I know exactly what it is...and I can tell you we need to get rid of it immediately."

Eliza was about to ask him to explain further, but he went on by saying, "This is Jotnar tech."

"Jotnar? As in...?"

Another nod. "Ice pirates."

Just his words made an icy finger of concern trail down her back. The juxtaposition of the ice vampires and this mysterious unit had all kinds of alarms going off in her head.

Turning to Dr. Vu, Edwin insisted, "Have the guards take it down to a cargo bay and load it onto a Bird immediately. I'll ask Tommy to oversee the operation, and I'll be down shortly to confirm it's been done."

Veronica looked appalled. "We can't get rid of it, my Lord! We have yet to scan it. This could be one of the most exciting finds this Congress has ever made! The tech alone could be worth a fortune to you."

"I'll save you the excitement. What's inside is not something you want to ever scan. And it's not worth shite. It's best launched into deep space."

Veronica looked ready to protest when Edwin calmly added, "Dump it. That's not a suggestion, Doctor. That's a command from your Lord."

Looking disappointed, Dr. Vu nodded. Eliza wondered if she was going to comply.

"If that's all." Edwin sounded grumpier than usual as he exited the lab. Once they had removed their protective gear and stepped back into the anteroom, Eliza put her hand on his arm. "How do you know so much about the Jotnar and their tech?"

He glanced back at the coffin-like structure visible through the large pane of glass…and sighed tiredly. "At one time, I was married to one."

* * *

On their way back up to Eliza's quarters, Eliza gave her husband a hard look and said, "You are going to have to clarify that statement you just made."

Edwin nodded. "I know." He took a deep breath and let it out slowly. One of the things they had promised each other years ago was that there would be no more secrets between them. And when the two of them came up with the Plan, Eliza had re-emphasized this point. They couldn't execute the Plan properly if there were unforeseen factors that might sabotage it.

It hurt, if she was being honest. She thought they had moved past the point of Edwin having deep, dark secrets. Obviously, she'd been wrong.

Edwin stared at his feet a long moment before he began. "You know that when I worked for Foxley, he had me turn all kinds of tricks. I was his heavy, his whore, his weapon, whatever he wanted. I had to do whatever he asked me to." He gave a little shudder and then shook his head. "Truth was, I *wanted* to do those things. It was fun, being his Enforcer, and I thought it made me a good Heir. I'm not proud of that."

She nodded. Many of Edwin's stories of his time in service to Foxley were nightmare fuel. Foxley had used, manipulated, and hurt him in so many ways that it made her heart ache. And all in the name of his mad ambition to accumulate an obscene amount of wealth to build the *Gypsy Queen*. Perhaps Edwin had been a willing participant in many of those horrors, but she found she couldn't judge him. She, too, had been an Heir for a short time—an Heir to that monster Summersfield. And she understood more than most the insane desire to please her master. It was something no human could understand until they'd been taken and manipulated by a Vampire Lord.

Edwin looked up at last, but his eyes turned inward as he spoke. "One of those things was an arranged marriage between me and the princess of the Jotnar. Princess Yrsa, her name was. She wasn't even the firstborn of Skarde, the King of the Jotnar—I think she was his eighth born, if I recall correctly. But she had Skarde's ear. She was his favorite. And that was important to Foxley. Important to his plans at the time."

Eliza watched the lighted buttons on the lift's panel as they descended. "So...Foxley made you marry this princess?"

He sort of shrugged. "It was more of a business arrangement. The Jotnar had some tech that Foxley wanted. Yrsa fancied me, and Foxley decided to offer me up as a bargaining chip as a means to establish trade between his Court and theirs." Shaking his head, he explained, "He wanted to invent a safe way for vampires to enter true cryogenic sleep, the kind that could last for centuries. And he wanted to capitalize on it. At the time, it had become fashionable to hibernate for long periods of time, but even a vampire won't sleep indefinitely. Unfortunately, the tech never worked correctly, all the field tests failed, and he eventually abandoned the project."

She stared at him long and hard as certain pieces fell into place in her head. "That containment unit?"

Edwin nodded. "Aye. I think the Jotnar never abandoned Foxley's project. I think they perfected it even though it took them some time."

"So," she said, trying to keep her voice reasonable and not hurt or trembling, "you were married once long ago."

When he didn't immediately answer, she felt her stomach fall faster than the lift they were riding. Raising her head, she stated, "Oh, god. You *are* married."

He grimaced. "After everything went down and Foxley decided the tech was not worth his time, I tried to get it annulled, lovey, I swear, but Yrsa wouldn't accept my terms and she threatened to have me excommunicated from the Roman Catholic Church if I tried. By then, Yrsa had gotten rather…attached to me."

Eliza sighed. "Let me guess. *El Mal de Amor*."

"Something like that. But it was never a real marriage. Back then, no one married for love anyway. It was all business all of the time."

She thought about that a moment. "So…are you still married to her?" She knew Edwin well enough to know he was a very devout Roman Catholic. She didn't share his beliefs, but she respected that his beliefs were his own.

"Er, well…" The doors opened on her floor and he said, "I think we should discuss this at length at a later point."

"Yes, I agreed." She stepped out onto her floor and turned to face him.

He gave her his big, sad puppy dog eyes. "I'm sorry. I know I should tell you these things."

"Yes," she agreed. "You should." She wished he were not so handsome and charming and didn't look so good in his fitted dark suits. It made it hard to be angry with him. With a deep sigh, she asked, "What happened to the princess?"

He started to say something but his words were drowned out by the ship's emergency alarm system. The lights in the corridor turned red and began to flash. At the same time, both of them got a mind text from Tommy, who was down in the loading bay.

—Sir, you need to get down here immediately!—

"What's happening?" Eliza said, glancing around at the general bedlam. She had never seen this kind of response from their ship before.

Edwin said it out loud *and* in mind-text. "What the bloody hell is going on down there, Tommy?"

—It's the unit, sir. We were loading it onto a Hummingbird per your directives when it suddenly…opened up.—

| viii |

It was a trap, Malcolm Whitby realized. The ship. The creatures. All of it.

It was a trap and they had fallen right for it.

Malcolm was in his quarters, playing with his youngest son, tossing Simon up into the air and catching him to the sound of the toddler's delighted squeals, when the thought hit him like a train.

"Anjou?" he called. "I must speak with Lord Edwin immediately!"

He and Anjou had been in a domestic arrangement for close to seven years now. Werewolves did not recognize human marriage or any of the complicated Court arrangements that vampires did. All that was required for two werewolves to commit to each other was a simple handfasting. He was a little surprised when it happened, considering her past relationship had been abusive. Malcolm had dethroned the ex-Alpha of the Youngbloods to win her and become head of the pack. And because he genuinely loved Anjou and, more importantly, respected her, he avoided pushing her into a new commitment. It was she who had asked him.

And now they had two small children, and Malcolm couldn't imagine being happier.

Simon howled like crazy when Malcolm tossed him high one last time, then caught him in his arms and held him close, rumbling deep in his chest, a sound that delighted and comforted his children whether he was in wolf form or human.

"What did you say, Malcolm?" Anjou stated from the doorway of their bedroom. She was getting dressed for the day and looked very beautiful in her slim white suit with its flaring tailcoat, her curling reams of black hair tucked up into a chignon. Her face was keen and slightly bemused by Malcolm's sudden outburst.

When they first joined Lord Edwin's Congress, with Malcolm representing the werewolf part of that arrangement, they were offered every luxury possible. Lord Edwin, an almost foolishly generous vampire, gave them a lavish twelve-room suite that rivaled even his own inner sanctum. He offered the Youngbloods all of the protection their pack would ever need and even gave the wolves jobs aboard the gyro so they would feel useful.

Malcolm had remained Edwin's Dog of War, his strategist, his general, while Anjou was offered an administration position in the Learning Center.

Malcolm made his voice soft so he didn't alarm the giggly baby werewolf in his arms. "I had a thought. A dark one."

Anjou tilted her head. "Tell me."

"What if the *Abraxas wasn't* left derelict, my mate. What if it was set up that way so the humans would find it, explore the ship, and become infected with whatever disease those Poppets and crew had? They might then take the infection down to Earth."

Anjou's eyes grew dark and concerned. "I see."

Simon, on spotting his mother near, began to fuss hungrily even though he had been fed only an hour before. He was growing large like Malcolm and never seemed satisfied.

Malcolm carried him over and waited patiently while Anjou undid her jacket to breastfeed their baby. It was a lovely, primal picture that always filled Malcolm's heart with love for his son and his mate

—so much so that he sometimes thought it should burst from being so full. Meanwhile, Briar, their little tomboy, came zooming into the room, black box braids bouncing around her face, one of her toy airplanes in hand. She quickly began to circle Malcolm's legs, making enthusiastic plane noises. She was only five, but the girl was convinced she wanted to be a pilot.

Standing there, he watched his little family, the warm feeling deep in his bones warring with the icy chill riding high up his spine. "I feel this was a trap. My instincts tell me none of this was coincidental."

Briar pretend crashed her airplane into Malcolm's legs with great special effect noises while he explained his fears. He first wanted to hear Anjou's opinion before taking this to Lord Edwin.

"The Jotnar are clever...and they've stayed out of Supe politics for centuries. But perhaps that was only because they were developing their tech and planning their moves." He added, "The containment unit is evidence. Aye." He shuddered as all of the little pieces of the Jotnar's plan fell into place in his warrior's mind. "It's what I would do."

Anjou looked worried at last. "But we intercepted it first."

"We did."

She rocked their baby, who was full of milk and nearly asleep now. Anjou seemed calm, but he saw her eyes moving erratically as the wheels turned in her head and she weighed the danger to her pack—and to their family. "So, that containment unit...?"

"Aye. I believe it was loaded onto the *Abraxas* at some point prior to the disaster that took the ship. Then, after the attack, whatever is inside emerged to claim the survivors. A clever gambit—attack from within *and* without. I believe it may have been controlling the ice vampires."

"In that case, you should—"

The ship's emergency protocol suddenly went off, turning their suite a lurid shade of red. Malcolm stiffened at the noise and Briar stopped doing airplane rolls in the air and looked up at him, her beautiful brown eyes wide with fear.

Anjou, suddenly looking like she was splashed with blood, said, "If you have these fears, you should get down to the cargo hold and warn Lord Edwin immediately."

Malcolm nodded. Anjou, besides being his mate and the Pack Mother was, first and foremost, a pragmatic woman.

* * *

On the lift down to the dock level, Edwin had a thought—and not a good one. He'd had a bad feeling about the mission on board the *Abraxas*, a feeling that things weren't quite right. Or, more specifically, that things were *too* right. Too...aligned. That they should find the ship with those ice vamps waiting...

He immediately mind-texted Malcolm, who was also on his way down. —It's a trap...—

—I know, my Lord. —

As soon as they converged in the corridors, they hurried toward the loading bay. Tommy was already there, but he was lying motionless in a big metal heap on the floor when they arrived. Edwin spotted him first and rushed to Tommy's side, Malcolm hot on his heels.

His Enforcer was crumpled up defensively the way someone who was injured and trying to protect himself might, his large, awkward, metallic body twisted painfully into a semi-fetal position. Edwin glanced around but noted that no one else was in the bay—as if his staff had fled the scene, leaving poor Tommy to fend for himself. He impulsively started to grab Tommy's shoulder to roll him over but yelped when his fingers encountered the solid sheen of ice coating Tommy's whole body.

Pulling his hand away, he looked at his bloodied hand and saw some of his skin sticking to Tommy's shoulder. "Don't touch him!" he warned Malcolm, who stopped mid-motion, his hand extended. "He's frozen bloody solid!"

Malcolm backed away while Edwin stood up, his hand smarting where he'd encountered what felt like dry ice.

"What happened to him?" Malcolm demanded to know, looking around.

"I don't know, mate."

"Is he dead?"

"I don't bloody know! But I'm going to make whoever did this pay through his bleedin' teeth," Edwin growled, gripping his injury. He'd had about enough of this wankery. He could feel his eyes bleeding black, and his wings were uncurling against his back, threatening to tear through the back of his shirt and suit jacket. He needed to pound something to dust—preferably the twat who'd done this to Tommy.

As the red emergency lights continued to flick on and off, he spotted several people scattered about—dock workers, technicians, and the runners that got the good where they needed to be. Perhaps ten or twelve of them, all crumpled up on the floor in a state similar to Tommy's. All of them frozen—like Tommy, their bodies twisted in pain and covered in white hoarfrost.

Edwin moved to the first few to look for vital signs, then swore violently at the massacre. First Tommy…and now this. His staff. The people he'd sworn to take care of when he became Lord of this stupid ship. They had given him their fealty, and this is what happened to them.

"NEWTON, shut down the emergency system."

"Shutting down, sir." The normal white and blue bay lights immediately sprang up, the sirens were cut off, and Edwin looked around in horror, then toward the loading bridge where the containment unit had been placed.

It was facing him, gaping open. He didn't bother casing the bay before he walked up to the empty containment unit and looked at the padded inside. If someone was lurking, he would have sensed him. Several powerful straps—obviously used to hold a body immobile inside the unit—were hanging loose. Otherwise, there was nothing to see. Whoever, whatever, had been inside had already exited the unit and attacked his people and his Enforcer before taking off into the depths of the ship.

Malcolm came up behind him, grunting, "I was afraid of this."

Edwin turned to him. "The trap? Aye. The Jotnar wanted someone to find the ship. And we did." Edwin immediately commanded NEWTON to scramble security, not that they needed it. They probably already knew because of the alarms and the AI.

Malcolm nodded. Seconds later, they both heard screams for the first time.

***

Oliver knew every single hiding place aboard the ship. And because he had the tools—either because Mum let him have them or the school gave it to him—he could get into every nook and cranny. He regularly removed the cover on the ventilation shaft in the floor of his room and slid down the tubes that would take him to almost any floor without needing to use the lift. Even though the tubes and shafts were pitch black—at least according to Ariel, who sometimes accompanied him—he always managed to find his way. Nothing was ever one hundred percent dark to Oliver.

Of course, he never told anyone besides Ariel. He knew his mum wouldn't approve.

Everyone thought he was a baby and couldn't take care of himself, but Oliver could. He wasn't afraid of anything and he was exceptionally strong. He discovered that one day when, while crawling through one of the shafts, he heard a rumbling noise, probably the engineers soldering above his head, and a part of the tube gave way, almost slamming into him.

It had startled him, but Oliver reacted automatically, throwing up his hands and catching the whole tube before it could crush him. There wasn't any room to get around it, but he was able to shove it back up and into place, and he figured it probably had to weigh a lot. Another time, he encountered one of the ship rats. They made their home down here, feeding off whatever crumbs they could find. A particularly hungry one jumped at him, and even though it was dark, Oliver still caught the creature by the neck and tossed it aside. It banged around the tubes pretty hard. He thought maybe he'd even killed it.

Nothing really frightened him. With the Walking Man about, there wasn't much that fazed Oliver. And now, after years of traversing the tubes, he was both fast and accurate. He could go from Mum's quarters all the way down to the loading bay in a matter of minutes. Which was where he was going now. Ariel had mind-texted him and said something really scary and exciting was going on down there. Naturally, he wanted to know what. She said her dad, who worked security on the ship, said that it was all hands on deck in the loading bay. That something had gotten out of the metal box that everyone aboard the ship was afraid of.

—What kind of box?—

—Daddy doesn't know, only that it's dangerous. He said it looks like a space coffin.—

—A space coffin? For a space vampire?— Of course, Oliver wanted to see the space coffin that maybe contained a space vampire. So, it was no issue getting down to the loading bay where the coffin was supposed to be loaded onto a Hummingbird. As soon as he got home from school, he told Mum he was going to do this homework but instead used his tools to access the tubes and climbed down to the loading bay, popping out through a grate in the wall in the supervisor's office. He then hurried down the corridor to the bay, hoping they hadn't loaded up the space coffin yet.

Oliver slowed down when he heard a scream coming from just beyond the intersection ahead. Sliding against the wall, he moved carefully and peeked around the bend. He sucked in a quick breath at the sight of the creature standing in the corridor beyond. It was extremely tall—maybe nine feet!—and as muscular as a barbarian. Its skin was bluish-black but its hair and beard were stark white. It looked mostly like a man, but its eyes were yellow and red, almost reptilian in appearance. It wore black armor.

The space vampire! Dangling from its gigantic fist was one of the security guards—though not Ariel's dad, thankfully. The man, choking because his throat was in the vice of the giant's fist, was pedaling his legs uselessly as the alien creature lifted him even higher so the top of his head almost touched the ceiling. The blue man growled, and the guard screamed, but not for long.

Oliver watched a sheen of frost seemingly crawl over the blue man's hand and then over the face and head of the guard, creeping steadily downward. It happened quickly; between one breath and the next, the man went stiff, frozen solid, and the giant blue man dropped him.

Oliver flinched when the security guard's body shattered like fragile glass on the floor and a too-loud gasp came out of his throat. But he couldn't help it. He'd never seen anything like that before!

The blue man turned and glared at him with those weird eyes. Oliver froze up and then, slowly, he began to tremble. He'd never really been afraid of anything until that moment. Suddenly, he wanted to go home. He wanted his mum.

The monstrous creature started marching toward Oliver, his eyes narrow and angry, and Oliver backed up—right against a wall.

* * *

Oliver was missing!

"Ollie?" The moment Eliza saw the empty room, a bad feeling formed like a hard pit in her stomach. "Ollie, where are you?"

She circled his room, then ripped the covers off his bed like he might be hiding underneath. Finally, she looked in his closet. No Oliver, though she was sure he said he wanted to get a jump on his homework before dinner.

Eliza finally found the open grate in the floor after moving his bed. She knelt beside it, her heart hammering painfully in her chest. "Oliver!"

* * *

Edwin had found himself in some dodgy situations over the two-plus centuries of his existence, but when he rounded the bend and found himself staring down a very long corridor at a Jotunn holding his son captive by pressing his huge hand against the small boy's chest, pinning him helplessly to the wall, all of his past misadventures paled by comparison.

He had never in his eternal life been so terrified as he was right now.

Nothing had ever experienced had prepared him for being a father or the terror he would feel at the sight of his child being threatened. All of his good sense fled him in that moment. "You!" he roared in the Jotnar language, pointing at the creature hurting his son. "Let my boy go and face me!"

The Jotunn turned and glared at him with its virulent eyes. "Lord Edwin," it said with amusement. The warrior smiled. "Your boy? What a find. Captain Yrsa sends her regards."

Turning back to his son, he grabbed a trembling Oliver by the front of his uniform shirt, the young boy's reed-thin form looking like a rag doll in his hands—and lifted him easily up off his feet.

Oliver turned his head and looked pleadingly at Edwin. There were fearful tears in his large azure eyes, something Edwin had never seen before, and something that tore at his clockwork heart. He didn't think. He lunged at the giant warrior. He was willing to do anything to prevent the monster from hurting his child, but he already knew he was too late—and too far away—to save his son from harm.

Then something happened. Something very strange.

Before Edwin could reach him, his boy's eyes turned stark black in the way of full-blooded vampires. No irises or pupils. Just black. Tears in those black eyes, he turned and looked back at the Jotunn, who was glaring down at him, the ice already beginning to crawl over the back of his hand and toward him...

As fast as he was, Edwin knew he would never outrun the cold streaking up the Jotunn's hand to reach his son. But Oliver didn't seem to even care. He stopped trembling and the blackness did not stay to just his eyes but instead crawled vine-like from them and over Oliver's cheeks and down his face. It crawled down his neck and into the collar of his school uniform. Then the blackness on his face swiftly expanded, turning Oliver's skin the color of shiny obsidian so only his clothes and the red rims of his eyes stood out. The rest of him looked like a living shadow.

By then, Edwin had reached the Jotunn and leaped, but the giant turned and backhanded him into the opposite wall, crushing his body into it in a cartoon-like outline. The blow was so powerful it temporarily knocked his breath from his lungs. Edwin tried to move, but he was temporarily stuck in the actual wall.

The Jotunn turned his full attention on Oliver. The ice had finally reached his son, but even as it began to touch his skin, Oliver's shadow self—Edwin didn't know what else to call it—reached out for the Jotunn at the same time...

And the giant, blue-skinned warrior began to scream. He screamed as if Oliver's shadow was toxic, and that shadow stuff—whatever it was—seemed to quickly overrun the ice and burn it up. Steam poured off the Jotunn's hand and arm as if Oliver were on fire. Unable to hold Oliver any longer, the Jotunn dropped his son like he was a hot branding iron.

Oliver fell into a nimble hand-and-knee crouch on the floor at the warrior's feet, his head up and his attention centered on his nemesis in a distinctively non-childlike way.

The Jotunn wheeled away from Oliver, clutching his burning arm, a look of devastating pain etched across his harsh features. He seemed to be searching for an avenue of escape.

By that time, Edwin had finally yanked himself from the wall and Malcolm had joined him in the corridor in giant wolf form. The Werewolf of Whitby had stationed himself at the intersection of the corridors, cutting off any chance that the Jotunn might escape into the depths of the ship. The giant black wolf's mane stood on end like black quills, and as the Jotunn turned to face him, Malcolm dropped his mouth open, growling and showing off his fearsome teeth in anticipation of the kill. Despite towering over even the giant werewolf, the Jotunn stopped as he reconsidered approaching the feral-looking creature.

The Jotunn suddenly decided a better option was to turn and face Edwin, who had moved to block the other way. The creature looked down at his own hand, which now had those black vines of Oliver's crawling across it. His skin was still smoking from whatever his son had done to him. "You disturbed our trap," he told Edwin, confirming what he and Malcolm had suspected earlier. "You ruined our plans, vampire!"

"Too bloody bad!" Edwin moved sideways in the narrow hallway. He wanted to try and place himself between the Jotunn and Oliver, but he also didn't want the Jotunn to escape down the corridor and into the depths of the ship where he might hurt more of Edwin's people.

Thankfully, the Jotunn decided for him by moving back toward the loading bay. It allowed Edwin to edge around so he was better able to shield his son. At the same time, something about putting his back to Oliver concerned him.

The boy had finally stood up from his crouch, but he hadn't returned to normal. He seemed worse than before, completely black except for his shining red eyes that looked like bloody gashes in his face and his white teeth, which looked longer and sharper. A number of strange, black, smoke-like tendrils smoldered off him, and when one of those tendrils drifted too close to Edwin, he jumped at the sensation of heat or electricity that crackled in the air. Edwin had never encountered anything like it.

"Oliver," Edwin said, trying to draw his son's attention. But Oliver's glowing ruby eyes were soldered to the Jotunn, and he was grinning, showing off his shark-like teeth that Edwin was sure hadn't existed before today. He felt a sharp tingle of fear, and he knew—just *knew*—that it was not advisable at the moment to get between Oliver and the Jotunn. He was terrified his son might rip right through him to get at the giant warrior, so intent was his look.

Changing tactics, Edwin swung around so he faced his son, cutting off the view of the Jotunn completely. "Ollie?" he said again. "Ollie, can you hear me, mate?"

Oliver's attention briefly switched to Edwin, but he was again distracted when the Jotunn warrior behind him emitted a horrendous roar of pain. When Edwin glanced back, eyes wide with alarm, he saw the creature clutching his infected hand. The black, spider-like tendrils had climbed all the way up to the Jotunn's clavicle. He started gasping for breath. Spinning away, the creature toppled to one side and lay on the floor, spasming in pain.

It was fortunate he'd collapsed because Edwin couldn't be bothered kicking his ass. He had more important matters to attend to. Ignoring the Jotunn, he turned to face Ollie and reached out to take his boy by the shoulders—then stopped himself. What if whatever toxin Oliver was generating infected him, too? He had no idea if he was immune to it or if it would put him in as much agony as the Jotunn. So, he crouched down and looked his son in the eye. "Ollie...Ollie, lad, look at me."

Even though Oliver was breathing harshly, he did. His eye looked like they were bleeding red light through his coal-black skin. He bared his fearsome teeth at Edwin like a feral dog and clenched and unclenched his fists as if he was thinking of grabbing him.

"*Ollie!*"

Eliza's voice cut like a blade through the chaos and caused the boy to turn and look at her standing at the end of the hall. Malcolm the wolf was stationed at her side, and even partly wrapped around her. Her expression went from concern to horror when she took in the sight of her son. She took a step forward but then stopped. She raised both hands imploringly, her voice small. "Ollie...Oliver."

Oliver's eyes softened suddenly at the sight of his mum. The darkness suddenly faded away, his teeth receded, and his eyes cleared and returned to their normal light blue. In seconds, he was just their ordinary little boy again. And seconds after that, tears were dripping from his eyes and he was sobbing tiredly as he ran toward his mum and let her enfold him in her arms.

"Ollie...sweet pea," Eliza said, holding him close and tucking his head against her chest. She stroked his head but then looked up at Edwin worriedly.

He recognized that look. Her eyes were full of darkness and terror for their son.

| ix |

The Queen's Gambit, one hundred years from now

The latest campaign had left Edwin ragged and bleeding—inside and out. After speaking to one of his Enforcers about their next move, he dismissed her and retreated to his quarters on board the ship to rest, drink, and contemplate how profoundly fucked they might be.

He nodded to his bodyguards as he let himself in. They reacted not at all, standing straight and tall and metallic in their station outside the doors of his personal quarters. He knew they would not move until relieved. They would die before they left him unguarded, such was their loyalty to him.

That was something, at least. In the last few decades of this seemingly endless war, he had won back the fealty of all on board the ship. And not a few off. They loved their Lord Edwin and recognized him as the supreme power, the last levee to hold back the encroaching darkness the Ancients presented to the world. But he often wondered if loyalty was enough. If *he* was enough.

Eliza would say he was. She would insist he could do this.

Thoughts of his wife left his heart feeling heavy and profoundly broken.

It was dark and quiet inside his inner sanctum. His crew made certain his quarters were always clean and neat and that the lights were kept low to help with the damage to his eyes that the various battles in the war had caused. They were fastidious to the point of obsession in their efforts to give him small comforts even though he never asked them for anything. A stocked bar. A soft bed. He knew they felt obligated for all he and his Congress had done for them—for the various freedoms he had won them. He appreciated that. But the silence, the utter stillness—the *emptiness*—always haunted him a little when he retreated to his quarters to rest.

Without bothering to change out of his ruined clothing, Edwin moved to the wet bar and poured himself a tall glass of blood laced generously with gin. It was the real stuff; these days, he needed more strength than substitute blood could give him. He drank it down in one gulp, the gin warming his dead-cold body, then poured another.

He looked up at the etched mirror positioned above the bar and studied the scars on his face, his oily hair tied haphazardly back in a tight queue, and the dark rings under his eyes. His eyes were full of grey cataracts, and his hair, once a dark, rich auburn, was almost stark white. Nasty and damaged though he was, he could still mostly see out of one eye.

"You are one ugly git, mate," he snortled. At least he could still find his sense of humor. That, at least, wasn't dead yet.

He spotted movement from the corner of his eye, but he wasn't unduly alarmed. He had been expecting this.

"How did you get past my guards?" His voice was ragged and coarse these days, filtered through too much pain and a fuckton of cigarettes. He certainly did not sound or look the regal Vampire Lord in any way—unless you were blind or squinted a lot.

Too much had come to pass.

"Those wankers?" said his uninvited guest. "Easy. I made them let me in. Then I made them forget the whole affair."

"You've learned new tricks." He was acutely aware of his guest's accent. It sounded similar to his own from many, many years ago. Having spent decades with Eliza—the best years of his life, though he didn't know that at the time—Edwin eventually lost much of his old-timey Bowbell brogue. These days, he sounded more like Eliza had. But his guest's accent had yet to fade.

He stepped into the adjoining room where his guest was sitting by the small port window, his long, long legs up and the heels of his boots balancing on the simple, two-person table that Edwin almost never used. His guest was dressed entirely in black, and, Edwin knew, under his long coat, all of his weapons were similarly painted black. That, combined with his blue-black obsidian skin and spiky hair left only his eyes glowing. They were white, as were his teeth—spiky shark teeth with the power to shred flesh, human and otherwise.

The creature looked like a malignant shadow.

"Oliver," Edwin said by way of a greeting and inclined his head. As a well-respected assassin, his son deserved that respect, at least.

"Hallo, Dad." And Oliver gave him that smile. That hideous nightmare smile.

It was unnaturally wide, almost slicing his entire handsome face in half like a shining sickle. And, yes, it was full of those white, pearl-like teeth, all of them slightly pointed inward.

In the dimness, Edwin could see few details of his son, but he knew from experience that his child had grown into an astonishing being of lethal grace. Tall and long-limbed, beautifully agile. He could move like a serpent, and his features, though difficult to discern at the moment, were a perfect symphony of his and Eliza's. Oliver had his hook-like Briton nose but Eliza's full lips and almond-shaped eyes. His long, blue-black hair, slightly curling and as thick as leaves on a bush, was secured with a thong and brushed the small of his back.

He was a real heartbreaker once upon a time. It saddened Edwin to realize that Oliver could have had any man or woman he wanted, but that no lover could compare to the devotion he felt for the armory under his coat—his first and truest love. His little boy preferred ripping hearts out by the roots and eating them whole rather than breaking them.

"What do you want, son?"

Oliver was currently fingering a small, slender knife—possibly a throwing dagger of his own design. He turned it idly in his fingers while he watched his dad with those keen eyes. "You look thin, Dad."

Edwin raised the flask in his hand in salute. "Worried about your old man's health?"

Oliver laughed at that. It was not a sane sound.

Edwin took a long draught directly from the flask. "To what do I owe the pleasure?"

Oliver, that damnable smile still in place, said, "I expect you have not heard. But then, why would you? You're too busy fighting the Forever War." His smile slipped only a microsecond before he announced, "The High Courts have put a contract on your head, my Lord. Were you not aware?"

Edwin snorted at that—actually, he was snorting at both Oliver's choice of words as well as the sheer pretentiousness of the High Courts to try and off one of their own. Still playing their insipid little games when no one alive cared about them any longer…it was pathetic. "They've wanted me gone for centuries, Ollie. You'll have to do better than that if you want to impress me. Suppose you want me afraid. Sorry to disappoint, son."

That horrid smile again. "You might be interested to know I've taken the contract."

Edwin took another draught from his flask before speaking. His throat was parched, and he hoped the drink would help with the pain in his barely mending bones. It didn't. He might need to visit his Poppets' quarters later this night and let their blood repair his many internal injuries. But right now, he stood up soldier straight, determined not to let Ollie see how hurt he really was. "*Have you now?*"

Oliver's smile grew even wider, if that was possible. "Surprised?"

"I shouldn't be, I reckon." Setting the almost empty flask down on a nearby table, Edwin turned to face his son—his heart, his enemy, his greatest regret. "It was inevitable. You have never forgiven me."

"For which offense? I may need to revisit the list."

"Oliver, please…"

His son set his feet down on the floor and stood up, giving Edwin a long, venomous look. "No, let's review them all, shall we? We'll begin with you lying to me for most of my childhood and then move on to how you sold me like chattel to the enemy. After that, we'll finish with what you did to Mum."

"Guilty on the first charge," Edwin admitted, his voice slowly rising in pitch. "But the second…Oliver, you don't understand how it was…what kind of a situation we were all in…"

Shaking his head, he spat, "Don't you dare! You chose your little empire over me! Were it not for Trasch, I'd still be a prisoner of war…"

"You're not being fair!" Edwin cried, the pain of the past lancing him deeper and more thoroughly than the weapons the enemy had stuck into his body only a few hours prior. "I did what I did to protect you. We both did."

"I don't want to hear your pathetic excuses, your justifications for what you did…*Dad*. Why don't we just jump to Mum?"

Edwin gasped air that sounded like a sob. "I did *nothing* to your mum that your mum did not ask me to." The words almost choked Edwin up. "I loved her, Ollie. I *still* love her."

For a moment, his son seemed completely overwhelmed, at a loss for words. And then he said in barely a whisper, "And still you put her on ice. How is that *love?*"

Edwin breathed in and out, in and out. His lungs felt on fire and his attention was already drifting to possible weapons in the room. He did not like where this was going, and he had no idea where Oliver had stashed that knife of his now.

What did it matter? Oliver was a vampire hunter, High Courts trained. He had decades of practice and a legendary record of kills, one that rivaled even Chimera. He probably had a thousand pockets with a thousand weapons in them—and he knew how to use every bloody last one. If he wanted Edwin dead, it would be done.

Reason then. He would use reason on his wayward child. "You don't understand anything, Ollie," Edwin explained tiredly. "You never have. And now, you're letting your rage blind you. Take it from me, son. That is a very dangerous way to operate."

"Then explain it to me!" Oliver reached for the table and tossed it across the room as if it was made of feathers. It smashed into a thousand fragments against the far wall.

Edwin flinched. He was taller than even Edwin, whippy and powerful. Oliver's vampire and Poppet genes had intersected in just such a way that he was nearly unequaled in all he did. And yet, despite his power and prowess, Oliver's voice shook a little when he whispered. "Explain it to me as though I'm a child."

Something about Oliver's desperate tone made Edwin stand taller, as if that would help. He could feel his own anger rising—his anger that Oliver would push for this. "I can't do that, son. What Eliza did"—he had to swallow down a lump of pain that never quite went away—"that is your mother's secret and her burden to carry. She wanted it that way."

Oliver's eyes flared. "Mum is dead!"

He moved so fast that Edwin never saw it coming. Suddenly and without warning, Oliver struck him in the shoulder with his fist, and together, they flew back across the room. In microseconds, Oliver him up against a wall, a set of blades between his knuckles embedded in the plaster beside Edwin's head. The weapon was unique, like brass knuckles but with corkscrew attachments. Black iron. Deadly on contact with vampires. Oliver, an accomplished metallurgist, had probably designed the weapon himself.

Oliver leaned close, his breath stinking of blood. "Her secrets mean nothing now. They're as dead and frozen as she is."

"Oliver." Edwin, not afraid now—the pain and never-ending fatigue he felt was all-consuming—reached up and set both hands on Oliver's chest. He could feel the tense strength of his son's musculature under his coat. "The words in your mouth are not your own. They were put there by Trasch—"

"Then tell me the truth and maybe I'll believe you."

Edwin licked his lips nervously. He didn't want to say it, but he also knew Eliza would not want her son in such pain. "You're not my Heir...and neither was she."

That stopped his son from driving him into the wall—and possibly ripping his head off in his hungry rage. In fact, he felt surprise pouring off Oliver's tall, gangly black form.

He didn't respond at first.

"That's what you really want to know, right?" Edwin said, baring his own teeth in a fearsome grin of bitter regret. "What you have always wondered. Whose Heir you are? Well, if you must know, lad, it's not me."

Oliver opened his mouth, then closed it with a click of teeth. Words failed him. Finally, after a few uncomfortable ticks of silence, he eased back a little and said softly, "The Walking Man."

"Eliza asked me to ice her when she realized who her master really was. And yours. She couldn't bear the idea of being his…of being that *thing* he created." Edwin narrowed his eyes as he felt them go all black with his rage—it was so familiar now. A permanent part of him that he drew on often whilst in battle. "And she knew a time would come when Summersfield would come for you as well. When he would take you and change you. And that, my son, is why she asked me to ice her."

Edwin sighed, his voice trembling with fatigue. "She hoped she could contain him within herself. She hoped he would follow her into death and leave you alone. But I can see now that she was so very wrong…"

Oliver, looking suddenly afraid, said, "I don't believe you. You're a liar!"

"I don't care what you believe, Ollie. You're not my son any longer. You stopped being my son when you gave your allegiance to Trasch…"

Oliver roared and, baring those long, fearsome teeth of his, raised his fist and plunged his weapon toward Edwin's face…

***

Back to the present

"How is he?" Edwin asked from the doorway of Eliza's quarters.

Eliza was sitting in a chair at the small, two-person table before her port window, a cup of untouched tea cooling in front of her. She turned her head when she heard Edwin enter but couldn't seem to focus. She blinked slowly, her eyes still burning from the crying she didn't want him to see. "He's resting in the guest bedroom. No vents in there. He looked exhausted."

She swallowed against the lump in her throat and said more to herself than to him, "I locked him in the room, Edwin, like...like some evil nanny in a gothic novel. What kind of mother does that?"

He stepped to the table, fists clenched and concern etched into his face. He looked at her helplessly. She knew he wanted to help, wanted to take this pain and horror away from her, but he didn't know how.

She sat up straight, trying to not break down. Christ, she felt like she had been crying for years—ever since Oliver was born. She was being as strong as she could, but, finally, she could feel her resolve starting to break down. First the *Abraxas*, now Ollie. And right now, they had some kind of space vampire locked in Veronica's lab. How much more would they be forced to deal with?

She swallowed down a sob. "Edwin..."

"I know." He sat down at the table across from her. He set his hand on hers. "I know, love."

It felt good to feel the weight of his hand there, but she couldn't seem to stop *shaking*. Wanting to change the subject, to just stop thinking about Ollie for a moment, she asked, "What's going to happen to the Jotunn?"

"He'll stay locked in cold storage in the lab. He won't get out. He can't." Edwin nodded and swallowed hard, adding, "He's too injured. And besides, he was wearing a device under his armor that keeps his body temperature low and allows him to survive in our much higher temperature. I had my guard take that. If he escapes, he'll overheat in minutes and die."

She nodded and took a sip of cold tea. Small comfort. But at least the big scary, blue man couldn't tear their ship—their home—apart.

With a small sniff, she asked the difficult question. "What...what is he, Edwin?" She didn't mean the Jotunn. "Is he some kind of mutation? A monster?"

Looking up, she said, "He's part vampire and part Poppet. A living vampire. How can something like that even exist?"

Edwin sat thinking about that for a long moment. He didn't patronize her. He didn't tell her that things were going to be all right when he didn't know for sure. She appreciated that about him. "I really don't know, Eliza. I spoke briefly with Dr. Vu when I delivered the Jotunn's device for analysis, and she said she's only ever seen something like what Ollie did once before in a collector's zoo, and it wasn't even exactly like that."

Eliza felt a stab somewhere near her heart. She didn't want to ask the inevitable question but she had to know. "What did she say she saw?"

Edwin pressed his lips together before speaking. "She said it was a rare form of vampire. A 'krsnik,' she called it."

He pronounced the difficult word "kroosnik." The word, so foreign and alien, frightened her to death, and she felt the pinprick of fresh tears spring to her eyes. "Krsnik? What does that even mean?"

Edwin looked up at her, his eyes honest but dour. "She said it was a kind of super vampire. And she said that...that the krsnik she saw could only survive by consuming other vampires. It could only survive on their blood."

Her emotional dam broke.

"Oh, my god!" Eliza didn't care that it might make her seem weak, she started to cry, which made Edwin lean forward to try and hold her. She drew back away from him for a moment. For some reason, she couldn't bear his, or anyone's, touch. "My baby is a monster, Edwin. You're saying my baby is a monster!"

"I'm saying no such thing!" he insisted. "And he's not a monster!"

"Did you see what he did? How he hurt that Jotunn?" Which made sense, seeing how the Jotunn, like all Fae, were the distant cousins of vampires. This was so much worse than she imagined.

Numb and speechless with horror, Eliza got up and walked to the opposite side of the room to pour herself a stiff drink from the wet bar there. Edwin started to get up, to follow her, perhaps to hold her and comfort her, but she just couldn't at the moment.

She rounded on him, her sudden anger so great that it made the lights in the room flicker. A pop of electricity made the Tesla bulb explode over the table. "Get out, Edwin! Just get out! Just leave me alone!"

| X |

Dr. Veronica Vu took frantic notes as she observed her patient through the window of the glass specimen box in her lab. Though she was a high-ranking doctor aboard Lord Edwin's ship who had many staff members under her direction, she did not mind completing the task herself. The Jotunn was a fascinating specimen! And, she reminded herself, she was possibly the first human to make contact with a Jotnar in a millennium.

As a bio-designer with a postgraduate degree in Supernatural anatomy, she understood a good deal about how vampires, werewolves, and even the Fae operated. But she knew very little about what made the ice pirates tick. Over a thousand years ago, the Jotnar, or Frost Giants, were excommunicated by all of the other races for some kind of minor offense, or so the story went. The other races were also extremely prejudiced. The Jotnar were a hybrid species—somehow both vampire and Fae at the same time. They contained aspects of both—though how that came about was still a mystery.

As a result of this, the Jotnar sailed off in their fleet of (at the time) primitive flying dirigibles resembling galleons and were not seen or encountered again except in whimsical stories and questionable accounts of "ice pirates" stealing cargo airships and killing crewmembers—never verified. Some even speculated that the species had died out or was on its way. Obviously, they were wrong. She was looking at one of the ice pirates right now.

Gorm, his name was, Veronica had discovered. He admitted to being a low-level grunt. He'd taken the job to infiltrate the *Abraxas* because he needed the coin to support his family—a story as old as time. Right now, he sat quietly on a bench while the arms of the robot in the room—the device controlled by the AI—worked on dressing the grievance injury inflicted upon him by Edwin's son.

Oliver had paralyzed the giant blue warrior with just a touch. Another mystery Veronica planned to unravel at a later date.

Inside the glass box (as they called it), the Jotunn grunted and swiped at the robot arms, making Veronica very glad the guards had stripped him of the harness he had been wearing under his armor. Veronica had examined it briefly and discovered it was more Jotnar tech—though rather advanced. It kept his core temperature no higher than minus forty degrees, which allowed him to step out of the temperature-controlled containment unit and walk around Lord Edwin's ship. But he would not be leaving this glass containment cell anytime soon, not until Lord Edwin decided what they were going to do with him. It was impenetrable except, perhaps, by a nuclear warhead.

Gorm had been surprisingly open about the Jotnar's plans. After the initial assault on the *Abraxas*, the Jotnar queen ordered Gorm to contaminate any survivors on the *Abraxas*. The infected crew would then spread the infection elsewhere, eventually taking it to Earth. That was what Veronica learned so far.

When Lord Edwin contacted her by mind-text to report on what she knew, Veronica explained what she had learned from their guest, adding, —The Jotnar are surprisingly advanced, and Gorm hasn't been shy about his objective. The only thing I don't understand is why they are doing any of this.—

—Great work, Doctor. I'm sure we'll figure it out.— Lord Edwin sounded impressed, which gave Veronica a little tingle of delight. —But please take care. I don't trust our guest.—

—Always, my Lord.— She clutched her tablet to her, thrilled her Lord was pleased with her. She still had so much to learn from Gorm! And she wanted desperately to impress Lord Edwin with her findings. If she could mine Jotnar tech, just imagine what she could bring to him!

Every day was an adventure aboard the *Queen's Gambit*.

Veronica had no regrets about giving up her respected but boring career at university. She had come to think of this ship as home, and Edwin's family as her own. And, of course, she secretly hoped that Edwin would one day see her as more than just the doctor working to find a cure for his wife, though she'd never admit that to *anyone*. She didn't want to ruin the friendship she had established with Miss Eliza, but she also wasn't naïve—though, sometimes, she wondered if Eliza was. Everyone knew that Vampire Lords took many Brides over the countless years of their existence, and it was only a matter of time before Edwin wandered. She just hoped that when that day arrived, he wandered toward her.

She'd never had a boyfriend in high school or college. Boys seemed too intimidated by her intellect to ask her out. And though she'd gone on a series of dates since, she'd never found anyone who satisfied her. But Lord Edwin...well, he was dangerous and sexy and exciting. Definitely not the type who'd ever noticed her in the past. But Edwin respected her work. He *saw* her.

Veronica turned back to Gorm, who was watching her carefully from behind the unbreakable safety glass. Over the next hour or so, she learned much more about Gorm's people. Some of their tech was borrowed from the vampires—the greatest engineers in the world. But some had been created by their own people. Because of their special anatomical needs, they rarely left their transports, which were temperature regulated to allow their species to survive at the exceedingly low temperatures their bodies required. Unlike the other Supe species, most of which used gigantic gyros as their bases of operation, the Jotnar lived much like the Roma in smaller, more maneuverable ground-to-air transports called Sky Sharks.

Overall, the Jotunn did not seem overly interested in the affairs of the Vampire Courts, the Werewolf Clans, or even the business of the Fae. Perhaps that was due to bitterness on their part—their anger with the racism their cousin species had shown them. In addition, Gorm and his people did seem more than a little hostile to the human race—which concerned her.

Gorm leaned forward, indicating he wanted to speak. "You are a slave of the Devil."

"The Devil?"

"Lord Edwin," Gorm clarified, a look of wariness in his eyes.

It took her a moment to recall that many of the Supes referred to Lord Edwin as the Devil. She was surprised his sordid reputation as a gangster and general hellraiser had reached as far as the Jotnar. "I am not a slave to Lord Edwin. I am free, and I work as a doctor and biologist aboard board his ship."

Gorm nodded, though he looked surprised. "You have many species on board?"

"We have a number." She didn't want to give their enemy too much information. To bring the conversation back around to his purpose, she said, "I understand you meant to infect the humans on the *Abraxas*, who would then take the virus to Earth. Why would you do such a thing? Are you interested in Earth's resources?"

They were now moving into territory better fit to an interrogation room, and she did not expect Gorm to reveal state secrets—

assuming he even knew what they were and wasn't simply a grunt following orders blindly.

But Gorm surprised her. He snorted. "The human's steam machines are making the upper atmosphere hotter. It is growing difficult to live there."

She found that very interesting and decided to mind-text Lord Edwin a request for an audience when this was over. Just wait until he learned how well she had done!

"I see. The *Abraxas* was your way of stopping the humans and their machines. I appreciate the information you have shared, Gorm, and I promise we will do you no harm. You are a prisoner of war. As such, you are entitled to certain rights."

Gorm nodded once. But he never took his eyes off her.

* * *

She noted that Lord Edwin looked exceptionally tired as she stepped into his personal office.

He was slouched in his chair, rubbing his eyes, but he immediately sat up straighter.

Veronica was sure that recent events had taken their toll. He seemed different since coming off the *Abraxas*. Older...more beaten down. The loss of the two vampires, the injuries to two of his most important crewmembers, and the multiple deaths down in the loading bay had all taken something out of him.

Still, despite the recent string of tragedies, her admiration for Lord Edwin remained unchanged. He was such a unique creature! She admired his empathy for both his own kind as well as others, including humans. It was a rare thing in vampires. He was also devilishly handsome, and he had a reputation as an intense lover. She longed to know if *El Mal de Amour*, his power to bestow mind-blowing orgasms through his bite, was as potent as all those who had experienced it claimed.

She also feared for him. Vampire Lords, she knew, did not have the luxury of being sentimental. They usually found themselves facing enemies on all fronts all of the time. They had to be strong and cold and endlessly ruthless. It was the only way their Courts—in Lord Edwin's case, his Congress—could survive the deadly, ongoing underhandedness of the Vampire Court system.

What if Lord Edwin—what she secretly thought of as *her Edwin*—was too soft for this business? What if his little love Eliza wasn't strong enough to prop their Lord up emotionally? Veronica knew she would need to keep an eye on him, and if the day arrived when she decided he was slipping, well, Veronica would need to act. She wasn't sure what form that act would take, but she was willing to do almost anything to save her Edwin.

"My Lord," she said from the doorway.

Lord Edwin stood up—he was quite a bit taller than Veronica's four-foot-even frame—and that stopped her dead in her tracks and made her heart quicken. Even tired, he cut an imposing figure in his dark suit, sly amber eyes, and scorching red hair and goatee. The only things that softened his appearance somewhat were his spare freckles and generally goofy demeanor. It gave him an almost boyish charm. His eyes, that peculiar shade of dark gold that she'd been told were natural to him and not vampire-made, always made her voice catch a little in her throat when she looked into them.

She tipped her head to him properly. Was she his "slave" as Gorm had accused her of being? Veronica didn't feel that way. She had interviewed for this position—changed her whole life around for it. It had excited her—the prospect of working on Eliza's issue and living aboard a vampire's gyro. Soon enough, Lord Edwin elevated her to head of her department. It was a noble calling. Still, did that make her *his* creature?

"Doctor," he said by way of a greeting.

"Thank you for seeing me, sir." She moved to a chair opposite his desk, but Edwin didn't sit back down.

"Can't stay long, Doctor. I must go see my people in the med ward."

That disappointed her. He could send someone to look in on them, but he insisted on doing it himself. Veronica had played with the idea of telling him how she felt about him. But this was dashing her intention. "I spoke to Gorm at length, and it seems his people aren't being motivated by Earth's resources as we suspected. Rather, it's a form of eco-terrorism."

She gave him a rundown of what he'd said while Lord Edwin paced uneasily back and forth across the office, hands behind his back.

He nodded when she had finished. "I'll be sure to contact their flagship as soon as possible and work out their issues. Call a parley, if possible. After all, we have something they used to have and likely want back."

"Gorm?" she asked. "But he's a grunt. I doubt the Jotnar care very much what happens to him."

Lord Edwin shook his head. "The harness. It's Jotnar tech. And I know they don't want that getting out. Tech is the only thing they have that they can trade with at this point."

"Ah." Veronica nodded. The thing about Lord Edwin was, he let people think he was goofy and not very sharp. But then he surprised them the way he was surprising her now. It was like his secret weapon.

"Thank you, Doctor. That's all for now." He reached for his suit jacket lying over the back of his chair—he seemed in a hurry to visit his injured crewmembers—but suddenly lurched against the wall behind the chair. Well, not so much lurched as slammed into it with his shoulder as if he'd lost his balance.

Veronica sprang forward to steady him. His arm, which she grabbed, was incredibly cold through his clothes. "My Lord!"

He turned, a crooked smile on his handsome face. It took a second for his eyes to focus properly. "Apologies. Didn't see the wall that jumped in my way."

She frowned at that. "My Lord, are you all right?"

"Yes. Perfectly fine. I think I need some rest."

"Yes," Veronica agreed. "I think you do."

***

Once Edwin was safely alone in the lift, he sank to the floor and drew his knees up to his chin. He rested for a few moments while the car carried him down and around to the medical ward so he could visit his people. Despite what he had said to Dr. Vu, he was probably not all right. Ever since his encounter with the Jotnar, he'd felt off. Well, more off than usual.

He was exhausted in a way he hadn't felt since he was a young mortal man. And there was a dark, disconcerting halo hovering at the edges of his vision. It had made finding the door to exit his office difficult. He put his hand upon his chest and felt the click of his clockwork heart beating as usual, but its rhythm was labored and irregular. It seemed to be skipping beats.

"You're completely overwound. If you don't rest and reset, you'll lock up," he repeated Eliza's words from long ago. He hadn't been sleeping. That was true enough. And his feeding schedule was erratic at best. But none of that was unusual for him. Ever since he became Lord of the *Queen's Gambit*, downtime had been haphazard at best.

No, he thought, it was something else. Ever since the Jotunn knocked him into that wall, something had changed. It shouldn't have even been an issue. God knew he'd taken much worse lickings from his various enemies over the centuries and walked them off with a laugh and nary a scratch. But this time, things were different.

As the lift settled, he struggled to his feet. He made his posture tall and strong as the doors opened. The night nurse on duty in the medical ward stood at absolute attention when he walked in.

She glanced at her tablet to confirm her patients' statuses. "Tommy is currently being thawed out by the flesh mechanic in Ward C of the engineering lad. They are anticipating minimal damage. And Chief Navigator Narissa had emergency surgery on both eyes to stop the bleeding, but..." She hesitated.

"What is it, nurse?"

The night nurse bit her bottom lip. "It looks as if the Chief Navigator has lost her left eye."

Edwin let out his breath in a shuddersome sigh. He asked her to lead the way.

First, he looked in on Tommy, who was still deactivated and in recovery in the mechanical lab. He was laid out on a hospital table while a flesh mechanic busily removed damaged sectors of his body and replaced them with new parts. The sight was fairly surreal and gruesome, and when Edwin glanced up at the large screen on the wall where NEWTON was guiding the mechanic, he got a good internal look at how very little of Tommy was organic—just the brain, spinal column, and the branch-like ganglia. Tommy was really just...nerves. He swallowed against his discomfort.

Next, the nurse took him down a warren of corridors to Recovery. Narissa was sitting up in her hospital bed, staring down at her dinner tray but eating none of it. Edwin hovered at her open door, watching her. A large bandage covered half of her face, including her left eye, and there were bruises and long scratches covered in shiny medical ointment on her opposite cheek. He didn't immediately go in.

His and Narissa's history was...rocky, to say the least. They had met under strained circumstances, and she had joined his crew reluctantly and mostly because despite being a brave warrior capable of great things, the Faes' Unseely Court had no use for her. Born into Court slavery, they considered her the lifelong property of vampires—tainted.

Maybe, he thought, it would be for the best to just leave her alone.

As if sensing she was being observed, Narissa raised her head and their eyes met. He expected anger, resentment, all the things she likely deeply harbored for him. Instead, he saw only pain and...determination. "Lord Edwin." She nodded and waved him over.

Tentatively, he stepped into her room, afraid she might use something as a weapon to throw at him, like her uneaten tray of hospital food. When that didn't happen, he approached her more confidently. "Narissa—"

She cut him off. "No niceties, vampire. Did you get him? Did you get that big blue bastard?" She radiated rage...just not at him.

He nodded as he reached her bedside. "Aye. He's in the lab, under watch. He won't be wandering anywhere for a while."

"Good. That's good news." Glancing around, Narissa started to slide out of bed in just her hospital johnny.

"Hold up! Where do you think you're going?"

She scrunched her face up the way she did when she was peeved—which was almost all of the time. "I'm returning to Navigation. The nurses won't let me go, but I know if you tell them to stand down, they'll listen..."

Taking her by the arm, firmly but gently, he pushed her back into bed. "You'll do no such thing! You stupid chit, you need to recover."

"I'm fine!" she cried, putting up a fuss. She pushed against him to get him to release her. "I'll be fine as soon as I get back to—"

And that's when it happened. That's when it hit him.

One moment, he was wrangling his chief navigator back into bed; the next, he saw the floor coming up to crash into his face. Hard. But he never felt the impact. He was already gone. He was floating down a deep, long tunnel into darkness. And Edwin stayed in that place for a long, long time.

* * *

From inside his glass prison, Gorm watched Dr. Vu move around the lab as she took notes and hummed to herself. And he smiled.

| xi |

The moment she heard what happened, Eliza threw herself into a lift, her heart thudding to the beat of a low-grade panic. As soon as the doors opened, she started racing down the corridor to the medical ward.

Malcolm was already there, waiting for her. It seemed whenever she needed support, he was there. "Please, my lady." He tried to slow her down, but Eliza shrugged away from the large, burly werewolf, then stopped herself cold and nodded. Without Malcolm, she realized the guards might not let her in to see Edwin.

Together, the two of them passed through three security checkpoints before they reached Edwin's private room.

It was dim but there were pale blue runner lights along the walls, giving the space a soothing but surreal feel. She was reminded of how gyros were essentially low-altitude spaceships. At the moment, her brain was doing all kinds of mental gymnastics to keep from dealing with the current crisis.

She sucked in a deep breath before approaching the hospital bed. They had laid Edwin out so he appeared peaceful, a sheet drawn up to the level of his bare chest, where someone had attached a series of electrodes that were sending signals to the various machines surrounding him. There were dark, sleepless pockets under his closed eyes, and his hair was a mess. She looked at the main monitor, which was silent. No heartbeat or blood pressure. But, she reminded herself, that was Edwin's normal resting state.

"Do they know what happened?" she asked the nurse on duty.

The nurse, who didn't really know who she was, said, "Should you even be here, madam? The Poppet's quarters are on floor sixty."

"I'm not just some Poppet. I'm his wife!" She looked to Malcolm for support.

He nodded. "Lady Eliza is Edwin's wife and Bride. She has a right to be here."

The nurse's eyebrows shifted all the way to the top of his forehead while he digested that information. She had just outed herself, true, but she couldn't care less at the moment. This was too important.

"Lord Edwin was speaking to the chief navigator when he suddenly collapsed," the nurse explained. "No vital signs, and only the slightest brain activity, so we don't think he'd dead dead. More dead-ish." The nurse made a face at his rather loose assessment.

Letting out a weary sigh, Eliza moved to the side of Edwin's bed. She pushed some hair off his forehead before touching it. He was ice cold. But, again, that wasn't so unusual. He was always dead cold when he slept. It took her winding up his heart in the morning to bring him to life and put a flush in his cheeks.

"I'm going to try and wind him up," she told Malcolm, taking the old-fashioned scarab key from under her dress collar that Edwin had given to her many years prior. The nurse observed it with interest. If the ship needed any further proof of what she'd claimed to be, this was it. She pressed it through his flesh and into the mechanism that acted as his pacemaker, gave it five turns, and stepped back to listen to the escapement turn over. It made one full rotation before clicking—but not in a normal way. More of a chaotic clickety-clack sort of way.

This was normally when he sucked in a sharp breath and maybe swore at the uncomfortable way he was being forced back to life. But, this time, he didn't react.

He didn't do anything. He just lay there, looking like a very dead vampire.

Feeling a tinge of true panic, Eliza looked to Malcolm, then tried the operation again. This time, the key went in but wouldn't turn at all. It felt like his clockwork heart was all locked up. "Something is wrong, Malcolm," she whispered, her voice shaking like her hands. "Something is very, very wrong."

Malcolm nodded. "Is there any way you can fix the mechanism?"

Malcolm thought she was smart—smarter than she really was. And though it was true she had an affinity with mechanical devices, Foxley's clockwork heart was an analog contraption. Neither she nor Edwin had ever really understood how it worked. For all she knew, it could be as much alchemical as mechanical.

"No, Malcolm. I don't think so." She had to keep her voice steady so it wouldn't break. "I've never seen anything like this in all the years I've known Edwin. And this device is completely alien to me—old-fashioned. It's like the Antikythera mechanism. I can't connect with it at all."

The irony of ironies, she thought fretfully. She could talk to any device on this ship. She could even control most of them, probably including the ship herself, if she had to. But the device that Foxley had created to save his favorite Heir was invented in a time before modern computers and was totally beyond her reach.

Malcolm grunted. "Is he...? I mean, could he be really dead?"

"I don't think so." She swallowed hard and turned his wrist over to examine his color. He had yet to gain the bruised hue of the truly departed. "Not dead. Dead-*ish*," she said, using the same word as the nurse.

"I suppose we could contact Foxley and see if he has a solution." The thought sat heavy with her. She wasn't opposed, but—

From the doorway, Dr. Vu said, "It may not help."

She glanced up at her friend. "What do you mean, Doctor?" She was trying very hard not to panic very badly now.

With a sigh, Dr. Vu stepped toward them, her tablet in hand. "I looked at the scans we took of your husband, Miss Eliza." She looked Edwin over, a deep mark puncturing the place between her eyes. "I wish I had better news, but we just don't know what's happened to him. The device in his chest is unlike anything we've ever seen. It doesn't even look like Foxley's tech."

"I don't understand." Eliza glanced back at Edwin. "I know Foxley created the device. It saved his life when Chimera shot him!"

"Foxley may have commissioned the device's design—but he didn't create it," Dr. Vu explained. "All of Foxley's tech—and, let's be honest, it's all over this ship the same as on every other gyro—has a certain look and feel to it. You can see Foxley's handiwork in everything he created. This isn't Foxley Industries tech. It's stranger than that."

"Do you have any idea what's wrong with the device? Any theories?"

Dr. Vu shook her head. "Edwin's clockwork heart is something I've never seen before. Something none of my engineers or flesh mechanics have ever seen."

"You mean Lord Edwin," Eliza stated.

Dr. Vu looked up. "Yes, of course." She looked down at her Lord sadly. "In fact, I'm not sure even Lord Foxley himself can help us."

"As far as I'm concerned, that psychopath can sink into hell," Eliza told Dr. Vu, her anger mounting. He might still be useful, sure, but Foxley's very name had the power to induce in her a rage unlike any she had ever felt except for Summersfield. Foxley was a plague upon her and Edwin's lives. That monster had caused them nothing but unending suffering in all of the years they had known him. "But if you can decipher the tech, maybe discover who created it, I'd greatly appreciate it."

Veronica looked surprised by her vehemence but dutifully nodded and left, which relieved Eliza greatly. Unless the doctor could suggest a viable solution, she was in no mood to discuss options with her.

* * *

Eliza stayed with Edwin for the next couple of hours while Malcolm fetched Oliver and took him up to play with his own children in their quarters. He was happy to keep an eye on her son, and that relieved Eliza immensely. During that time, Dr. Vu ran several more tests and scanned Edwin one more time, all with similar results. Her small team of experts just didn't know what to do.

Resolved and thinking a little more clearly now, Eliza decided to move Edwin to her personal quarters and seal him inside one of the Hydraulic Protection Compartments that the vampire population on board used whenever they needed to be shipped on and off the gyro and wanted to remain safe from the sun and other dangers. Veronica seemed disappointed by Eliza's decision but didn't argue with her. The compartment Eliza chose was made of lead-lined titanium steel, and it was much safer than leaving Edwin exposed and vulnerable.

Once they were alone in her quarters, Eliza carefully dressed him so he was presentable, then she and Malcolm laid him to rest in the HPC. Before she locked the lid—impenetrable to everything short of a nuclear warhead but fitted with an inside lock should he awaken on his own—Eliza tried to wind Edwin's heart up one last time, but the mechanism was completely frozen at that point.

She looked down at his face, which was ashen grey, a strange, unnatural contrast to his auburn hair and goatee. He had collapsed with his eyes open just like a person who had died suddenly, but they were closed properly now—she had been forced to use a bit of tape—and he lay comfortably inside the compartment in the spare bedroom of her personal quarters. She had dressed him in his favorite dark forest green suit and combed his hair properly. He looked perfectly beautiful and ready...for a funeral.

The sight of him made her choke up, and she had to work hard not to break down in tears. They had talked about this possibility in the past. How his body might one day reject his clockwork heart. How she might be alone and without his protection. They had made plans for it. But she never thought she'd see the day. Edwin seemed so bloody invulnerable!

No crying. No despair. Time to find a solution, she told herself as she sniffed back her tears. She had to be strong for them both.

"I'm sorry, lovey. I'll be waiting for you when you wake up." She kissed his cold, stony cheek, feeling very much like she was at some awful wake, and then locked the HPC, which gave a sharp, hydraulic hiss as the many safety mechanisms engaged. Afterward, she sat alone in a chair beside the compartment, feeling like some wretched widow in black, trying to decide what to do next.

"Just get out, Edwin! Just leave me alone!"

Those were the last words she'd spoken to him. The last words he'd heard her say. She covered her face, shaking slightly, and finally let herself cry it out. There was no way she was moving forward without first letting this weakness out of her body.

What an awful thing for her to say! In her heart, she had blamed him for so much even though she knew it wasn't fair to him. Perhaps she'd always blamed Edwin for Oliver—for his part in making him what he was. For making him at all. And it was all so damned ridiculous because wasn't she the one responsible? It was her body that had done this to Oliver. It was her blood curse that had likely doomed their son. Her infernal and eternal connection to Summersfield.

She was wiping the tears from her eyes and the unladylike snot from her nose when she made a very difficult decision for them both—for her and for Edwin. She made it because someone had to, and if she didn't—if she stuck to the Plan at this point—everything in their lives was going to fall to chaos. And, after all, it was only fair she was the one who took control of the situation.

She did not want to do this, but she had no choice now.

She was going to step out of the shadows at last. And that would be hard. But what worried her more was the second part of her plan. Because she had also decided to summon the Devil himself.

***

The Vampire Bride color was red, no surprise there. So that was the color that Eliza chose to wear. A bright red tailcoat embroidered with flames and birds that had a flowing tail that reached her heels. Under it, she wore a fitted white blouse with pearl buttons and a pair of stark black trousers. She included tall, red buccaneer boots with sensible heels. Most Vampire Lords were old enough to have some kind of family seal or coat of arms. But since Edwin had never had one of those, he had simply made one up—a red and orange phoenix on a black shield. Eliza wore a pewter phoenix brooch at her throat to signal that.

She stood nervously in a lift on her way up to the bridge. She kept pulling at her lace sleeves, her mind worrying at the many repercussions of what she was about to do. It would either save Edwin or doom their entire Congress. At this point, things could seriously go either way.

You've got this. You can do this.

When she reached the bridge floor, the doors opened and she sensed the soldiers patrolling the hallways stop to assess her. These were the top officers who guarded the bridge and engineering rooms and did not allow any of the passengers to remain on this level who were not on the VIP list. That list was incredibly short and consisted of only Edwin and his inner circle.

One soldier eyed her critically, concern stamped into his face. Up until a half hour ago, she wasn't someone on the VIP list. As part of their cover, she had requested that Edwin leave her off it. But things had changed. She was now, for all intents and purposes, the Sitting Lord of the *Queen's Gambit,* a position normally held by a Lord's Bride or Enforcer—whichever he trusted more.

The officer eyeing her moved toward her, to bar her way, but one behind him reached out and grabbed him by the arm and shook his head.

Eliza stepped bravely off the lift. As she did so and the officers got a good look at her and her Bride uniform, they drifted back against the walls the way they would if Edwin had arrived. Some looked her over, sizing her up in a disconcerting way. They were still digesting the new order of things. She was pretty sure the nurse down in the medical ward had been wagging his tongue like crazy, and theirs was a small ship, relatively speaking. Surely, everyone knew by now.

Eyeing the officers warily, Eliza focused her attention on the situation despite her nibbling fears. Standing tall, she said, "VIP request to enter the bridge." She met the eyes of each officer down the line. "Please."

The head of security, a soldier by the name of Timms, stepped forward to address her. "Name?"

She cleared her throat and said clearly, "Lady Eliza McGillicuddy, the Bride of Lord Edwin McGillicuddy. Also, the current Sitting Lord of the *Queen's Gambit*."

After a heated moment, he inclined his head. "Request granted...my Lady."

"Thank you, Timms."

Timms then did the unexpected and went down on one knee, leaning forward slightly to take her hand. She wore Edwin's ring, which Timms examined before kissing it in a gesture of fealty. "Your Ladyship."

She allowed for it and waited until he was standing once more to make her request. "Timms, I need to hail the gyro the *Gypsy Queen*. I wish to send a message."

"Yes, my Lady. Please follow me." He led her to the Communications Room where several officers sat at consoles in a semicircle. Their duties consisted of sending and receiving messages from a dispatch on Earth, as well as communicating with other gyros and craft. They essentially controlled who was let on and off the ship.

She made it halfway across the vast room before an alarm went off unexpectedly.

Timms stepped up to the closest officer. "What's happened, Lamont?"

The officer, a young man with sandy hair cut military-style, bit his bottom lip. "The captain is reporting that a ship has uncloaked and is hailing us, sir. It looks like a modified Hummingbird, but we can't be sure. I've...never actually seen this type of ship." He looked over and dipped his head in respect to Eliza. "My Lady."

"I see. Let me see the readout," Timms began but Eliza interrupted.

"That's a Sky Shark," she told Timms, frowning at the murky image on the screen. She, like Edwin, had read Dr. Vu's report, the results of her little talk with Gorm. "It's a modified Hummingbird. Jotnar tech."

Timms nodded. "What Lady Eliza said. Lamont, we are going to Code Yellow."

"Code Yellow, sir."

He turned to another officer not occupied. "Franklin, I need you to take care of an errand for me." He glanced at Eliza for direction.

Eliza cleared her throat, tore her eyes away from the terrifying things happening on Lamont's console, and said, "I need you to contact the *Gypsy Queen* and extend a boarding pass to Lord Henry Foxley."

Franklin, apparently familiar with Lord Foxley's shady reputation, glared at her for a full two seconds before dutifully nodding, not questioning her command. "It will be done, My Lady." He glanced down at his console as he prepared to send the invitation. "Any note attached?"

"Yes, please include the following: 'Edwin needs you.'"

***

While her invitation was being sent out, Timms escorted Eliza to the bridge, the place where all of the decisions were made on a daily basis—the ship's navigational course, the roster of who was let on and off, and all of the orders were executed that helped to support their little world.

It was a place Eliza had never been before, and, to his credit, Timms didn't treat her like a child, simply presenting the large, hangar-like room with a domed ceiling and perhaps a hundred active computer stations positioned around the room—some on floor-level but also some elevated on large mechanical arms. Almost all of the stations were occupied, which gave her an idea of the staggering number of staff members required to run the ship.

The "floating stations," those suspended like cherry pickers from the walls, were used for navigation and could move with the constant rotation of the gyro, Timms explained. They made sure the gyro stayed to course. The ones at floor level were communication consoles and what he called "active war" stations.

That gave her a little shiver.

In the very center of the vast space was a horseshoe of a dozen seats facing a large, convex display monitor perhaps fifty feet tall and twice that wide with a long, complex computer console before it. The display showed the upper atmosphere, cloudlike water vapors situated over an Earth that looked very far away. This was the Captain's Station, Timms said, and the captain required her input.

As she approached, Captain Enzokuhle stood up and took her hand to bow over it. "Ma'am." With his British accent, it sounded more like "mum" to her.

"Hello, Captain. I'm honored to be here," she told him.

"The honor is mine, ma'am, I assure you." He glanced up at her, the warmth in his eyes telling her much. "However, I'm very sorry about the circumstances and doubly concerned about Lord Edwin."

"I have a team on that," she said only, not wanting to give away how worried she was. "Timms said you require me?"

He escorted her to the main communications console. "The Jotnar are hailing us and we need to answer them. Normally, I would ask Lord Edwin to attend to this, but..." He made a vague gesture.

The idea both surprised and terrified her. "I'm not so sure I should be the one doing this."

Captain Enzo shook his head. "You must. Even as the captain, I don't have the authority to speak to our enemy. The sitting Lord must do that."

She let out her breath in a little gasp, afraid she had bitten off far more than she could chew. *You can do this. You can handle this.*

"All right. What do I do, Captain?"

He indicated the speaker mike and controls. "Greet them. Ask them what they want. They may want to negotiate. You don't have to do that. Simply gather intelligence. Keep things simple." He smiled encouragingly.

She nodded. "Thank you, Captain." She stared at the large convex screen that now showed the Sky Shark in real time. It was as aerodynamic as a Hummingbird but had been re-engineered into a longer, more bullet-like craft in gunmetal grey. It sported fins and even a razor-sharp dorsal line. Along one side of the screen flashed a line of stats: This craft, a flagship called the *Midnight Sun*, was idling 400 parsecs from their current position. It was much larger than a traditional Hummingbird, probably capable of transporting, or even housing, hundreds of people comfortably. She looked for any evidence of weapons, even asked NEWTON, but if any existed, they were internal and well hidden. NEWTON said he couldn't detect any heat signatures at all—for any weapons *or* people.

Captain Enzo leaned in and said, "The internal temperature of the Sky Shark is around minus forty Celsius, roughly the temperature of the deep Arctic in the dead of winter."

Oh my! she thought. Adjusting the height of the microphone, she said clearly into it, "*Midnight Sun*, this is the *Queen's Gambit*. Lady Eliza McGillicuddy speaking." She grimaced, afraid she sounded horribly rookie, but Captain Enzo nodded her on. Leaning forward, she added, "We are responding to your hail."

The picture of the Sky Shark remained on the huge screen, but now it was accompanied by a soundwave pattern. A deep, powerful woman's voice responded: "*Queen's Gambit*, we have received your transmission."

Eliza said into the microphone. "I'm glad we can speak with—"

The woman's voice quickly cut her off. "This is Captain Yrsa speaking from the bridge of the *Midnight Sun*..."

Yrsa! That was Edwin's ex-wife (still wife?).

"...and we require your immediate surrender. Lower your defensive shields, *Queen's Gambit*, and prepare to be boarded."

Eliza sucked in a quick breath. "Now wait just a minute...!" She winced when she saw Captain Enzo shake his head.

Eliza shut down the mike and turned to him.

Captain Enzo explained, "I'm not trying to tell you what to do, my Lady—"

"No. I need you to tell me exactly what to do, Captain. I am totally out of my depth here."

He nodded. "I suggest not antagonizing the Jotnar. We believe they have unknown weapons in the hull of the Sky Shark—incredibly advanced weapons. That little ship out there crippled Lord Emmerdale's gyro in one short blast."

Eliza felt a deep shudder go up her back. With a nod, she took a deep breath and turned the mike back on. She could feel herself starting to sweat. "*Midnight Sun*, we have received your request but must decline your boarding pass. You may not board the *Queen's Gambit*. I repeat you may not—"

"That is entirely unacceptable!" came Yrsa's voice. It was deep and smoky and made Eliza want to clear her throat. And then: "As Captain, I wish to speak to your Lord: Edwin McGillicuddy."

She didn't know the protocol to responding to that, so she just did the best she could. "Lord McGillicuddy is indisposed at the moment, but I speak on his behalf."

A pause. "Who are *you*?"

The question was so unexpected and hostile that Eliza didn't know how to respond for a moment. Ah, to hell with it. She leaned into the mike. "I am Mrs. McGillicuddy, Edwin's wife and Bride."

"That's impossible," Yrsa insisted, sounding annoyed. "I am Edwin's wife and Bride!"

"Yes, well, welcome to the Lord Edwin wife club." She saw Captain Enzo flinch at that.

Captain Yrsa demanded, "I demand to speak to Edwin immediately!"

"And I told you that you can't. You have to speak to me!"

An officer on one of the floating stations signaled to Captain Enzo. The captain nodded, looking concerned. A second after that, Eliza felt an impact rattle the floor. Sirens went off on the bridge. Enzo immediately turned to the officer on the floating station and demanded he report.

"The Sky Shark launched a small projectile into the *Gambit*'s hull, Captain." He gave a series of coordinates that corresponded to where the damage was located, followed by, "Damage minimum. No serious impact, no engineering issues, but we have a shallow breach."

Captain Enzo nodded. "Warning shot." He turned back to Eliza and nodded for her to proceed.

Eliza turned the radio back on. "Uncalled for, *Midnight Sun*. You have violated aether etiquette and may have just committed an act of war."

Yrsa grunted over the airwaves. "You committed an act of war when you took my officer off the *Abraxas*, Mrs. McGillicuddy."

Eliza had to keep from growling into the mike. "We took a containment unit off the damaged ship *Abraxas*. We did not know it contained your soldier. But I'm certain you already know that, *Mrs. McGillicuddy*, seeing how you planted him there and altered the crew of the ship to obey your commands." She took a deep breath before delivering the coup de grace. "When you attacked the *Abraxas* and her crew, you committed an act of war against the whole vampire race, and now you have brought down upon your heads the displeasure of the High Vampire Courts."

Captain Yrsa laughed as if that was funny. "This may surprise you, little vampire's plaything, but I care not a whit what the High Vampire Courts think of the Jotnar."

"That may be so, but the High Courts have the authority to court martial you and your crew and to shut down the *Midnight Sun* and your whole fleet." She had no idea if they could actually do that, but she also knew that, for whatever dubious reason, Lord Trasch had an interest in these current affairs, and he had the ear of the High Courts. He'd probably do it for spite alone.

More alarms started to sound, and the officer who reported the hull breach suddenly went a shade paler. Captain Enzo said, "Officer, report—"

But Captain Yrsa interrupted. "Thank you for this pleasant little discussion, Mrs. McGillicuddy. While we have been speaking, it has given our device time to dry freeze your control system..."

Eliza whipped around to look at different computer stations. The occupants looked besieged as they worked frantically over their keyboards. She then turned to Captain Enzo, but he ignored her for a moment as he spoke rapidly to his people.

"I need a report from the engineers..." he began, and even before he finished the first sentence, NEWTON spoke up.

"The damage was almost nonexistent to the hull, Captain, but the Control Room is experiencing several navigational issues."

"What kind of 'navigational issues?'"

"We've..." NEWTON's voice degraded into a coil whine, followed by a whirring noise that sounded extremely troubling. He disappeared offline.

"NEWTON?" the captain called.

One of the officers at a floating station jumped in. "Captain, NEWTON's offline, and we've begun drifting off course."

"Go to manual."

"I can't, sir." He checked his screen. "The gyroscope won't respond and its programming seems to have been damaged by some kind of unknown virus. Artificers have been summoned..."

"Life support?"

"Holding, sir."

The room erupted into low-grade panic, and for good reason. The gyroscope was the beating heart of the gyro, the device emitting the false gravity that kept this ship afloat. If it was damaged severely enough, they were all doomed...to fall out of the sky.

| xii |

The *Queen's Gambit* had been effectively immobilized by the computer virus the Jotnar had literally injected into their ship. Although their life support and basic functions still worked, NEWTON and their navigation was "completely borked," as one of the engineers put it so succinctly when the captain called down for a report. They still didn't know if the gyroscope was damaged or not.

The ship at this point might as well be a hunk of metal floating aimlessly in the stratosphere.

Captain Enzo moved around the bridge and exchanged damage reports with several crewmembers before returning to the pilot officer who had delivered the troubling news. Eliza gripped her elbows and waited for the captain's prognosis.

"Shut the gyroscope down. We'll sustain her on torque until we have a more extensive report and take it from there. Where are those artificers you promised, ensign? What's their ETA?"

"They will be up from Earth in an hour and a half, Captain," the soldier announced.

"Shutting down the gyroscope, Captain," another of his crew answered, a woman sitting high up in one of the floating stations. Her fingers flew nimbly over her keyboard until Eliza heard the clanging alarms change in tone. Everything suddenly became very still—eerily so.

"Gyroscope currently disabled. Awaiting orders, sir," said the crewwoman.

Captain Enzo nodded. "Thank you, pilot officer."

Turning back to Eliza, he said, "I do not mean to disrespect you, my Lady. But I need to brief Lord Edwin on this issue."

Eliza didn't know how to explain. She certainly did not want anyone here to know how badly wounded Edwin was. If it got out, it wouldn't help matters. It might even make them worse. She knew in her heart that probably the only thing preventing the *Gambit* from suffering the same fatality as the *Abraxas* was Yrsa's attachment to Edwin. If she thought that Edwin was dead, she'd probably tear their ship to shreds in her fury.

Clenching her fists at her sides, Eliza said, "No, let me handle this."

The Captain looked torn. He knew what she meant to Edwin and that she had proper autocracy aboard the ship, but the way she'd handled things just now? Yes, she would be doubting herself too. Lifting her head, she added, "Please, Captain, you need to trust me. And I need your help."

"What do you need?"

"The harness the Jotunn was wearing. Can you retrieve it double quick?"

He looked her in the eyes and considered whether or not he trusted her. She knew it was going to be a challenge. After all, he did not really know her. And if he decided not to listen to her, there was little she could do about it.

Finally, he nodded. "It's in the evidence lockers in the guards' station, but I can send someone to retrieve it."

"Please do. And quickly." Turning back, she looked over the stats attached to the Sky Shark, studying the schematics that NEWTON had retrieved before he'd been neutralized. Although it was obvious the Jotnar had re-engineered the ship. It didn't look much different than a Hummingbird, and she was familiar with that design. She had "tapped" into the control system of one of the shuttles long ago.

While she was waiting for the Jotnar's device to be retrieved, a new image came up on the large main screen, that of the Captain of the Jotnar, who had apparently decided she wanted to gloat in living color.

Her appearance took Eliza by surprise. She knew the Jotnar were a peculiar hybrid of vampire and Fae, but Yrsa's dark blue skin, shock of white hair wound up around her head, and yellow-rimmed scarlet eyes made Eliza lurch inside a little. The Captain of the Jotnar looked positively alien in appearance. Not unattractive, and certainly fascinating, but her species was one of the odder-looking ones.

Eliza had expected Yrsa to be dressed in military garb as befitting her station, but instead of a uniform and armor as she'd seen the grunt soldier Gorm wear, she was dressed in some kind of low-cut baby blue ballroom gown with puffed sleeves and glitter all over it. Over that, she wore what looked like a shaggy white fur coat that might have been made of bearskin. Gems glistened in her pointed ears, at her throat, and on her wrists and fingers. She looked more like some fancy Disney princess than the military ruler of the Ice Pirates.

Yrsa must have been analyzing Eliza as well, because she said after a second or two, "You look very short and very brown, Mrs. McGillicuddy. I do not believe Edwin would marry someone like you. He prefers tall, pale pretties." She made a gesture with her hands to indicate herself.

First, Eliza got angry. Then she sighed. She was growing tired of Yrsa making this personal—though of course it was. She also realized she needed to create a diversion until Enzo's runner had fetched the harness up from the lockers, so she tried to take control of the conversation. "You are aware your marriage to Edwin was a sham? Arranged by Lord Foxley so he could get his greedy little paws on your tech?"

Yrsa laughed. "Is that what Edwin told you?"

Eliza forced herself not to react. Yrsa was just baiting her anyway.

The Jotunn's smile split her face nearly in half in the manner of the Fae, but her teeth were mostly human looking except for her canines, upper and lower, which were freakishly long and sharp like a vampire's. "Sham or not, it didn't seem that way on our wedding night. Do you know the tricks that sweet little undead ginger can do with his tongue? It's truly supernatural."

Eliza clenched her teeth, then forced herself to relax her jaw. The doors had just shushed open behind her and a young officer almost totally out of breath rushed toward her, the harness in his hands. She glanced askance at him and took the large black, metal harness—it was heavier than it looked—and set it on the station in front of her.

"I wouldn't know about that, *Mrs. McGillicuddy*," she answered Edwin's ex. "My husband and I don't need silly tricks to get it up in the bedroom. I suppose that tells you something about how he felt about you."

Captain Yrsa lost her predatory smile. "Enough games. Again, I formally request a boarding pass to your ship. If you don't comply..."

Eliza didn't hear the rest of the woman's demands. The way the Jotnar had attacked the *Queen's Gambit* had given her an idea.

She set both hands on the harness draped over the station. At first, she felt only a dim humming under her fingertips. But that quickly grew in volume as her strange techkinetic powers went to work on the device and it came alive at her command. As she had suspected, it was wired remotely to the network aboard the *Midnight Sun*, giving her an open electronic pathway to Yrsa's ship. Of course, that was something the Jotnar hadn't worried about or even considered. They likely figured their tech was so alien from everyone else's that no one could hack it. But when you stripped tech down to its basic elements, it was all just binary code. Language. And she could access that with no problem.

Closing her eyes, Eliza listened to the music of the circuitry and allowed it to carry her across the airwaves to the Jotnar's ship. It took seconds, if that.

Then she was inside and moving swiftly along the electrical byways of the ship. She could see all of the internal workings of the vessel and could twist and turn through it efficiently. Once, she had done this same thing while aboard the *Gypsy Queen*, taking it over completely and repairing it from the inside out so it would not fall on the occupants of New York City.

Captain Yrsa stopped speaking when one of her crew slid up beside her and whispered something in her pointed ear. Eliza peeked one eye open. Yrsa grunted to the crewmember and then suddenly cut the transmission.

Excellent.

Eliza continued to feel her way through the Jotnar's vessel like a little virus, moving through all kinds of electronic back doors. A few seconds later, the *Midnight Sun* hailed them again, but this time, Yrsa looked livid, with red spots high up on her cool blue cheeks.

"What are you doing to my ship, you little bitch?" she demanded to know.

Eliza noticed Captain Enzo looked surprised at the news. She smiled widely at Yrsa before responding. "It sucks when you have a wounded ship, doesn't it?"

Yrsa leaned in so close that Eliza could see the literal red of her eyes. "Whatever you are doing, Poppet, stop it immediately or we will fire upon you and rip your ship apart!"

"Yes, could try that, I suppose, but you'll note I've tapped into your defense system, Yrsa." She paused for effect. "And that's not the only thing. Check your life support. You might say, we have a little contest going—see who can destroy whose ship the fastest."

Eliza checked the readings on the large screen. "I see you keep your ship at a frosty minus forty degrees, depending on the level." She noticed certain areas of the *Midnight Sun* were kept slightly warmer than others by ten or twenty degrees. She suspected those might be nurseries, and it gave her no pleasure to imagine the discomfort the Jotnar babes might be experiencing, but she had no choice. The *Queen's Gambit* was counting on her to save it, and she had to call Yrsa's bluff. "Be a shame if your cooling system suddenly failed and it became very warm in there very quickly..."

She urged the temperature up by ten degrees. "I hope your people have those containment units to hide in. I'll leave those untouched for you lot to place your children in."

She hoped they would. She hated the idea of hurting the little ones of her enemies—the innocent ones.

Yrsa seethed. "How are you doing this?"

"That's for me to know and for you to not know."

When she commanded the temperature on Yrsa's ship to rise another five degrees, she sensed all kinds of alarms going off. *The Midnight Sun* was now in deep distress, and the Jotnar people were mobilizing to get the young, vulnerable, and infirm to the cooler parts of the ship. Eliza's heart clenched when she imagined hurting these people—even if they were her enemies. This wasn't her style. Still, she had to carry on.

Captain Yrsa, all but growling, looked like she might punch the screen, then stopped herself and smoothed out her face and hair as she considered her options. Something about her spoiled little princess routine amused Eliza. "I understand," she said in a more reasonable tone of voice. "You are some kind of machine woman, aren't you? A new kind of Mechi-person?"

"I'm really not, Captain. I'm just a Poppet standing in front of a Jotunn, asking her to be reasonable."

The Jotnar leader glowered, then shook her head. "That's not possible. Did you upload some kind of virus?"

Actually, Eliza *was* the virus, but Yrsa didn't need to know that. "Oh, look, your majesty, the ship just increased another ten degrees...!"

"Fine," Yrsa finally conceded, and on the huge screen, Eliza could see the small veins popping in her face. Turning to a crewmember beside her, she uttered a command before turning back to Eliza. "I deactivated the Icepick's virus. Now let my ship go."

"Is that what it's called? An Icepick? Interesting."

"I did what you asked. Now release my ship!"

It was one of the hardest things she had ever done, but Eliza commanded the *Midnight Sun* to raise the temp another ten degrees. Ten years ago, she was a fearful little thing and would have given in easily. She would have folded like a house of cards. But a decade of living with Edwin and dealing with his people's particular level of political hostility had taught her well. She couldn't afford to be a wimp...and she had to put her ship and her family first. Everyone here was counting on her.

One of Yrsa's soldiers reported from his station. Yrsa, her face twisted with frustrated rage, roared, "I deactivated the virus! What more do you want?"

Eliza turned and glanced at Captain Enzo, who, in turn, looked up at one of the floating stations. The woman piloting it gave him a thumbs up. "The virus appears to be neutralized, Captain. NEWTON, however, is still currently offline."

Eliza sighed, turning back to the screen. "Thank you for that. But as a reminder, I'm leaving the temp at minus thirty-five degrees—a five-degree difference. Consider it a demerit for attacking our ship unprovoked. And, if you make any further moves against the *Queen's Gambit*, or do anything untoward at all, you'll earn another five-degree demerit for every infraction."

"What about my soldier? And my tech?"

"You'll get that back if you can prove to be good little Jotnar and behave. If you can't...well, you'll never see either of those things ever again."

Captain Yrsa suddenly laughed, which took Eliza by surprise. "I like you, little Poppet. You're spunky. No wonder Edwin made you his Bride. Still..." Her grin remained in place even as she delivered the final blow. "I could easily abandon this flagship and summon another. I could summon a hundred more. Can you control every one of my ships? My whole fleet? If not, then neither of us has any long-term advantage."

"I..." Eliza began, but she didn't know what to say. Just holding onto Yrsa's flagship was taxing her powers terribly.

"Little Poppet, we absolutely must meet in person! So, unless you are capable of destroying my whole fleet immediately, I demand a parley."

Before Eliza could respond, Yrsa cut the transmission.

* * *

"My Lady, you don't have to do this," Malcolm insisted, jogging to keep abreast of Eliza's quick steps down the corridor. She had invited him to accompany her to her meeting with the captain of the Jotnar. She felt it would make her look strong—to have a Dog of War at her side. But, if she was being honest, she wanted him there because she needed his strength and expertise. She couldn't afford to make any further mistakes.

As they got into a lift together, she reflected. The idea of sitting down to a parley with the leader of the Jotnar scared the living hell out of her. She wasn't talented this way, and there was so damned much riding on her doing well.

She rubbed Edwin's ring on her ring finger like it was some kind of magic charm that could help her. This ring wasn't the bloodstone he'd given her when she agreed to be his Bride. That had been lost when she was arrested all those years ago. Edwin had spent years trying to track it down with no success. Bloodstones—pink diamonds—were especially rare. Her ring was probably in a very rich person's collection, never to see the light of day again. But he said he didn't care about that, and he'd replaced it with a new ring, a Claddagh ring. The heart symbolized love, the hands friendship, and the crown loyalty.

Her Claddagh wedding ring was set with a Connemara marble, Ireland's ancient gemstone that Edwin said was 900 million years in the making, no two pieces the same. It was also considered lucky—which she needed badly at the moment.

Malcolm looked her up and down, his eyes lingering over her form in a way that was perhaps a hair too personal. "You look beautiful, as always, my lady. Queenly."

"Thank you." She smoothed her jacket down and tried to stand up taller—or, as tall as her five-foot-five frame would allow. Once, long ago, she had fooled onlookers into thinking she was a Vampire Lord. Now, she needed to fool the Jotnar into thinking she was the leader of this little floating world.

She lowered her head. She didn't feel like a leader. She felt tired and bleak. Edwin was dead to the world and the Jotnar wanted to destroy their gyro and, likely, the entire planet. And somehow, she was supposed to fix this. She sniffed and tried to suck back on the fearful tears filling her eyes.

"My Lady...Eliza." Malcolm stopped the lift with the emergency brake, drifted forward, and took her familiarly into his arms. He enveloped her small form completely, and his grip was huge and warm and comforting in a way no one else's was. Long ago, he had asked her to be his pack queen. At that time, a time when she hadn't known Edwin all that well, she had been tempted oh so badly to let him have her. One bite and she could be a werewolf and his pack mate...forever. She could leave the world of vampires and their deadly, underhanded politics behind.

A different life. Maybe a better one?

She sniffed a few times again his chest, breathed in his foresty scene, and used it to strengthen her resolve. Soon, she looked up. "Thank you, Malcolm. Thank you for being my friend."

"I will be with you the entire time," he reassured her. "You need only stick to the script."

"I understand."

He nodded, smiling an assurance at her. "If Captain Yrsa tries to take you down an unfamiliar bargaining road, just bring her back around. You can handle this, my queen...Eliza."

She nodded.

"And remember," he added after starting the lift up again, "you do not need to do this at all. Not now, at least. You could call off the parley."

She bit her lip as she drew back and looked up at her tall, handsome protector. She didn't *want* to do this, but she had no choice. "I'm afraid if I don't, if I just stand around waiting for Edwin to wake up or someone else to step in, Yrsa will make another move." After a moment, she added, "No...I know she'll make a move.

"Payback—if for no other reason than because she thinks I stole Edwin from her."

The thought made her heart skip a beat. "Malcolm, what if she declares war on the vampire species? Or rips this ship apart? What happens to our people? Our Congress?" She swallowed against those possibilities. The Jotnar might not be as numerous as other races, but they had superior tech, extremely effective weaponry, and a lot of unspent anger. "Oh god, one wrong word, and I could get us all killed."

"Perhaps we should contact the High Courts for advice."

"Trasch and his kind?" His suggestion surprised her. It spoke of Malcolm's desperation. "We don't know if the High Courts will even take an interest. And if they do, it might take days or weeks for them to act. And even then, that means they may look more deeply into our Congress."

That last thought frightened her almost more than the Jotnar. She knew if the High Courts thought Edwin's Congress was weak, they would move against them. Effectively speaking, their Congress now had enemies on all sides.

Then one last horrifying thought: "And if they become interested, they may turn their sights on Oliver—especially now that I've outed myself." She shook her head. "I can't take that chance. You understand as a father. You understand we have to protect our children, Malcolm."

The big werewolf nodded as the doors of the lift opened. "Aye. I understand that. I understand family." Then his wolfish eyes darkened. "But I do not trust Yrsa to be honorable."

* * *

Mum told him he could go play with Ariel while she went to have an important meeting. It was Saturday morning, no school, and that always excited Oliver. He liked to be alone to work on his robots. Sometimes, it got lonely after a while, especially if Mum was busy, but when Ariel was there, they always had fun together.

While he worked, he tried to remember what had happened the day before. It was hard to piece together. He remembered Ariel telling him about the space vampire in the hold. He remembered visiting it via the ducts he knew so well, but what happened after that was like a badly broken-up dream. Sometimes small bits made themselves known, but none of it made any sense to him, so he decided he wasn't going to worry about it just then.

He was putting the finishing touches on his robot's motor and testing its mobility, showing Ariel the wires he was tying together, when his best friend suddenly sat up straight on the floor and turned to glance down the corridor. He felt the static electricity in the air make his hair stand on end and realized rather suddenly that Ariel had stiffened in fear.

Oh no, he thought. He hoped it wasn't the Walking Man.

Turning, he glanced at where she was looking.

Thankfully, it wasn't the Walking Man standing at the end of the corridor, but it also wasn't someone he recognized. Ariel turned away from the stranger and looked at him worriedly before getting up and scrambling down the corridor toward the lift that would take her home. She was so afraid of the stranger that she didn't even say goodbye!

Oliver, annoyed that the stranger had chased Ariel off, sat up straighter and scowled at the figure. He might even have gotten to his feet to confront him, but something stopped him. The figure wasn't tall but somehow filled the whole space with his presence.

The stranger at the end of the hallway started toward him. He was only a kid, but one Oliver didn't know. He was sure the boy didn't go to his school, though he did wear a school uniform—dark blue shorts, a white shirt, and a blue blazer with his school's insignia emblazoned on the left-side pocket. A striped red and blue tie was knotted up under his chin. The boy looked eleven or twelve, with ashy blond hair that fell in a wave over his face, almost concealing one eye. His eyes were bright grey and lively, and his complexion, though pale, peachy at the cheeks.

He stopped a few feet away and waved to Oliver. "Hi!" His voice was deeper than Oliver expected.

Forgetting the robot, which had begun to walk off, Oliver pulled his back against the wall, an instinctually defensive gesture even though the boy looked human and harmless. Still, he didn't like the way the boy's eyes moved or the depth of understanding—*of years*—in them.

Feeling suddenly shy, Oliver made the sign for "Hello."

The boy had reached him. He wasn't very tall, maybe two inches taller than Oliver. "You sign?" said the boy, leaning down slightly, his hands on his knees. "That's cool, bro. I sign too. In fact, I invented it!"

What a strange thing to say. But while the strange boy was talking, he was also fluidly signing all of the words as if it was second nature to him.

That made Oliver relax somewhat. He liked that the new boy knew his language. Making a show of looking him up and down, Oliver said, *Are you new to school? If you are, you have the wrong uniform.*

The new boy plucked at his shirt. "Do I? That's a shame. But yeah, I am new. New here, anyway." He glanced around. "Not too many grownups about, eh?"

Oliver shook his head. They are having an important meeting with the other ship.

"The Jotnar? Yeah, I heard that was happening. But I'm not here because of that."

Why are you here?

"Your mum invited me." The new boy grinned.

That interested Oliver. But before he could ask for more details, the boy turned his attention to the walking robot and exclaimed, "Oh, wow, that is *so* cool! Where did you get that?"

Made it.

"No way!" The boy plopped down on the floor on his belly, his head cradled in his hands so he could watch the robot move at eye level.

Feeling more relieved—even excited that the new boy liked his robot—Oliver, grinning hugely, glad the boy liked and understood his robot. He spent the next few minutes showing the new boy how he'd built the robot's frame from spare parts and what it could do.

The new boy followed along and kept asking really important questions about his design. When Oliver mentioned an issue he was having with the robot's AI, the way it seemed incapable of choosing a direction when it came to an intersection in the hallways, the boy made a really good suggestion about how to reprogram it.

You know a lot! Oliver said. He was happy to have met the boy, who was now sitting cross-legged in the hallway next to him while they worked on the robot together. He had almost completely forgotten about Ariel.

How do you know so much? Oliver asked him.

The new boy hummed to himself. "I'm an engineer."

Oliver nearly squeaked in excitement. He wanted to be an engineer, too, or maybe an artificer. He was so excited by the news that he'd totally forgotten to ask the boy's name or how he knew his mum.

But when he did, the boy said offhand, "It's Henry. I don't know your mum very well, but I know Lord Edwin."

Wow, Henry was *so* cool and smart!

After a few more minutes of tinkering with the robot, they got it working. As it toddled off a little unevenly, Henry looked up from under his almost unruly waves of blond hair and said, "Hey. Want to know a secret, Ollie? It's a really cool secret."

Oliver nodded enthusiastically.

Henry signed, *We're family. You and I.* "That's probably why you're so smart," he added verbally. "You get that from me."

That intrigued Oliver. As far as he was aware, Mum was his only family.

Are we cousins? He'd never had a cousin before but liked the idea of it. He was a little jealous of Uncle Malcolm and his large family and extended pack. He wondered what it would be like to have a brother or sister or just some cousins to play with.

"Nope." Henry picked up the robot, played with a servo in its back, and then set it down. It started motoring more fluidly around the floor. Smiling, he glanced up and said, "You might not believe this, but I'm your grandad."

Oliver crossed his arms and tapped out, *I don't believe you. You're way too young to be my grandfather...*

He stopped when he saw Henry smile, saw all his small, perfectly sharp teeth. He had a bad moment when he thought about getting up and running back to the apartment and locking the door behind him the way his mum told him to if he ever felt threatened, but then he decided against it. Henry seemed nice...for a vampire. And Oliver didn't want to lose his robot.

He held his breath and waited, but the child-like vampire didn't do anything scary. He just tilted his head and said, "You don't like vampires much, do you, Oliver? That's smart, considering what they're capable of. But also ironic...considering what you are."

Oliver felt a small shock somewhere deep inside. He didn't know what the vampire who looked like a boy meant. But Henry must have sensed his surprise because he set a gentle hand on Oliver's shoulder and said more kindly, "Don't be alarmed. It isn't anything scary or terrible. In fact, you're quite extraordinary, Oliver. One of a kind."

Oliver sucked in a sharp breath.

"Your mum and dad never told you, did they?"

I don't know what you mean. Tell me what? Oliver shifted away from the vampire's touch and back against the wall. Now, he couldn't decide if he liked him or not. He looked around the corridor, wondering if he should get help.

"Who he is. Your dad."

Oliver's attention snapped back around to Henry. The vampire boy was now watching him quietly with his pale grey eyes that didn't look like a kid's at all.

"Da...d?" Oliver said suddenly, the name sticking in his throat. It was his first word in perhaps two years.

Mum said he didn't have a dad. Well, he did, technically, but she said his dad died long ago before he was born. She didn't have any pictures to show him.

As the robot slipped smoothly by Henry, the vampire boy snatched it up and held it in the air. Oliver watched the robot struggle in Henry's grip, rotating its legs like a frightened animal in the claws of a predator. The AI, now working perfectly, made the robot say, *"Let go let go let go...!"*

But Henry didn't. "I believe we have much to discuss, grandson." He grinned.

| xiii |

In retrospect, the parley was doomed to fail from the start.
When Eliza and Malcolm arrived at the Embassy Consulate Hall where she would be negotiating with Captain Yrsa, she saw the tables were barely set up and the staff who were in charge of preparing the room were standing around, whispering to each other. Agitated, she clapped her hands and said, "I want this place ready now!"

A message had arrived from Yrsa's ship stating she would be arriving in the company of her Royal Guard in just over an hour. Since parleys were traditionally held on neutral ground, it was agreed upon by their two Courts that it should happen in the Embassy suite aboard the *Queen's Gambit*.

That worried Eliza some. She didn't like the idea of Yrsa and her men boarding the ship—even under the Embassy's neutral banner—but Malcolm informed her she had no choice since Yrsa's fleet didn't have an Embassy. As such, she wanted to present a professional front to the General of the Jotnar…and the disarray presently in the room did not in any way show professionalism.

One of the unformed workers turned to look at her dolefully. He said after a moment's consideration, "Where's Lord Edwin?"

"Not here. But I am."

There was a bad moment when Eliza feared a mutiny. She knew the staff would never have pulled this kind of stunt with Edwin. She might be Edwin's Bride, but she was also a Poppet, and only a Poppet—one of Edwin's *property*. Malcolm, standing behind her, put an encouraging hand on her shoulder. He wasn't riding in to save her. She needed to fix this herself or the staff on board the ship would never respect her.

Raising both hands, palms out, she let her frustration filter down into her weird affectation for static electricity. And as small sparks jumped from her hands and lit up the dim room, she saw the staff's eyes grow luminous.

"I want this room ready in five!" she told them, and they scrambled.

Working double quick, they finished the room in just under the time she'd given them, and good thing, too, because mere moments after they had set the final chair and adjusted the lighting, a courier ran up to her to tell her Yrsa's transport had docked.

Taking a deep breath, she turned to Malcolm. "Here we go."

A short ten minutes later, the Court Guards escorted the leader of the Jotnar and her advisors and bodyguards into the room. The Court Guards were large, retired military men that Edwin had hired because no one else was willing to give them a chance and no enemy was stupid enough to give them a hard time. They were hard men, toughened by war but essentially alone—no family and few friends. Many suffered from severe PSTD. Still, even being large, burly military guys, they looked tiny compared to the eight-foot-tall Jotnar who lumbered into the Embassy suite.

The sight of them ducking through the doorway, their massive, dark blue bodies encased in shiny black armor like the carapace of dangerous monster insects, their shining white hair hanging to mid-back in braids, made Eliza's heart sink to her shoes. Having not seen Gorm in person, she'd had no idea how large and formidable the Ice Pirates were. How in hell was she ever going to negotiate with something like *that?*

Malcolm, perhaps sensing her sudden fear—or even smelling her light, sudden sweat—leaned in and said, "Each of them is wearing harnesses under their armor. And, without those harnesses, they would die of overheating within minutes of being on this ship. They are more fragile than they seem. Remember that."

Eliza nodded as she stepped forward to greet Captain Yrsa in person for the first time.

The guard parted to allow their captain to step forward.

And there she stood in real-time: Captain Yrsa, glaring down at Eliza with her reddened alien eyes. She was perhaps only a few inches shorter than the smallest male surrounding her, which still made her tower over Eliza by at least two and a half feet. For the occasion, she wore a white lace, almost see-through gown with an extra-long train that looked like snowflakes sewn together. Beneath the translucent fabric, she wore very little. Eliza spotted a cooling harness similar to what Gorm had been wearing, though this one was far more fashionable and resembled a black leather underbust corset. Her voluptuous figure was rather openly displayed, and she wore only a thin, black leather thong.

Yrsa's voluminous white hair was pinned up in a gigantic beehive and held with a decorative comb with frozen blue flowers. Her eyes actually seemed to glow faintly.

Eliza had to admit the woman was quite stunningly beautiful. Her mind immediately turned to Yrsa and her husband married…probably having sex on some gigantic bed covered in white wolf fur. She couldn't decide if the image in her head was sexy or utterly terrifying.

From behind her, Malcolm muttered low in her ear, "She looks like a gigantic BDSM Smurfette." And that made Eliza smile far too widely as she stepped forward to greet the leader of the Jotnar.

Yrsa looked her over critically, making a show of how small she was, but Eliza offered her hand all the same. The Jotunn leader took it in her enormous black-gloved one and gave her a single shake. "Even smaller than I expected," she said loud enough to make it a permanent statement.

Eliza thought of a thousand comebacks but decided that no petty revenge on her part was worth putting her Congress at risk. Instead, she decided to turn things on their ear. "That's a beautiful gown."

Yrsa cocked a bemused eyebrow at her sudden compliment. "I wore it on my wedding night." Her smile grew half an inch and her tongue flickered in the corner of her mouth like a lizard's. "My first night with Edwin. I thought he would appreciate seeing it again. And what's underneath it."

Eliza nearly rolled her eyes. For the first time, she understood that Yrsa too felt threatened—and perhaps a tad desperate. After all, Eliza was the one married to him, not Yrsa. Otherwise, why would she be wearing a ludicrous, diaphanous *nightgown* to a parley? "All right then. We've had our fun. Let's get on with it, shall we?"

They sat down on opposite ends of a large oval table with a hole in it. Malcolm and several security guards stood behind Eliza while Yrsa's men stood glowering behind her seated figure. They looked savage and unpredictable. The Consul was supposed to lead the negotiations—in this case, Emerson, Edwin's snaky attorney—but before the little conniving vamp could even open his mouth, Yrsa laid out the Jotnar's demands in three parts.

One, they wanted their man Gorm back; two, they wanted their tech back intact; and, thirdly—and most surprisingly—they wanted Eliza to hand over the keys to the *Queen's Gambit*.

That threw Eliza for a moment. She couldn't believe the Jotnar's audacity! But instead of losing her cool, she remembered what Malcolm said earlier: This was a negotiation. Yrsa was working high, trying to get everything she wanted all at once. And, anyway, this was how the Ice Pirates operated; they stole or otherwise negotiated everything they owned. It was how they had made incredible leaps in tech. He also advised she appoint a speaker—him—to appear more in power.

She nodded to Malcolm, who was acting as her Second, and he stood up. He leaned forward, fingertips just touching the top of the table, and announced they were agreeable to the first two demands, but only on the condition that the Jotnar cease their objectives, returned to the *Midnight Sun*, and made no further war advances toward their Congress, the humans, or any of the other races. They too were aiming high.

"Unacceptable," Yrsa insisted. Her eyes looked lighted from within as she spoke—not to Malcolm but to Eliza. "Your Congress killed many of our kind aboard the *Abraxas*. I demand blood. Satisfaction."

It took Eliza a moment to realize she was referring to the ice vampires. "Your *kind*? Excuse me, your highness, but you unlawfully infected the members of Lord Emmerdale's Congress and turned them into hand puppets. Those people were never *yours*."

Yrsa leaned forward and narrowed her eyes. "They became Jotnar after their infection. And, after all, isn't that how the vampires propagate? And the wolves?" She glanced up to include Malcolm. Looking back at Eliza, she added, "How do the vampires make more of their kind? They infect *humans*."

"Humans who choose to be vampires," Eliza countered.

"All of them?" She paused for dramatics, knowing full well that not every vampire was made an Heir in accordance with their own will. "*Mrs. McGillicuddy*, you don't seem to understand our position. We have been exiled for centuries by the other species. Cut off and isolated. This is our boon. This is our *birthright*. To propagate and to expand our empire. We are owed this."

Well, now, this was territory she better understood because, as a Poppet, she was quite familiar with the rules of Court Etiquette. "Under the laws of the Paris Accord, no species on Earth—vampire, werewolf, Jotnar, or otherwise—may force a human being to join with them. That must be done voluntarily. It may not always be this way, but forcing a human is still considered a punishable crime. I would have you remember that."

Yrsa sat back, looking stung. "We were not there to sign the Accord, as you recall. We were living in exile at that time."

Emerson interrupted. This was, after all, his wheelhouse. "Whether or not you were there, Captain, is irrelevant. The rules still apply. Ignorance of the law does not excuse one from breaking it."

Yrsa gave the lawyer a deadly look. "You will stay out of this, little vampire. I am the queen of my kind. As such, I always get what I want."

Oh, my god, she even sounded like a spoiled princess!

Something occurred to Eliza. Edwin had mentioned Yrsa's father, Captain Skarde, the former military commander of the Jotnar. Yet he was curiously absent. "What happened to your father, Yrsa?" she suddenly asked. "Why isn't he here, acting as one of your advisors or whatever?"

Turning back to Eliza, Yrsa spat out, "My father was weak. He was removed from his position."

"By you?"

Settling back, Yrsa gave her a gratified smile that spoke volumes. "Yes, in fact."

"You deposed your own father?"

"He was old. Set in his ways. He did not understand that the Jotnar's time to act was now."

Eliza shook her head. "So you...what? Murdered him?"

"Something like that. He was exiled to the Dasht-e Lut salt desert to die."

Eliza was both surprised and...somehow not. That jived with Yrsa's personality. "And now you want me to turn my ship—my *Congress*—over to someone like you? Someone who feels nothing about murdering her own father because he wouldn't get behind her decisions? Am I following this correctly?"

Emerson glanced at her, eyebrows raised in subtle admiration.

"Anyone who disobeys their leader deserves punishment," Yrsa stated simply.

"My Congress," Eliza repeated. "A fragile alliance between the humans, the vampires, the wolves, and the Fae. Do you not understand how precarious a Congress is? How easily this alliance can be shattered and, as a result, produce an act of war that could last centuries between the races? And you wish for me to turn this rare, fragile thing over to someone willing to dispose of her own kin when they displease her?"

A low rumble of voices filled the room as people—vamps, werewolves, and Jotnar—spoke amongst themselves. Out of the corner of her eye, Eliza spotted Emerson giving her an appreciative thumbs up.

Yrsa snorted. "Mrs. McGillicuddy, what would you know about controlling a Congress? Aren't you merely the Bride of the Lord of this ship? How long have you been in power?"

Yrsa's men backed up her statement by beating on the table with their fists.

Eliza didn't know what to say for a moment. Emerson stepped in and told the Jotnar to hush. To her surprise, they listened to him. Then he nodded to Eliza to continue.

At a loss as to how to approach this sticky situation, she decided to circle back to the issue at hand. "The two situations are not the same, Captain. Getting back to what you were doing with the *Abraxas*. Humans first choose and then are chosen by their Vampire Lords to become Heirs. Your Jotnar either murdered the denizens of the crippled *Abraxas* or turned them into Jotnar against their will. However you want to defend your decision, it was still a violation against the Accord and a potential act of war—one that the High Vampire Courts are already aware of."

She paused before delivering the coup de grace. "If you take this ship—even if I gave you the keys myself—the High Courts would refuse to recognize your sovereignty. They would reject your claim on the *Queen's Gambit*. Of that, you can be assured."

Her eyes gleaming, Yrsa said, "How do you know you have their ear? Can you trust they will listen to you?"

Eliza stumbled on a reply, hating how wily Captain Yrsa was. How easily the Jotnar Queen saw through her bluff.

Yrsa's eyes cooled. "Enough pettiness and lawyerese. We can debate for days what is right or wrong. I demand a Le Troc. Are you willing to comply, Mrs. McGillicuddy?"

Confused, Eliza leaned back into Malcolm. "What's she talking about?"

Emerson explained instead. "A Le Troc is an ancient system wherein two warring tribes of Supernatural must exchange goods of equal value, thereby forming an alliance of sorts and neutralizing any ill-will. The goods can be anything, evening something symbolic. Not necessarily earthly goods."

"An alliance?" Eliza said almost too loudly. "Why would we want that?"

"Because if we are aligned, we cannot, by law, make any further war moves against one another's Courts."

She swallowed hard, unsure.

"It's an acceptable solution, my Lady. It will delay any further attacks until we figure out a better, long-term solution."

Speaking up, Yrsa said loudly from across the table, "It wasn't just a virus the Icepick injected into your ship. You also have a cryo-bomb in your engine, Mrs. McGillicuddy, one your engineers and artificers will find very difficult to remove, especially without your AI to guide them. If you don't want us to detonate it and freeze your engine, you'll listen very carefully."

Eliza turned, sucked in a sharp breath, and said, "An explosive?"

"A reverse incendiary device capable of cracking your ship in half."

She hadn't expected that. Letting out a shuddering breath, she asked softly, "What do you want, exactly?"

Yrsa, smiling wryly, produced a black data stick and held it up. "This contains information and a schematic of the maximum security prison rig Oublies, also known as the Vault."

Eliza looked at the stick, her brows knitting together. She knew what the Oublies was: the most impenetrable prison in the world, created to hold only the most dangerous criminals—specifically, Supe criminals of all kinds. The rig—a huge, floating Alcatraz—was full to brimming with monsters of all kinds. But before she could even open her mouth to question Yrsa's objective, Yrsa continued.

"It may help you, Mrs. McGillicuddy, or it may not. The prison guards, the Mechi-people, may have changed much of the layout of the ship by now. But if they have not, it will guide you to retrieving Dr. Arturo Pretorius, an artificer who has been incarcerated there. He is one of our top artificers."

She tried to digest all of this info as quickly as she could. "Why would we help you to retrieve this criminal...this Dr. Pretorius?"

"He is important to us and our future. If we cannot have your gyro, then we must have him. Consider it an even trade."

Yrsa held up a hand to stay any more of Eliza's questions. "We need Dr. Pretorius to perfect the cooling tech we need to keep our world hospitable to the needs of the Jotnar. Without him...well, as you can see, our original plan to convince your people to stop heating the Earth has failed. This is our Plan B, so to speak. Dr. Pretorius is the only artificer who can accomplish what we need done."

She smiled. It was almost a human smile. "Retrieve the good doctor, and we will deactivate the cryo-bomb in your engine. Fail to do so, and...well, we'll send your gyro plummeting in pieces to the Earth below, killing millions of people and launching nuclear winter."

Her smile stayed in place as she added, "Either way, we win."

Eliza nearly popped up out of her seat. "Now, wait just a mo—"

But Yrsa ignored her. She set the data stick down on the table and stood up—all seven-plus feet of her. Her head came precariously close to brushing the ceiling.

Eliza, nearly shaking, just stared at the data stick. "You're insane. If you blow this ship, it will kill *everyone*."

"Everyone...on Earth. Thankfully, my people have long since taken to the sky and are self-sufficient. I'll be in touch. Good day...Mrs. McGillicuddy." With a curt nod, Captain Yrsa and her men stalked from the room, all of them wearing satisfied smiles on their alien blue faces.

* * *

Eliza was virtually vibrating with fear and rage as she stepped out of the Embassy Room and into the hallway and headed to the lifts, accompanied by Malcolm and Emerson. The vampire was yakking on about what a great job she did at the negotiations, but it sure as hell didn't feel that way.

She looked at them both, feeling hollow inside. "I don't know what I just did in that meeting, but I'm fairly certain Edwin could have handled things much better. He probably would have batted his eyes at Yrsa and had her eating out his hand."

"This was good," Emerson insisted, almost cavorting with excitement. "And you did well, my Lady. Edwin was unlikely to have done much better. Sometimes, I think that husband of yours is a mite soft in the head." He tapped the side of his head to emphasize.

She ignored the lawyer, leaned against a wall for support, and tried to stay the tremors in her hands. "NEWTON?" she asked somewhat randomly.

She was surprised when the AI answered. "Yes, my Lady Eliza."

"You're back!" She felt a glimmer of hope.

"For the moment, yes. The Jotnar have restored me."

The first thing she did was ask about the cryo-bomb, but NEWTON said he couldn't dislodge the Icepick without tripping the device.

"But never fear, Lady Eliza. More artificers are set to arrive from Earth today to assist and advise."

Eliza thought about the possibility of making gentle "contact" with the Icepick via the harness, but when she floated the idea, NEWTON said there was a virtual tripwire on the device. "I believe if you tamper with it, it may go off prematurely."

Hanging her head, Eliza headed for a lift. "I wish Edwin was awake so I could ask him what to do."

Malcolm suddenly came around and blocked her way. He reached out and took her hands, which were shaking badly. "You did very well, my Lady, given the circumstances."

"Did well? I'm pretty sure I just made things worse for all of us." She stepped around him and into the lift, but before Malcolm could trail after her, she said, "I need to see my son, spend time with him. Go see to your family, Malcolm."

Relieved, he bowed his head, leaving her in the care of Emerson.

The small, neat, utterly lizard-like vampire stood beside her, his fancy, monogrammed attaché case tucked under one arm while she leaned against the wall. It suddenly occurred to her that as the new head of this Congress, Emerson would now be her eternal shadow. She didn't know how she felt about that. He looked like he both wanted to help her and bite her at the same time.

While they ascended to her apartment level, she touched the data stick in her pocket. God, she was so out of her depth on this!

"Emerson, what the hell do I do?"

Emerson took a deep breath as he considered their options. "Well, now, my Lady, we have much to discover and more to discuss. I believe our next move should be to see if we can't at least get Lord Edwin up and activated. Perhaps Lord Foxley can help."

"Lord Foxley. God help us."

Emerson grinned like a viper. "I assure you God had nothing to do with creating Lord Foxley."

* * *

She stopped as soon as she stepped inside her quarters, paralyzed with fear. Lord Foxley sat on her sofa, reading a book to her son, who was lying with his head in Foxley's lap. All of her worst nightmares coalesced around her, plus a few she wasn't even aware of, and Eliza had to make a conscious decision not to short out every device in the room with her sporadic eruption of fear and outrage.

"Oliver!" she said, her voice somehow sounding both hoarse and screechy at the same time. Her instinct was to rush forward and snatch her son away from the monster who had him, but she was afraid Foxley would do something to Oliver, so she stayed rooted to the spot, just gaping at him. "Oliver, it's me! It's Mum!"

Oliver, who had been half-asleep and listening to Foxley read *The Carpathian Castle* by Jules Verne, opened his eyes and turned his head. When he saw her, his eyes widened, he sat up suddenly, and said in a sleepy tone, "Mum?"

He looked unharmed. No bite marks on him. So far.

"Oliver," Eliza repeated, moving a few cautious steps forward while Foxley watched her, a supremely amused expression on his face and the open book in his lap. He was wearing one of his absurd school uniforms.

"Ollie, come here, sweet pea."

Rubbing at his eyes sleepily, her son got up and walked to her. She resisted grabbing him by the shoulders too quickly. She didn't want to frighten him after all he had been through.

Foxley sat up, crossing his legs, which just barely touched the floor. He smiled nicely, his white-blonde hair tumbling across his brow and into his ghostly grey eyes. "I assure you, madam, Ollie is entirely intact. We were enjoying an underappreciated classic, he and I." He indicated the book in his lap.

Clutching Oliver a bit too tightly, Eliza said, "What are you doing here?"

Foxley gave her his big facetious eyes. "Madam, you invited me aboard."

"Aboard the ship. Not to my apartment! Not to see my family!"

Meanwhile, Oliver was squirming under her tight hold. "Mum...stop!" he said, pushing at her hands. It took her a moment to realize Oliver was speaking. Actually talking. She couldn't believe it! With tears in her eyes, she turned him around and went down on one knee, still keeping one eye on Foxley. "Oliver! How long have you been with this...man?"

"Grampa? Hours, I guess." He shrugged and rubbed at his sleepy eyes again. "Dunno."

Her breath caught at the sound of the words coming out of her son's mouth. "And he didn't hurt you? Didn't...make you do anything?" She recalled all too well that Foxley could physically manipulate people through their own blood. Once upon a time, he'd held her down and threatened her in front of Edwin.

Oliver shook his head. "Grampa is cool. We made robots."

"That man..." She pointed to Foxley. "...is *not* your grandfather!"

Suddenly, Oliver's eyes darkened in a way that worried Eliza. "He said he's Lord Edwin's dad. You never told me about Edwin, Mum! Never told me—"

"Quiet..." she said, hoping no one could overhear them from the hallway. "We don't have the time to discuss that right now, sweetie. But I promise—"

"You should have told me!" Oliver said, his eye flashing black in a way that made her heart lurch into her throat. Those were vampire eyes.

"Grampa says Lord Edwin is my dad. Is that true?"

She opened her mouth, then closed it, unsure how to respond.

"Why did you say my dad was dead?"

"Oliver...baby!" She tried to hang onto him, but he was unnaturally strong for a little boy and wrestled his way far too easily from her grip. Before she even knew what to do, he turned and fled out into the hallway...and crashed right into Malcolm's legs where the big werewolf was standing outside her door.

Malcolm, always so good with children, didn't even question what was happening. He just clutched her son against his legs for a long moment. Eventually, he glanced up at her, and Eliza shook her head, helpless tears in her eyes.

She mouthed, *He knows.*

Nodding, Malcolm dropped down to his haunches and whispered something to her son, something that caused his tears to lessen. Putting his big hand atop Oliver's head, he looked him in the eye and said, "How does a sleepover sound, Oliver? I know Briar likes to hear about your robots. We can even invite Ariel and make it a proper party."

Oliver's sniffles stopped and he turned to look at Eliza, still on her knees in the family room. It wasn't a friendly look he threw her. After a second, he turned back to Malcolm and nodded.

"Good." Malcolm stood up and took Oliver's hand in his. Looking over at Eliza, he said, "We're going to have a sleepover at our place, my Lady."

Feeling sick and on the verge of crying again, or possibly throwing up this time, Eliza nodded. "Please take care of him."

With a sharp nod, Malcolm turned and led Oliver away.

Eliza watched her little boy go, then got up and closed the door. She sniffed and straightened her shoulders as she prepared to face the devil himself. She had to pick her words carefully. As much as she hated Foxley, she also knew they needed him.

Taking a deep breath, she turned to face one of her oldest enemies. "How could you? That was low, Foxley...even for you. I extended an invitation to you, and this is what you do? You prey on my son?"

Foxley had migrated from the sofa to the wet bar and was clinking through the collection of bottles there—mostly wine and blood substitute labels. He seemed to find nothing to his satisfaction. Finally turning, he met Eliza's eyes, and she felt some of the old fear filter back into her.

It was impossible not to be afraid of Foxley. The last time they were together, Foxley had pinned her to a floor, locked her in a cage, and repeatedly threatened her in an effort to manipulate Edwin. She reminded herself of how dangerous he truly was—and how no move was beneath him.

"Madam, there was no 'preying.' As Oliver stated, we simply built robots."

"Right. Sure."

"Ollie had questions." He shrugged, finally settling on the best bottle of wine on the bar. He poured himself a drink "I simply answered them."

"No, you ruined his life. And mine. And Edwin's."

"I'm honestly surprised you never told the boy about his illustrious father. 'Tis a shame. Do you really believe the High Courts won't put two and two together in time?"

She glared at him as she worked to get her temper and her fear under control. How she wanted to strangle the life out of Edwin's bastard maker. But, ultimately, she knew it would do them all no good. They needed Foxley, as loathed as she was to admit it.

"I don't want anything to do with the High Courts," she stated purposefully. "I don't want those bastards' interference in our lives."

"In that, madam, we have a common goal." Foxley sipped from his glass and made a face.

Swallowing hard, she changed tactics. "Edwin—"

"I know about my Heir." He gave her a look of annoyance as he leaned against the bar. "I'm his maker and master, little Poppet. I feel every beat of Edwin's heart. And every moment it does *not* beat."

"Then you know—"

"He is not dead," Foxley stated, then frowned as if catching himself in a half-truth. "Not in the traditional sense. The clockwork mechanism didn't malfunction, by the by. It simply locked up due to some other cause. Impact damage, perhaps. Edwin is in the vampire equivalent of a self-induced coma."

She sucked in a sharp breath at the news. She wasn't sure if that was better or worse. "What does that even mean? He put *himself* under?" Edwin was a lot of things, including once, a long time ago, a gangster. But he was no coward.

Foxley contemplated that. "Not voluntarily...more like his body shut him down to allow it to heal from some catastrophe. The Cronus Clock is not broken. In fact, it is working exactly as it was intended. It is saving his life."

It took her a moment to digest that. She didn't know Edwin's clockwork heart had a name. "So the...Cronus Clock could start up again? He could wake up on his own?"

"He will need a cold reboot, so to speak."

"What does that mean?"

"It means what it sounds like. He needs to be shocked awake."

She contemplated that. "Can you do that?"

"No."

That surprised her. She went and sat down in a nearby chair before she fell down. "I don't understand. I thought you invented his...Cronus Clock?"

He returned empty-handed to the sofa and looked at her archly. "I'm an engineer, not an artificer. I work in broad, practical strokes. *Engines*, little Poppet. It's in 'engineer.'"

His tone annoyed her, but she let him continue.

"The man who created Edwin's clockwork heart was commissioned by me. He was a watchmaker artisan named Fortescue, a vampire hundreds of years steeped in his craft." Returning to the wet bar, he poured himself another glass of wine before returning to the sofa. Foxley's utter casualness made her want to scream. "Fortescue's Cronus Clock is as much art as design—and it is not *my* specialty. You would need to speak to the artificer himself to understand how to revive Edwin."

"And where do I find this Fortescu—this vampire artificer?"

Foxley examined the wine in his glass by holding it up to the light. He scowled at the vintage. "He died aboard the Oublies more than thirty years ago."

Eliza felt her hopes die inside her. "Died in prison? In the Vault?"

"Well, he was a criminal."

Foxley *would* have had a criminal vampire artificer working for him. That was just his speed. "Were there plans or schematics? Surely something of his work remains?"

The little bastard shook his head. "Fortescue destroyed all of his plans before he went to prison. The mysteries of the Cronus Clock perished with its maker, I'm afraid."

It was all she could do to keep from crying, and she did not want to do that—not in front of *him*. It seemed no matter what she did, there were ridiculous obstacles to overcome. "Without Edwin, we're all dead in the water. We have no protection from the Courts."

Foxley turned his head strangely in that way he had, sort of sideways, but his eyes never left her. "I would not allow that."

"I doubt you could prevent it."

"You underestimate me as usual." Rising, he moved toward her, his hand extended. "Take my protection for the time being."

Eliza lifted her tear-stained face and edged back a little in her seat, glaring at him. Looking for the deceit in his eyes. "As if you care what happens to my family."

"It's true I find the power you hold over Edwin...distasteful. But we are, after all, allies of a sort in our mutual love for him, as well as our distrust of the High Courts. If they harmed Oliver, that would break Edwin's heart for the last time—and that I do not want."

She tried to decide if she believed him. One thing was for certain: Foxley had never been shy about how he felt about his Heir. Or his carnivorous desire to try and win Edwin back. Foxley would go through anyone for that—including her. His obsession was as monstrous as the rest of him.

Looking at him steadily, Eliza finally took his hand and shook it. It was cold and dry. "This is a temporary alliance. A ceasefire. And we're not 'allies,' Foxley. Not after what you did to Oliver." She took a deep breath for courage and prayed they all made it through this. "I need whatever help you can lend us regarding Edwin, but after that, I want you off my ship."

He watched her a long moment, saying nothing. She could not tell if the expression on his face was one of insult or amusement. Foxley was impossible to decipher at the best of times.

Finally, he said: "I did not do anything to Oliver but uncover the truth you have so deeply buried since his birth. Oliver has every right to know who his father is. And what he is."

"Oliver is a little boy," she insisted.

"Oliver is a vampire-in-waiting, madam," Foxley said, an evil twinkle in his eyes. "And he is not the only one."

| xiv |

As soon as she learned that Tommy was up and about, Eliza decided to go down to the labs to visit him. She needed as much backup and as many advisors as she could find right now.

She was headed to a lift when she spotted someone familiar loitering in the corridor, his back to her while he charmed up one of the staff—a young, handsome courtier named Darcy, who was blushing profusely.

"Cesar!"

Her old friend turned to face her, and Eliza felt her heart flutter at the sight. She almost didn't recognize him. He was dressed in a pricey, fitted grey business suit, and his hair was longer and fell in tame but rakish blond curls over his shoulders. He was smiling boyishly as he was wont to do—still the young, beautiful man in his late twenties that Edwin had made his Heir almost a decade earlier. His eyes, once a deep ocean blue, had lightened over the years in the way of vampire eyes everywhere and now looked much paler, almost silvery.

Even as she ran up to him and threw herself into his arms, she reflected on how in a few centuries' time, his eyes would look nearly ghostly.

"Miss Eliza!" he said, swinging her around a couple of times before setting her down. Then he pulled her close and buried his face in the side of her neck. She stiffened for one second before she reminded herself of how safe she was in Cesar's arms. They were best friends and had lived together for over two years following his transformation at Edwin's hands.

Pulling back, he looked down into her eyes sympathetically. "I'm so sorry about what happened with Edwin."

"Did you feel it?" she wondered. "Did you feel what happened?"

He nodded. "It hurt. A lot. I texted you, but you didn't answer. Then I learned from Foxley that you had a lot of other problems to deal with."

Tears filled her eyes—and guilt her heart. "I'm sorry. I should have answered you," she sniffed. "It's been insane here. I saw your text, I just..." She shook her head and then felt the corridor take a half-turn around her.

Cesar caught her before she collapsed. "You're exhausted. Do you have time to eat something? You look like you're starving yourself."

She laughed weakly. "I can't remember the last time I had a meal."

"Come on. We'll hit the food court. Or one of the fancier restaurants on the ship. Yeah, let's go with that!"

They took a lift down to the Bazaar, where there were dozens of high-end restaurants, open-air eateries, and not a few bars and taverns. Eliza pointed out her favorite, a teashop called Tea Junkie, owned and run by a lovely young merchant named Kimberly Richardson.

As soon as they stepped inside, Kimberly shushed over in her long skirts and greeted Eliza. "I have your usual spot, my Lady." Previously, she had always addressed Eliza by her first name only, but now things had changed. It seemed everyone aboard the *Queen's Gambit* was up on their gossip now.

Once they were seated in a cozy corner booth, Cesar leaned in and said, "So, it's true. You're...out of the closet, so to speak. About being Edwin's Bride, I mean."

Eliza nodded while Kimberly served her an amazing (and rare) pot of Da Hong Pao tea with its own tea cozy and a three-tiered plate of cucumber sandwiches. Kimberly served Cesar a specialty of hers, a blood-substitute-based tea mix, without even asking. "Not by choice, but with so much going on, someone has to take the helm." She nodded a thanks to Kimberly as she shushed away.

Cesar, stirring his teacup, nodded. "I'm really worried about Edwin."

She nodded, then realized she had bolted down four cucumber sandwich triangles in succession without even thinking about it and forced herself to chew more slowly. A thought occurred to her and she swallowed hard and said in a very low voice, one only vampire ears could hear, "If Edwin...died...or, at least, didn't wake up, would you be all right?" She knew that young, bloodbound vampires often perished if they lost their masters. Some didn't but went irretrievably insane.

He glanced up, his eyes shining brightly in the dim tearoom. "I don't know. I don't think it would end well for me." He shrugged at the thought. "At the very least, it would hurt. A lot. I mean...I love Edwin." She saw him swallow hard. "It would destroy me to lose him."

She nodded. Reaching out, she put her hand on Cesar's wrist. She could feel his cold even through his jacket and shirt sleeve. "How are you, Cesar? Really? Working for Foxley must be its own special brand of hell."

His eyes softened at her concern. "It's not a party, if you know what I mean. But it's not terrible, either. There are benefits." He laughed suddenly. "God, the money that flows through the *Gypsy*

Queen is positively obscene. The businesses on board. The tourism. Whatever else Foxley finagles. That little parasite has his fingers in everything! I doubt he even knows what he's worth."

She pressed her lips together. "You look like he's taking care of you. Though I know that doesn't mean much. He took care of Edwin, too, and Edwin still carries the scars of his service. He hasn't hurt you? Done things to you?"

Cesar shook his head. "Mostly, he treats me like I'm not there unless he needs me to do something for him. He's currently obsessed with buying up or otherwise stealing tech, so he has me bully his competitors and other artificers into selling their devices' patents to him."

"That's awful."

When he saw her worried expression, he added, "It isn't what you think. I mostly just stand next to him and act threatening. I rarely have to do anything more exciting."

"That's something, I guess." She shook her head. "Still, two hundred years is a long time to work as a thug for that psycho."

Cesar held up a finger. "One hundred and ninety-two years. I've already served eight of them."

They laughed about that, not without a touch of bitterness, before exchanging a few current anecdotes. Cesar detailed some of the disastrous dates he'd been on lately. Eliza talked about her equally terrible parley skills. When she thoughtlessly brought up the fact that she'd run into him on her way to see Tommy in Recovery, Cesar grew very somber suddenly, but she understood why and had to kick herself for mentioning it.

Tommy had suffered and become what he was because of Cesar. She briefly considered asking him if he wanted to see his ex-lover but then thought better of it when she saw the pain still stamped so deeply into his eyes. Instead, she asked if he needed a refill.

"No, thank you. This is enough." He indicated his virtually untouched drink. Then added, "With all of the Poppets on board Foxley's ship, I rarely even need to drink this stuff anymore." He shook his head. "You lose your taste for it after a while."

She was nibbling a chocolate digestive biscuit off the three-tier tray but set it down on a napkin. "You've been feeding on Foxley's Poppets?"

He gave her a funny look. "Doesn't Edwin feed on his Poppets here aboard this ship?"

"Sometimes." She hesitated. "But it's a volunteer-only program. He never forces them. Or even seduces them, really."

He nodded. "But they still do it. They want to feed him because they love him."

He wasn't wrong, but it still left her uncomfortable. Unlike what she imagined went on aboard Foxley's ship, everything was consensual on all sides with Edwin and his Poppets. That was the house rule for all vampires in Edwin's Congress, and the policy for any vampire who visited the ship, and she explained that to Cesar so he understood.

"But because Edwin is kind, and also because of that power of his, the Poppets line up for him, right?" he asked

Again, she felt a twinge. He usually had more Poppets than he knew what to do with. She opened her mouth to say that, but Cesar cut her off with his next request.

"Are your Poppets open for visits?" Smiling and showing perhaps more teeth than he meant to, he eyed Kimberly in passing as she saw to another customer, then switched his attention back to her. "While I'm on board, I would love to visit the Poppets' quarters, if that's permissible."

She wasn't sure how to answer that. She hadn't expected Cesar, who had spent the first few years of his vampirehood living on synthetic blood, to ask. Just to be polite, she said, "I can put in a request and see if someone can accommodate you."

"'A request?'" He laughed at that. Then he leaned in close and said, "They're Poppets, Miss Eliza. It's a little beyond them to decide if they want a visit, don't you think?"

"No," she insisted, suddenly unhappy with the turn of their conversation. *She* was a Poppet, after all. "The Poppets here know exactly what they're being asked to do. They go to school now. They make their own decisions. They have rights aboard this ship." She stopped herself. She was sounding defensive and soapbox-y when Cesar was simply asking what every other vampire asked when they boarded the *Queen's Gambit*.

She saw him sipping the blood substitute, his eyebrows raised in surprise.

Forcing a smile, she repeated, "I'll put in a request and let you know. In the meantime, will you be staying? I have to hold a meeting about recent events. I wouldn't mind you there." She added, "You're ex-military. I'd appreciate your input."

Setting down his teacup, Cesar wiped his mouth with his napkin and said, "Anything for you, Miss Eliza."

***

"We're really going to do this, then?" Malcolm asked as Eliza loaded the data stick into the projector that controlled the sand table in the center of the room.

"We will if I can get this junk working."

The two of them were gathered in Edwin's War Room—a separate and never-used chamber in his personal offices that few of them had ever even visited up to this point. It was large enough to hold a crowd but felt cramped from being used for storage. She had asked the Court Guards to clear the sand table covered in boxes of office supplies and to fetch chairs. The others filtered in even as Eliza rattled the old 3-D projector to get the ancient piece of machinery working.

Finally, the machine, which had been in mothballs for at least a decade, warmed up enough to spit out a giant schematic on the table—the data on the stick that Captain Yrsa had given her. The guests she had invited to this meeting—Narissa, Malcolm, and the now-functional Tommy—glanced with interest at what Eliza assumed was the layout of the giant prison gyro known as the Vault. It was so large that the sand table had reduced the image to fit. With all of its thousands of corridors and byways, it resembled a mad little labyrinth.

"That's it?" Narissa said while Tommy powered up to the table. She was leaning against the table but had to shift to allow Tommy to fit. "That's the Vault?"

"The rig Oublies, yes," Malcolm announced.

Narissa looked it over. She wore a patch over her missing eye but was otherwise looking well. Tommy was moving slowly and saying nothing, his eyes on the floor. "I've heard of it, of course, but never saw it in the flesh—so to speak. They don't allow pictures or videos."

Eliza nodded and shifted her attention to Tommy. "How are you, my friend?"

He nodded. "Functional."

At the same time, the one remaining person she had invited stepped into the War Room—Cesar. He had changed into a dark blue, military-inspired suit with silver buttons. Not his dress uniform from the Air Force, but one that hinted at some distant ghost of it. It made him look especially dashing. Enough that everyone noticed him, including Tommy, whose eyes swiveled up and then down again as he chose to ignore his ex-lover.

Eliza could feel the tension in the air as Cesar smiled sadly at her and chose a spot as far away from Tommy as he could—which, incidentally, was in the far corner.

Leaning in, Narissa said, "Why is he here? Isn't he Foxley's Enforcer?"

"He's not, actually," Eliza explained, hoping the Fae warrior would not give her too much lip the way she did Edwin. "Cesar is Edwin's Heir and former Enforcer. And I need him—both for his expertise and because he's the one person on board this ship who can connect with Edwin in his current state. He can tell us what's going on."

Narissa looked unconvinced but chose not to comment.

Eliza was relieved and looked to Cesar for info.

"I haven't reached him quite yet, but I'm getting closer. Working through layers, you might say."

Nodding, Eliza started the meeting by thanking everyone for being here, then went on to brief them about the objective—that of finding this Dr. Pretorius and getting off the rig in one piece. There was some mumbling about that, but she diligently turned to the 3-D diagram on the sand table. "I've given this a lot of thought, and I think the best way to proceed is to have a small group infiltrate the Vault."

She paused to spin the schematic to give them a better view. "That group, once aboard, should split off. One group to distract the military police on board the ship while the others search the ship."

She pointed to a spot on the schematic marked with red lines. "Yrsa believes he is being held on what's known as the Blue Level—the part of the ship reserved for terrorists and revolutionaries—but she isn't certain where. It will require a sweep search end to end."

Malcolm, resting his shoulder against the wall, raised his hand politely. "What kind of distraction are we talking about, exactly?"

She smiled at his question. "Over the years, Edwin has received many invites from corporations who want floating offices here. It's how a Vampire Lord generally finances their ship." She added the last for the benefit of anyone who didn't know. "One of the inquiries we received about a year ago was from the Oublies. I plan to use that as a cover for visiting. I...I'll occupy the Warden and his guards while the rest of you search the ship."

"The Oublies proposed you?" Narissa said with raised eyebrows.

She nodded at Narissa. "The Oublies is a corporation like anything else."

Cesar raised his hand and then suddenly spoke up. "Won't Core-Civic"—he stopped and glanced around—"that's the Oublies' parent company, by the way." He returned his attention to Eliza. "Won't CoreCivic find it suspicious you're responding to their inquiry at this time?"

"I don't think so," she explained. "Edwin has been struggling to keep the *Queen's Gambit* a Black Box for years. But his lawyers have been in a panic about his finances for a while. We only have enough funds to keep this pile floating for maybe fifty or sixty years. So, Edwin needs to start responding to queries. I've asked Emerson to draft a response to CoreCivic as if Edwin has an interest. And, since corps like them love to make a show of inviting Vampire Lords to tour their facilities, it should be an easy and logical in..." She sighed. "There's only one small issue."

"What's that?" Cesar cautiously asked.

"Emerson doesn't know we'll be infiltrating the Vault while he's negotiating the contract on Edwin's behalf. And he *can't* know. No one outside this room can know about anything we're discussing here today." She looked around the small circle of people she trusted—possibly with her life.

All of them nodded in response. They all knew Emerson was a tool.

"This could also be extremely dangerous. So if anyone wants out, now is the time to leave." She glanced at each of her friends, but no one left the room.

Finally, Cesar stepped forward. "Sounds easy. So, how do we do this?"

Eliza blushed and said in a small voice, "I don't really know. I haven't gotten that far yet."

Cesar looked over the room. "Would you allow me to work out the fine details?"

"Please."

Nodding, Cesar laid out his plan. He felt there should be three teams. One team to distract the Warden and the guards, and two others to canvas the ship. "The Oublies is huge—close to the size of the *Gypsy Queen*. More ground can be covered that way. But we should keep the teams small. A large group may feel invasive to the Warden."

She nodded. "If you can make this work, Cesar, you have my blessing."

***

They spent the rest of the night going over the sand table, fine-tuning their plan and trying to cover any contingency that might arise. Whichever team found the doctor first would retrieve him and neutralize any threats on their way back to the shuttle. Simple.

But Eliza wasn't sure if she was comfortable with that part of the plan. She'd heard that all of the officers working on the rig were synthetic—Mechi-people. CoreCivic used officers who could not accidentally or intentionally "bond" with their prisoners. Stockholm syndrome was not conducive to running a for-profit floating prison. That meant security would be especially tight. She wasn't sure if anyone here, Supe or otherwise, was strong enough to put a Mech down, and unlike the Mechs that works in other industries, the security guards on board the rig were not programmed to hesitate at taking a life.

"I have to go," Eliza insisted when several of her friends insisted she was too valuable to be put in such a vulnerable situation. "I may be able to tap into the Mech's computer mainframe and help you."

"But distracting the Warden...won't that be dangerous?" Cesar said with concern. They all knew that, unlike the Mechs, the Warden was a vampire. Unpredictable.

Eliza swallowed and nodded. "Yes, but I'm a Poppet. Or, was a Poppet. I'm uniquely trained for this type of thing."

Her friends looked concerned but nodded. At her insistence, they would rest tonight in prep for the six-hour flight to the rig first thing in the morning.

On her way out of the War Room, Cesar jogged up alongside Eliza. "Can I talk to you in private, Miss Eliza?"

She expected this. He was probably going to try and talk her out of coming along. "Sure. Let's use Edwin's office."

Once inside and alone, Eliza locked the soundproofed door and turned on the lights. She hesitated when she saw one of Edwin's suit jackets hanging haphazardly across the back of the executive chair he used at his large oaken desk. She knew it would smell like his aftershave, and that caused her to suck back on the fearful tears in her nose and throat. She had no idea what she was doing. She had no idea if Edwin was even truly "alive" anymore.

"He's not dead," Cesar insisted, reading her face. "I mean, he's not alive either. He was never 'alive' for as long as I've known him. But he isn't *gone*."

She nodded, sniffed, then wiped at her nose. God, she was so damned tired of crying. "Thank you. I appreciate that. If it's Tommy you want to talk about—"

"No," he interrupted, shaking his head. "My situation with Tommy is mine to resolve...or not. I hope you understand that."

"I do." With one more sniff, she straightened up and hoped she didn't look like the hot mess she felt like. Lord, Cesar was so much more confident than when they'd first known each other. It occurred to her that he was very good at being a vampire. It suited him well.

Nodding to himself, he wandered to the desk, his eyes on Edwin's coat as if he was as drawn to it as she was—maybe more so. Of all of the people aboard this ship, Cesar was the one closest to Edwin. He was more a part of Edwin than even she was. They were of the same blood.

He almost touched the jacket, but stopped himself inches away. "Remember when I said Foxley was hot on collecting tech?"

She nodded.

"Well, he has some medical tech that I think may be of interest to you and Edwin."

She felt a little surge of hope. "Can it fix Edwin's heart?"

"Not like that." He smiled sadly. "But I still think it can still be of use. I'd like to show it to you, but it's aboard the *Gypsy Queen*, which is docked over Pennsylvania right now. About an hour's ride west as the bird flies." Cesar made a little swooping gesture with his hand. "Would you fly out with me tonight? I promise to have you back in no time."

So far, Cesar had been brilliant, so she nodded. "I'll go grab my coat!"

XV

Not long after his heart failed him, Edwin woke up in a large, ornate neoclassical bedchamber of the kind usually reserved for nobles in French novels of romance. It was beautifully wainscoted, with tall, rounded windows showing a sweeping fantasy landscape just beyond. Three huge glass chandeliers hung from the ceiling, and the four-poster bed, made of dark wood and carved with mythological creatures, dominated the space and was large enough to hold an orgy.

But though he noted the elaborate windows, he saw there was no door. No way out. That was the clue that told Edwin this place wasn't real. He was in hibernation mode—what the vampires used to call a "fugue" back in the old days.

He'd never experienced a fugue before, though he knew about the condition through the tales of his fangier friends. Sometimes, when a vampire was greatly wounded, they shut down to heal. Other times, it was ennui that drove them into hibernation mode for weeks, months, or even years. The injury could be either physical or emotional. Not that a vampire ever truly "shut down." It was more like they created a lucid dream to live in, to heal themselves in, for a while.

He went to the window and spotted Eliza and Ollie sitting on a large blanket out in the garden, having a tea party under the fierce noonday sunshine. They looked so happy as they cut their slices of chocolate cake and clinked their cups of tea together. He waved to them, but he couldn't seem to get their attention. Then he realized they were merely part of the landscape—his lucid dream.

So...this was the fugue his mind had created for him. Blimey, it seemed cruel.

He sat on the floor and watched them until the sun went down and the moon rose. Time passed in his carefully constructed dream world. Reality seemed to bend a little more with the days and nights that seemed to come and go, though he had no idea what the real passage of time was like. Days? Weeks? Maybe years? There was no way to measure time from here.

Granted, it was a lovely fugue, beautiful and peaceful. But lonely. He missed being with his family. His beautiful, strong-willed wife. His brilliant but troubled little boy. He went to the windows often to watch them frolic in the garden. Sometimes he saw Ollie flying a kite. Other times, Eliza swung gracefully from a belt swing. The pain grew just a little more intense each time he observed them from afar.

Turn it off.

He wanted to turn off the fantasy. But he wanted the pain. He didn't want to forget.

"This is not real," he told himself. He said it often. He even wrote it on the wall of the bed chamber with a feather pen from the inkwell on the desk so he would not forget.

THIS IS NOT REAL.

He couldn't afford to forget. And no matter how many times he looked out the window and saw Eliza and Ollie and felt that pain, he couldn't afford to turn away from it He knew his real family might be experiencing terrible trials while he lay in state, unable to move.

But as time passed, it became increasingly difficult to remind himself that this wasn't a dream. The ink on the wall began to fade, and the inkwell ran dry. He told himself this was a fantasy, that he was really dead in a box, over and over. He even made a mantra of it, but, after a while, he wasn't so sure. He wasn't sure he wasn't really dead and this wasn't his personal heaven...or hell. He could feel his mind slipping into a deeper darkness.

No! Focus!

To keep his mind sharp, he made certain the fugue began to lose all of its luster. The garden became overcast and rainy, and his family no longer showed for their daily picnics. His bedchamber became ugly, dark, and dusty as his mind went to dark places. He paced endlessly, and even pounded on the walls, hoping for some sign that he could get out of there, or a clue as to how to wake up, but nothing ever changed.

The day Cesar appeared in the room with him, looking like a pale ghost standing near the hearth, his breath caught and his heart rejoiced. He had silently been calling out to those of his bloodline, hoping someone would make an appearance. At that point, he was even willing to entertain Foxley.

What a delight to see his Heir—to see someone he loved! He ran to Cesar and tried to touch him, but his hand passed through his image, leaving behind a trail of smoky wisps.

"Is this real or are you part of this blood stupid fantasy?" Edwin asked the young vampire.

Cesar tried to speak. No sound came forth, but Edwin was able read his lips well enough. *I'm real. Well, as real as this place gets.* Cesar looked about the bedchamber, which had decayed considerably. The furniture was now tarnished and ancient, and cobwebs hung like torn silk from the ceiling. All the books on the shelves on the far wall had moldered.

"So you're not part of my fugue?" Edwin asked worriedly.

Cesar frowned at the inhospitable conditions. *I'm not created by your mind, if that's what you mean. I'm contacting you from outside. The real world.* He gestured vaguely. *It's taken me some time to get through. I've never done this before.*

"How long has it been?" Suddenly, Edwin was terrified that years might have passed. What if his family wasn't even alive any longer? "How long have I been in state?"

Cesar tried to speak, but, to his horror, he dissipated, causing Edwin to go down on his knees in despair. He only returned much later. How much later, Edwin didn't know, but he was sitting in defeat in a corner, his arms wrapping around his knees, trying hard not to give into his own darkness.

Cesar, once materialized again, gestured to him like some wayward spirit. He said he had a plan to help Edwin escape the fugue. *Just be patient. I promise I will get you out of this place.*

Edwin nodded, trusting in Cesar's capabilities. He had no other choice, after all.

* * *

It felt surreal to be back aboard the *Gypsy Queen*. Eliza recalled being a prisoner here and running up and down these hallways once upon a time as she desperately searched for a way off Foxley's ship. Now, here she was, a registered guest, walking confidently down a corridor to one of the many tech labs that Foxley's gyro hosted.

Cesar, the second most important member of this Court, and the one escorting her, said, "You can talk to the techs when we get there. I don't understand these things very well, just being the hired muscle and all, but you probably will."

Eliza guffawed. "Why does everyone think I know all about this stuff? I'm not educated in it, you know."

"But you're very smart. Intuitively so. You came up with that plan back in the War Room." Cesar held a door open for her. "Edwin doesn't appreciate you enough."

Eliza blushed at that.

When they finally reached one of the research labs, Cesar used his top private clearance to get them inside. "There's someone I want you to meet," he said, swinging open one final glass door for her.

Inside, a small man turned to greet them. Eliza recognized him from the various tech journals she read as one of the top flesh mechanics in the world, Dr. Hans Rickman. When he stepped forward to take her hand in greeting, she let out a little gasp.

"You must be Herr Cesar's friend," the man intoned, staring up at her. He was as diminutive as a six-year-old child and almost completely bald with large glasses and a quick, easy smile.

Eliza leaned down a little to shake his hand. "Eliza McGillicuddy," she said. "And I know who you are, Dr. Rickman. I'm a huge fan, actually."

He laughed at that. "The feeling is mutual, Frau McGillicuddy. I have heard much about you." He hesitated. "Or is it Lady McGillicuddy now?"

"Call me Eliza."

He brightened considerably. "Then you must call me Hans."

She grinned. "It would be my honor."

"Let us go proceed inside, *ja?*" Hans said, leading the way into the inner lab.

As they navigated the corridors to the inner workings of the lab, Hans explained that his research facility was a separate entity from Foxley's worldwide corporation. He emphasized that Foxley "did not own him." Like many Vampire Lords, Foxley leased his gyro's med floors to a rotating assortment of research companies. This year, it was Abbot Laboratories, an enormous enterprise working toward general improvements to everyday life like upgraded medical devices, vaccine production advancements, and (their specialty), the fusion of organic tissue with biomechanical devices like prosthetics that could be controlled with the brain and spinal column.

Eliza found that last part particularly interesting, and she knew Dr. Vu had likely used some of Dr. Hans's basic medical advancements (available free to the public) to help her construct the Colossus that now housed what was left of Tommy.

Dr. Hans showed her what he called the Wasp Room. It was a huge, rounded, and domed room with honeycombed walls and ceiling and a complicated air ventilation system that droned on endlessly—probably how it got its name. In the center loomed a very large device similar to an MRI machine but with a lot of upgrades. A sliding table was attached to one side. On the other was only a small slit cut into the enormous, wheel-like apparatus.

"When I heard what happened to your husband, I immediately asked Cesar to invite you aboard," Dr. Hans explained, approaching the machine, which lighted up automatically like a carnival ride as he approached. A ring of lights blinked to life in a circle around the device and a new hum filled the room. "Lord Edwin is severely injured, *ja?*"

Eliza glared at Cesar, surprised he would share such sensitive information with anyone outside Edwin's Congress, but Cesar turned and said to her, "I only told Dr. Hans about Edwin because I think he can help. I asked him not to share that info with anyone else."

She surely hoped he did not. But, since the cat was officially out of the bag, she turned to Dr. Hans and said, "Please don't suggest a biomechanical suit. As a vampire, such a surgery would not work."

Dr. Hans watched her carefully for several seconds before saying, "I agree. Vampire anatomy and genetics are…tricky. But, that is not what the Wasp Machine does." He turned to touch it delicately with his purple-nitrile-gloved hand before going on. "I am afraid to say, Frau Eliza, that I do have enough knowledge of Supe biology to help with what has befallen your husband. This device works entirely differently."

He explained what it did, which she found just a little hard to believe. He described it as if it was a giant 3-D printer. When she said that, he laughed.

"*Ja*, the tech is not so different. In this case, however, we will be copying biological material." He turned to her companion. "Did you bring the sample, Herr Cesar?"

He stepped forward and produced a LoBind Tube from his jacket pocket, a metal capsule for carrying a blood sample when a tech needed to protect it from contamination. He glanced at Eliza as he explained, "I had to charm it away from your Dr. Vu. I'm sorry about that."

Eliza couldn't help herself. She blurted out, "This is…insane. How can you grow a human from a blood sample?"

Dr. Hans glanced at her. "Consider it…more a carbon copy."

She looked at the vial, knowing exactly what it was. "Edwin's blood."

"*Ja*," Dr. Hans said with a smile and a hearty nod. "And I believe it will be enough."

***

Dr. Hans used the Wasp Machine's robot arms to transport the sample to a slide and the slide to the machine because, he said, it was imperative that no living being come in contact with the sample while it was being delivered into the machine. That would produce recumbent DNA, which would be a disaster.

The machine rejected the sample on the first try. Dr. Hans had to go back and recalibrate it. He said it was having difficulty "digesting" Edwin's DNA, likely because it was designed for human use and not used to the complexities of Super biology. They had only tested the machine on lab mice and, once, a human corpse donated to the lab for study.

Eliza stood back and watched in wonder.

The second time the robot insert the slide, the Wasp Machine began the process of analyzing the genetic code. Dr. Hans stood over the machine, fidgeting nervously, while Cesar sidled up to her and whispered, "Dr. Hans explained that if this works, what the machine will produce won't be Edwin, exactly. More like a facsimile."

"What do you mean?" Eliza asked in concern.

"It uses materials preloaded into the drum—real biological "fabric," as he calls it—but it's not Supe fabric or anything." He hesitated and looked at the machine beeping along.

Dr. Hands explained, "The machine is compensating for the differences. It's why it failed the first time. It couldn't read Lord Edwin's vampire DNA. It has to "translate" it into something it *can* read. Something...human."

Eliza nodded. "So, if this works...what will come out won't be a vampire."

"No, but...imagine if it works!" In a hushed voice, Dr. Hands added, "We began this work because Lord Foxley wanted a new form of transport. You load your DNA at home into the machine and it spits out a clone somewhere else via a vast network. You could be in two places at the same time."

"But...would it be you?" she asked.

"It will carry a neural imprint of who you are and what you know. It will be a perfect *copy* of you."

Eliza marveled at the idea. "So, people who are ill could have a second chance. A new body."

"Well, no. It carries an exact DNA copy of what you are, including any flaws. Adjusting the DNA or changing it in some way is still many years off."

Together, they waited almost two hours for the machine to complete its task. When Dr. Hans jumped in the air with a whoop and clapped his hands, she knew it was done.

Moving as a group to the opposite side of the Wasp Machine, they waited while the machine made some final adjustments and the stainless steel table finally slid out. Eliza gaped down at it. A very naked but extremely accurate copy of her husband lay there, gasping, his eyes wide open.

* * *

After Dr. Hans finished his physical exam of the Edwin clone, he stepped out of the private room, tablet in hand, and nodded to her. "He seems in good health, Frau Eliza, all things considered. You may see him now."

Eliza hesitated. "What do you mean...all things considered?"

He glanced down at his tablet where he presumably had Edwin's medical record. "You are aware of his history as a human?"

"I know a lot of it," she admitted.

He nodded. "He was not in perfect health at the time that Lord Foxley made him his Heir."

"I know that." A cold shock went through her. "You mean...the..." She found she could not bring herself to say it. It felt so shameful even though she knew it should not be.

Dr. Hans smiled encouragingly. "I have given him antibiotics for the syphilis. It was congenital, in case you were wondering. He was exposed to it at birth, but he was apparently a very strong youth, and the disease remained in remission far longer than I would have expected from someone suffering from such poor nutritional deficits."

He saw her terrified expression, took her hand, and gave her a sympathetic look. "It is not as terrible as it seems, *mein* Frau. We can treat such diseases now, and I expect him to make a full recovery, but he has permanent scarring of the lungs as a result, and, I am afraid, will suffer from asthma for whatever time this body holds up."

A thought hit her, an insidious one. "What if...Edwin's body doesn't hold up? What if he falls ill or dies while human? Will that affect his vampire body?"

For the first time, the good doctor looked perplexed. "I do not know. The psychic shock could damage his vampire body. It could even kill him. Or it could shock it back awake."

When he saw her horrified expression, he gave her fingers a squeeze. "I will see to it Lord Edwin is well taken care of. He will have an inhaler and script before he leaves my care."

Asthma. Edwin was asthmatic. It was hard for her to bend her mind around that. She was so used to him being strong and near-invincible. No physical flaws. But if that was the worst of it, she'd take it, and they would both just have to deal with his condition.

She didn't know what to expect when she walked into the private room, but, to her surprise and delight, Edwin was sitting up in bed, now covered in a hospital Johnny and a blanket, a large tray of hospital food in front of him. He was shoving the food around his tray with his fork like he didn't know what to do with it, but when she cleared her throat, he immediately set his utensil down and looked up, his eyes brightening.

"Lovey."

His voice sounded strange. Hoarse. The sound of someone speaking for the first time with vocal cords that had never before been exercised, she reminded herself. Still, she hung in the doorway, too terrified to approach him for the moment. "Edwin?"

"Aye, lovey," he said and squinted at her. She thought he might be a bit myopic.

She put a hand to her mouth as she looked him over. He looked like the Edwin she knew. Still redheaded pale with auburn hair. No goatee. His new body hadn't grown that out yet. His eyes were the same dark golden hue she was used to. And he had freckles—she hadn't expected that.

He looked...human. More real somehow. This was how he looked, she suddenly realized, while he was still alive.

Moving closer, she said, "Is it really you? Are you *my* Edwin?"

He glanced around like she might mean someone else, then said, "Aye. It's me."

She wondered about the neurological link. The doctor said he would have the same memories and personality that he'd had previously. But what if there were gaps? Or what if something went wrong?

And then she stopped herself from overthinking it as she came to a halt by his bedside. She might not be looking at the Lord Edwin the vampire she had always known. But as he smiled up at her in greeting, she realized this was most definitely *her* Edwin.

He nodded as if he was easily reading her concerns. "I have his memories...er, my memories."

"All of them?"

"Every bloody one." He frowned. "Including what happened in the cargo bay." Refocusing on her, he said, "How is Ollie? Can I see him?"

She didn't want to lie to him and tell him Ollie was perfectly fine. She knew that wasn't true. But she also didn't want him to worry in his presently fragile state. "Ollie is recovering all right. We'll be seeing him soon."

Edwin's eyes filled with tears. "Oh, Eliza. Does he hate me?"

"Oh, god. It's really you." And pushing aside his hospital tray, she jumped on him.

He oofed as she landed on him, then suddenly laughed when she kissed him.

It was a long, arduous kiss. When she came up for a breath of air, she rubbed his face and hair, barely believing he was real. "Your hair and eyes are darker."

"Are they?"

She nodded. Feeling a twinge of concern, even guilt, she said, "I'm sorry, Edwin. Sorry for what I said...before. I shouldn't have been like that." Tears filled her eyes now. "Can you forgive me?"

He looked her over, and his expression was both loving and thoughtful. No anger. "No worries, love." Reaching out to play with the white lock of her hair that wound through the black, he added, "I know it's been a shock. What you've had to do and put up with while I was...you know..."

Leaning down, she kissed him again. Oh my, she thought. His skin and lips were warm! She wasn't used to that!

Over the next few minutes, it seemed they couldn't take their hands off one another. Finally, he whispered in her ear, "Don't take this the wrong way, lovey, but...my condition..."

The syphilis.

She smiled, touched by his concern. "I'm a Poppet, Edwin. We're extremely disease resistant, remember?"

He grinned at that. "Go lock the door. The nurse isn't slated to be back for her rounds for an hour."

"Ah hour, eh?"

He got that wicked gleam in his eye, so she went and hurriedly closed and locked the door to the private suite, then started tearing at her clothes. After they had satisfied each other in every intimate way possible, she sat cuddled against him in the narrow hospital bed, her head on his chest. "Do you need anything?" she asked, while he played with her hair. "What can I get you, Edwin?"

He thought about that for one moment before answering. "A pizza. I want a pizza. And then some chocolate cake."

She laughed.

| **xvi** |

On the shuttle ride back to the *Queen's Gambit*, Edwin sat between her and Cesar, eating fish and chips out of a bag and talking about his plans to repair things with Ollie. He looked tired but otherwise had been cleared by the doctor for the ride home. Eliza had his inhaler in her pocket and an antibiotic script at the ready, but she wasn't convinced he was fit enough to jump back into things.

Dr. Hans warned her that Edwin's health was still precarious. He even suggested that should something happen to this body, the trauma could cause his real body to die the true death. Or it might wake him up. The tech was so new, they didn't know yet what might happen.

Cesar kept looking over and sometimes even rubbing Edwin's shoulder or arm like he was trying to convince himself that his master was really sitting here, inches away. Eliza knew he was reacting to Edwin's closeness—a need to be near his master—though she had no idea if the urge was biological, psychological, a Supe thing, or some combination of all three.

"I was thinking perhaps the ship is no place for him. While I was in the fugue, I had a lot of time to just think, Eliza," Edwin told her thoughtfully as he chewed on a chip. "Do you think we are doing wrong by him? Perhaps a boarding school on Earth is kinder?"

She didn't like that idea. She hated the idea of her Ollie being so far away. But Edwin had a point. Ollie's safety was their top priority. Still, she didn't want to discuss that right at the moment. "Can we talk about this later?"

He nodded as he popped another chip into his mouth.

She shook her head and sighed at his display. "Edwin, if you keep eating like that, you're going to make yourself sick." He had so far put away half a pizza, two burgers, three milkshakes, and two pieces of cake. She'd had no idea he had such a robust appetite for human junk food. As a vampire, he never seemed to have much interest in nourishment past the essentials.

He looked up, still chewing, and smiled, then brushed some crumbs off the clothes he had borrowed from Cesar. "I'm just making up for lost time, love."

"For two hundred years of not eating?"

Edwin grinned and stuffed another chip into his mouth.

Cesar, smiling, mouthed to her, He has a fat person inside him trying to get out.

"I heard that," Edwin mumbled. He looked down at Cesar's hand sitting comfortably on his thigh, then glanced over at her. She sensed other hungers emerging—very human male ones. "Mrs. McGillicuddy, may I have your permission?"

She knew what he meant. He, too, was suffering his profound separation from Cesar—his Heir, his child. They used to do this all the time while they lived in their snug little townhouse in New York. He would ask her permission, and she would grant it because she trusted him. Her friends sometimes warned her that making such allowances would invite trouble. They assumed Edwin would wander romantically. But he never had. On reflection, her friends had never fully grasped how incredibly polyamorous he was. But, perhaps because she was a Poppet raised in the Vampire Court system, she saw it. It was a concept rather mundane to Eliza. She had grown up in such environments.

Unfortunately, her natural leniency and lack of jealousy also meant she'd had to spend many a night listening to Edwin and Cesar giggling like randy teenagers through the bedroom wall. Sometimes, she wondered if that made her a strange girl—that it never bothered her much that Cesar got a small part of her husband. Then again, Edwin was an amorous creature. There was more than enough to go around in her opinion—sometimes even too much.

Nodding, she said, "You may, Mr. McGillicuddy. But only if you leave me something for later tonight."

"It's a date, my Lady!" He kissed her hand. Then, with a happy, crumb-filled grin, Edwin set his bag of chips aside, turned, and briefly boxed Cesar against his seat while he squirmed into his Heir's lap. Their eyes met, the old connection was made, and Cesar gained the same big, goofy smile.

Edwin pinned him to the back of the seat and ran a hand through his hair, mussing it. "I've missed you." He started to kiss his Heir with all of the pent-up passion he no doubt felt due to their long periods of separation.

"Missed you, too." Cesar squirmed in delight and Edwin playfully bit him with his human teeth. Eliza watched them go at it like silly gooses. She rolled her eyes and leaned back in her seat to catch a few much-needed Z's before they tackled the next issue on their to-do list.

***

"Dr. Vu, something has happened to the Jotunn."

The young tech stood in the doorway of Veronica's private office, worry lines creasing his face.

Veronica sat up straighter and stopped typing her latest report. "What do you mean, Carl?"

"I mean...I don't think he's breathing."

Pulling off her glasses, Veronica stood and charged out of the office, staying on Carl's heels until they reached the glass box. Carl was right to be concerned. The Jotunn—her Jotunn—was lying deathly still on the bench inside. She couldn't see any evidence that he was breathing or that his chest was rising or falling.

"NEWTON, what's happened?" she asked the AI, but she only got white noise as a response.

Carl, standing next to her, said, "The AI's been going in and out all day."

She was afraid of this. Ever since the Jotnar damaged their ship, nothing had been working correctly. And when she checked the temperature in the glass box on her tablet, she noted it had fallen by ten degrees. Her Jotnar was overheating! Nodding to herself, Veronica reached for the keycard around her neck. But before she could slide it, Carl reached out and took her wrist in his hand. She immediately stared at it and he let her go.

"You aren't going in there?" Carl asked, a deep dent between his eyes.

"If Gorm has stopped breathing, I may have to do CPR."

"All right, but we should summon a Court Guard to go with us."

"Not us, Carl. Me. You keep an eye on him from out here."

"Dr. Vu!"

"I don't have time to wait for a guard. My Jotunn might be dying!" Veronica swiped her card and the security door slid open, letting out a blast of freezing cold air that momentarily shocked her. And then she was inside the glass box. The cold inside—a frosty minus fort—immediately burned her skin and made her eyes water, but she couldn't worry about her own discomfort. She didn't even bother to check Gorm's vitals. She immediately began chest compressions.

It was difficult because Gorm was built like a brick house. She could barely impact his burly, heavily-muscled chest. "Carl, bring the paddles!" she shouted, not letting up. She couldn't afford to lose Gorm. How would she explain that to Lord Edwin?

While Carl was off fetching the defibrillator, Veronica continued compressions as best she could. A few seconds later, though, she noted Gorm's eyes were open, his red-rimmed peepers taking her fully in. A small smile played across his lips.

Veronica opened her mouth to shout for Carl, but Gorm reached out and grabbed her by the throat with his giant hand. It was like being in an iron vice. Veronica could only choke out a polite cough.

By the time Carl arrived, pushing the defibrillator cart ahead of him, Veronica was lying on the floor and Gorm was breathing regularly again. "Dr. Vu!" He threw himself on the floor and elevated her head on his knee, even used the penlight in his lab coat to shine a light into her eyes.

Veronica blinked at the brightness and pushed his hand away. "I'm all right. I slipped and fell. Ice on the floor."

Carl looked over at Gorm, who appeared to be asleep, then back at his boss. "Let's get you out of here."

He threw her arm around his neck and helped walk her out of the glass box and back into the warmth of the lab, closing and bolting the door behind him. Veronica indicated a nearby chair and Carl helped her to sit. She leaned forward and put her head between her legs, breathing deeply for a few seconds before sitting back.

"Are you all right, Dr. Vu? I could fetch a paramedic."

Veronica nodded then shook her head no. "I think the cold got to me. Minus forty. That's cold enough to throw a bucket of water into the air and watch it freeze." She snorted at that.

"I'll get you some hot tea and a blanket."

After Carl was gone, Veronica took a few deep breaths and coughed out the cold. Her entire body felt numb and, at the same time, tingling from the cold. Also, her arm had begun to hurt—a deep, burning ache that caused her to roll up the sleeve of her lab coat.

She felt a dull wave of nausea when she spotted the deep red teeth marks in her skin.

***

Edwin had been made a vampire young, only nineteen years old. As a result, he'd spent so many years being undead that he had completely forgotten what it felt like to be human. Or, perhaps, he had just never fully realized it.

Being human was…strange. Different. He was forever either hot or cold. He never felt quite comfortable the way he had in his more impenetrable vampire skin. He felt a little bit vulnerable all of the time. He was hungry—again, all of the time. And everything he put into his body also had to come out at some point. Blimey, he'd forgotten all about *that*.

And…it was wonderful.

This was something he never thought he would get to experience again. He could walk around the ship deck in the sunlight. He didn't need the UV-protected windows to keep him apart from the world during the day. He could eat modern delicacies like Twinkies and Key lime pie—though he was thinking he might let off on that last bit as his stomach was starting to get after him about eating too much sugar.

He thought about all of these things as he stepped into his offices aboard the ship. The world was no longer quite as bright and he had to turn on the lights to see properly.

Eliza followed him in, explaining the situation with the Jotnar. She was quite distraught over how things had come to pass even though he was immensely proud of how she'd handled herself while he was down. She didn't know it, but she was a natural Lord, more inclined to the subtle nuances of running a Congress than he was.

Honestly, despite the life he had found himself living, it wasn't for him. He liked the idea of having his little family and spending his days writing his pulp novels. He was a simple type of bloke. Being the Lord of a Congress—being in charge of so many souls so dependent on his every decision—never really appealed to him.

When it seemed Eliza was on the verge of tears, he took her in his arms and told her how well she had done. She just looked sad at that and said, "Thank you for your vote of confidence, Edwin, but I'm pretty sure I just made things worse with this Le Troc."

"Love, things would have been worse if you had done nothing."

"I don't know about that. Now, we have to infiltrate the Vault. The Vault, of all things." She led him into the War Room and showed him the sand table. After detailing her plan to nick Dr. Pretorius—she added, "I don't even know if this will work. I could get someone hurt. Or worse."

Edwin glanced over the 3-D diagram of the Oublies, anchored to Mount McKinley in the Densmore Mountains, near the center of the Alaska Range—one of the most isolated places on Earth. He had to squint some, and he realized he was likely in need of glasses. "It's very odd, all of this," he said with some weariness. "None of this sounds like Yrsa."

"What do you mean? How could this not be like her? She deposed and murdered her own father."

He glanced up, surprised. "Now, I know something is wrong." When he saw how confused she was, he explained, "Yrsa was a sweet and naive girl when I knew her. Devoted to her father."

"I don't understand."

"She was petty and spoilt, aye. But there wasn't a mean bone in Yrsa's body when we were married. She was as much a victim as I was. She even carried around this little white wolf dog like Paris-bloody-Hilton." He pantomimed cradling a tiny animal. Shaking his head with exasperation, he turned back to the sand table.

After looking it over some, he pointed out a few key issues with her plan that Eliza didn't really consider—mostly to do with the Warden. "He doesn't have much use for those of the female persuasion...if you know what I mean."

Eliza went to retrieve a notepad and jot down some notes. "I didn't know that about him." She glanced up in surprise when Edwin told her the creature running the rig was a former member of the High Courts—and in no way mentally stable.

"Don't worry about the Warden. He's a wanker, but I know him. I should be able to distract him long enough for you to get the good doctor out."

Eliza stared at him, appalled. "You can't think for one second you're up to joining us."

"Of course I am." Edwin instinctively stood up straighter. "I'm not letting you go alone, lovey. And I am mostly certainly not letting you be alone with the Warden."

"Edwin, you're still sick. And you're asthmatic."

He gave her a biting smile. "I'm human, love, not dying. And I'm well enough to go. Plus, I have an inhaler now."

She shook her head. "No, I mean you absolutely *cannot* go. If the Warden knows you, Edwin, he'll expect you to be...well, Lord Edwin. The vampire. And you're not."

Edwin sighed. She made a good point. But the idea of his wife going in with a team and infiltrating the Vault while he stayed home and stuffed his face and slept off the side effects of his antibiotics was intolerable. But before either one of them could come up with some kind of suitable plan, they both heard a knock on the open door of the War Room.

They turned, and the sight of Foxley leaning in the doorway, dressed in his ludicrous schoolboy uniform, rendered them both speechless for a good ten seconds.

Finally, Edwin said, "What the bloody hell are you doing here?"

Foxley smiled, pale eyes alight, fingers laced together villainously. He didn't even look surprised to see Edwin walking about. "I was invited."

"Get out," Edwin said angrily. "Get off my ship!"

"It was me. I invited him," Eliza confessed, her cheeks reddening profusely. "I'd hoped he might be able to help wake you up, Edwin." She glared at Foxley. "He couldn't."

Edwin shook his head. "I don't care if he's Father Christmas, here to spread holiday spirit. I don't want him here. Leave, Foxley, now!"

Foxley didn't even have the good grace to look offended. He just smiled more. "Or you will do what exactly?" He looked Edwin up and down. "As a vampire, you were never my equal. As a human, you are less bothersome than a flea to me."

Edwin swallowed, trying to get his anger under control before he did something incredibly stupid. Like rush Foxley and get himself—this body, anyway—murdered right in front of Eliza. But before he could respond, he felt a tremendous rush like an invisible hand was pushing him backward and down into a nearby chair.

He tried to resist, to stand up, but countering Foxley's bloodkinetic power was like trying to escape a riptide. There was nowhere to go.

Eliza, a smart chit, flinched and withdrew as Foxley entered the room. "My goodness," Foxley exclaimed, glancing over the sand table before centering his attention on Edwin, trapped in the chair. "I have the good grace to let you borrow my Enforcer *and* my tech for your wife's insane mission, and you, my boy, try to throw me off your ship? That's not very hospitable."

Eliza visibly swallowed hard. "You knew what Cesar was up to with Dr. Hans, didn't you?"

Foxley just looked annoyed as he glanced briefly at her. Edwin had known the little tyrant for over two hundred years, and still, he had never gotten used to that crafty look on his master's face—that look that hinted at how ancient Foxley was. And how much contempt he had for everyone. "People consistently underestimate me. I know everything that happens aboard my ship." Throwing Edwin a nasty side-eye, he added, "The Wasp Machine is *my* tech. I financed it. And, by the way, you're welcome."

Edwin grunted at that. "You let Dr. Hans experiment on me like some lab rat."

"I needed to know if my tech works. Surprise! It does."

"I hate you. Just so you know."

The ancient vampire laughed at that. "And yet, for all your protests…all that false outrage…I may still be of further use to you."

Edwin doubted that but was willing to entertain whatever insane plot was running around Foxley's corrupt skull if it meant he would just go away and leave them in peace. "Can I get up now?"

Foxley grinned. "You may." He made a gesture like a magician performing a magic trick, and suddenly, Edwin found the pressure was gone and he could stand up again. He did so cautiously.

Turning back to the sand table, Foxley looked it over with interest. "To infiltrate the Vault safely, my boy, you need a vampire to make you his Heir."

Edwin noted how Eliza stiffened at that suggestion. He felt the same way. Having escaped vampirism, he had no desire to return to that life. Not if a different one was possible. Maybe a human one with his wife and child.

Foxley climbed up onto the sand table and settled there, looking ridiculously innocent in his schoolboy uniform. His feet didn't quite touch the floor and he started to swing his legs just for effect. "Don't give me such a surprised look. You need that vampire body of yours, and I am all you have. Cesar and all of your other vamps on board this ship are too young or weak, and Emerson, though older, is not a Lord and cannot make Heirs. I'm the only one who can make you a vampire."

Foxley patted the table beside him, his smile growing. It was a sweet and innocent smile—until you saw his teeth. Edwin wasn't fooled at all. "Come sit with me, child. I will make it quick and painless, and then you will be strong again."

Slowly, Edwin shook his head. At the same time, he felt his very human blood run cold in his veins. "I would rather do this as a human and struggle than ever let you touch me again."

Foxley sighed. "You are being dramatic, as usual. It wasn't that bad the first time around."

Edwin bristled. "You held me against the floor like a common rapist. You never even asked—!"

"We had a deal." Foxley's voice couldn't possibly be that loud, yet both Edwin and Eliza flinched like someone had cracked glass in their ears. The monster eyed him virulently before adding in a new, deeper—darker—voice, "Child, your eternal indignation wearies me. You agreed to be my Heir. You always knew what that entailed."

Edwin started shaking his head, but Foxley wasn't finished. "Can we please dispatch with this tiresome dynamic? You were nothing. Less than nothing. I made you great. I made you a god. I did that." Finally, Foxley bared his teeth. "You agreed to my contract, and you enjoyed the power I gave you. You reveled in it. Any anguish you experience now is merely a byproduct of your current and questionable choice of companion." He eyed Eliza like this was all her fault.

Edwin had to steady himself against the table. He didn't like where this conversation was going, and he didn't want Eliza knowing too many details about that part of his life. She already knew Foxley was a monster; Edwin didn't want her knowing how much of one he'd been for a time.

"Nothing to say? Cat got your tongue, you unappreciative little brat?" Foxley warned.

To steer things back to the present, Edwin said, "What you've suggested has given me an idea. You said I was an experiment. So, let's run with that." He turned to address Eliza, who was partly scrunched into a corner of the room. "I want to reorder your plan, love. A small team consisting of you, me, Tommy, and Emerson. When we meet the Warden, we'll explain my condition as Foxley's latest technological experiment."

Eliza nodded as she slowly straightened up, though she never took her eyes off Foxley. "I can see that working. We can explain you off as a Lord enjoying Foxley's newest toy. A device that allows Vampire Lords to recapture the past glory of their human lives for a while."

"The Vampire Lords are just bored enough to find something like that interesting," Edwin postulated. He didn't add that it meant he could stay human for at least a little while longer.

Foxley considered that. With a slight smirk, he said, "But to be convincing, you'll need me to accompany you. After all, I am almost always on site when I test out a new toy. Plus, I can pilot us to the Oublies."

"Now, wait just one moment—" Edwin began, turning back to his former master.

But Foxley ignored him. Still smiling, he jumped down off the sand table and moved smoothly to the door in a way that only the really old ones could. Turning, he rubbed his hands together. "It's settled, then. I will see you in six hours." He sighed happily. "Another little adventure! I simply cannot wait! This is going to be so much fun!"

He was gone like the wind.

Eliza turned to him and said, "Edwin, what have we done?"

Edwin only tilted his head to the ceiling and cried, "Fuck!"

| xvii |

"Do you want to talk about it?" she asked Edwin during the flight to the Vault. It was midmorning, the sun burning bright orange over the sharp white pyramids of the Alaska Range, and they were sitting near the rear of the transport. Tommy and Emerson were seated near the front, just behind the pilot's seat where Foxley was navigating—not without skill but in such a way that it made her stomach fall a little at his near-suicidal speed and hairpin turns.

Currently, Edwin was studying the Vault's layout, which Eliza had transferred to a tablet. He turned the device this way and that while he followed the highly-detailed labyrinthine corridors of the giant floating prison.

She waited for him to open up about their earlier encounter with Foxley—she knew he was still thinking about it—but he surprised her. Looking up, he said softly and with great concern, "I'm worried about Oliver, love."

Sighing, she admitted, "Me, too." Before leaving for the mission, she had spent the morning with their son while he ate his breakfast. She had kissed him repeatedly, much to his annoyance, and told him to be good for Uncle Malcolm, whom she was trusting to protect him. But Oliver didn't have much to say. He had gone silent once more and simply read the back of his cereal box like she wasn't there. It was breaking her heart. "I've been thinking about your suggestion. The boarding school?"

Edwin's eyebrows slid up his forehead with interest.

"I don't think it's a terrible idea. Maybe we should get Ollie off the ship. Especially now. Make less of a target of him."

"And I'm rethinking my suggestion," he said. "The farther away he is from us, the harder it will be for us to protect him. I mean, we can't send a werewolf bodyguard off with him to Eton College. That would look ridiculous." Like her, he trusted Malcolm to protect their son with his life. But they couldn't be sure he would be safe even at school.

She nodded at that, closed her eyes, and listened to the drone of the engines. "Maybe we're approaching this all wrong."

"How do you mean, love?"

"Our primary concern is the High Courts and what they might do to Ollie. But they wouldn't be able to touch him if you were a part of them—influencing them, I mean."

Edwin thought a moment. "You want me to run for a place on the High Courts' Council?"

"Would you win? If you ran, I mean?"

"I don't bloody know." His eyes drifted to the port window as he considered. "Maybe."

He didn't say it with pride or even much interest. He sounded weary. "The old reptiles would see it as a boon, I reckon—a convenient way to keep tabs on my Congress and keep me in check. But I would need to play by their rules. They would have their fingers in our business, our ship. Everything. Our Congress would essentially *belong* to them."

"Sounds terrifying. Forget I said anything—"

"No, it's not a terrible idea. Just complex. It might protect Ollie. And us." He made a face. "No matter what horrors the Old Ones come up with, the one thing they always do is stick up for one another. Power in unity and all that shite."

She nodded her understanding. "In that case, and if you think you can handle them, then I trust you. I mean, if you think you can take on the likes of Lord Trasch." She visibly shuddered. Vampires had always made her nervous, but there was something positively alien—malignant—about Trasch. And she had heard things about him, that he was monstrous in ways that went beyond simply being a vampire. Some said that while he was alive, he was some kind of serial killer.

"Let me think on it," Edwin said. "Once I sort this business with the ship and this body..." He put a hand on his chest. "...I'll see what I can do."

A few tense moments later, Foxley announced they were entering the Oublies' airspace.

Eliza turned to the port and gasped at the impressive sight of the giant floating prison, gunmetal grey and as ominous as an alien moon in the sky ahead of them.

* * *

Back in the day, the United State's most infamous prison had been Alcatraz Federal Penitentiary, an extremely secure facility located off the shores of San Francisco. During that time, The Rock contained some of the most dangerous supernatural criminals in the world. However, there was a communal outcry from the citizens living not far from the island. They lived in terror that the Supes might one day escape to terrorize them. After all, it was a facility originally built to hold human prisoners.

As a result, CoreCivic built the Oublies and hung it in the sky. That was sometime around the early 1960s. But since then, the prison had been filled with what was considered the worse of the worse supernatural threats—terrorists and serial killers, mostly. The unredeemable. And since most of the occupants were immortal—or nearly so—the rig was built to last nearly forever. The addition of synthetic guards made it that much more secure, and it soon gained a reputation as being impossible to escape from. In time, it became known as the Vault.

The Oublies rig was enormous, even larger than the *Gypsy Queen*—widely considered the largest gyro in the world. Unlike other gyros, however, the Vault was stationary, hence its definition as a rig. It hung in the sky over Mount McKinley like a giant cobalt moon, millions of lights flickering over its surface. A massive metal net completely covered the surface of the rig, and this, in turn, was connected to thousands of gigantic ship chains that were, themselves, embedded in the mountain peaks below. Due to its size alone, it could not move, though it did utilize the usual gyroscopic technology of other gyros to keep it afloat.

That was the info Edwin had gleaned from Yrsa's data stick, plus what he'd been able to research online. But none of it made him feel any better about what they were about to do. The place looked as friendly as...well, a prison.

A prison built to contain supernatural threats of all kinds.

Foxley warned them about air turbulence as they motored over the frozen white tundra on their way to the ship. The land was beautiful and wild, green under the heavy blanket of snow. The Hummingbird shuddered slightly as he increased altitude and then swooped down closer to the rig. Foxley always flew like he was tempting fate, but the flight was rocky even by his standards. Edwin, always a nervous flyer, grabbed one of the straps hanging from the ceiling and asked what was happening.

Foxley said he was getting warnings there was an electronic "field" around the rig, likely to sense incoming guests, and was adjusting to accommodate it. "Just think of it as a carnival ride," Foxley said and laughed.

Edwin feared he might toss his cookies.

A transmission came in and a female-sounding voice asked for their transport's clearance code. Emerson leaned forward to offer it, then reminded the Oublies that CoreCivic was the one who invited them aboard and they were expected. He had sent a request ahead that morning.

It took a few minutes to get their docking clearance, during which Edwin saw Eliza fidgeting and staring out the port.

"Clearance granted. Please proceed with normal docking procedure," came the female voice while the Oublies grew to fill the entire screen of the Hummingbird. Soon, a pair of open bay doors appeared. Foxley shot down the tunnel at an uncomfortable speed and set her down in a designated bay.

They deplaned in the visitor's bay, some of them staggering after the rough flight. Edwin, being the Lord, took the lead, with Eliza and Tommy to both sides and a step behind him, as was customary. He could tell that Emerson was annoyed that Eliza occupied the left-hand space as his Bride and Tommy his right as his Enforcer, forcing the vampire lawyer to trail behind like a petulant child. Foxley brought up their rear, looking amused and unperturbed. Foxley gave not one whit about appearances, as usual. Edwin wondered, not for the first time, if they were going to seriously cock this up because of him.

Waiting for them in the bay was a small coalition of guards consisting of five Mechi-people marching in an arrow formation. Edwin's steps slowed as he approached the group of synthetics. They were much larger than he'd anticipated, at least seven feet tall, and constructed not unlike Tommy in that their bi-metal forms were coarsely banged into humanoid shapes. Little more than metal golems, they had small, bullet-shaped heads with simple depressions for eyes and a hole for a mouth. Their bodies were obviously designed to both look menacing and still function well: round barrel bodies, long arms, large hands with dexterous fingers, and stout legs.

This lot had been around a while. Their metal bodies were rust-pitted and tarnished from age, but they still managed to maneuver with ease. Unlike Tommy, they wore no human clothing of any kind, though they did sport bandoliers across their bodies featuring various achievement metals and a wide belt with large firearms and a series of knives hanging from them.

The Mech in the front stepped forward and said in a female voice that surprised Edwin, "Greetings, Lord Edwin McGillicuddy. My name is Commander-in-Chief Fuyuko, Head of the CoreCivic Outer Guard, Fourth Division. It was requested that I meet you and escort you on your tour of our home—the Oublies."

Fuyuko had a surprisingly soft, feminine voice, which was completely at odds with her fearsome appearance. It was the same voice that had guided them during their landing procedure.

It took Edwin a moment to recover. "Hallo there, mate...er, Commander-in-Chief. So good that you could meet us."

"Of course, my Lord. But please call me Fuyuko. It is quite a pleasure!" She looked him over curiously while her fellow Mechs swayed light behind her, awaiting orders, perhaps.

Before he could say anymore, Foxley took the initiative and moved to the front of the group. "Fuyuko, my lady!" he said, making his voice pleasant and light. "It is good to see you again!"

Fuyuko's eyes lit up. "Lord Foxley! I did not expect that we would meet again—and on this tour, no less."

"Yes, well, my Heir here"—he indicated Edwin—"was kind enough to invite me on the tour after I shared my technology with him." He went on to briefly explain his new Wasp Machine, a technology that could allow vampires to holiday away their own bodies for a time.

Edwin saw Fuyuko's eyes virtually shine at the prospect of being in human skin for a while. Leave it to Foxley to get his hooks into everyone—even a living bloody machine. After a few minutes of idyll chitchat, Foxley added, "I noticed the Warden is conspicuously absent."

Fuyuko tilted her head. "The Warden is currently occupied but will join us shortly. He has asked that I begin the tour ahead of his arrival." Straightening up, she announced over the group, "I welcome you all! And that includes you as well, Lady McGillicuddy." She nodded at Eliza, who offered her a stately bow in return.

The rest of the Mechs began singing some sort of rallying song about CoreCivic. It was all very strange and off-putting. But once it was done, Fuyuko slammed her hands together like an exuberate child and announced. "*Konnichiwa!* I do believe we will all be the best of friends. Shall we begin the tour?"

* * *

A pair of shiny, high-end, open-air EVs were waiting for them. Eliza noted that they were much larger than the ones aboard their own ship, probably to accommodate the gigantic Mech bodies that patrolled these endless corridors. Their crew easily fit in one vehicle, which appeared to be on some form of autopilot. Or perhaps they were controlled remotely. Whatever the case, she, Edwin, Tommy, Emerson, Foxley, and Fuyuko got into the first one, while the second one, carrying the four Mechs that had accompanied Fuyuko, brought up the rear.

She glanced in the side mirror at the second vehicle, wondering why the additional Mechs were there. For their perceived protection, to impress Edwin, or perhaps because the Mechs were suspicious by nature and this was the easiest way to keep an eye on guests? Edwin saw her looking and took her hand, giving it a reassuring squeeze.

As they motored down a wide, funnel-like corridor toward a brightly lit room at the end, Fuyuko kicked up a rather flirty-sounding conversation with Tommy. "I don't know *you*, sir. Where were you manufactured?"

It took Tommy a moment to catch on to what she was implying. "I'm not a Mech. I was created as a Colossus in Lord Edwin's Congress, Commander-in-Chief."

Fuyuko was very interested in that. "A Colossus! How innovative. You have organic parts? What percentile?"

"Correct." He did not mention how much was synthetic and how much organic. "And you?"

"I was created in the CoreCivicCenter Laboratories. I am seven percent organic. Brain and ganglia, including this arm." She indicated which one.

Eliza was surprised by that information. "You're not wholly synthetic?"

"No, my Lady." She seemed proud of that. "After serving thirty-four years out of my eight life sentences, I was given the option for an upgrade. I'd rather be a guard here than a prisoner. Now, I am *useful*."

Eliza had to about sew her jaw shut. "You were a prisoner here?"

"Some of us are allowed to upgrade as a way of shortening our sentences. It is both an honor and an opportunity." Fuyuko paused and seemed to muse. "I have no regrets. Serving CoreCivic has become my passion, you might say."

She saw Tommy shirk a little at the Mech's enthusiasm. Eliza imagined the idea of willingly becoming something like Fuyuko just to lighten a long sentence made him cringe inside. He'd had no choice in the matter and, given a choice now, she often felt he would have preferred a human death. Lord. She'd had no idea that the corporation behind the Vault turned their prisoners into synthetic guards. The idea was...macabre.

The EV emerged into a large, welcomingly bright auditorium and came to an automatic stop. The chamber was lit by electric chandeliers and wall sconces and filled with several banquet tables full of goodies of all kinds—foods for those who could consume it and carafes full of various, high-end blood substitutes for the vamps. One whole section was set aside with rows of chairs in pew formation before a large wall screen bearing a welcoming message for Edwin's Congress.

Fuyuko pointed out the screen and said, "This is the meeting hall. When you are ready, we have prepared a presentation as to why CoreCivic is the best corporation to ally with your Congress, my Lord. You will learn about its humble beginnings on Earth, what we do to help protect humans from Supernatural threats, and how we have grown into this incredible floating wonder."

Eliza was dubious. She wouldn't exactly call a giant prison full of supernatural monsters a "floating wonder."

The other members of Edwin's Congress came up beside them, looking around and mumbling about the enormity of the place while Fuyuko added, "After the reel and refreshments, we will be happy to walk your people through the halls of the various wards." Producing a large tablet, Fuyuko presented a schematic of the Oublies not unlike the one that Eliza already had.

They were presently in the visitor's area, an enormous, hundred-story building block that shot up through the center of the rig like the core of an apple. Off this central tower were the various prison wards—hundreds of them going in almost every direction, all of them color-coded. "We will be touring the safest ones, of course. Orange security, not blue."

She leaned in. "Blue is where we keep our more dangerous guests."

Eliza groaned internally. This was going to take forever. She saw Edwin search for a way to move things along, but it was Emerson who came to their rescue, to her utmost surprise.

"That is all well and good, Commander-in-Chief." The little vampire nodded at the tablet, his ratty eyes flashing. "But my client and I would like to speak to the Warden as soon as it is feasible. I think we have made up our minds already and would like to begin the paperwork." He glanced aside at Edwin for confirmation.

Ah, he was afraid Edwin might turn down this very luscious offer. As always, Emerson smelled money and was turning rabid about following the trail.

Edwin, suddenly coming alive, said, "Aye, that's correct. I would like to speak with the Warden now, please, Fuyuko." He even gave her those sly eyes of his.

Fuyuko fumbled for a response, obviously thrown off her game. Eliza could tell she was very proud of the Vault and wanted to show off its achievements. But then she recovered, lowered the tablet, and said, "Ah...yes, of course. I see no reason to delay! We can tour afterward. Just this way!" Fuyuko said with forced glee, indicating that the group should follow.

"We are off to see the Warden!" She said it like she might break out into a show tune.

| xviii |

Cesar was still smarting from being left behind on the mission, but as soon as Foxley got wind of it, he knew the little creep would want to have another of his "little adventures," as he called them. Back aboard the *Gypsy Queen*, Mr. Stephen, with whom Cesar had kicked up a casual open relationship, warned him it was a frequent thing with their Lord.

"Something will take his fancy, and then off he'll pop. Might not be back in days, weeks, or even months," Mr. Stephen warned him one night in bed after a round of especially ardent lovemaking. He was using a mirror to admire the bite marks in his shoulder. "You'll get used to it, vampire."

Still. It hurt to be pushed around like this. Like he was furniture. Foxley made a point of making Cesar acutely aware that he was there for no other reason than as an emotional gut-punch to Edwin. Cesar was used to it, but that didn't mean it didn't hurt.

As a result, Cesar was wandering between the outside kiosks in the Bazaar, taking in the wares and people. There were peddlers selling everything from food and tech to clothes and trinkets. Anything and everything the crew aboard Edwin's gyro might want or need. There were even bars, clubs, and strictly regulated houses of prostitution.

The *Gypsy Queen* had a similar level, called the Leisure Hive, but it was about twice the size of Edwin's Bazaar and offered everything here plus more. Certainly more vice. Down in the Leisure Hive, there were gambling halls, posh hotels situated right next to seedy bars and old-fashioned-looking taverns, high-end clubs of every kind serving all kinds of eclectic needs—and, of course, dozens of brothels.

When he first started to work for Foxley almost a decade earlier, Cesar had been shy about visiting the Leisure Hive. It was densely populated, and the people were loud, bawdy, often drunken or high, and it was nearly impossible to pass through without getting hit up. Because he was a vampire, and one of high rank on board the gyro, everyone wanted a piece of him. The problem was, Cesar wasn't that type of guy. He was more the type to stay home with his lover and make a homemade meal and watch a movie—boring stuff. The Leisure Hive felt overwhelming, and the scents and sights of it caused him to want to fang out at times, something he had strictly trained himself not to do as a tribute to his master, Edwin, who was an extremely disciplined vampire.

But as time passed, and the frustration and boredom set in, Cesar began to warm to the Leisure Hive. He made friends aboard the *Gypsy Queen*, and he and his workmates often spent their time off having fun down in the Hive. As Foxley's Enforcer, he had an open tab and didn't have to pay for anything. He could have as much synthetic blood—or real blood from Poppets and even willing human guests—as he liked. Everyone wanted to sleep with him. He was Foxley's vampire, a celebrity. People aboard the gyro loved him.

Now, he made a point of visiting certain brothels and clubs. He had a rotating system of Poppets and human sex workers who serviced him whenever he crooked his finger. The humans tasted amazing, but the Poppets were simply divine, genetically engineered to be both delicious and incredibly nutritious.

When Lady Eliza hesitated about letting him visit the Poppets' quarters aboard her ship, he was disappointed and even slightly annoyed. He knew she meant well and was only looking after her fellow Poppets, but he expected her to trust him. And not having fresh Poppet blood was starting to get to him.

The synthetic stuff was trash, to put it plainly. He needed the rush of hot, fresh blood, fruity from the source. And the added bonus of a beautiful, virile Poppet laid out on his sheets, face turned away in a nest of soft hair, willingly offering up his throat—or any other body part—was more than Cesar could resist these days. It was what he dreamed of. What he lusted for day and night.

It made his mouth water even now just thinking about it. He swallowed hard as he cut a swath through the vendors, his throat clicking drily...emptily. Perhaps it was best he hadn't been chosen for the mission. He hadn't drunk fresh Poppet blood in more than a day and he was shaky and headachey. Piloting a Hummingbird would have been difficult.

"Hey, handsome!"

He turned at the sound of the voice cutting through the crowd and spotted Kimberly the lovely tea lady standing at the shop she owned. She was setting up her outside café, opening umbrellas on the patio, but stopped to wave to him.

He sauntered over and gave her a big smile. "Lady Kimberly! Nice seeing you again!"

"I spotted you wandering around like a lost soul," Kimberly said with a wide smile. "Are you lost in the Bazaar?"

"Uh...no. Just walking." He didn't mention the hunger, the constant hunger. Plus, he thought it was possible that seeing Tommy again in his altered form during the conference in the War Room had done him no favors. He had seriously considered taking Tommy aside to try and apologize once more to him. But there were no words. He couldn't think of a single thing to say to the man that would come close to how sorry he felt for the part he played in hurting the love of his life. How did you apologize for destroying someone so completely?

Shaking his head, he refocused on Kimberly and put an artificial smile on his face. "I couldn't sleep. Actually, I don't sleep much anyway. I was curious to see more of the Bazaar."

Kimberly, looking radiant, said, "Well, sir, may I offer you a cup of my special brew as you partake in your travels?"

That seemed like a perfect plan and, smiling genuinely at last, he let Kimberly guide him inside the teashop and to the long coffee bar at the back. He took a seat and let her prepare that special combination of tea and blood substitute that she excelled at.

While he drank, he asked her what there was to do aboard the *Queen's Gambit*.

"We have a new movie house that plays classics every day all day long. It's to honor Lord Edwin." Kimberly beamed her smile. "He likes classic movies."

"I remember. But are there any clubs?"

"We have a book club. And a sewing club, too! It meets on Tuesdays."

"Hookup joints," Cesar clarified as he took a sip of the brew. It wasn't half bad for fake blood.

Kimberly looked slightly uncomfortable but continued to be helpful. "The Casino Royale is the biggest nightclub in the Bazaar. I'm sure you could...find someone there."

Had he overstepped in some way? When he first arrived, he'd assumed that Edwin's gyro would be positively crawling with clubs and brothels. Edwin, after all, wasn't exactly a Puritan. Then he reminded himself that the *Queen's Gambit* was a Black Box. It didn't host tourism or even welcome guests in any great number, and since Lady Eliza was unquestionably the queen bee here, there probably weren't many hookup spots. She seemed rather protective of her Poppets.

After thanking Kimberly for the tea, he went in search of the casino, finding it at the far end of the Bazaar and within walking distance of the theater she recommended. As much as he enjoyed watching old movies—they reminded him of his cozy days with Edwin, curled up with him on the sofa in their New York townhome—he hoped there were some Poppets somewhere willing to accommodate a hungry vampire.

The place was packed, but it didn't have the same air as Foxley's many dens of iniquity. The people—employees who worked on the ship—acted more like a giant family. There was no rowdiness or disagreements. They served spirits, but it was mostly wine, beer, and a few fancy umbrella drinks.

People sat enjoying Blackjack or poker at tables or played penny ante pool in the back under the large, stained-glass table lights. A long bar ran in an S-pattern through the main floor, with two barkeeps on either side and a scattering of round tables all around.

Cesar took a seat near the wall and checked out his options.

No prostitutes were roaming about, but he did spot some pretty male servers in snug red and white uniforms. Not bad pickings. He felt a warm surge when a young stud came over and asked him what he wanted.

"What subs do you have?" he asked, referring to the various brands of blood substitutes.

The male server rattled off the names. Cesar picked one at random.

When the young man brought the bottle over, Cesar glanced at his name badge, which read "Tyler," and asked him outright when he was getting off his shift.

Blushing profusely, Tyler said, "Not for another hour. You'll probably be gone by then."

"I'll wait," Cesar announced, lounging in the booth in an inviting way that made Tyler look over continuously to see if he was still there. It drove the humans wild to know a powerful vamp wanted them and might even do things to them.

Seducing human prey was painfully easy.

Cesar nursed his drink and waited. Over the next hour, Tyler dropped his tray twice and fumbled through the remainder of his orders. After his shift was over, he returned to Cesar's table, still in his snug, sexy uniform, positively stoked. Cesar told him to sit.

Tyler obeyed, looking Cesar over with interest. "You're Foxley's, aren't you?"

"I work for Foxley as his Enforcer," Cesar informed him. "But I'm Lord Edwin's Heir."

Tyler sighed, a hand on his cheek. "He's so cool. Lord Edwin, I mean. You're hot, too. Lord Edwin is just..." Tyler fanned himself.

"I know what you mean. I felt the same way when he chose me as his Heir."

Tyler leaned in, impressed. "You must be special for Lord Edwin to do that. I would do almost anything to be chosen as one of his Brides. Most of us here would."

"You ever dream of making it with a vampire?" he asked, using almost the same words that Edwin once plied him with when he was human.

Tyler's eyes lit up, and within moments, they had retired to one of the side lounges where they had more privacy. Cesar pinned the young man against the wall near a billiards table and soothed him into submission while he kissed and licked along the length of Tyler's neck. He tasted of the day's sweat and smoke. But Cesar could taste the young man's own fresh flavor—his blood—racing just beneath the surface of his skin. Tyler moaned while Cesar swirled his tongue around, finally settling in to suck a bite of skin between his lengthening eyeteeth.

Cesar bit and Tyler suddenly yelped and jumped, the back of his head clunking against the wall. Cesar stopped and drew back, startled by the young man's reaction. "You all right?"

"I just..." Tyler reached up to touch the marks that Cesar's sharpened teeth had left. A bead of blood had welled up in each of the small but deep holes. He looked at the blood on his fingers, which were shaking. "I...I just...I don't know about this. That hurt."

"That's what makes it fun." Cesar dove back in, drawn to the beautiful taste of Tyler's neck, his blood. He mouthed the wound, but Tyler squirmed and put his hands up against Cesar's chest, separating them.

Tyler laughed nervously. "No, that really hurts."

Cesar smiled through the blood taste on his lips. "Pain makes you feel alive."

"No, come on." He started to squirm in earnest, so Cesar shoved him back against the wall hard and held his head by the hair. Hunger had made him mean. He didn't like the idea of Tyler leading him on. What exactly did the kid think they were going to do in this room alone? Play pinochle?

Cesar, growling, tightened his hold on Tyler's hair, and Tyler whined in response and started to shake. Despite Tyler's struggles, Cesar lowered his head, drawn back to the amazing taste of Tyler's blood—

And that's when someone grabbed him from behind.

The other bartender, an older man with a lot of muscle and a graying beard, stood there, the fist of one hand bunched in Cesar's jacket. His other hand held a pool cue, which he had raised threateningly over Cesar's head. "We don't do that here, vampire. Tyler said no, man. No is no!"

Cesar looked at the way the human had grabbed him. The threatening way he was holding the cue. He had a lot of nerve grabbing a high-ranking vampire like that. Didn't he have any sense?

Baring his teeth, Cesar said, *"Get away. He's mine!"* But his voice was barely human and growled forth like a hungry animal.

"No," the older bartender told him. "Let Tyler go."

Cesar snarled in response and he saw the older man's face turn dead white as he tried to decide what his next move should be. Then his eyes shifted to a spot to the side of Cesar.

Cesar was just about to turn that way when he became aware of another presence—one of the many uniformed Court Guards that patrolled this area. He was wielding a long, black shock stick. The guard didn't even hesitate as he thrust it into Cesar's side and a burst of electricity shot through Cesar's body, lighting up his sensitive nerves.

The guard said, "Nighty-night, Mr. Vampire."

Cesar's entire body seized up. And when the burning pain finally stopped, he found he could do nothing but clench up and drop to the floor in a semi-conscious state. The last thing he heard was the older bartender saying, "Take this jerk to the brig and let him dry out. Fuckin' vamps...can't trust 'em."

* * *

Over the last few days, Veronica had struck up some interesting conversations with Gorm. He told her many interesting things about his life and family. She, in turn, told him about her duties aboard the *Gambit*, as well as some of her more long-term ambitions. He seemed interested.

"You like him," Gorm said while they were conversing.

She glanced up, stared at him through the glass partition, and scratched at her itching arm, but didn't immediately respond.

Gorm gave her a sympathetic smile. "Lord Edwin. You are in love with him."

Her first instincts were to deny that statement, but in Gorm, she was finding something akin to a kindred soul. Like her, he was a low-ranking member of his crew. No one cared about what Gorm wanted out of his life. He was just a moving part, a cog in someone else's machine.

She grunted in acknowledgment. "Doesn't matter. He only has eyes for that little Poppet." She meant to change the subject to something less personal—less *painful*—but the frustration she felt was bubbling up in her, no doubt exasperated by the fact that she'd slept badly last night, tossing and turning and sweating all night long.

"I really don't know what he sees in her, if I'm being honest. She's not an artificer or a doctor. She has little education. I mean, she used to be his secretary, for Christ's sake. She pounded *keys*." She let out a frustrated breath. "Lord Edwin seduced his secretary. How clichéd is that?"

They talked at length about their respective lives' disappointments. Lost opportunities, past loves. The minutiae of their lives were surprisingly similar. But when Gorm humbly requested his harness, Veronica was naturally suspicious and, at first, she turned him down. But then she recalled how precarious his existence was in this glorified freezer on a ship where the AI wasn't even working correctly, and decided to send the order up to fetch Gorm's harness. It wasn't like she was going to let him out, and what if he collapsed again? She couldn't afford to lose him.

The ship's concierge was understandably upset. "I would prefer to have Lord Edwin's approval on this," he said. They spoke in his office on the administrative floor, with the old man stationed behind his desk and shuffling papers. "If you get his signature, I will do whatever Lord Edwin asks of me."

Like everyone else on board, he was loyal to a fault to their Lord.

But Veronica knew that wasn't going to happen even after Edwin got back from his mission. Gorm had attacked Edwin's son, Oliver. Even though she knew Gorm wasn't strong enough to escape the glass box, Edwin wasn't likely to allow it for personal reasons.

At the same time, Veronica knew in her heart that an alliance was possible with the Jotnar. Hell, Lord Edwin had managed to bring together the vamps, the shifters, *and* the Fae all in one fell swoop. In doing so, he created the first Congress in half a millennium. Granting Gorm his simple request was the first step to negotiating with his people. And having the Jotnar on his side would be a boon. Were Veronica able to achieve that for him, surely he would recognize how important she was to his Congress? To him?

It was surprisingly easy to forge his electronic signature. Veronica had minored in computer science and could create a passable deepfake. A few hours later, Gorm got his harness back, though she promised herself that she would be careful. Gorm would not be allowed to step outside the glass box. She explained that to him.

"I understand, my friend," he granted her. He expressed his gratitude to her and promised he would not give the guards, or her, any trouble. "We are, after all, a universal people."

She nodded and smiled and scratched at her arm. His words greatly relieved her. But as soon as he had the harness back on, she'd begun to have doubts about what she had done. Still, she went to bed that night with a little smile on her face. She had bonded with this young soldier, one she hoped would serve them well in the future. When Edwin—her Edwin—returned from his mission and saw how well-behaved Gorm was, he would surely forgive her for the forgery and upgrade her status on the ship.

She imagined herself Head Ship Doctor, Edwin's right-hand person. The one he relied on, even confided in, on long, dark nights of the soul. He might even choose her for his next Bride the way he had Lady Eliza and his Heir Cesar.

The next morning, she woke invigorated, though she had a headache by the early afternoon. It continued all through the evening and into the night, when she finally discovered she was running a fever. She was hot at first, but soon she grew extraordinarily cold. She went to bed early the following evening dressed in flannel pajamas and a heavy robe, but the cold never seemed to leave her no matter how high she set the thermostat in her personal quarters.

She was shivering and her teeth were chattering when she got up the following morning. When she looked in the mirror, she saw her face was pale and there were black rings under her eyes. She had definitely picked up a bug. The blackout incident in Gorm's cell from a few days earlier worried her, but when she checked the bite mark on her arm, it was completely gone and she decided she might have hallucinated the whole incident. She and Gorm had an understanding; she didn't think he would hurt her.

At work, Carl noticed and asked if she was all right.

"I think it might be the flu," she told him, wiping at her sweaty face and hair.

"Oh, no," he told her. "God, I hope not! I hate the flu!"

She felt sick after lunch and locked herself in the ladies' bathroom, rolling up her sleeve. When she saw the black veins twining under her skin, she felt a dull, sick shock. She knew she could deny it no longer. She decided to take a sample of her own blood down to the labs for testing. She would try to get ahead of this thing. But on the way down, a sudden onset of dizziness sent her reeling to the floor of the lift, and it took all of her coworkers in the lab to help her back to her quarters to rest.

Veronica, now pale and lethargic and so frozen in bed that she could barely speak, infected one of her coworkers when the virus, which had mutated in her system, became airborne. Cynthia, the worker who helped her into bed, carried the bug back to the lab and medical wards with her. Several of her coworkers, along with several guards, carried the infection with them to other parts of the gyro. By then, Veronica could no longer move or speak, only chatter from the cold freezing and contorting her body.

Over the next couple of days, the infection Veronica had picked up from Gorm continued to mutate, spreading faster and faster throughout the ship. It didn't much care for the Supernaturals who worked on board Edwin's gyro—it found itself rather incompatible with their anatomy—but it was quick to infect anyone human, something Veronica would have discovered through blood work if she hadn't turned so quickly.

As a result, almost half of the crew suffered no symptoms in those first days and, indeed, they didn't even notice that was something amiss until their human coworkers stopped showing up for their shifts. A few chose to look in on their coworkers and friends, but since the Supes on the ship were an insular species, generally distrustful of humans, it took a few days for the crew to realize how many humans on the gyro were ill. By the time anyone began to have real concerns, the bug had already spread far and wide.

Alone in his comfy frozen quarters, Gorm, who had finally accomplished the mission he had been sent to the *Queen's Gambit* to do, smiled to himself, listened to another of the human guards outside his glass box collapse, and silently told his Queen, "It is done."

***

Fuyuko had been yammering on for ten minutes straight about the Oublies. It was all Edwin could do to keep from telling the mechanical chit to shut up.

They were all standing inside one of the oversized lifts on their way to the Warden's administrative floor. The lifts on the Oublies, just like his own, didn't just go up and down but left or right on a complex grid system that covered all parts of the gigantic spherical rig. Their car had made several turns and ascensions already.

"Here we are!" Fuyuko stepped out of the lift and ushered the others after her.

Another corridor. As they started down it, a Mech guard passed them going the other way, this one accompanied by a large, fearsome-looking creature that walked on all fours but had no head. It was vaguely canine-shaped, and Edwin feared it might be a dog version of the Mechs. He hoped it had not been built on the remaining ganglia of a real dog. He liked animals.

Eliza, walking close beside him, shirked a little at the sight of the creature motoring past, its joints making disconcerting grinding noises and its small, toe-less metal feet clicketing against the industrial flooring as it slowed to briefly divert its headless attention their way.

Fuyuko laughed at her reaction. "Those are doggones. Doggo plus drone. Get it? They help us keep the guests in line. But they are no real threat to anyone who doesn't belong here."

Eliza looked unconvinced and kept the creature in her peripheral vision as they moved past it. "Guests?"

"That's what we call them here aboard the Oublies. We do not use the word 'prisoner' here. They are our guests and we are rehabilitating them." She clomped to the end of the corridor and used a keycard to unlock a large double set of doors.

Edwin expected an office suite of some kind, but the space was set up like a large octagonal auditorium, a vast, cold, grey room as comforting as a dungeon. In some ways, it reminded Edwin of the White Room, the battle royale chamber aboard the Fae's rig, where visitors were sometimes pitted against the Faes' Green Man. In the dead center of the room was a small dais sporting cuffs that fit on the ankles and a pair of long, smooth, tube-chains that hung from the ceiling, also ending in cuffs that fit on the wrists.

Chained upon the dais was a large but scrawny-looking werewolf in half-wolf form. He was bent almost double as he hung from the chains, sweat pouring off his scabby, befurred body and drool pooling from his panting mouth and falling between his bare feet. Blood speckled the floor all around him.

Edwin and Eliza stopped short at the sight. Standing before the werewolf was the Warden, a sonic whip in a holster on his side.

Lord Wincott, long since exiled from the High Courts, turned at the sound of their approach and had the actual nerve to smile a wide welcoming smile full of sharp brown, rotting teeth. He was a tall, thin snake of a creature in a powdered wig, a ruffled, blood-stained broadcloth shirt, and a brocade waistcoat that hadn't been laundered in probably forever. His undead face was heavily powdered and made-up, though sweat had smeared his makeup into a hideous caricature. He looked utterly mad.

"Edwin! My old friend!" he declared, his voice an annoying, high-pitched whine that made Edwin's nerves sing. He held open his arms as if to embrace him.

Edwin stopped and glared at the creature. They had met only once before. And they were most certainly not old friends.

The last time they were in the same room together was nearly a hundred years ago, during a fete at Foxley's manor in the English countryside. Edwin watched Wincott beat to within an inch of his life a servant who had dropped his beverage. Earlier in the evening, he had worked to maneuver Edwin into an empty bedroom. Once alone, the letch stuck his unwelcome hand down Edwin's pants, and when Edwin told the wanker to fuck off, the creature grabbed his family jewels and wouldn't let go. An altercation ensued, and Wincott threw him so hard against a wall, Edwin partly blacked out. When he finally came around, Wincott was trying to stick his dick down Edwin's throat.

Edwin secretly swore the next time they met, he would kill the bastard.

"Wincott," he said only now, his voice a low growl.

The creature stopped and looked him over, making his interest obvious. "You have changed, Lord Edwin!" He offered Edwin a grandiose bow.

"You," Edwin pointed out, glancing briefly at the brutalized werewolf hanging in his chains, "have not, I see."

Wincott laughed, a high, frenzied noise that made Edwin's stomach turn and caused Eliza to shrink against him. Edwin was tempted to give his wife a reassuring squeeze of the hand, but he didn't want to alert Wincott to her importance to him.

Biting his tongue, he said only, "CoreCivic sent a request for office space aboard the *Queen's Gambit*. I'm here to negotiate those terms. Well, Emerson and I." Edwin indicated the impatiently fidgeting vampire to the left of him.

"The terms...the terms," Wincott intoned emptily. His eyes moved erratically up and over the walls of the torture room. At the same time, his hand moved to scratch himself in a way one's parents always said not to do. "Oh, yes, we want to have you. Your lovely Congress. Your lovely, beautiful people. We would love to have them all!"

He was probably using the royal *we*.

Eliza swallowed so hard, Edwin heard it. Under her breath, she said, "Dear god."

Wincott started to laugh that whinnying again, drew his sonic whip, and flicked it on. It started to hum, and he cut the air with it like a silent blade as he swished it about. The werewolf trembled and peed on the floor at the sight of it.

"Wincott, I would like to get on with that now, if you wouldn't mind," Edwin insisted, hoping to get the fool back on track—and get them all out of this place.

The vampire stopped laughing like a button had been pushed. He eyed Edwin with red-rimmed, hungry eyes. "And we...we would love to have *you*."

Eliza looked like she might be sick.

Wincott grinned broadly, maniacally, before spinning around to face one of the Mechs standing like a silent sentinel nearby. He indicated the half-dead werewolf in chains. "Take our guest back to his accommodations, won't you, my dear?"

"Yes, Warden," said the Mech, his voice carefully neutral, though Edwin detected something distasteful in it all the same. The Mech climbed the steps of the dais to remove the half-conscious werewolf and swing its tattered body easily over its shoulders.

Turning to address Edwin once more, Wincott cut the air with the whip one last time, the weapon making a hissing noise that set Edwin's teeth on edge and left an aftershock in the air. "And you and I, little Lord, will have our tet-a-tet in my boudoir. Come along!"

xix

Eliza knew the importance of their mission. Still, she had a terrible feeling about leaving Edwin along with Wincott. The vampire was totally cracked and, in her opinion, capable of almost anything. And despite the brave face her husband was putting on for her benefit and that of his crew, she knew he wasn't well. She could hear his breathing—harsh and labored. And he had a cough he was trying to conceal. All of the walking through these damned endless corridors was taking its toll on him.

Before they parted ways—Edwin and Emerson to Wincott's office and she, Tommy, and Foxley to the tour she had agreed to take with Fuyuko—she dragged him aside.

"Are you going to be all right with…that thing," she whispered low, eyeing Wincott, who was now down on the floor on his hands and knees, busy licking up the spilled blood of the werewolf he had so recently tortured.

"I have Emerson with me," Edwin insisted. "I'm as safe as I can be."

"Emerson? Emerson is about as useful as an elephant in a mine field!" she said almost too loudly. She closed her eyes and got her temper under control. "He's not going to protect you, Edwin. Take Tommy at least!!"

"You need Tommy to help you take down that mouthy walking clanker!" he whispered, referring to Fuyuko. He started to cough again and grabbed his inhaler from his inside jacket pocket.

"Take Foxley, then." She shuddered at the suggestion. Who was more dangerous to Edwin, Wincott or Foxley? It was like a case of the frying pan or the fire...

He grabbed her arm gently and looked into her eyes. "Have faith, Mrs. McGillicuddy. I was a street brawler long before I was a vampire. I know how to handle the likes of Wincott."

Her lips trembled as she tried to answer. She knew there was no getting through to him. He was going to do this stupid hero shite with or without her blessing. "At least let me go with you, then. I'm not stronger than a vampire. But, as a Poppet, I'm stronger than a human. I'm stronger than you—no offense."

"None taken." He took her hand and patted it, his eyes, watering from his coughing fit. "But I need you, Tommy, and Foxley to find that wanker Pretorius. It's the whole point of this bloody mission. You know that."

"Yes, but..."

"And you may need both Tommy and Foxley to hold back those walking garbage cans. You're the one in danger. Not me."

She knew he was right. But she still didn't like it one little bit.

* * *

Eliza felt Fuyuko was enjoying the tour a little bit *too* much.

They would go a hundred feet past various cell doors in the Orange Wing and Fuyuko would swing around and start rattling off facts and figures about CoreCivic and operations aboard the Oublies, making it all sound like Disneyland. She had really drunk the Kool-Aid.

The Orange Wing, which was not orange in any way—it was the same drab grey of the rest of the rig—stretched on seemingly forever. The doors of the private cells were all closed and securely locked. They each had small slits cut into the tops. If Eliza stretched to tiptoes, she found she could catch a quick glimpse inside the cells.

They were mostly occupied by Supernatural criminals of the white collar variety—Fae and shifters, primarily—all dressed in orange jumpsuits and reading or staring at the walls. Much of the wing was dedicated to a debtor's prison of sorts, where the creatures, having hit skid row, had fallen behind on their debts. A few had embezzled or defrauded. They were working their sentences off here simply because the human prisons on Earth were too afraid to hold them.

Eliza found it distasteful and even racist. And she sensed Tommy felt the same way. He walked with his head down, barely able to look at the doors. Unlike them, however, Foxley skipped along, looking exuberant even though he had done much, much worse than anyone here ever had.

"Oublies," she found herself saying to Fuyuko. "That's a French word for a 'place of forgetting.'"

"That's correct, Lady Eliza!"

"Hundreds of years ago, they used to throw French prisoners down into holes and forget about them."

Fuyuko threw her arms out joyously. "Justice!"

"Is it?" she asked, then kicked herself. She didn't want to get into a moral debate with a walking pile of metal trash. "I'm sure they are not all bad people here. Just people with problems."

"They're not people. They are monsters," Fuyuko stated and moved to the next corridor to show them the mess hall.

This tour was taking too long. She kept hoping that Foxley would jump Fuyuko, but he seemed content to follow behind, looking amused and saying nothing. There had to be a way to turn things around.

Ignoring Fuyuko's canned speech, she turned to Tommy. "I bet the Blue Wing is more interesting than this."

Picking up on her idea, Tommy swung his head around. "Yes, my Lady, I have heard there are some interesting and dangerous criminals there."

Fuyuko, sad they weren't paying attention to her, turned and said, "We will not be visiting the Blue Wing. The criminals there are far too dangerous."

"But…they're all locked away securely in cells, no?" Eliza asked with interest.

"Correct. But we do not tour the Blue Wing. There are risks."

"I understand, Fuyuko. If there was an incident, you would no doubt be unable to handle such a crisis on your own." She indicated that it was just the four of them—her, Tommy, Foxley, and Fuyuko herself. "You could be seriously hurt."

"I am perfectly designed to handle *any* crisis, Lady McGillicuddy. It is simply not advisable."

Eliza nodded as they came to a halt before the mess hall where, through an open door, she saw more petty criminal prisoners working the counter and kitchen, most with their heads down. "Yes, despite your great combat skill, something could always go wrong that you would not be able to handle. I understand."

Fuyuko hovered, fist clenching and unclenching as she contemplated Eliza's offhand accusation. It took her a moment to respond. "I will have you know we do have tours of that wing. Most guests simply do not enjoy them."

Eliza sensed Fuyuko was lying. She was still an organic being. A real person capable of human feelings and reactions, and it was obvious she was smarting from Eliza's backhanded insult. Eliza indicated the mess hall. "It has to be more interesting than this place, which looks like a school cafeteria." She glanced at Tommy, who nodded. "And we can always invite a doggone alone for extra protection if you're concerned, Fuyuko."

"I do not need a doggone!" Fuyuko insisted too quickly. And then she seemed to check herself. "Very well. If this place is not *exciting* enough for you, Lady McGillicuddy, we will tour the other wing. Come along."

"Yes, ma'am," Eliza answered with a small half-smile on her face as she followed Fuyuko to one of the many lifts.

* * *

Wincott escorted Edwin and Emerson to his French Revivalist-inspired boudoir.

It was an unholy mess. The delicate once-white furnishings were rubbed raw from use and covered in castoff bits of clothes. Surfaces bore serving trays with old decanters of dried blood on them, many of which had attracted flies. The wainscoting bore bloodstains and black handprints. Wincott's desk—what Edwin thought *might* be his desk—groaned under the weight of a disarray of unfiled papers and yet more serving trays. There was garbage strewn everywhere.

But the most disconcerting thing was the young, naked faun crouched in one corner. Fading handprint bruises covered his face on one side, burn marks were evident on the inside of his forearms and his thighs, and one of his antlers looked like it had been savagely broken off. That was in addition to the dozens of bite marks all over his body, some in delicate spots that gave Edwin a sick shiver. He stood up slowly as Wincott entered and lowered his head submissively.

Wincott, not even flinching at the sight of the young faun, said, "Pagniash, retrieve some refreshments for my guests here." He turned to eye his guests with those red, rheumy eyes of his.

Emerson spoke up. "Blood. Real, if you have it."

Edwin only swallowed hard and said, "I'm good."

Pagniash bowed his head and bounded from the boudoir and into another attached room that Edwin assumed acted like a kitchen or pantry of sorts.

"You have a faun," Emerson commented, a bloodshot gleam in his eye. "I hear they are quite tasty."

Wincott grinned. "They are! Their blood has that magical zing that you can only get from the Fae!" Wincott turned and eyed Edwin. "Are you sure I can't get you something, Lord Edwin? Surely, that human body requires nourishment? You must need *something* in it." He leered, showing off those brown, broken teeth of his.

Edwin squared his shoulders and tried not to let the shudder of revulsion show in his body. "I'm right as rain, Wincott. Shall we attend to matters?"

"Let us have a drink to celebrate our union." He grinned at Emerson, who foolishly grinned back. "Pleasure first! Then we will attend to the very dull matter of business."

* * *

The five of them took a very long lift ride in several directions to reach the Blue Wing. When the doors finally opened, Eliza wondered if it was possible the corridor that stretched ahead was even darker and more depressing than the other ones she had seen.

She stepped out, but her thoughts were back with Edwin. She dearly hoped he would be all right, surrounded on two sides by vampires as he was. She knew he was more delicate than he seemed.

"And this is the infamous Blue Wing," Fuyuko announced, gesturing grandly. "Where we keep some of the most dangerous criminals in the world."

There were more doors here, but no windows. She hadn't expected that. She wondered how they were ever going to find Dr. Pretorius's cell in this maze. Yrsa said he was in the Blue Wing, but that the Jotnar didn't have any details past that. She looked over at Tommy, whose head was swiveling this way and that. She felt he was likely having the same thoughts.

An idea surfaced and she turned to Fuyuko. "Can you tell us about some of the criminals here?"

Fuyuko looked surprised but then recovered. "Certainly." She stopped at one of the cells, checked her tablet, and announced, "This is the criminal known as the Kobra." She began rattling off details that Eliza cared about not at all.

She just stared at the tablet in Fuyuko's hands. After a few moments, she glanced over at Tommy and said, "That is very interesting."

Tommy intoned, "Indeed, my Lady."

"Fascinating," Foxley said, sounding utterly bored. He was looking down at some device in his hand like a child who couldn't be persuaded to set down their mobile device.

They moved to the next cell and then the next. Each time, Eliza asked about the criminal behind the locked door. Fuyuko looked slightly irritated but humored them every time. In the meantime, Eliza kept an eye out for what was going on in the corridors around them. She could hear the distant thump of feet as the giant Mechs passed down other hallways. Sometimes, she detected the distinctive clicketing of doggone feet, but that was distant.

She and Tommy grew very still and paid serious attention to Fuyuko's narrative when one Mech, walking with a doggone, passed them by before taking a sharp turn. She waited until she couldn't hear the distant click of feet before she turned to Tommy to give him the code that they were going to act. "I think we've seen enough."

Tommy nodded. "I agree."

He stepped forward, moving much faster than he seemed capable of, and put a hand on Fuyuko's tablet to rescue it. Fuyuko looked up at him, a hint of surprise in her posture.

She never got a word in. She was a Mech, yes, but Tommy was a Colossus, larger and more durable than she was. He swung his other arm up and clenched his hand about her neck. Fuyuko started blurting out a sound, but Tommy used all of the power in his hydraulic body to force her against the wall between two doors. At the same time, he crushed her neck into a mangled mass.

She tried to speak anyway, but what came out was a muddled response. She raised both hands automatically and grabbed Tommy around the shoulders, but then grew absolutely still as her body suddenly malfunctioned and froze up.

Tommy let go of Fuyuko's neck and set both of his giant hands on either side of her head, cupping her cheeks. With a twist and a spit of sparks, Tommy turned her head a full 180 degrees so it was facing the wall before ripping it right off—not cleanly, though. Once her head came off, Eliza spied the base of her human spinal column. She sucked in a deep breath at the sight of the human bones sticking out of the machine body. It was macabre.

She thought Fuyuko's grip should lessen on Tommy, but it didn't. Even as the head dropped to the floor with a clank and then rolled down the corridor a few feet, her hands clamped down even tighter on Tommy's shoulders, and she pushed.

Her strength was terrifying, and she easily pushed Tommy against the opposite wall, the hard thump making Eliza grimace at the way the sound echoed down the corridor. She quickly looked around, sure she would spot another Mech turning the bend. None did, but that didn't mean one wouldn't appear soon.

Fuyuko, unable to speak, was awkwardly grappling Tommy against the wall, and she was much stronger than she seemed. Her giant fingers clenched, actually denting Tommy's shoulders. Tommy growled in response and tried to fight off her headless body, but that just made her go into a frenzy of pushing and shoving as she tried to get his gigantic body down into a submissive hold.

The two machine people grappled and twisted violently in the corridor, gears grinding and feed stomping, bodies banging against the walls. Eliza had to jump out of the way lest she be smashed flat. She turned to Foxley, leaning against a wall and playing a game on his phone. "A little help here, please!" she hissed.

"I think not," Foxley responded without looking up.

"What the hell do you mean?"

"The Mechs are made of metal and contain no blood of any kind." He glanced up, his eyes cool and bored. "How do you expect me to control them?"

Eliza gaped. "I expect you to do something!"

"Your literal boy toy has it handled."

She glanced back at Tommy, now shoved against the wall with the headless Mech clenching his throat with her fingers. She could hear Tommy grunting as Fuyuko applied pressure. Down the corridor, she could hear Fuyuko's head spitting out facts about CoreCivic like nothing was amiss.

Meanwhile, Eliza heard distant thumps as the Mechs, alerted either by some kind of collective consciousness or only noticing the tussle on a hidden CCTV she wasn't aware of, began to mobilize.

Good fucking lord, what in hell was she supposed to do?

* * *

"Come, Edwin, sit with me." Wincott patted the seat of the divan beside him. "Before we begin, we should become re-acquainted." When he saw Edwin wasn't moving an inch from his spot near the door, he added, "Pagniash, go prepare Lord Edwin some human sustenance. Surely, we have something in the stores."

"Yes, my Lord," Pagniash answered, almost dropping the serving tray he held before racing back to the kitchen.

Edwin glanced over at the desk where Emerson was settling his briefcase and getting out his files, oblivious to the obvious danger that Wincott posed. Edwin's job was perhaps the hardest and most dangerous because he needed to create a diversion and keep Wincott and Emerson occupied while Eliza, Tommy, and Foxley found Dr. Pretorius in the Blue Wing. He didn't think that was going to be a problem for him. He only dreaded what it entailed.

You've done this before—and as a human, he reminded himself.

He'd never gone into too many details with Eliza, but she was well aware of what he did before he became Foxley's Heir and Enforcer. Yes, his duties included looking after the ladies of the brothel and protecting them from the clients who would harm or even kill them. But he also entertained a small clientele of his own, mostly the noblemen and women of the realm who enjoyed "slumming it" by today's standards. He knew intimately how to take care of someone's needs, having been taught how to entertain company when he was still a preteen.

Still, the idea of letting Wincott touch him was both revolting and utterly terrifying. As a vampire, he could have endured almost anything, but he was all too aware of how fragile this current meatsuit of his was.

"Lord Edwin…" Wincott singsonged, languidly gesturing to him with a crooked finger.

Sucking in a deep breath, Edwin stood up straight and went to sit beside the vampire, though he made sure to leave a few inches of space between them. By then, Pagniash had returned with some very questionable-looking food on a serving tray. Edwin was no chef, but he didn't think the food was supposed to move like that.

He looked up at the faun, who was shaking badly, his one eye mashed shut and bruised. Their eyes met, and Edwin felt the rage in him redouble at the terribly battered sight of the sweet-looking boy standing before him.

Wincott noticed. "He's quite delightful and has a wonderful squeal," he announced, reaching out to trickle his dirty fingernails down Edwin's arm. "Do you like him, Lord Edwin?"

Edwin couldn't help himself. He reached out and put a hand on Pagniash's arm, but softly. He wasn't sure if he could communicate it, but he wanted to say, *When we get out of here, we will take you with us, mate.*

Pagniash's entire countenance seemed to brighten suddenly as if he knew. Perhaps his Fae powers had picked up on Edwin's thoughts.

Turning back to Wincott, Edwin said, "He's lovely."

Wincott ran a hand up and down Edwin's shoulder and arm. Edwin made a monumental effort not to punch the bastard in the face. "As are you, my Lord. So pretty and delicate. And this human body is warm! What will Foxley think of next?"

Before Edwin could say anything, Wincott turned to Emerson. "You may prepare the contracts, counselor. I wish to examine this human body in private first. It is perhaps something I may want to experience at some point."

Edwin turned to Emerson and opened his mouth to protest, but he was oblivious. In the meantime, Wincott jumped up, took Edwin by the arm, and dragged him off the divan and into an adjoining room—a large bedchamber of some kind decorated in the French style like the rest of Wincott's quarters, except this one had a gigantic four-poster bed covered in white sheets drenched in old brown bloodstains.

The room reeked of blood and death, and Edwin noticed flies and other creepy crawlies moving along the mattress of the bed. He had to breathe through his mouth to keep from retching. "Look, Win—"

"Hush. We were interrupted last time we were together." Wincott dragged him close. His voice was no longer high and breathy like a young girl's. Now, he growled like an animal. He leaned down to sniff Edwin's face and hair. Edwin was paralyzed with the fear that Wincott would kiss him. Instead, he propelled Edwin toward that terrifying bed. His strength was such that Edwin had no choice. It was like being shoved by a machine.

Blimey, he hated being a human!

When they reached the bed, Wincott pushed him down into its stinking squishiness. Edwin immediately tried to pop up, but Wincott rested his long, claw-like hand in the center of Edwin's chest and held him down so he was supine on the mattress. Something tickled along Edwin's scalp. Edwin, suddenly bursting with fear, began to squirm He even landed a kick to Wincott's legs, but Wincott never even reacted.

"Get...off me...you wanker!"

Smiling through the blood and lip rouge smeared all over his face, Wincott said, "Yes, you may fight if you like, Lord Edwin. The results will be the same, but I enjoy the stimulation."

Edwin, his human body propelled into a panic, began to twist as he tried to get out from under Wincott, but he was no match for a vampire's strength. One of his flailing hands hit Wincott's face, his fingernail catching the corner of his eye. With a growl, Wincott backhanded him.

The blow felt like a brick to his face and knocked Edwin back down on the bed, stunning him. His vision was full of red and black, and he moaned from the pain of what was surely a broken nose. Meanwhile, Wincott, being far less gentle about it now, tore at the front of Edwin's trousers in a frenzy of greed and lust.

His heart pounding furiously in his chest, Edwin grunted and tried to escape, but he was like a rag doll in Wincott's hands, being pushed this way and that. Squinting up through the pain in his face, all Edwin could see through his bleary eyes was Wincott's demonically overpainted face and shark-like teeth as he laughed.

XX

The Colossus that was Tommy and the headless Mech that was all that remained of Fuyuko were trading blows and/or throwing each other against the walls. Their huge bodies clanked and their gears ground. The corridor sounded with blows and the stumbling of the giant machines' feet. Tommy grunted from each blow that Fuyuko dealt with her huge fists, but Fuyuko's head just continued to mumble on the ground a few feet away while her body charged Tommy again and again like what it was—a machine that refused to quit.

Eliza hovered undecidedly, afraid Fuyuko was really hurting Tommy, who seemed to take longer after each blow to recover. She wanted to help her friend but she knew getting anywhere near the two battling titans was dangerous.

Down the way came the stomp and clatter of feet as the other Mechs and a few doggones headed their way. They knew, finally, that something was going on. Eliza feared all the Mechs were likely wired together into a giant group consciousness. It made sense to do it that way so that if one was in trouble, the others knew where their co-worker was and could rush in to help.

But she couldn't afford a horde of Mechi-people descending on them. Defeating one Mech was proving nearly impossible. They didn't stand a chance against an army of them. She glanced around, hoping to spot Foxley. Maybe he could create a diversion of some kind, but as was typical of him, he was gone, leaving her to deal with this mess.

Resting at Eliza's feet was Fuyuko's tablet, fallen when she attacked Tommy. Eliza quickly snatched it up and clenched it in both hands—her neural link to the Mechs and the rig. Not for the first time in her life, she closed her eyes and allowed herself to connect with this virtually alien technology. The jolt was sudden and almost instantaneous.

Performing this little trick was never pleasant. It always felt like she was being slowly electrified, and she knew that one day, she would push herself to a dangerous brink. But the spark of a connection was made as she hoped it would be.

It felt like falling and floating at the same time. With a fierce sunburst upon her mind's eye, she saw inside the neural network that controlled the Mechs and the rig, though she quickly cut that part off. She'd learned in the past that it was easy to get lost in the long, fiery tubes that connected everything aboard a gyro. If she tried to see everything (and control everything), she was likely to burn it all out. She could cripple the whole rig—or give herself a stroke. It wouldn't be the first time.

Instead, she gently felt along the edges of the Mechi-people's group consciousness. They were miserable creatures, the lot of them. Trapped and silently weeping inside their metal bodies that were no longer their own. Most were full of painful regrets for the decision they had made to allow CoreCivic to do this to them. But it was too late, and their actions—and much of their minds—were no longer their own to control. They lived inside a small, dark box deep within themselves while the corporation controlled almost every action they performed throughout the day.

As the horde of Mechi-people and doggones closed in on them, some of them shouting commands, Eliza wrote and sent out a single command line of code that translated simply as *FULL STOP*.

The half dozen Mechs who had nearly reached them, guns drawn, simply froze in place—though she could see their huge metal bodies vibrating, wanting to break through the command line but unable to.

Turning, Eliza concentrated on Fuyuko, commanding her to halt as well. Her actions slowed even as she delivered another stunning blow to Tommy's solar plexus, almost doubling Tommy over. But, unlike the others, she didn't stop so easily. Instead, she withdrew a few steps and seemed to consider the situation as she decided on her next move.

"Something's wrong," Eliza told Tommy. "I can't get her to listen like the others. I think she's too damaged!"

Tommy, grunting from the latest stunning blow, stumbled back against a wall. He leaned against it, looking exhausted. "Can you…can you…?" Tommy was unable to finish the thought.

Fuyuko stood up and took stock of her headless self. She clenched both huge fists as she prepared to charge Tommy once more.

Eliza knew she had to do something before she killed Tommy. She didn't want to hurt the Mechs, but she had no choice. Being on the neural network let her know that the corridors of the prison were rigged with an electrical charge system. It worked well to stop criminals if they somehow escaped their cells, sort of like a taser they could not possibly escape. But the charge could be adjusted high or low or concentrated in certain spots. That way, it could stop an organic being without harming the Mechs or any of the other prisoners.

Eliza just cranked the charge up and let it go, the crackling energy flowing through the floor and under Fuyuko's feet, causing the Mech to pop right up and into the air, her body, sizzling with electricity before smashing down to the floor at Tommy's feet. Some part of her synthetic body came apart at the seams, and she continued to convulse for a few moments before finally lying still, arms and legs twisted at weird angles.

Silence descended over the corridors. From beyond the securely locked doors of the cells, Eliza heard some of the "guests" inquiring about what was happening. A few feet away, Tommy crouched against the wall, head down as he worked to recover from the many blows he had taken. Eliza ran to him and put her hand on his arm. "Are you okay, Tommy? Can I help you in any way?"

He looked up, one of his eye holes crunched inward. He was badly dented and one arm no longer seemed to work and hung uselessly at his side. He swiveled his head around to face her. "I think...I think I'm all right, my Lady."

Still holding his arm, she let her power flow over his metal body and into him. Once, long ago, she did a quick fix of Foxley's gyroscope with this trick, pasting it back together with figurative bubblegum and fishing wire so his whole gyro wouldn't nosedive into New York City, and she used it now to mend the most broken parts of Tommy's Colossus body.

It was, as always, a rough fix. She did the best she could, fusing broken tubes and torn wires, but at least it allowed him partial use of his damaged arm. She could not fix the dents and holes in his synthetic body or whatever internal damage he had suffered. When she asked him to test the arm, he was able to slowly clench and unclench his hand into a fist and partially raise his arm into the air.

"Thank you," he said, sounding truly grateful for the patch. Looking around, he took stock of the Mechs standing so still and silent that they looked as lifeless as statues, then noticed the tablet in Eliza's hands. "Can we use that to find Dr. Pretorius? I know Fuyuko was using it on her tour."

She nodded at his excellent idea. "I'll try."

Unfortunately, the tablet seemed pretty damaged. It was a good conduit for contacting the neural network, but its data had been badly scrambled amidst the fight and the damage that followed.

They were getting no help that way.

* * *

You have one job. Just lay back and endure it.

Edwin's whole purpose here was to distract Wincott, let the monster have its way with him, but something snapped inside him. And instead of focusing on the ceiling and letting Wincott have him, his body started to panic. His arms flailed and he found himself reaching above his head, his hand coming down on something cold and hard and solid—a serving tray left derelict in the center of the bed.

He snagged it tight, lifted it, and brought it down resoundingly on Wincott's head. The tray bent and Wincott yelped and withdrew, eyeing Edwin savagely. His jaws split open like a wound and his jaggedly broken teeth gleamed in the low lighting and filled Edwin with paralyzing dread for a moment.

But only a moment. Edwin was a dirty fighter. Always had been. It was the first thing he ever learned living in the East End. And it was the one thing he'd never forgotten even after two centuries of unlife.

As Wincott reared back, preparing to strike like a snake at his throat, Edwin raised both fists, drew one back to the level of his chin, and swiftly jabbed a punch into Wincott's exposed throat just above the dirty ruffles. Even as a human, Edwin was no weakling, and he felt the cartilage of the vampire's throat crumble under the forceful blow.

Wincott gasped and started to choke, his long, purplish tongue unfurling from his mouth.

Edwin followed up with a second shot to Wincott's eye, snapping the creature's head back and sending his body tumbling off the bed and to the floor.

"Wanker!" Sitting up, Edwin jumped off the bed. His undone trousers fell down, but Edwin didn't have the time to worry about such trivial annoyances. He knew instinctively that the vampire would be up and back at him in seconds.

Instead of worrying about his belt and trousers, he reached for some ugly knickknack on a nearby table—it appeared to be the disturbing porcelain head of a frog with an open mouth to hold your smoke—and swung it around, slamming it into Wincott's face just as the creature sprang up and at him like a demonic jack-in-the-box. The porcelain figurine shattered and Wincott snarled as the pieces tore the skin of his face. He knocked Edwin's hand away, then backhanded him—a glancing blow that knocked Edwin halfway across the room and into a wall.

Barely conscious, Edwin sat up. But, for a moment, he wasn't sure which way was up, and his head was full of a whining static. Glancing around, he focused on the door to the office and started crawling that way, though his undone trousers tangled him all up.

"We'll have none of *that*, my Lord," Wincott snarled from a few feet away.

Panting with fear, Edwin tried to crawl faster out of his pants, hands screeking over the filthy wooden floor, but the belt got stuck down around the edges of his boots. By then, Wincott was recovered enough to spring into the air.

Edwin, letting go of the idea of escape, twisted around just in time to find Wincott sitting on top of him and pinning him to the floor. The monster was drooling out of his broken mouth and cracked teeth as he attempted to grab and pin one of Edwin's wrists to the floor. Edwin lifted his other wrist to his mouth, ready to bite and create the blood whip that had gotten him out of so many uncomfortable situations, then remembered he wasn't a vampire any longer. Bloody hell! He hated being human! He tried to throw a punch instead, but Wincott caught both of his wrists in one hand and easily forced them down to the floor above his head.

"You won't escape this time, Lord Edwin," Wincott growled through the blood and foam in his mouth. "Hell, after that impressive display, I might even make you my Heir." He ran his free hand down over Edwin's chest and over the extra-soft equipment in his trousers. "This body of yours anyway. Then we can be together forever."

Edwin twisted this way and that, a fearful whimper caught in his throat, but there was nowhere to go. And he wasn't strong enough to fight a vampire, especially now, with his body laboring and his breath coughing through his damaged lungs...

Just as Wincott lowered his disgusting, stinking mouth to Edwin's neck, the door slid open behind them, the light from the other room spilling in and over them both. Edwin prayed it was Emerson here to save him. But he was wrong.

Pagniash stood in the doorway, his face twisted into a snarl and darkened by shadows. And he had a long iron fireplace poker in one hand.

Edwin, lying prone on the floor, gasped up at the sight of the boy's face—his wounded, weary, rage-filled face—as he lifted the poker high over his head and, with a scream, drove it down, right toward the two of them.

***

Eliza, now fully fused to the neural network that controlled the Mechs, could freeze them on the spot. It didn't take too much work, either. As long as she and Tommy had a few seconds advanced warning that a troupe of the Mechs was heading their way—and, frankly, they could hear them from quite far off—she could activate the port that controlled that "pod" and tell the soldiers to halt.

She didn't feel they were in any pain as she and Tommy squelched between the frozen Mechs in the corridors. The Mechs' faces and postures were, as always, neutral, and their minds seem to be sleeping. Perhaps they were even enjoying the rest.

But she worried it wouldn't last. The more Mechs she put to sleep, the more of a strain it was on the whole network, which was not enjoying her interference. Although she had discovered there were no humans on the Oublies controlling the network—it was entirely Mechi-people operated and controlled—she could tell it was starting to detect her presence in the same way it might a computer virus. It was only a matter of time before someone flesh and blood from the home offices of CoreCivic down on Earth activated a powerful anti-virus program to combat her interference. Then the Mechs would be released all at once.

And that would be very bad for them.

She and Tommy were now hurrying down the seemingly endless corridors, no longer walking as they had. Tommy was a very fast Colossus—even with carrying Fuyuko's disembodied head in his hands. Once Eliza found the tablet was useless, she got the idea to take Fuyuko with them—well, this part of her anyway—since the Mech had memorized the names of every one of the "guests" in the million-plus cells the Oublies contained. She knew where Dr. Pretorius was located, and, to Eliza's surprise, she was even willing to cooperate. The problem was, Fuyuko was damaged and kept misremembering which cell the good (bad?) doctor was in. Eliza had to keep reminding her to concentrate.

"This is highly unorthodox. Home office will not approve this," Fuyuko said for the hundredth time. She had once again forgotten about the skirmish in the hall that had damaged her, and she was once more unsure about their identities—though whether that was the result of her mechanical damage or something happening to her organic, dying brain, Eliza was unsure.

Tommy turned the heavy Mech head to face Eliza.

It gave Eliza a shiver to see the detached metallic head with its organic spine and ganglia hanging out, but she forced herself to say in a reasonable voice, "Yes, I agree. But we must move Dr. Pretorius to a new cell. Dangerous criminals are looking for him."

"You are from CoreCivic?" Fuyuko asked her (not for the first time), sounding confused.

"Correct. I am the System Operator of CoreCivic." Eliza showed Fuyuko one of the electronic badges she had taken off Fuyuko herself. "Tommy is a Mech like you and my assistant."

Tommy turned the head briefly so Fuyuko could see him. Then he turned her back to face Eliza.

Tommy's presence seemed to placate her. "Who is it trying to remove our guest?"

"Some infamous criminals from Lord Edwin McGillicuddy's Congress. They want to free Dr. Pretorius to commit an act of bioterrorism. We must find him before they do." It was both a lie and a truth, depending on your perspective.

"I understand. Lord Edwin McGillicuddy is a monster. Please proceed down the next corridor, turn left, and take the lift to the C Level," Fuyuko explained, sounding concerned.

Once they were on C Level, the process started all over again, with Fuyuko forgetting who they were once more.

"Blood hell, this Mech is grinding my gears," Tommy mumbled under his breath.

Eliza nodded her agreement. "We have *got* to be almost there. How big is this damned place?"

They both stopped dead in their tracks when they spotted a doggone rounding the bend ahead of them. It had moved silently, but the moment it spied them in whatever headless way it did, Eliza saw the canine drone pause as it considered them, then coil to strike, a long, metallic shock stick emerging from within the confines of its "collar." It bleated a warning just before it launched itself forward.

It moved so fast! Eliza raised her hand to command it to stop, but it was already airborne and heading right toward them, its shock stick crackling with deadly energy. With a cry, she turned away, sure it would crash into them, but Tommy moved to block it. The stick connected with him and he made an alarming noise close to a scream as his entire body vibrated with the electrical shock passing through it.

At the same time, Eliza turned back and, instead of trying to stop it, which would require more concentration than she had at the moment, she simply threw her arms out, commanding the ambient energy in the room to return to its host.

The doggone lit up, shaking horribly as the shock passed over and through it. After a few sparking, terrifying seconds, it dropped to the floor, its circuits grinding and locking up, its body trembling and burning. It almost seemed to whine like a real dog.

Eliza ran to Tommy, now sitting on the floor, his back to one of the cell doors. He, too, was trembling from the shock but otherwise seemed unharmed. His Colossus body was a true marvel. "Are you all right? Tommy!"

He turned his head this way and that, then nodded to her. "I...think so. Her...not so much."

They both looked down at Fuyuko's head in his lap. Her voice was small and tinny, and she kept making the same bleating noise over and over again. Eliza thought she might have burned out.

"Oh, hell!" she cried to the ceiling. Best laid plans and all that. So far, everything on this stupid mission had gone spectacularly sideways. Sitting there with Tommy, she ran a hand over her tired face. Looked like they were going to have to do this the old-fashioned way.

Getting up, she started going door to door, pounding on doors and calling "Hello?" to each of the prisoners and asking after the doctor. Few of them answered her. But one of the prisoners laughed and said, "If you're looking for that creepy wanker Pretorius. He's next door."

Eliza wasted no time moving to the next door and putting her ear to the heavy, securely locked, and windowless sliding door. She called, "Hello? Dr. Pretorius?" But no one answered. Weary and almost on the verge of tears, she pounded on it, hoping to get his attention, but her fists fell weekly upon the thick titanium steel. All she managed to do was hurt her hand.

Tommy was up and standing beside her. "May I?" he asked and she stepped dutifully back. Despite the solid craftsmanship of the door, it was no match for Tommy's titan strength. It took him a moment to sink his fingers into the almost nonexistent cracks in the edges, but once he had it, he peeled the door away like it was child's play.

The inside of the cell was dim, dank, and not what Eliza expected. She wasn't sure what her expectations were. A mad scientist's laboratory with chemicals cooking over a Bunsen burner like in the horror movies? Instead, the cell was surprisingly humid, with no furnishings at all. Most of it was made up of a small, deep, dark pool of water, the shadows of which speckled the tiled walls and ceiling. It reminded her of the pen at the zoo for the penguins or the polar bears. She took a tentative step inside, then another, being careful not to slip on the wet tiles.

Besides her, Tommy swore. "I don't understand."

"Neither do I." Yrsa never said what Dr. Pretorius was. She assumed he was a Jotunn like her people, but obviously, that wasn't correct.

"Dr. Pretorius?" Eliza called softly, trying to see through all of the gloom. Something made a splashing noise in response and she shirked, afraid a monster would pop out of the water at any moment. A few seconds later, something did surface, but not violently. Instead, the large, lumpy, shadowy looked at them both with dark eyes that reflected the water. It was no monster, but it was most certainly not human, either.

"What the...?"

The thing shot out at them with surprising agility, its enormous body speckled grey and white, its head full of shockingly drawn teeth. Tommy threw up an arm and the beast—Eliza saw after a moment that it was a very large leopard seal—clamped down on his synthetic forearm. It jerked him forward, almost dragging him to the floor before letting go and landing with a plop on the tiled floor. With a hoarse growl, it eyed them both hostilely.

Eliza stumbled back away from the dangerous-looking creature, eyeing it carefully. "That can't be...him." And then she remembered something Edwin told her many years ago, while on a mission with his old friend Captain Leo, a vampire liberator of creatures that the Vampire Lords had enslaved. At the time, they both struggled to free a pair of...

"Oh, no...oh, hell!"

"What is it?" Tommy looked baffled.

"I think it is him." Eliza swallowed. "I think Pretorius is a Fae. A selkie. How in hell are we going to get something like *that* back to the ship?"

| xxi |

The iron poker made a wet, crunching noise as Pagniash sank its sharp tip deep into Wincott's back, twisted it with vengeance, then twisted it some more as he finally drove it deep into the floor beneath the two of them. The sharp metal nicked Edwin in passing hard enough to make him grunt. However, Wincott, who had taken it straight through his torso, screamed much louder, his fetid breath scouring Edwin's face.

Edwin screamed now, too, certain the poker's deadly razor tip had gotten him as well. But when he started to wiggle, he found he could move. He could feel the poker, and there was a sharp, white-hot pain in his side, but he didn't think the tip had actually gone through his body.

Wincott let go of Edwin's hands to scratch desperately along the floor. Thrashing in earnest now, Edwin started wriggling out from under the gurgling, dying vampire. His clothes were stuck, but with a twist, his coat jacket and shirt tore as he squirmed his way free and then crawled backward away from the scene of the ongoing murder.

In the meantime, Pagniash, a crazed expression on his face, twisted and shunted the poker over and over. Edwin realized after a moment that the young faun had never stopped screaming, and the iron of the weapon was burning all through Wincott's body in a way both fascinating and horrible to watch. Edwin dragged himself into a corner and got his pants back up. He watched as small, lightning-like shocks of red light radiated out of the tip of the iron and reacted as it coursed through Wincott's body. Iron was an anathema to the Fae. For vampires, it was certain death if allowed to linger inside their bodies.

Edwin checked his side. The poker tip had jabbed him in the space between his ribs and hip. Thankfully, he was skinny as a rail and the weapon had only nicked the finite amount of meat on his bones. Still, he had a bad moment where he winced, worried about an infection, then remembered the irony of being human at the moment: Despite all of the trouble it was causing him, the iron of the poker couldn't actually harm him.

Pagniash, with a final cry, twisted the poker one last time and stepped back, spitting on the Warden, who had finally caught fire. The vampire screamed and whimpered a remarkably long time before the pile of burning clothes and bones finally shuddered and lay still, the lifeless skeleton smoldering and filling the room with a dry, crumbling stench that turned Edwin's stomach.

The young faun turned and looked at Edwin. Where before his face had been crazed with revenge, now it was still and almost lifeless. His eyes simmered with unspent tears. "I kept the poker hidden under the floorboard for when a time came when I knew I could use it. For when I knew...I could be free."

"I...don't understand," Edwin admitted. He felt slightly shell-shocked by this unexpected turn of events.

"When you touched me...I knew. I knew you were the sign to act. That you would save me." The tears in the faun's eyes began to spill over and onto his dirty cheeks. "Are you...are you going to lock me up again?" The boy burst into tired tears, sobbing like a child.

Edwin gaped at the sight. "No, lad." He got up, approaching the faun carefully. Removing his now-ruined jacket, he slowly wrapped it around the boy's naked shoulders, then, on impulse, gathered the wounded young faun against him. The boy cried and cried into his shoulder while Edwin rubbed his back. "You are most definitely going free."

Their moment was interrupted by Emerson, who knocked politely on the door before sliding it open. He looked over the carnage in the room with wide, unbelieving eyes. Leave it to Emerson to stay out of it until the danger was over. It was probably how such a weak vampire as he managed to last this long. "What the hell happened here? Why is there a dead vampire on the floor?"

Pagniash jumped in before Edwin had a moment to unsew his jaw. "It was Lord Edwin. He killed the Warden...to save me." He wiped away the tears off his face. "He's a hero. And that means he's also the Warden now."

Emerson blinked slowly before turning his attention on Edwin. Maybe Edwin hadn't heard right. "Wait...bloody *what?*"

* * *

Each time they tried to approach the giant leopard seal, he barked and lunged, showing off his lethal set of jagged teeth. Even Tommy was hesitant to approach at this point. The seal looked big enough to drag him under the water.

"Maybe we can knock him out?" Tommy suggested. "They must have tranquilizers of some kind around here."

Eliza shook her head. "I don't know where, and I'm not sure we can even get close enough to try."

"Maybe we can reason with him?"

"Does he look reasonable?"

The seal looked back and forth between them before growing quiet and relaxing its expression. *You'll take me out of here?*

It took Eliza a moment to realize the thought in her head was not her own. She looked to Tommy, who immediately said, "Aye, I heard it, too."

After summoning her courage, she slipped a step closer, remembering her time at Lord Ian's castle when the sleepwalkers—the half-Fae—were running about, causing havoc. The Fae, as she recalled, could communicate mentally with each other as well as other species—when they wanted to. Tommy laid a hand protectively on her shoulder, which she covered with her own. "Are you speaking, doctor?"

The seal's dark eyes flitted between them. Yes, of course! Will you take me off this floating brig? If you will, I shall come quietly.

"If you're willing to cooperate—to not attack us—then yes."

Dr. Pretorius relaxed visibly. Where do you plan to take me? I must know.

She looked at Tommy, then opted for the truth. He was going to find out soon anyway. "Uhh...to Captain Yrsa of the Jotnar. She says she needs your services. She sent us, in fact."

She watched Dr. Pretorius carefully, afraid he would simply jump back into his pool. They would never get him out then.

Yrsa! The leopard seal threw his head back and howled happily. *You have a deal. But first, I require something from Cold Storage.*

Eliza frowned at that. She vaguely recalled seeing that on the sand table map. "Cold Storage?"

It's the storage locker where they stow prisoners' possessions...as if they will ever get off this rig. Dr. Pretorius grunted. *I must have my human skin. I simply cannot leave it behind!* He made more of those grunting noises and added a flap of his flipper. *Find my skin and I will go willingly.*

Eliza felt a twinge. Cold Storage was in a completely different area of the rig. It was a huge delay and, so far, nothing was going to plan. "Tommy..."

"Let's just do it. Otherwise, we'll never get the hell out of here."

Sighing in agreement, she said, "I'll get it. You see to getting the doctor back to the ship."

"Wait...no. My Lady, it is far too dang—"

"No offense, Tommy, but you're damaged and slow. I'll be able to get in and out in no time." Before Tommy could protest further, she turned to Dr. Pretorius and said, "This is Special Agent Thomas Quinn, formerly of the DEA. Now the acting Enforcer for the Congress of Lord Edwin McGillicuddy. He will stay with you. Protect you. But I expect you to be kind to him."

Dr. Pretorius glared at the Colossus as if he was seeing just another kind of jailer.

She then turned to Tommy, who looked tired and injured, and said, "A word, please, Tommy."

They slipped back out into the corridor and Eliza said in a low whisper, "You have to watch him. See that he doesn't slip away. You're the only one who can do it." Glancing around, she added, "As you can see, bloody Foxley has dumped us."

Tommy sagged slightly. "But I can't leave you to such a dangerous mission!" He whisper-added, "Lord Edwin would annihilate me."

"I'll handle Lord Edwin." She patted his armored arm. "And if you see Edwin, and he asks where I got myself off to, just tell him I slipped away when your back was turned. He'll believe that."

* * *

Edwin sat on the edge of the deceased Warden's desk while Pagniash went about the task of bandaging the wound in his side, which, though ragged, wasn't deep, thankfully. After he was done, he dutifully cleaned the blood off Edwin's face from where his nose had been badly broken.

At the same time, the three of them were putting an interesting spin on Wincott's sudden demise.

"Lord Wincott came at me with the poker, but before he could reach me, Lord Edwin stepped in. He said, 'You won't be doing that here, chum.' Then he stabbed Wincott in the chest and my Lord just exploded." Pagniash explained as he finished up with the first aid kit. He was dressed in clothes they had found in Wincott's closet, and he had a blanket wrapped around his shoulders.

Emerson sat at the desk, his tablet in hand as he took down notes, looking from one of them to the other. Finally, he turned to Edwin and said, "And this is an accurate recounting of what happened, my Lord?"

Edwin winced and put a hand to his smarting nose. "No! I was—"

Emerson hissed between his fanged eyeteeth and gave Edwin a funny look. It finally dawned on Edwin what the bloodsucking bloodsucker was implying. If Pagniash was found to have killed his master, the High Courts would put the boy to trial in a kangaroo court and execute him. But if Edwin was the one who ended Wincott—perhaps because of some challenge or outrage—then, well, that meant...

Edwin sucked in a sharp breath and decided to play along. "Aye...aye, that was how it happened exactly. I stabbed him." He glanced at Pagniash, who nodded him on. "But only after I challenged him for control of the Oublies. The old boy didn't like that much."

Emerson nodded to this, his eyes shifting craftily. "And this was to save the young faun Pagniash?"

"And also because Wincott assaulted me once long ago. I was evening the score."

Another nod. "Excellent. So, what you're saying is you were offended by how Lord Wincott was treating his servant, and also for how he treated you once. You stepped in with a challenge for control of his court. Wincott accepted, and you dueled. You ended Wincott with this poker." He nodded to the weapon on the floor, still smoldering with Wincott's blood.

Turning to Pagniash, Emerson stated, "And you were a witness to this challenge."

"I was," Pagniash announced. He pointed to his face. "Will you be taking pictures?"

"I will." Emerson was stiff and businesslike as he typed up his report to the High Courts. "Will you swear an affidavit supporting your claim?"

"Yes." Pagniash nodded to Edwin. "Lord Edwin is my master now. And the Oublies belongs to his Congress."

Edwin felt his head spin—blood loss or the last few minutes, he couldn't be sure. "What just happened here?"

Emerson got that grin, that evil reptile grin that he only ever got when he knew he'd turned an otherwise terrible event to his favor. Getting up, he slapped Edwin on the shoulder. "You, my Lord, are now the new, proud owner of the Oublies, a for-profit prison whose revenue is over seventy-four billion a year—more than enough to support the *Queen's Gambit*. In fact, as of today—well, as soon as the High Courts process this report—you're one of the wealthiest vampires in the world, second only, perhaps, to Lord Foxley himself. Congratulations!"

Emerson showed Edwin his tablet and the Send button for the report. "You may have the honor, my esteemed Lord."

Edwin leaned forward and hit the button with a shaky finger, then stared at his lawyer long and hard. "I...I..."

"This is why you pay me the big bucks," Emerson stated. "You're welcome."

***

Eliza borrowed a tablet from a frozen Mech and summoned a diagram of the rig, looking for the Cold Storage Room. A part of her wished she could contact Edwin and tell him how their plans had changed, but all of them had agreed to radio silence for the duration of the mission, certain their transmissions could be intercepted. She was determined to finish before any of them were caught or, god help them, harmed, but it didn't make her worry any less.

Once she'd pinpointed it, she found a lift and took a long ride that went down, to the left, then to the right, then down again—for what seemed like hours. Soon, she felt like she was descending into the unknown depths of hell, and, for all she knew, she was. Basement level. Cold Storage. The place where the Oublies tossed their guest's belongings once they were incarcerated. Things that would never be found or claimed by anyone and were destined to rot for all eternity, or for however long the Oublies existed.

While on her way down, she started worrying about everyone once more. She wondered if she'd be able to save her ship, and if Ollie was okay even though she knew he was in excellent hands with his Uncle Malcolm. Most of all: Edwin. She couldn't help wondering how he was fairing, and she had to resist very hard the urge to open a communications line. She knew if she did, the CoreCivic home office would tap into it. No doubt, they already knew something was very wrong aboard the Vault and were sending a team to investigate. And the last thing she needed was their interference. At this point, they were probably in the process of rebooting the whole system to shake off her influence—because that was exactly what she would do.

Her fears were realized when the lift doors opened and she saw flashing red emergency lights in the darkened corridor. No sirens or voices or even any significant noises. But the lights were a dead giveaway that the rig was now on full alert—possibly even on lockdown. She had very little time to find what she'd come here for.

Racing down the corridors, she took a series of hairpin turns, trying to follow the badly worn etched marking in the walls that indicated where the labyrinth of hallways went. She panted, her feet pounding against the floor, her hair flying behind her, her eyes going everywhere at once. She didn't think security was going to be tight here; she didn't think anyone cared about this level.

She was wrong. She had to jerk herself to a sudden halt when she heard the familiar tapping of canine feet on the floor as she reached yet another intersection.

"Shit!" she hissed and ducked behind a corner.

The clinking noise grew louder. Eliza leaned against the wall to catch her breath, then slid closer to the edge and peered around.

A lone doggone was moving in a rickety fashion down the corridor. She wondered if they put the older models down here, or ones that just didn't work as well. It moved in a stinted, injured fashion, but it still looked intimidating with its large size and the way it stopped every few feet as if trying to sense if anyone was about. Maybe she could try zapping it the way she had the Mechipeople, but she couldn't detect any taser plates in the floor at this level. Shite, as Edwin would say.

The closer the doggone got, the more Eliza shirked against the wall. When it finally cleared the bend, she went stock still. She couldn't even breathe. She prayed it would keep going and not turn to look her way.

It took a few stumbling steps forward, then stopped, then a few more. *Click...click...clickety...click...*

Eliza's swallowed against her riding panic. *Keep going...please...!*

Unfortunately, it stopped almost as if it could hear her thoughts. She pressed a hand to her mouth to keep from breathing too loudly.

Another step. And then...it turned its body.

For one second, she was left staring at its strange headlessness.

It seemed stunned. Then a disembodied voice poured out of it: *"Stop, intruder. You are not authorized for this level."* It started toward her, but slowly in its limping way.

Eliza let out a squeak. "Authorize this!" She threw the tablet at the thing.

It was surprisingly fast. Before the tablet even connected with the doggone, its long shock stick emerged from its collar, lighting up the tablet in mid-air. Smoking and on fire, the device smashed to the floor.

Eliza stared at it all wild-eyed. Then she took off running.

* * *

Edwin, Emerson, and Pagniash were heading back to the transport, Edwin desperately hoping the others were waiting for them there, when they ran into Tommy and a giant seal in the corridor ahead of them. He and his companions skidded to a guarded halt to keep from colliding with the two giant beings.

Tommy turned, his eyes lighting up, and said, "My Lord!"

Edwin took a long moment to catch his breath—the strain of the running almost had him on his knees—coughed, and then cleared his throat. He turned his attention on the massive creature with Tommy. "What the fark is that?" And then it clicked. "That is not...not..."

"Dr. Pretorius."

It took Edwin a moment to digest that. Then he swore. "Right then. Where's my wife?"

Tommy winced. "Uh...that's an interesting story. She sort of...uh, you see..."

Edwin glared at his enforcer. "She went off on her own."

Tommy virtually cringed. "Lady Eliza has gone to Cold Storage to retrieve the doctor's human skin."

Edwin, stunned, took a moment to digest that. It was not a sentence he figured he would ever hear. "And you let her go?"

Tommy looked stricken. "She wouldn't listen to me!"

Edwin closed his eyes, pinched his nose, and then winced at the pain in his face. "Of course she didn't. Since when does she listen to anyone?" He then straightened up. He was the Lord of a vast Congress that now included a prison barge—though CoreCivic wasn't aware of that fact just yet since the High Vampire Courts needed to process the paperwork. It was time he acted like it.

"Right," he said, taking a deep breath and suppressing a cough. "Tommy, get everyone on the ship and wait for me. I'm going down to Cold Storage for Eliza."

Tommy nodded. "I understand, sir."

"And where the fark did Foxley go?" Edwin asked when he realized every member of his party was there except his favorite nemesis.

Tommy shook his head slowly. "I do not know, sir. He disappeared early on."

Edwin growled at the news.

Just then, the lights in the corridor started to flash red in warning. With a groan, Edwin turned. He couldn't worry about Foxley right now. He knew if it came down to it, Eliza could pilot them off this heap. He had to get his wife off this rig before his crazy chit wife got herself killed!

| xxii |

Eliza ran, and the fear ran with her.

Heart and feet pounding, she scurried down one corridor after another with no idea where she was going. All she knew was she had to lose the drone only a hundred feet behind her. The doggone was fast, but it was also off-kilter, its gait uneven—her only respite. She would race to the end of yet another endless grey corridor and hear the *tap-tap-clink-tap* of the doggone following, its voice calling out to her to halt immediately.

As if she would.

Ahead, she spotted a bank of lifts—no other escape. No side doors and all of the cell doors were securely locked. Swearing, she limped to the end of the corridor and smashed the button to open the lift. Then she heard the low moaning noise. The lift must have dropped from pneumatic pressure, which they often did on the *Queen's Gambit* when not in use. She hit another button on a different lift, then another. She hit them all.

Same. All the lifts were on the lower level!

Clink...clink...clink...clinkclinkclink...!

She felt the doggone at her back in the seconds before it sprang. But before it could, she swung around to face it—and the door of the lift shifted open behind her.

Eliza fell inward on her back on the grated floor of the lift, the doggone airborne for a moment as it landed atop her, its mechanical feet to either side of her head. Immediately, it lowered the shock stick toward her face.

Not knowing what else to do, Eliza reached up to grab the stick, a reflexive gesture, but one that saved her. The moment the metal pole touched her palms, she felt the discharge of electricity from the weapon. It was like a blast of radiant, painful fire that raced up both of her arms. Gritting her teeth to keep from screaming, she did what she had done many years ago while attached to an actual lighting rod atop Lord Ian's castle on the English moors while the Sleepwalkers attacked far below.

She couldn't create electricity, but ambient energy seemed particularly fond of her all the same. Catching the electrical fire in the shock stick, she molded it in her hands before sending it back to the doggone in one long, controlled burst.

The doggone lit up like a Christmas tree. Spark flew and chips of metal burned off and pinged off the walls of the lift. Then the entire drone burst into flames. Terrified it would catch her clothes or hair on fire, Eliza lifted both legs and kicked out, knocking the burning drone out of the lift and into the hallway beyond, where it crumpled into a pile.

She lay there, panting and smoldering slightly, listening to the doggone's tinny voice crying out in distress while the doors closed and the lift began to descend.

***

Edwin ran, and the fear ran with him.

The rig was an endless maze of corridors that all looked the same, and he decided that once all of the papers were signed and this pile was his, he would definitely get a team in to repaint these bloody annoying grey walls!

Ahead, he spotted one of the many locator maps on the wall, but this one, like all of them, was so old that it was nearly illegible. He traced the route to Cold Storage and saw he was nearly there. One more lift ride and then he had to go right and he would be right there at the doors!

"Right then." He took off running again, but this time it was more of a limping jog as his body labored and his bleeding cough came back. His side hurt like the dickens. He had to stop and take a dose off the inhaler before heading to the end of this corridor, the last leg before he reached the lifts.

A Mechi-person swung around the bend so suddenly that he barely had time to slow his roll before he plowed into it.

It eyed him savagely. Even though the rig was technically his, the guards didn't know that yet. "Halt, intruder!" it said, grabbing its shock gun and aiming it toward him.

Edwin had one moment to think. "Fuck it," he said and took off running right toward the Mech.

"Halt or die!" the giant Mech announced, its firearm making a threatening crackling noise as it cranked it to full capacity. Blue electricity danced along the stick—which was growing larger and larger in Edwin's vision as he dived at the guard.

"Halt now!" the Mech boomed and thrust the stick at Edwin, who, narrow and wiry, dropped to the floor with an oof, folded his arms, and slipped horizontally between the Mech's spread legs. The moment he cleared the Mech and skidded a few feet on, he popped back up, threw the Mech the bird, and took off running toward the bank of lifts.

The Mech turned, made a grinding, growling noise, and started after him. It was a fast brute for being a big tin can, and it covered ground much faster than Edwin could, but Edwin was ahead by several paces. By the time it reached the lifts, Edwin was already inside an empty car and waving at it as the doors closed and the lift began to descend.

* * *

Groaning with relief, Eliza threw the old-fashioned swing doors of Cold Storage open. She thought she'd never reach the place. But the moment she was inside the gigantic warehouse, she felt her earlier hopelessness return in spades.

The place was huge—easily the size of an airplane hangar—and immensely dark, lit up by only small lights very far up on the cathedral ceiling that shed hardly any illumination. Interconnected wooden cabinets created a new and even more elaborate labyrinth that cut through the dimly lit space. And they seemed to go on forever. In addition, books, loose papers, and various belongings were scattered throughout the place with no obvious rhyme or reason.

Eliza glared at the sheer walls of cabinets and the dusty junk heaped up everywhere and felt herself despair. How the hell would she *ever* find what she was looking for in this mess?

The slam of a drawer made her jump nearly out of her skin. Turning, she put her hands up, ready to fight if she had to even though she knew she was no match for a mechanical juggernaut.

A figure moved in the shadows to her left. She squinted through the moldy gloom, then hissed, "Whoever you are, I have a weapon!" Which was an outright lie.

An all-too-familiar laugh rang out. "No, madam, I know for a fact that you do not."

"Foxley?"

The monster himself stepped casually into a pool of sallow light. He wore an amused expression on his face, and tucked under one arm was a large stack of folders.

"What are you doing here?" she said, lowering her arms but not by much. Then she noticed the stack of files. "What are those?"

"Designs and patents."

"You're stealing them? From the prisoners?"

Foxley grinned cattily.

"Oh, my god, you are such a ghoul," she told him.

"And your intentions are, of course, altruistic," he said.

"I'm not stealing from the imprisoned, if that's what you mean." She consulted the locker number on her wrist that Dr. Pretorius had given her, then, without explaining further, went down the rows until she found the appropriate cabinet. She slid open the rolling drawers until she found what she was looking for—a metal security briefcase with a rotating lock on it.

She grabbed the handle and pulled, hefting it out—it was heavier than she expected—and then dropped it to the floor before putting in the code numbers. The briefcase made a hissing noise as it unlocked. She cracked it open and flinched at what was inside: pinkish-grey fabric all folded up.

Just then, the hangar doors banged open and Edwin charge into the room. He looked a mess, flustered and disheveled, with an ace bandage over his badly bruised nose. Scrapes and cuts decorated his face.

She gaped in a combination of happiness and horror. Happiness at knowing he was here. Horror at the sight of him. "Edwin! What happened to you?"

He took one look at her, limped toward her, and put his hands on her shoulders. His eyes brightened considerably as he kissed her quickly and then looked her in the eye. "Hallo, wife. Is that it?"

It took her a moment to respond. "Y-yes!"

He nodded and bent to pick up the briefcase. "Excellent. Time to go!"

"What?" She shook her head, perplexed.

He didn't respond, took her by the arm, and steered her to the door.

Seconds later, she, Edwin, and Foxley were back out in the corridor with the heavy briefcase swinging from Edwin's hand. Down a ways came the stomping of several pairs of feet. Edwin turned in that direction. "Bloody hell!"

"Edwin," she demanded, "what is going on?"

Without turning, Edwin explained. "The Warden is dead. The Vault is mine now. But our friends here don't know that yet because they didn't get the memo."

Eliza opened her mouth to ask just how in hell all of that was possible but then decided not to. Everywhere Edwin went, chaos was soon to follow, so she wasn't at all surprised by this sudden turn of events. "You're the Warden now?"

"That's correct."

"If you're the Warden, shouldn't you tell the Mechs? Make them obey you?"

Edwin shrugged. "I don't think these wankers can be reasoned with."

"You're probably right. We need to get out of here."

"Agreed."

The wankers he was referring to were heading their way. And they looked none too pleased: a solid wall of mechanical juggernauts, shock sticks raised high in their massive fists. Edwin shooed everyone back into the Cold Storage Room and closed and locked the doors.

All of them looked around for a possible escape route, but it was impossible to know which way to go. The room was crowded, dark, and too much of a bloody mess. If there was an exit, it was probably through the maze of cabinets. And there was no time to find it, either, as the army of Mechs was almost to the door.

Edwin moved to a cabinet and gave it a shove. It moved...minimally.

Foxley sighed at the sight, walked up to him, and eased him aside. Taking the cabinet in his arms, he lifted it off the floor as if it was made of feathers and flung it at the door, where it smashed to the floor and skidded ten feet to a stop.

Edwin gave her a nod, and Eliza jumped to it, pushing the cabinet, now lying on its side, the few inches to the door and against it. He joined her after the next cabinet was flung their way, and the two of them pushed that one against the other door. Foxley waltzed up to them with a third one in his arms and slammed it down on top of the first two. Edwin looked at the barricade, envy burning in his eyes. She could tell he missed being a vampire with all of the advantages attendant thereupon.

Stepping back, Edwin said, "I don't think that will hold them long."

"Just long enough," Foxley said, then added, "There's a door at the back, but I didn't open it."

"Why didn't you bloody say so?" Edwin cried, turning to him.

"You didn't ask," he answered and smiled, showing a hint of teeth.

With a growl of annoyance, Edwin took Eliza's hand, hefted the blood suitcase in his other, and swung around that way, letting Foxley take the lead. They followed the vampire through the weird warren of cabinets and into what seemed a deeper dark. Distantly, they both heard the slam of angry fists on the barred doors and the Mechs demanding they open them immediately. It made Eliza want to run headlong into the dark, but she could barely see the space ahead of them.

Foxley with his vampire eyes had an easier time navigating the darkness. There weren't just cabinets here but also large crates and boxes. Foxley periodically leaped to the top of a crate to check their location, then slipped down as smooth as butter and kept going, forcing Edwin and Eliza to limp along to keep up with him.

The pounding behind them was more insistent now. It was only a matter of time before the Mech stormed into the room.

"Where the bloody hell is this door, Foxley?" Edwin demanded, sounding testy in the near-perfect darkness.

"Not far. Just follow the sound of my voice."

He was moving fast now, twisting up and down the aisles, and Eliza, much smaller than Edwin, had to hurry to keep up. He was virtually dragging her by the time they reached a mostly straight corridor with some kind of door at the end. Eliza had to squint to recognize what it was under the too-dim lighting.

The door looked too small and was located several feet off the floor. She felt the first needlings of disappointment when Edwin reached out to grab the old-fashioned latch handle and rolled the door up. "That's..." she started and her fear was confirmed when she recognized the obsolete pulley system inside. "...a dumbwaiter."

Behind them came the sound of a bomb going off as the doors of the Cold Storage Room were ripped off their hinges and thrown into a bank of cabinets. Feet clattered across the floor in a military formation.

"Shite," Edwin whispered beside her in the dark. Turning to Foxley, he said, "Help me get her inside."

"No!" Eliza shouted above the crashing noises of the approaching Mechs as they shoved crates and cabinets out of their way. She started to fight in Edwin's hold. "I'm not going in!"

He pushed her toward the open dumbwaiter anyway. She grabbed his arm, her fingernails digging in, but even human and unwell, he was strong. "I'm not leaving you behind!" she insisted, twisting in his hold. "They'll kill you!"

"No, they will not," Foxley said calmly, watching the two of them struggle. He set his precious files down at his feet and stepped past them, stopping in the middle of the aisle. He slid off his uniform jacket and undid the cuffs of his shirt. He faced the corridor squarely, even kicked the ground. Turning slightly, he said to Edwin, "Put her in."

"Edwin, no!" she screamed.

She was still screaming when Edwin grabbed her by the waist and lifted her into the dumbwaiter. She fit well in a light crouch, but she gripped his shoulders, unwilling to let him go. He was insane if he thought he could face those machines!

"Please, lovey. Please," he insisted. He looked at her pleadingly with dark circle under his eyes and sniffed a few drops of blood that had started to drip from his broken nose. The sight of him sucked some of the fight out of her. "If something happens to me, who will protect Ollie?"

"That's not fair!" she cried, but her need to fight was starting to wane and she sagged. "Don't say that!"

"Just pull the pulley behind you. It will take you up," he instructed.

"Edwin!" Tears flew from her eyes. Her fingers clawed at his shoulders.

Tears shining in his eyes, he slowly let her go and stepped back. She didn't leap out. He was right. One of them had to keep Ollie safe.

Reaching for the briefcase, he set it down inside the dumbwaiter with her. "Tell Ollie I love him. And that I'm sorry!"

"Edwin!" The last thing Eliza saw was his sweet, battered face as he slid the door of the dumbwaiter down.

* * *

Forcibly blanking his mind of all thoughts of Eliza and Ollie, Edwin turned and faced the oncoming horde.

"This reminds me of Afghanistan and that opium dealer you upset so badly," Foxley said as the horde started down the narrow corridor of cabinets toward them.

Edwin, no fool, placed himself squarely behind Foxley. In another life, he would have stood shoulder to shoulder with his master, but he had no illusions about his weakened human body. He needed protection if he was going to survive this altercation.

"You slept with his daughter, didn't you?"

Edwin grunted as he rolled up his sleeves. There was a time long ago when everything seemed to be a delightful game. He sometimes missed those years of carefree, joyous chaos, but things had changed and the world had moved on, as it was wont to do. In just the last decade, he'd been forced to grow up fast. These days, he was a husband, a father, and a Vampire Lord. It was a sobering existence, not nearly as much fun as being Foxley's Enforcer, but he decided he liked who he had become. It suited him.

As the Mechs bore down on them, their footfalls shaking the whole room, he quieted his mind. He wasn't nearly as afraid as he'd feared he might be. Eliza was away, safe. He was doing this for her. And for Oliver. For his Congress. It was who he'd become.

The first Mech reached Foxley, a fury machine that towered high over Foxley's slender, boyish, five-foot-nothing frame. Foxley tilted his head up, looked the Mech in the eye—and grinned. It was the sadistic, shark-like grin that Edwin expected. The one that told him Foxley was going to enjoy this.

"I would not do that, child," Foxley said to the Machine-man.

The Mech laughed at him, at his use of the word "child," and thrust the shock stick in Foxley's face.

Foxley casually grabbed it, the voltage sparking along the metal rod and up his arm. He didn't seem to even feel the pain of it even though Edwin knew, even as a vampire, the voltage would have lit Edwin up like a Christmas tree. "That's the problem with you children. You don't respect your elders," Foxley said in a menacing tone. Turning in a surprisingly graceful pirouette, Foxley used the shock stick to lift the Mech straight off the floor, turned again to gain the momentum he needed, and flung the titan—easily half a ton in weight—at its fellows.

The impact was near-cataclysmic. The Mech struck the others like they were bowling pins, scattering them wide and knocking most into the cabinets all around. Those, in turn, exploded into shards of wood and flying sheets of paper and other debris. Edwin covered his face with his arm to protect himself. At the same time, the energy from the shock stick danced along the Mechs' metal bodies, making them jump and clash like a heap of garbage cans. It even arced briefly across the floor—though, because it was made of wood, Edwin only felt the vibration of it under his feet.

Foxley, in an act of utter contempt, picked up the shock stick and stuck it to the whole heap of Mechs lying together. The room lit up, sparks flying as the shock passed from metal body to metal body. The Mechs screamed in terrible pain and Edwin felt his hair stand on end. When the dust and debris cleared, he saw the dark heaps of smoldering metal bodies, some having melted together, and the wide ring of crushed and destroyed wooden cabinets.

"Bloody hell, Foxley!"

Foxley grinned. "That was fun."

They were barely able to recoup when the next wave arrived—Mechs accompanied by a half dozen doggones. The new Mechs took one look at the remains of their dead fellows and turned their rage-filled eyes on the two of them. The one in the front, some kind of appointed leader, pointed at them and gave the order to attack.

The doggones flew at the two of them.

Foxley, moving faster than Edwin had ever seen him, grabbed the first doggone by the collar as it lunged at his face. His fingers punched right through the metal and the drone whined. The second bounded over him and struck Edwin down, pinning him to the floor on his back. Edwin coughed in surprise and instinctively threw his arm up to fend off the drone, but there was no head or mouth to bite him. Instead, another stock stick emerged from its collar.

Edwin swore.

Seconds later, he sensed Foxley's presence. "You will not touch him," Foxley said in a deep, even, utterly terrifying tone of voice. He grabbed the doggone by the shock stick and twisted it around, bending the stick horribly. Electricity danced across his arm and lit up his face so he looked like some kind of demonic angel of electricity. Foxley didn't even blink at the pain. For one moment, he was captured in its illumination like he was wearing a halo. Then he wrenched the drone to one side, a gesture so violent, it ripped the doggone right in half. It sagged in his hand and Foxley dropped it in a burning heap, then turned his attention on the next one heading his way.

By then, Edwin was on his feet and backing away from two of the doggones who were working as a tag team to force him into a corner. Both had their shock sticks out, and the black balls at the ends of them spat with electricity that Edwin just knew could stop his heart on contact.

It sucked to have none of the vampire strengths that Foxley had. But then he recalled that just because he didn't have enhanced strength or flexibility didn't mean he didn't have skills honed from over two hundred years of life—much of it spent fighting one enemy or another.

Glancing around, he looked for a weapon he could use. Most of the debris scattered across the floor consisted of office supplies, but he did notice a banker's lamp lying on its side. He shifted that way, grabbed up the cord, and stepped on the lamp itself, ripping the cord loose in one gesture.

By then, one of the doggones was done playing and was airborne, heading right for him.

Edwin dodged left, missing a collision with the doggone by inches. That caused him to veer straight into the wall of cabinets on that side. Deciding to use that to his advantage, Edwin parkoured off the closest one, bounced the other way, and missed the second as it lunged. The second crashed into the first, and the two landed in a heap.

Foxley noticed and turned, a dead doggone dangling from his hand. "Nice."

At the same time, the last of the doggones sprang over Foxley, aiming for Edwin. He unfurled the cord in his hand, using it the same way he normally used his blood whip, and lassoed one of the drone's legs, slipping sideways and down and jerking the cord so the doggone twisted in midair. As soon as it was down, Foxley leveled a punch square at the center point of its body that caused it to explode into glittering metal shards that skittered off into the dark.

Edwin, having landed a few feet away from Foxley, dropped to his knees and wheezed with effort. The whole room teetered uncomfortably around him, and he wanted nothing more than to sink to the floor and into the nice, safe darkness leaking into the corners of his eyes, but the rest of the Mech army, looking enraged, started forward, guns drawn.

"We need to get out of here," Foxley insisted.

Edwin tried to get up but his footing slipped and he dropped back to his knees. "You go," he said. He wasn't going anywhere at this point.

Foxley went to him and gathered him into his arms like he was a child. Edwin flinched in alarm, but Foxley was surprisingly gentle. Leaning forward, he folded his wings protectively over them both.

Edwin sucked in a sharp breath when the Mechs opened fire with their boomers, the impacts making them both shudder with each massive punch. Foxley endured, grunting in pain, and after a few seconds, Edwin saw pinpricks of light as the boomers started to shred his wings. His master's head nodded forward and his eyes closed.

"Foxley!"

* * *

When Eliza pulled on the simple pulley line, the car of the dumbwaiter went up a few inches—but only a few. She had to pull and pull to get it up to the next level. But even though she was quickly tiring out, she knew she couldn't stop or even take a break. She had to get to the next floor so she could get out of this damned thing, find Tommy, and then the two of them could rejoin what was surely a frighteningly close battle down below. From the muffled ruckus, it sounded like trashcans being throwing thrown against the walls. She only hoped that none of the bodies being thrashed about were Edwin's.

She was panting like a marathon sprinter when she spied light peeking from a crack above. A few more hearty pulls in the musty darkness and she felt the car "settle" into place. Reaching out, she slid the rolling door up, emerging in some kind of small alcove full of racks of books and folders. A record storage room? She didn't know. She did hear metallic knocking and what sounded like a propane torch hissing from the next room.

Grabbing up the damned briefcase, she tiptoed in the dark, making it to a partially open sliding door. She peered into the crack. The adjacent room looked like a large operating theater of some kind. A metal table took up a great deal of the space, with a large, round surgical light hanging down over it and illuminating the body of one of the Mech-people laid out. Another Mech stood over the body of the first, working on an elbow joint with an acetylene torch. Sparks flew as the Mech worked, supremely intent on its work.

Was it repairing one of the Mechs she had broken? Or was this a brand new Mech?

Did the Mechi-people make their own soldiers here?

She didn't know. But it looked like a good opportunity to sneak past.

She couldn't make a run for it—not if she was going to smuggle the bulky briefcase out. Noting the placement of the surgical mirrors in the room, Eliza got down on her hands and knees and started worming her way past the furiously engaged Mech, trying to slide the metal briefcase across the floor as silently as possible. There was one moment when she was crawling directly behind it and it paused.

Eliza was sure it could sense her. She grew very still and felt the little hairs stand up on the back of her neck. Then the Mech leaned down even farther to concentrate on the joint. Taking a deep breath, she crawled faster, relentlessly pushing the briefcase ahead of her, until she made it to the door on the opposite side of the theater.

Scrambling up onto her knees, she gripped the door latch and slid it slowly open, peeked outside to make certain the coast was clear, and then crawled out into the empty corridor even as a huge wave of relief washed over her, making her feel almost giddy with victory. Lunging to her feet, she hefted the almost too-heavy briefcase and started to run full tilt toward a distant bank of lifts.

She didn't sense the presence until it was too late and the Mech appeared at the intersection of two corridors. This one was different from the others, newer. A tall, slender female, light on her feet, suddenly snagged Eliza by the hair.

"There you are!"

Eliza screamed and flailed. The briefcase flew out of her hands and slid down the corridor. She grabbed at the Mechi-woman's breastplate, her fingernails screeking over the metal. But the Mech didn't seem to care.

"Invader, you will be upgraded," it told her and started dragging her despite her kicking and screaming protests back toward the operating theater.

* * *

"Extreme prejudice!" one of the remaining Mechs announced, aiming his boomer at Edwin, who was lying on the floor, but he seemed less sure now.

Edwin swallowed hard—it felt like a walnut was stuck in his throat—and shifted back as the Mech and one of his fellows moved purposefully forward, skating around the eviscerated remnants of their chums to close in on him.

A battered Foxley slid in front of him, letting out a rattling growl that caused the Mechs to hesitate. In the last five minutes, Foxley had torn through the small army of Mechs like a junkyard dog with a toy, ripping limbs and even, in one case, a whole head off. Since then, the Mechs had slowed and begun to eye the two of them more cautiously.

Foxley, his wings shredded and bloodied and looking barely human, sank into a crouch, one hand flat to the floor. He spread his shattered wings demonically, his eyes all black as he eyed the next group of Mechs about to fall upon them. The front of his shirt was drenched in the greenish fluid that spurted from the Mech's ripped-open bodies, but there was also blood from his own injuries on his face, which he licked now with a long black tongue.

He'd been impressively relentless, like an unstoppable hydraulic machine that didn't know the definition of quitting. Edwin still hated his master with every fiber of his being, but he was seriously impressed by Foxley's fighting skills.

"I had no idea you were capable of this," Edwin squeaked out.

"I'm an Old One, one of the most powerful vampires in the world. Why do you think Trasch won't challenge me openly even though the old lizard wants me dead?" Foxley chuckled.

Edwin believed him—even if he did think Foxley was being pretentious.

The two Mechs in front rushed him as one.

Foxley casually stood up, making it look like a coordinated dance step, and stepped forward, moving with a lightness that belied the strength in his small body. As the two Mechs bent into their assault, he met them head-on so quickly that Edwin could barely follow the motion. Foxley grabbed both Mechs by the throats, and before either one of them could so much as raise their shock sticks, he lifted both giants off the floor and thrust downward, one Mech in each hand, so they crashed into the floor on their backs. The impact was so powerful, their bodies simply imploded from the force of the concussion.

Metal plates and circuitry flew in every direction. Their arms and legs simply disconnected from their bodies, leaving them helpless on the floor. The remaining Mechs moved more slowly, but they still managed to hem them in on all sides.

One of the shock sticks from the now decimated Mechi-people lay inches from Edwin's booted feet. He scooped it up and switched it on, and as one of the Mechs rushed him, he adopted the en garde position just as his instructors had taught him back in the day and thrust the stick like a rapier into the center of the Mech's chest, lighting it up and blowing a hole right through it.

Edwin leaped backward as it fell, but it wasn't quite done yet. It reached out with one massive hand and clutched his ankle, upending him. Edwin yelped and fell on his back. At the same time, the huge juggernaut moved faster than it had any right to, and, within seconds, it was upon him, its huge hand clutching his throat. Edwin choked as he felt his fragile human throat being pinched. He grabbed at the Mech's hands, but his pathetic human fingernails just slid off the metal.

As he began to choke, he also began to fight reflexively, but it was useless. The creature was too powerful. And as much as it was a machine, a part of it was human, he knew, and that part wanted revenge for what he and Foxley had done to its friends.

"You die now," the Mech rumbled and applied more pressure.

Edwin's mind whirled with regrets, mostly about not being able to see Eliza and Ollie again. He started to say a prayer, but then the pressure lessened.

The Mech was looking him in the eye, but the light in its eyeholes blinked out for a second, then came back on. All of the Mechs around him seemed to haze out for a moment. Then his Mech released its hold on his throat and Edwin could almost sense the shift in its posture.

The Mech suddenly started to shake, and its voice came out contrite. "L...Lord Edwin?" it said, sounding appalled by what it was doing.

Edwin, stunned, just lay there on the floor as the metal behemoth scrambled off of him and stood up, weaving slightly with the gaping hole in its chest.

"Lord Edwin," it said again after a few moments. It offered him its hand in a friendly manner. "We are at your service."

Gasping with relief, Edwin fall back, letting the back of his head clunk on the floor. CoreCivic had finally received the paperwork!

* * *

"Let go of me, you metal twat!" Eliza screamed as the female Mech wrestled her down onto the cold metal surgical table. She growled and twisted and even got a few good kicks in. But it was like kicking a metal flagpole. It hurt her leg but the Mech didn't seem to care at all.

"You will be upgraded."

"When my husband finds out you 'upgraded' me, he's going to kick your ass!"

The Mech put its big hand over her mouth, muffling her cries. It also kept her pinned in place as another Mech, the same Mech that had been soldering the broken guard earlier, tottered up to her. "The human is making strange noises. Is she a criminal?"

"She broke into the Oublies," the female intoned. "She is a criminal."

The other Mech looked down upon Eliza sadly. "I am sorry, human. Why would you choose this?"

The first Mech removed her hand. "I didn't choose it!" Eliza screamed.

"I am Violet. A new Mech," the female explained. "You must choose to be upgraded."

"That's what I'm trying to tell you!" Eliza insisted. "I didn't choose!"

"If you did not volunteer, what are you doing here?"

Eliza opened her mouth to answer, then realized she had no excuse.

"She has great spirit," the other Mech insisted. "I believe we should upgrade her."

Eliza was about to start fighting all over again when the two Mechs suddenly both stopped moving or speaking and their heads dropped down like they had been deactivated. Eliza didn't understand it, but here was the chance she needed to wiggle out from under the hand of the Mech working as a flesh mechanic.

Unfortunately, it was a tight squeeze. She wished she hadn't been so indulgent with those chocolate digestive biscuits that Edwin always gave her!

Finally, after really twisting this way and that, she dropped off the edge of the table and onto the floor on her hands and knees, scuffing herself up. With a grunt, she worked to get to her feet. If it was the last thing she did, she would get out of this funhouse of the damned.

She limped toward the door of the operation theater and then out into the hallway. And stopped.

"Oh, hell!"

The hallway was full of Mechs, all in frozen postures like they were listening to something only they could hear. Could she slip between their massive bodies? She supposed she had no choice...

Someone came up behind her. She spun around, then threw herself backward and away from Violet as the Mechi-woman approached her, her hands up to show she meant no harm. "Lady Eliza!"

Eliza hesitated and glanced around, wondering how Violet knew her name.

The Mechi-people in the corridor suddenly came to life once more. One by one, they straightened up and turned their vaguely humanoid heads to her. "Lady Eliza," they said, and "My Lady."

Eliza stumbled around, glancing at each of them, then turned back to face Violet. She had no idea what was going on. "Violet? What's happening?"

"There was an update...well, more like an upgrade from home office just now," Violent explained.

She gently, almost gracefully, dropped to one knee and bowed her head respectfully, a hand to her heart. Her eyes blazing with light, she said, "You are Lady Eliza, the wife of Lord Edwin, the

Warden of the Oublies. And we, the Mechi-people, live to serve you, my Lady."

| **xxiii** |

The Mechs insisted on escorting their "Lady Eliza" to her ship themselves, but she still didn't entirely trust them. What if their programming went haywire again and they turned on her? And yet, somehow, she trusted Violet, who was a very new Mech and seemed to be less under CoreCivic's control.

On the way to the Hummingbird, Violet explained that she had only been upgraded the day before. She did it to cut the one-hundred-year-plus sentence she had been handed down by the judge. "And you chose...this?" Eliza questioned as they made their way in the lift down to the loading bay.

Violet turned to glance down at her. "I served twenty-one years alone in a ten-by-ten cell. I just could not tolerate the isolation any longer."

Eliza almost commented that what Violet was living in now—her synthetic body—was as much of a prison as her cell but decided to hold her tongue. She had no idea what it was like to be thrown into a cell on the Oublies, the "place of forgetting," and be left to rot for decades. She had no right to judge Violet's decision to become a Mechi-person.

The doors of the lift slid open, and the first thing she saw was Edwin waiting for her on a loading dock in front of their ship. With a screech of triumph, she launched herself at him. He managed to catch her, but then both of them landed on the floor with her atop him.

He looked a mess, his clothes torn and bloodied, and he had fresh bruises on his face.

"What happened to you?" she asked in outrage.

He grinned sheepishly. "Almost died."

"I was almost upgraded."

"Right. You win."

She laughed and kissed him, and he laughed, too. It was perfect.

* * *

The Mechi-people, now under Edwin's control, announced they were loyal to him and his Congress. Violet even kissed his figurative ring.

The first thing Edwin did was arrange transportation for Pagniash, who wanted as far away from the Oublies as he could get. Next, he assigned a transport to Dr. Pretorius for his return to the Midnight Sun. The tall, shady-looking fellow, now wearing his human skin, looked positively bubbly at the idea of rejoining the Jotnar. At his side swung his trusty security briefcase, this time containing his seal skin.

Edwin assigned Mechi-people to pilot both transports. As a politically neutral people, he didn't think they would have any issue completing their tasks.

One of Violet's people offered to pilot Edwin's Hummingbird back to the *Queen's Gambit* since Foxley had disappeared after the battle in the Cold Storage Room—off on "another of his little adventures," Edwin guessed. He felt a kind of relief about that. If Foxley had hung around, he might have to thank him for saving his life, and he wasn't sure his pride could handle that.

Edwin and Eliza retreated to the back of the transport. Immediately after takeoff, she had Edwin lie down in one of the narrow bunks that could be used for sleeping during long flights. It wasn't the most comfortable, with a thin cushion to sleep on, but he looked too exhausted to care.

She was more worried about him than she wanted to say. Retrieving a first aid kit from off the wall, she set about doctoring his various scrapes and bruises. He winced more as a human than he ever did a as vampire.

"Reminds me of that time in the hotel," he said, referring to the first time she had done this, after his encounter with the Clockwork Man. It was also the first time they had made love, and it had lit up the room in both a real and figurative way.

"You need it more now than you did then. You're a lot less fangier."

He laughed at that, then started a fit of coughing while she applied astringent to a cut above his eyebrow.

"You're going to need your nose reset. They might even have to re-break it."

Ignoring her dire prognosis, Edwin curled an arm around her shoulders and dragged her down onto the bunk with him so he could rest his forehead against hers. "I'm glad you're here."

She moved to swab a particularly nasty gash on his cheek that might need a stitch or two, and he flinched and hissed a small curse through his lips.

"You don't enjoy being human very much, do you?"

He groaned and closed his eyes. "I've forgotten how hard it is...how much it hurts." He stayed quiet a long moment and then swallowed nervously before saying, "I have this thought. Do you want to hear it?"

"It's a three-hour flight back to the ship. I'm all ears."

"Hmm. Well, what if the three of us ran away—you, me, and Ollie."

"What do you mean 'run away?'"

"I have friends all over the world. People who owe me favors. We could abandon the Plan, leave the *Queen's Gambit* behind, and strike out on our own. I'm not saying it would be easy. But we could be a family. A human family." He hesitated before adding, "No High Courts. No vampires. No bollocks."

Her lips parted and she swallowed hard when she realized he was being serious. "Just walk away? But who would run the Congress?"

Edwin shrugged. "It's a Congress, lovey. Someone will take it over. There's too much of a power vacuum for someone not to fill it."

She swallowed hard when she realized he'd given this much more thought than she'd realized. "That's a lot of power—a lot of protection—to give up."

Another shrug. "We'll protect Ollie. We'll protect each other." Then he sighed. "I never wanted to be head of a Court or a Congress. I never wanted the *Gambit*. Or the *Abraxas* or the Oublies." He stroked his thumb down her cheek. "I only want you and Ollie. A simple life."

She smiled at that—a little wistfully.

"Imagine it. I could be a real dad to Ollie. Make up for all of the time that was lost to us. I could be a proper husband to you. And maybe I can get back to writing some terrible books full of sex and gunfights. That would be delightful."

She grinned as she imagined it, couldn't help herself. The three of them running off to have adventures of their own. Flying away to unknown parts of the world. Being a family at last—a *real* family. It recalled the good old days of them living in their humble townhome in New York. It was the last time they were truly happy.

The prospect of having no Supernaturals in their lives was beyond tempting. Foxley implied that both she and Ollie were vampires-in-waiting, and she knew in her heart that it wouldn't take much to activate their dormant genes. A terrible tragedy or an unfortunate accident. But if they were never put in a position where that ever had to happen...?

"But you're mortal like this," she whispered. "We both are. We'll die in time."

Edwin's eyes seemed full of light as he grabbed her hand and kissed her Claddagh ring. "No! First, we'll have grand adventures, then we will grow old together. And *then* we will die—after having raised our son into a good man. We will have had what every human on the planet longs for."

"What you long for?" she told him pointedly.

He grew silent at that, his eyes solemn.

She always knew it was in him—that need for a human life. Could she really deny him this chance? Should she even deny herself? She thought about that a long, silent moment. Edwin could shrug off the life of a vampire gangster that he never really wanted, and she and Ollie could be free of Summersfield's influence forever. Summersfield, or his essence—whatever it was that haunted them—could not come to collect them if they were never his. Never vampires. If she and Ollie remained human, if they died human, they would never be his Heirs.

Sitting up, she looked down at him. "It's a lot to consider."

"But you're tempted."

Settling back down beside him—the fit was tight in the narrow bunk, but she didn't mind—she kissed him gently so as not to aggravate his bruises. "Of course, I am." Turning slightly so she was on her back, she liberated the now crumpled envelope she'd been carrying around with her for days.

Edwin took immediate notice and said, "Is that it?"

She glanced aside at him and nodded. "I was going to wait until everything was settled, but after everything that happened today, I don't want to wait a moment longer." She held the envelope up as she slid the sheet of data out. Before unfolding it, she took his hand.

He helped her unfold it. There was a pie graph on one side with a stack of data on the other.

They looked it over together for some time, studying the genetic material that made Eliza who she was. Of course, the corporation that made her had drawn from a huge and varied pool of genetic material. But just because that was so didn't mean she didn't have real roots somewhere.

Finally, she spoke. "I'm seventy-one-point-four percent South African."

He added, "And fifteen-point-three percent Southeast Asian."

The other small remaining percentages were nonspecific European or unknown.

She didn't know why, but tears burned her eyes as she read over the information again, studied it, memorized it. "I'm African and Asian, Edwin." Looking over at him, she added, "I know that probably doesn't mean a whole lot, but...I have a people. I mean...I actually have a culture. A heritage. Like a real human."

"Of course it matters. And, I've told you in the past, you are real. A real human, lovey."

She pressed the DNA results that Edwin had so thoughtfully given her—the best gift she had ever received—to her heart. Her tears then were happy ones.

"Happy birthday to me!" she said before the two of them drifted off to sleep.

* * *

Eliza agreed to his crazy plan. She even called it "their plan."

They returned posthaste to the *Queen's Gambit* to learn Yrsa made good on her parley promise and deactivated the cryo-bomb embedded in their engine. It took the engineers a few hours, but they managed to safely remove the Icepick.

After overseeing the operation, Edwin snuck back to Eliza's quarters and, together, they finalized their plans. They decided to turn the operation of the Congress over to Malcolm and his wolves. They agreed he was the best man for the job. Then they took Oliver aside and explained what was going to happen next. Oliver was naturally sad to have to say goodbye to his friend Ariel, but Eliza promised him he could stay in touch with her by letter and mind text.

The very next day, Edwin, Eliza, and Oliver escaped the *Queen's Gambit* on board a Hummingbird and traveled around the world for a time, having all kinds of exciting adventures. They finally settled in north Cornwall, on England's rugged southwestern tip. There he and Eliza built their own little cottage by hand. It was situated on the rocky, black sand beach, with a beautiful view of the crashing Celtic Sea that they could see right from their windows.

Edwin continued to write in his *Doctor Blood* series, whose rights were eventually purchased for movies and television. It allowed them the financial freedom to follow their more esoteric dreams. In time, Edwin dedicated himself to serious mainstream novels, mostly epic historical dramas (which never got as popular as his pulp novels, but that was all right), while Eliza managed his properties. She was very good at entertainment law and eventually went back to school for her diploma, passing the bar on the first try. She even opened a private practice for a time.

Their son Oliver, extremely advanced for his age, left them at sixteen to study at the Imperial College in London. There he majored in mechanical engineering, eventually finding a rotating job as a flesh mechanic on board a number of gyros. He was very good at what he did and was in high demand. Eventually, he settled down with a delightful young man, and he and his husband raised their two sweet little daughters—Edwin and Eliza's grandchildren—who often came to stay with them when their parents were on extended missions.

Edwin adored his granddaughters. He loved spending time with them, giving them shoulder rides across the sand dunes and playing old-fashioned card and board games with them on rainy afternoons. He always let them win. They were the apples of his eyes.

Edwin and Eliza had grown older by then and were in their sixties. Retired. They didn't leave the cottage very often. Edwin needed bifocals to read the thousands of books he filled their home with. Eliza had never been much of a homemaker, but she tried. She often burned the pies and cakes she tried to bake. When it happened, Edwin laughed it off and just opened a window for ventilation. Eliza's grandbabies (and great-grandbabies) thought everything she made tasted good, and that was all that mattered.

At the end of the day, they could often be found sitting in matching rocking chairs on the back porch, facing the beach and the sea, Edwin with a book, and Eliza with her knitting. Sometimes, they held hands while they talked about the many mad adventures they'd had in their younger years. Eliza laughed because she couldn't believe they had survived any of it. Edwin just felt lucky to have the family he'd always longed for and the freedom he used to think was out of reach.

Edwin and Eliza died old, within days of one another, the one refusing to live without the other. They felt they were extremely blessed, for the supernatural had chosen to never again darken their door...

***

"Lord Edwin? Lord Edwin, we have a problem."

Edwin jerked awake to the sound of the sea still crashing in his ears. He sat up and looked around Eliza's bedroom, confused as to why he wasn't in the little cottage on the coast with Eliza. It took a moment for him to orient himself and remember what had happened. After he and Eliza disembarked the shuttle, he'd almost collapsed from blood loss and all of the exertion aboard the Oublies. Although he knew he was slowly getting better, he still wasn't quite himself. Eliza insisted he rest up in the upstairs bedroom of her personal quarters while she packed for their little family's great escape. She'd been excited about what adventures awaited them.

He squinted at the light pouring red and gold through the large, stained-glass portal window, then checked the bedside clock: He'd only been asleep a couple of hours.

Blinking up at his lawyer, he said, "What's happened, Emerson?"

Emerson opened his mouth and then closed it. There was blood on his hands and face and what looked like several tears in his suit. A horrifying deep bite mark shone red and black in the side of his neck. Eliza stepped into the room behind Emerson, looking concerned about the vampire lawyer's sudden appearance in her apartment.

Emerson looked even paler than usual and his eyes glowed feverishly in the dim room. "Sir...it's...I don't want to upset you, but...it's...uhh..." Emerson seemed to choke and a drop of black blood poured from the corner of the vampire's mouth.

"Bloody hell, Emerson!" Edwin demanded, sitting up and rubbing his face at the horrifying sight of his lawyer gurgling and finally flopping forward onto the bed. There were huge, shark-like bite marks in Emerson's lower half, and part of the lawyer's intestines unraveled onto the bed right in front of Edwin like sausages.

Edwin flinched and jumped up even though his human body ached terribly.

The last thing Emerson said before he succumbed to his injuries and fell upon Edwin was "Fr...frozen..."

| xxiv |

The Queen's Gambit, 24 hours earlier

Carl, Dr. Vu's assistant, was feeling literary like the dog's breakfast as he carded himself into the lab that morning. He hadn't slept, he had a massive headache, and he was certain he had picked up whatever bug Dr. Vu and the rest of the lab workers had.

His boss hadn't looked well the day before—pale, with dark rings under her eyes. Feeling sorry for her, he had brought her tea and aspirin, but it didn't seem to help. Finally, she had gone home, leaving Carl to finish their work for the day.

Now, Carl had it, whatever it was. He almost called off work, but there were so few workers on duty, he knew the healthiest among them had to show up, even if it was to med up on painkillers and sleep it off on the ratty brown corduroy couch in the employees' lounge.

"Dr. Vu?" he called as he stepped into the lab, his white coat over one arm. It was unusually cold in the lab this morning. He wondered who had tampered with the lab's temperature control. The temp flux probably ruined their samples from the day before, which made him grumble.

"Dr. Vu!" he said louder as he passed through the various rooms and headed for the research lab with the glass box in it where Dr.

Vu spent most of her time these days. She was seemingly obsessed with their Jotnar specimen, not that he could really blame her. And she was always the first in the lab in the morning.

His anxiety bounced up a notch when he stepped into the room. He could see right away that the door of the glass box was open, cold air steaming out into the relative warmth of the lab. He gaped at it for a long moment before dropping his coat on the floor. It took him a moment longer to find his voice. "D...Dr. Vu?"

"Carl?"

He swung around suddenly, expecting to find his boss standing there. Instead, she was crouched low to the floor and glaring up at him. Her skin was dark blue and her eyes bright white. He almost didn't recognize her.

And standing beside her in all his towering blue fury was their Jotunn. Gorm. He was watching Carl carefully with his red-rimmed eyes and, at the same time, petting Dr. Vu on the head like she was a pet dog.

"Dr...Vu?" Carl choked on his words but eventually figured out a way to try and scream for help. Unfortunately, the Jotnar moved much faster than he could. A simple swipe of his giant hand ripped the bottom portion of Carl's jaw off in one move. Carl choked on his own blood and screams and fell back onto the icy floor, blood pouring from his face.

Dr. Vu, no! was what he would have said, had he a mouth to say it.

Dr. Vu, or the thing Dr. Vu had become, skittered forward, clicking her teeth together ravenously at the sight of the pool of blood forming under Carl's head. Her jagged-toothed smile was the last thing Carl ever saw.

* * *

The Queen's Gambit, *now*

Edwin, his blood thudding uncomfortably loud in his ears, looked down at the dead and eviscerated vampire lying across his bed, then turned to Eliza. She was still standing in the door, rooted to the spot in shock and confusion. After a moment, Edwin said in a surprisingly calm voice, "Where's Ollie?"

"He's at school."

"Get him and get to a Hummingbird. Now."

Eliza's paralysis broke and she nodded. "What about you? Are you coming?"

"I have to warn the crew. Get a distress call out. But I'll be right behind you."

He was horribly afraid she wouldn't listen, that she would insist on staying with him, but since someone had to fetch Ollie, it wasn't even a contest. "I expect to see you in the passenger bay," she insisted. "I won't leave without you."

"I'll be there," he promised, slipping on his robe and tying it over his pajama bottoms. He had no idea where his slippers were, but he wasn't going to sweat the small details. Not with this emergency. "Now go fetch Ollie!"

Once she was gone, Edwin turned to look at Emerson, who was lying half on and off his bed. Bite marks and razor-deep scratches covered his body. He had bled out from the most grievous of his wounds. Edwin didn't even need to question what had caused them. He recognized the wounds as similar to the ones the bodies carried on board the *Abraxas*.

"Hell," he whispered as he pulled the bedcovers up and over his dead solicitor. He never liked Emerson, but he didn't deserve this.

Squaring his shoulders for the battle ahead, Edwin hurried from the bedroom.

Eliza wasted no time getting to a lift and hitting the right button for the Learning Center. The ride, which in reality maybe lasted three minutes tops, seemed to take forever, and she found herself muttering under her breath, urging the lift to hurry, hurry.

The ship was infected. Somehow and in some way, the ship was infected.

The lift doors were not even fully open before she shouldered her way out and dashed down the corridor, which was usually crowded with students and teachers at this hour of the day. Only a few people were staggering around—human guards and a few parents who looked ill and on the verge of collapse. She banged between them like a pinball, some of them reaching for her blindly as she slipped by. All of them looked pale and icy, their eyes swimming in their faces as they slammed into walls and each other.

Whatever it was, the infection was spreading. It had been spreading for some time.

Ice, Emerson had said. *Ice vampires...*

As soon as she reached the Learning Center, she slowed down, sucking in a sharp breath as she burst through the doors and into the hallways. She spotted Anjou, Malcolm's mate, who was already there. The woman was being forced back against a long line of lockers by Ms. Stafford, Ollie's teacher, who had her hands wrapped around Anjou's throat and was snapping her jaws in Anjou's face.

Without even thinking about it, Eliza launched herself at Ms. Stafford, colliding with the woman and kicking her down onto the floor. Ms. Stafford immediately sat up but seemed to be having trouble finding her feet. As she started crawling toward Eliza on hands and knees, making an unnerving sound by clicking her jaws together, Anjou jumped in and grabbed the woman by the head, snapping her neck with her preternatural wolf strength so the woman gurgled and went limp in her arms.

Anjou's eyes were bright and wild as she released the body and turned to Eliza. "Eliza! Have you seen—?"

"I know!" she said, looking down at the body of Ollie's teacher. She was vibrating with fear and trying very hard to keep from panicking. She glanced around the hallway where several more teachers lay, some with terrible bite wounds in them. "The whole ship is infected with that virus. Where's Ollie?"

"We have all of the children in the art room. They don't seem to be infected." Anjou sighed as she glanced down at the remains of Ms. Stafford. "Malcolm is watching them. I volunteered to see if the coast was clear."

"Obviously not!"

"How is the rest of the ship?" Anjou looked to the double doors that led to the lifts.

Eliza recalled the people in the corridor who were grabbing at her as she passed. "We can't go that way. It's filling up fast. We'll need to take the stairs."

Nodding, she said, "Stick with me."

Together, they headed to the art room. All fifty-plus kids from the school were crammed into it. The older ones were in the back, comforting the little ones, who were coloring or playing with Legos. Malcolm paced the room in wolf form, guarding everyone.

Ollie's eyes lit up on spotting her and he started running to her.

She felt a wave of relief such as she'd never known before. She gathered her boy against her, hugging him against her furiously pounding heart. She couldn't help herself; she kissed his head even though she knew he hated public displays of affection before turning to face Anjou, standing beside her. "Thank you," she sniffed, tears in her eyes. "Thank you for keeping them safe."

Anjou nodded. "We just learned about the infection about a half hour ago," she confirmed. "We decided we had to get the children down to the visitor's bay and off the gyro, but we didn't know how bad the infection was."

Malcolm, who had quickly shifted back to human form, was buttoning up his shirt and pants as he approached them. "We did not want to risk the children's safety out in the corridors if things had gotten bad."

Eliza nodded to him, touched by his consideration not just for his own children, but for her son and the others. "It's good you stayed," she said voce sotto as to not upset the children any further than they already were.

Letting go of her boy, she took Anjou and Malcolm aside. "Those things eviscerated Emerson." She took a deep breath and swallowed before voicing her worse fear. "And I think they've begun to mobilize like on the *Abraxas*."

Anjou looked horrified by the news and went to scoop her infant son up off the floor where he was chewing on a wooden block. She turned to Malcolm. "We need to do something!"

He nodded as he finished dressing. His eyes drifted to where two of the younger children had started a fight on the floor, both of them on edge. "I don't think we can get all of the children safely out of here. Just our own might be doable, but the whole school...?"

"We're not leaving *anyone* behind," Eliza insisted and Anjou nodded. "We'll barricade the doors. Hold them off as long as possible until reinforcements arrive."

Anjou, nodding, turned to Eliza. "Agreed. Making our stand here makes more sense. Where is Lord Edwin?"

"He's gone to warn the rest of the ship and to try and get a distress call out. But I don't know if he succeeded." She swallowed as a terrible feeling rushed through her. "I don't even know if he's well enough to do that."

Malcolm perked up at that news. "If you and Anjou can protect the children, my Lady, I can go find Lord Edwin and lend support."

Anjou, pale and narrow-eyed, turned and sank her fingernails into the front of his shirt. "Malc, I don't want you out there! What if those things get in?"

"They won't get in if you barricade the room after I'm gone."

Eliza nodded, her eyes already shifting to the heaviest furnishings like the filing cabinets and the teacher's desk. "We'll build a good barrier," she assured Anjou. "They won't get in. I'll die before I let those things get our children."

Malcolm looked on her with pride. "My Lady," he said, taking her hand. "I swear I will find Edwin. And I will protect him."

* * *

Edwin was almost to the bridge when Tommy suddenly appeared, falling into lockstep with his master. He was carrying a large sonic rifle over one shoulder, and he looked like he meant business.

"Ship's infected," Edwin informed him.

Tommy grunted in acknowledgment.

"I expect you're immune?"

"I believe so, sir. You?"

"No farking way. I'm pretty sure whatever is affecting the humans is airborne. Also, I'm human now."

Tommy gave Edwin a concerned look.

"We'll worry about that later. One crisis at a time, mate."

Tommy nodded.

Together, they hurried to the bridge, marching past several of Edwin's former guards, most of which were either staggering around ill or sitting or lying on the floor. Some were twitching and gurgling, their skin darkening moment by moment to that weird, alien indigo-blue color he associate with the ice vamps. The ensigns in the floating stations looked to be holding on by a thread.

One of the bridge guards made a grab at Edwin as he made his way across the floor, but Tommy's reflexes were on point. He grabbed the man and flung him away like he was a rag doll, allowing Edwin to approach Captain Enzo, slumped over in his chair. He was rambling into a microphone as he tried to record a captain's log for the black box. Edwin did not take that as a good sign.

As he came upon the man, he put a hand on his shoulder. "Captain...?"

Enzo struggled to glance up. He looked pale and feverish, going fast. He muttered some words but none of them made any sense.

"Lord Edwin!"

Turning, he spotted Narissa standing at the door of the bridge, motioning to him. As he approached her, she said, "Are you...well?"

Edwin touched his face, which was warmer than it ought to be. He'd felt lightheaded since waking up abruptly. He was sweating, and he was certain he was running a low-grade fever, but he hoped that having been off the ship up until a few hours ago meant he had more time than the others before he turned. The antibiotics he'd been taking might also hold off the infection for a little while longer. "Aye. Well enough."

She nodded, accepting that, though she looked concerned. "When I first noted what was happening, I sent a distress signal to Earth. The answer I got basically said no one is coming. They don't want to risk someone coming up here and taking the infection down to Earth. They suggested we appeal to the High Courts for aid."

He grunted at that. It was the answer he expected. Anytime a Court was in distress, the answer was the same from the humans: Go jump, vampires. Not that he could blame them, he supposed. It was pretty obvious they needed to be quarantined until they beat this thing.

Edwin looked his navigator over, noting that she was still wearing a bandage over her eye. Otherwise, she looked solid. "How are you, Narissa?"

She stood up straighter and opened her mouth to speak. But in that moment, Enzo turned and lunged at them both, a frighteningly feral sound rattling out of his throat. Edwin only had time to shirk away. Narissa, a lifelong warrior, casually stepped in, grabbed him by the shoulder, and shoved him to the floor, pinning his arm so he couldn't move or attack anyone in the room.

She bared her teeth in a fearsome grin. "Well enough and ready for action, sir." Looking up, she added, "Put me back in, coach."

He nodded to her and then looked the bridge over and its occupants. He had Narissa and he had Tommy, two beings who were unlikely to be infected. But Captain Enzo and the other humans would need to be evicted and put in lockup where they couldn't hurt anyone. Narissa, who had the most experience with the equipment, would need to man the gyro. Tommy would need to fulfill his duty as Edwin's Enforcer.

After he gave the order, everyone scrambled. Once the bridge was cleared except for the three of them—him, Tommy, and Narissa—Tommy came alongside him. "What are your orders, my Lord?"

Edwin's mind jumped around for a second for a solution to all of this madness before landing on the obvious one. The only one. The humans were useless; the High Courts even more so. He had few options. Looking between his two friends, he said, "I'm going to negotiate with Yrsa. I need you two to watch my back."

He hesitated, suddenly fearful that Tommy and Narissa might rebel. He'd never been entirely sure they trusted him to be the Lord they needed. But Tommy grunted and glanced over at Narissa, who gave him a thumbs up from her station.

"Yes, my Lord," she added. "It will be done."

* * *

Between the two of them, Eliza and Anjou managed to get every piece of furniture in the art room in front of the door as a barricade—the long folding tables used for art projects, the heavy teacher's desk, the cabinets, and even the small collection of student desks. Little Briar, Anjou's daughter, kept asking them what they were doing, so Anjou told her it was a game the grownups were playing and that she could help if she wanted to, which seemed to satisfy the little girl. She ran to a corner to drag some chairs over to the door.

Eliza found it brilliant the way Anjou was keeping the children calm and occupied with various tasks, toys, or treats. It was what made the woman a great pack alpha and an awesome administrator. When Simon began to cry from his highchair, Anjou turned to Eliza and said, "Could you find something for Briar and the children to do?"

She offered an apologetic smile as she began to undo her jacket. "Growing werewolf."

"Of course!"

Eliza hurried to the group of children, many of which had begun to cry fearfully, and asked one of the older girls to lead in a sing-along. While most of the kids started to get into it, she noticed Ollie standing off by himself.

"Ollie, what is it?" she said as she came upon him

He spelled out Ariel's name.

She glanced around, finally realizing she wasn't among the other children. She thought about going out there and looking for her, but she was afraid to leave Anjou and the rest of the children alone.

"Baby, I don't know where she is. She could be *anywhere* on the ship at this point, and we can't go out there."

"Why can't we go outside?" Briar asked innocently, drifting toward them.

"It's the game, baby. We have to play the game."

Ollie shook his head furiously. It's not a game! And I want to find Ariel!

His violent gestures set Briar off, and the little girl began to cry. While Eliza tried desperately to comfort the girl, Ollie started storming off in the other direction. She grabbed his arm to stop him. "I need you to stay here!" she barked at him, not wanting to upset him but needing him to understand. "We might need you to help us!"

Ollie, red-faced, finally blurted out, "You don't care about me! You lied to me!"

"Ollie!"

He pulled away from her—he was unnaturally strong for such a little boy—and went to hide in the adjoining room where they kept the art supplies.

For the hundredth time, Eliza tried to send Edwin a mind text, but she was still getting a network error. Anjou stepped back into the room, Simon on her hip. Eliza could tell from his sweet baby smell that he was newly changed, but he was still overtired and fussing. Anjou did her best to nurse him while walking back and forth across the room, head slightly down and worry lines cutting across her face.

"He'll be all right," Eliza reassured her friend. She sat down in a chair and had Briar sit on the floor while she did her hair in box braids. That seemed to calm the girl. "Malcolm is a tough guy. Nothing can get to him."

"He's doing this for you, you know," Anjou said as she swept by, and Eliza paused.

She hadn't expected that and felt a dull shock at Anjou's words.

Anjou eyed her in a funny way. "He's putting his life on the line to save Lord Edwin because he wants to impress you."

Eliza stopped parting Briar's hair and said in a soft voice, "That isn't fair, Anjou."

"Isn't it?" She lifted her head, her wolf eyes suddenly bright. "Isn't it why he does everything he does?"

"Anjou...don't do this."

"You speak. He listens. You crook your finger. He comes running like the dog he is."

Eliza felt her cheeks burn at Anjou's accusation. "He loves you!" she countered. "He had children with you!"

Anjou lowered her eyes as she bounced Simon in her arms. "He had children with me, yes. But he'd do anything for you."

Eliza couldn't bear to hear another word of this nonsense. She never expected this of Anjou. Getting up, she moved to the front of the room and looked at their barricade, her hands clenching and unclenching. Why did Anjou have to say that? It wasn't fair. While she had always felt an attraction to Malcolm, she had *never* acted on it—not once since Malcolm met Anjou! Malcolm's feelings for her, whatever they were, were not her responsibility!

When Briar started to cry again, Eliza chose to focus on that, hurrying to see what was the matter. "Ollie wouldn't let me!" Briar protested. She was sitting on the floor near the adjoining room, hugging her favorite toy, her bear-bear, tears in her eyes. Eliza sensed she was overdue for a meltdown and got down on her knees, pulling Briar against her and rubbing the back of her head.

"It's okay, baby. It's all right."

Briar sniffed and added, "But he wouldn't let me play!" She gestured to the supply room, and when Eliza went to investigate, a wave of fear ripped through her to the point of making her ill. There was a wall vent in the room, and it was askew.

* * *

The sight of Yrsa's pale, cool, familiar face on the screen dragged a cold finger down Edwin's spine. She was a beautiful woman when Foxley ordered him to marry her. Not the sharpest tool. She was silly and spoilt, always wearing the most up-to-date fashions and carrying that little white furball around with her. She laughed at all of his jokes, even if they were stupid. On the night of their honeymoon, she'd been so sheltered she'd barely been aware of what went where.

"Yrsa, we sent Dr. Pretorius to you." He kept his voice modulated to sound professional even though every fiber of his being wanted to scream at her and ask her what in hell she was doing. "We kept our part of the bargain."

"Yes, dear. That was very sweet of you," she answered, smiling wryly. "And so did we. Since the return of the good doctor, we've deactivated the cryo-bomb in your ship."

"You infected my ship!"

"Your pretty little wife did not negotiate that part."

He growled internally. "Don't bloody make this personal, woman!"

She loomed over him on the huge screen, her reddish eyes beaming malcontent. "All of this was always personal, and you know it!" Taking a deep breath, she let it out in a rattling hiss before letting him have it. "You up and left me. Walked out on me, Edwin! We were married and it meant nothing to you!"

He clenched his fist to keep from driving it into the screen. "It was never a real marriage and you knew that! Foxley set us up. Your own father sold you to me like chattel!" he snarled, which led to a fit of coughing. After a few moments, his eyes were watering and his head felt like it was in a vice. If he had any doubts he was ill and getting worse, that was gone now.

Yrsa gave him a sideways look. "What's wrong with you? You look terrible, little Lord."

He had to grip the side of the console to stay upright. The room was starting to spin on him again. "I'm bloody sick from the virus your man gave my ship!"

She opened her mouth, then closed it. She looked confused. "I don't understand. It should not have affected you! He said...he said..." Yrsa's eyes suddenly blanked out like she was having a seizure.

Edwin eyed his ex-wife in utter confusion. "Who said? What did they say? What are you talking about, Yrsa?"

Yrsa eyed him strangely before slumping forward on the screen.

"Yrsa? Yrsa, talk to me!" Edwin demanded.

Someone from off-screen reached out and dragged her head up by the reams of hair atop her head. When Edwin again saw her face, he realized something was very wrong with Yrsa. Her face was as pale and blanked out as a doll's. No, no...a puppet. She looked like a painted puppet.

The person behind her appeared on the screen. When Edwin saw who it was, he was both horrified and yet...not surprised at all. A part of him always expected this. He just never really believed it could be true.

"You," he breathed out low.

Crouched behind Yrsa, bent and twisted, one crooked hand latched onto her shoulder, the other sunk deep into her updo to keep her head upright, was Lord Trasch. The old lizard eyed him malignantly. "Lord Edwin, I see you're up and about." His voice was light and breezy, little more than a hiss of air.

Yrsa made a croaking noise and her head started to fall forward again. Trasch reasserted his hold in her hair and pulled her head back so far that Yrsa was left staring dead-eyed at the ceiling. Trasch eased himself back, and now, finally, Edwin saw the cool purple blood and other substances on his lips and chin and smeared across his face. He grinned at Edwin purply with his sharp teeth.

They didn't call Trash the Mind-Eater for nothing.

Edwin said in a low growl, "What did you do to her, Trasch?"

"We formed an alliance of sorts, the captain and I."

"Let. Her. Go."

"Captain Yrsa invited me aboard her ship. I am her honored guest," Trasch insisted.

All the pieces were falling into place. He might be fevering, but his brain was working just fine, and he realized he'd been had. His whole Congress had been manipulated.

"Did you set this up, Trasch?" he asked in a sibilant whisper. "Were the Jotnar even interested in Dr. Pretorius or global warming or any of that rubbish? Or was it an excuse to occupy us while your man infected my ship…?"

"Your accusations wound me, my Lord," Trasch said in a plaintive voice. Snorting in disgust, he added, "You are but a child, yet you play at being Lord of a vast Congress, the first in half a millennium. Quite the boon. Quite the conceit." He grinned, showing off those rotted, bloodstained teeth of his. "I'm simply giving you a crash course in Court politics, you little upstart—what you can look forward to as you attempt to 'run with the big dogs,' as they say."

Edwin clenched his fists, his whole being seething with his hatred. He had never before actually seen red. But he was doing so now. "Why use her? Why use Yrsa?"

Trasch gave him a bemused look. "Why not? To wound you would be but a moment's delight. But to wound one of your pretty pretties is far more satisfying…" He traced a long black fingernail down over the curve of Yrsa's cheek and she visibly trembled under his touch. "I wonder what your other pretty pretties taste like..."

Roaring suddenly, Edwin slammed his fists on the console, making the whole thing jump and almost knocking out the screen. He wanted to rant and scream at Trasch, rip the bastard to pieces, but he couldn't do much of anything because another coughing fit dropped him to the floor like a sack of concrete.

Narissa, who was standing only feet away, rushed to him. "My Lord..."

He motioned her back, tilted his head forward, and a spurt of blood dripped out of his nose and mouth, making a dark, unhealthy pool on the floor between his knees. He wiped the human blood away and eyed it with disdain. This body was nearly finished. The thought depressed him terribly.

It all made sense now. Trasch had been behind it all from the very start when he issued the order that Edwin take the *Abraxas*. The bastard set him up. Trasch had crippled his Court, hurt his exwife, and put his family in danger? And for what reason? To teach him some *lesson*?

"Please, my Lord," Narissa pleaded.

He let Narissa help him back to his feet—Narissa, who would have been his enemy in some other life. She looked terrified for him. For all of them. Grabbing the console to keep himself upward, he glared up at the ancient vampire in the blood-red robes. "I'll wreck you, Trasch. I will make it so you curse the day you were made the monster you are."

"Is that a promise?" Trasch asked, sounding interested.

"It's a prophecy." Weaving on his feet, he vowed, "And not just you. I'll wreck the High Courts. I'll make all of you Old Ones pay for this."

He might have said more, but something in Yrsa's eyes stirred, and, rather suddenly, she straightened up and became animate. Seemingly recognizing him, Yrsa gave a small, kitten-like cry, and her eyes filled with tears. In that second, he recognized the woman he'd married once long ago. "Edwin!" she cried suddenly. "Edwin, I'm sorry! I didn't mean...Edwin, he's hurting me! Save me, Edwin...!"

Trasch didn't let her get any more out. Turning to her, he grabbed Yrsa's head with both hands, his thumbs pressing into her cheeks to keep her from resisting, and snapped his jaws down on some unseen wound on the back of her head. While Edwin watched, Trasch began to feed, his ragged teeth crunching deep into Yrsa's skull while her blood and brain matter ran freely over his face and dripped off his chin.

Yrsa moaned deliriously before her eyes fluttered in pain and then blanked out. Thankfully, within seconds, she seemed to lose all consciousness.

He couldn't bear to watch this...couldn't...and yet he forced himself to. He knew if he had any hope of defeating Trasch, he would need to see this... remember it... burn it into his fucking brain for all time...

By the time Trasch was finished, so was Yrsa. She slumped away, falling to the floor off-screen. By then, Edwin was trembling and bent over the console. It was Narissa who leaned forward to cut the transmission so he didn't need to experience any more of this nightmare. He shook horribly and watched the drops of his blood—black and infected—fall from his nose and to the controls.

Narissa said in a tiny voice, "I'm sorry. I'm so sorry, Edwin. There was nothing you could do for her." After a long pause, she added, "What do we do now?"

Tommy came up along his other side, silent but stoic as always, but Edwin could feel his Enforcer's low-grade panic. They were supremely fucked, and everyone was looking to him for answers, and he didn't know what the hell to do. He could barely think through the horror he had just experienced.

And then, looking on the Colossus standing beside him, he suddenly knew exactly what to do.

He sucked in a sharp breath and, his hand, still shaking like he had a palsy, reached for the communication controls before letting them go. He realized he didn't have a good grasp of how the tech worked. Glancing aside at Narissa, who, over the years, had learned to do almost every function on the bridge, he said, "Help me. I want to hail the Oublies. I want soldiers sent here posthaste. Can you do that for me, officer?"

| **XXV** |

Marco Mayfield, one of the officers who guarded the brig, was writing his wife a goodbye letter on his tablet when he realized something was very wrong. He was telling her that he loved her, that he was sorry about what happened last week, and wanted her to get herself and their children off the *Queen's Gambit* as soon as possible, but paused when he heard someone call out from down the corridor where the cells were located. He tried to send the e-letter but got a No Signal. NEWTON had been going in and out on the ship for days, making mind-texting impossible, but he hoped he might get a letter through. No dice.

"Hello? Marco, are you there?"

He glanced up at the bank of security screens, searching through watering eyes and a crushing headache for the one he wanted. There. Third on the right. The one they had been keeping the vampire in.

His good friend Chappie was signaling to him from the inside CCTV, which made no sense. "What the hell, Chap?" he said, kicking his feet down off the desk.

When he got an alert that the ship was under attack by some kind of zombie-like creatures, Marco decided to hole up here and wait it out. He did love his wife and kids and all that, but he had no delusions about the dangers involved in searching for them on the ship. Marco had seen enough zombie movies to know it never went well. Right now, his wife and kids were on their own.

Then, about a half hour ago, Marco realized Chappie was gone. Probably went to do his rounds and check on the vampire. They were under orders to keep an eye on him, and Marco knew the great and mighty King Edwin would come down hard on their asses if something happened to it, which was important to him. Since then, though, Chappie hadn't returned.

"Chap, man, what the hell's going on?" he asked himself, looking at the footage, which showed Chappie pacing around the vampire's cell. No vampire. He didn't want to go anywhere near that grotty bastard, but he couldn't just leave his friend in the thing's cell.

When Marco pushed himself out of his chair, the warden's room took a half-spin around him, but he quickly regained his balance against the wall, then proceeded down the corridor to the cells. He moved slowly so as not to irritate his vertigo. He knew he was sick with whatever bug was going around, but he was also too damned afraid to step outside the brig to visit the medical ward.

When he reached the cellblock, he looked in through the bars and saw his friend standing there, looking annoyed. "What happened? Why the hell are you in there, dude?"

Chappie, who looked rumpled and banged up, slowly shook his head. "When I went to check on the grotty, the bastard grabbed me, banged me against the bars, and took my keycard!" He snorted with disgust. "Then he locked me in here."

"He got out?"

"Yeah, man. I'm sorry, man."

Marco glanced around, suddenly worried the bastard might jump him. "So, he's out?"

Intellectually, he knew that was unlikely. The grotty was Lord Edwin's Heir, Cesar Whatshisname. The stupid drunk bastard got himself in the brig after acting like a jerk—something Marco himself was guilty of on occasion. He didn't think the vamp was that much of a threat. Still, the idea of a potentially hungry vampire on the loose was almost more frightening than whatever was happening on the ship.

Chap shook his head. "He's long gone, man. You got your card? Can you get me out of here?"

"Y-yeah." Marco pulled his keycard on its stretch wire and ran it over the sensor, unlocking the cell, then pushed the door open for his friend. But Chap continued to stand there, not moving much. "Are you all right? He didn't bite you?"

Chappie's body did some weird thing where it almost seemed to ripple like an illusion. Marco frowned as he approached his friend, trying to figure out if what he was seeing was real or only a figment of his fevering imagination. "Chap...?"

It was only when he was inches away from his fellow guard that he realized his mistake. Chappie had called in sick today, some kind of virus. Marco had forgotten that, the fever having turned his brain to thought soup. By then, though, it was too late.

Chappie's eyes shifted from brown to blue. The face and body blurred as well. Microseconds later, the vamp grabbed him. Marco made a noise of surprise, but by then, it was over. The vampire—or shapeshifter, or whatever the hell the grotty was—had him by the throat.

Its cold hand was like an iron vice around his neck. Marco couldn't even cry out for help.

Another ripple flowed through the figure that was Chappie, changing it into the tall blond vampire with its icy white skin and startling blue eyes. "Sorry, pal," it said, sounding genuinely remorseful. "I have to get out of here and help Lord Edwin and the rest of the ship. You understand."

Marco moaned out a noncommittal response as the vampire lifted him high, his feet leaving the floor.

"Still, I wouldn't mind a snack to keep me going."

Marco started to scream as the vampire turned and thrust him back against the wall of the cell, pinning him there with no effort at all. Marco caught sight of its hungry black eyes and starbright teeth. The last thing he saw that wasn't bright red.

***

Anjou's tablet in hand, Eliza made her way as quietly as possible down the empty corridors of the ship. Even though the network was going in and out erratically, she'd managed to find an employees' directory on it. It gave her the floor and suite number of Ariel's family—the only place she could think of that Ollie might have gone to rescue his friend. After that, it was a quick ride up the lift to the fortieth floor where most of the staff had their quarters.

On the ride up, she thought about the last conversation she'd had with Anjou before she asked her to help her shift the barrier away so she could slip out the door.

"It isn't safe," Anjou told her as if she didn't know that already. "If you go out there, you'll be a sitting duck for those things."

"I don't care," she told her friend—or maybe ex-friend. She didn't know where she stood with Anjou anymore. Still, she didn't need or want Anjou's approval. "I'm not leaving Ollie to fend for himself."

She was glad she had the tablet even if it wasn't working properly, because the moment the doors of the lift opened, someone lunged in at her. She saw white eyes and bloodied hands as they closed in, trying to snag her. Under normal circumstances, she might have reacted differently, thrown herself back, or even screamed, but at the moment, all she could see was red. If these things had hurt her baby, she was going to lose it all over their asses...

With a growl, Eliza stood her ground and brought the tablet down with both hands over the ice vampire's head. She was a

Poppet. Her strength, though not nearly that of a Supernatural, was still formidable—still more than that of a human. She was built incredibly tough by her creators, able to withstand the preternatural abuse of vampires.

The ice vamp made a croaking noise as she staved its head in with the tablet. It went down hard. But then she continued to beat it over and over again until the creature stopped moving. She realized after a moment that she was screaming obscenities at it and had to stop herself before she attracted any more attention.

Panting and shaking, she took a step back. She looked at the mess she had created, then eyed the corridor ahead. It looked empty. "Ollie!" she called. She dropped the broken tablet and bolted from the lift.

* * *

"Yes...Lord Edwin, we...there..." Violet said. Her metallic face and voice were going in and out sporadically while the overstressed ship's network struggled to stay online.

"Violet?" Edwin leaned earnestly over the console, his frustration mounting. "Violet, can you hear me?"

"...we...four hou...and..."

The transmission cut out.

"Dammit! Narissa, can you get her back?"

Narissa seated at one of the ground-level stations, tried a series of switches. "No, my Lord. I had a downed network."

"NEWTON?" he called.

No answer.

"Can you get NEWTON up?"

She tried a few more things before shaking her head. "NEWTON's offline."

"Shite," Edwin said, breathing out harshly. Turning his head, he rubbed his face. "Did she get the request?"

"I think so," Narissa said, looking heartsick.

"She said four hours," Tommy said, standing sentinel by the door of the bridge and guarding it with his big gun. "That's how long it took to get back here from the Oublies. That's a good sign, right?"

"I hope so..." Edwin never finished his thought because a rumbling interrupted them. A moment later, a part of the ceiling suddenly collapsed over their heads, raining down wires and debris, and, with it, a number of ice vampires that had apparently been crawling through the ducts began to drop through the hole.

A pair of vamps fell upon Tommy, and one dropped down to the floor in front of Narissa, who immediately raised her arms in defense. Two nearly landed on Edwin, who stepped back reflexively, hitting the communications console. He twisted away as one reached for him with blackened, frozen fingers, a gesture that sent him sprawling across the floor of the bridge.

They chittered and leaped at him, moving incredibly fast. Edwin flipped the other way and grabbed a laptop lying on the floor, throwing it at the closest ice vamp, but it bounced off its face, barely even annoying it. The two started crawling awkwardly across the floor toward him, working in a weird tangent.

Swearing and sweating, Edwin crawled backward as quickly as he could, which wasn't very quick at all. His body was weak and he was growing more disoriented by the moment. The creatures hissed and crawled after him on their knees and elbows. It seemed they were only barely mobile at the moment. He realized after a moment that the horrific chittering noise they were making was their teeth clattering together—whether in cold or hunger he had no idea. Their milky white eyes rolled crazily in their heads before centering in on him.

"Shite shite shite!" he spat, squeaking against the well-polished floor as he propelled himself back. His should hit another console, and, with nowhere left to run, he tried to get to his feet, but one of the vamps swiped at him, ripping at his pajama leg and the skin beneath. He cried out.

One of the vamp's heads suddenly burst into black soup and the body dropped to the floor inches from him. He stared at it, then up at Tommy, who had fired upon it with his boomer rifle.

"Thanks, ma—" he started before the other one jumped on him, latching on like a giant tick, its teeth sinking into his shoulder. Edwin screamed in pain and outrage.

Seconds later, it too exploded before slumping forward. Tommy ripped the vamp off Edwin, who was panting on the floor, the fiery pain in his shoulder keeping him down. "Can you get up, my Lord?"

"Uh...." Edwin struggled to his knees, a hand clamped to his bite wound, but slipped in all of the blood on the floor. Tommy grabbed him and pulled him gently up. The whole room was spinning dangerously around him but he tried hard to focus. He was vaguely aware of Narissa shooting other vamps dropping down from the hole in the ceiling with her own smaller boomer, which she kept in a holster on her side. He focused on Tommy's hand on his arm. "Th-thanks, mate."

"You need to get out of here, sir. You're no good to us."

Edwin agreed. Bloody useless—this version of him, anyway.

Swinging around, Tommy called out to Narissa, "I need you to cover him!"

"Got it!" She swung around and started firing toward the door, picking off vamps near the exit.

"Go...go!" Tommy swung around, his boomer already taking beads on other vamps, and propelled the badly wounded Edwin toward the door.

***

"Ollie?" Eliza pounded on the door to Ariel's apartment, stopped to listen, then pounded again. "Ollie, are you in there? Can you hear me?"

She heard dim, shuffling noises from behind the door but no answer. She leaned against it, trying to get a read on whether the noises were human or not. In her hands, she clutched an umbrella she'd found lying discarded on the floor several corridors back. It was pathetic but also her only weapon.

When a hand fell on her shoulder from behind her, she nearly jumped onto the ceiling. She immediately turned and raised the umbrella high, ready to cave in the face of whatever monster had crept up on her.

"Stop! Please!" Cesar stood there, his arm raised as he caught the umbrella and stopped it from connecting with his head.

She trembled. "Cesar?"

They looked at one another for a long moment before Eliza burst into tears of fatigue and threw herself into his arms. He welcomed her, hugging her tight against him so her feet almost left the floor.

"Bad day?" he asked softly.

"The worse!"

After he set her down, she gave him a quick rundown of what had happened and how she'd lost Ollie in the ship somewhere, though she was certain he was with his friend Ariel in her parent's quarters. Cesar explained he'd been in the brig for the past two days, but it was okay. He'd been treated well.

"Why were you in the brig?"

He laughed it off. "I partied too hard. But the point is, when I heard the figurative shit had hit the fan, I knew I had to do something. Now, let's see about this door."

Letting her go, Cesar turned to face it. He slid his fingers into the crease where the door met the casting and ripped the whole thing right off, crumpling it like it was made of paper. Eliza gasped. Even after a lifetime of dealing with vampires, she never got over how damned strong they were. It seemed nothing could stop them.

The interior of the flat was unlit and utterly black. Eliza couldn't see a thing, but Cesar had no problem piercing the darkness with his vamp eyes. He recognized the signs of danger immediately. His eye grew wide, and he suddenly twisted around, grasping Eliza and driving her to the floor, shielding her as two ice vampires leaped out at them both.

Cesar grunted as the monsters pummeled him with their claws—Ariel's mother and father, Eliza assumed—but he didn't stay down long. Lifting himself slightly but still maintaining a barrier, he grunted out, "Go...go!"

Eliza scrambled backward and out from under him.

As soon as she was clear, Cesar did the unexpected and released his wings. The razor-sharp edges of the twin bronze fans ripped through his clothes and cleaved the head right off one of the vamps—which continued to scream as it flew across the corridor and hit the opposite wall, plunking down right next to Eliza in a muddy black puddle, making her jump. But he missed the second vamp, who went into a frenzy, perhaps because it scented the blood of its fellow.

Cesar cried out as the remaining creature tore a long, bloody gouge in his back. He flipped around unexpectedly to face it head-on, which gave the monster access to his face. It scratched and bit at him, but Cesar threw his hands up, lodging one forearm in its mouth. It tore at his sleeve and the flesh underneath. Cesar roared in pain.

Eliza scrambled up, almost falling in all of the blood, and snatched up the fallen and now bent umbrella. Bracing herself, she brought it down with all of her might over the head of the ice vamp, thumping it several times. Its white, pupil-less eyes rolled crazily in its head and, finally, it looked up at her, shifting a few inches up to take her fully in. Its lips parted and it made that disconcerting clicking noise before bracing itself to jump at her.

Eliza cried out, dropping the umbrella and stumbling back.

"Oh, no you don't!" Reaching up, Cesar plunged his fist into the creature's chest, the corridor echoing with a dense, wet, cracking noise. He then jerked his hand out, his fist raking over its shattered rib case. In that fist he clutched its soft, black jelly heart, which slowly turned to liquid that splashed over his face and chest, making him gag.

The creature shuddered once before falling upon him. Cesar kicked it off and got quickly to his feet.

Eliza lay slumped against the wall, her brain reeling with the absolute horror of what had become of Ariel's parents. She turned to glare into the flat. "Ollie! Oh, my god, Ollie's in there!"

Nodding, Cesar wasted no time diving into the room even though he was splattered with rotting ice vampire guts and looked like he wanted to heave. Eliza followed more tentatively into the chilled dark, her hand brushing repeatedly over the wall until she hit the light switch.

The lights flicked ominously before coming up, bathing the flat in a cold, bluish light. Eliza glanced around at the demolished living room. Chairs and tables were overturned, and even the sofa and loveseat had ragged claw marks in them. She felt her breath catch and she had to work hard not to scream in horror. "O-Oliver! Ollie!"

Cesar stepped out from the back rooms, shaking his head. "He's not there."

She didn't want to cry. She didn't want to panic. But a horrid chill flew up her spine and into her brain. Her baby...where was her baby?

A clashing noise made her jump and turn. She even raised her hands to defend herself. Then she spied the vent cover near the floor in the corner. Someone had pushed it out. Seconds later, Ollie climbed out. He knelt on the floor, looking dizzied and unsure.

"Ollie!" Eliza rushed to him and scooped him up, pulling him against her. Then she went to one knee and looked him over for any injuries. He looked all right.

"Ollie?" came Ariel's voice from out of the vent. "Can I come out now?"

Crawling to the vent on her knees, Eliza peered in. "Yes, baby, you can come out now."

While Ariel crawled out of the vent and joined Ollie and Eliza in a little huddle, Cesar made another circuit of the room before migrating toward the door. He looked on high alert, his wings shifting nervously around him. Considering his elevated hearing and senses, Eliza didn't like the look on the vampire's face.

"Cesar, what's happening?"

His eyes shifted around and, finally, he drew back into the room, though he looked regretfully at the crushed-up door. "They're coming, Eliza. I can hear them. The vamps are coming."

| xxvi |

Malcolm in his wolf form had been loping up and down the hallways of the floor that Lord Edwin occupied when his ears pricked at the sound of running water. It had become a singular sound on a floor that was almost completely abandoned and full of fallen personal items and loose papers. Still, he cased the corridor back and forth as he followed the sound, looking for signs of danger.

When he reached Lord Edwin's personal quarters, he slowed to a trot. The door was ajar and the interior of the flat was dark, though a shimmer of light flashed across one wall. Malcolm sniffed for signs of danger. Finding nothing too unusual, he stepped inside.

Lord Edwin's quarters were neither large nor elaborate, which was unusual for a sitting Lord. Usually, the ship's Lord had the largest quarters on the ship, rooms and rooms full of the Lord's monetary conquests and other signs of their status: Jewels, museum pieces, the best and most plush furnishings, dining halls, ballrooms, and, of course, the gloriously decadent Poppets' quarters, where the Lords indulged their deepest and darkest desires.

In contrast, Lord Edwin's quarters weren't much larger than most officers' on the ship, and he'd furnished it himself with the things he had once had in his townhome—his leather smoking couch, gangster posters, and wet bar. His only indulgence was a large, vaulted, two-story library adjacent to the main room for his extensive collection of books.

There, and when he had the time, he sometimes still worked on writing his pulp novels. It featured an extremely cluttered desk, which his servants tried in vain to organize, and an antique typewriter he was extremely attached to and wouldn't let anyone touch. He once said it was the same one Lady Eliza once used to type up some of his books.

Malcolm padded slowly through the library, down a hallway, and toward the shifting lights, finally arriving in the doorway of Edwin's bathroom. His servants adored him in a unique and wholesome way, and they, without being asked, had renovated the bathroom into a kind of Grecian paradise for him, with a large soaking tub, beautiful stained glass windows set high up that let in the carefully UV-diffused sunlight, and even some greenery hanging down from ledges. Thick white candles sat on several surfaces, but only a few were lit tonight.

Edwin sat on the edge of his beautiful glass tub while water plashed out of the handcrafted brass taps in the shape of a swan. He was swirling his fingers in the smoky warm water but looked up as Malcolm, a huge wolf, fitted himself into the limited space. "My war dog. I'm happy to see you."

Malcolm tilted his head, sniffing the air. He could smell the sickness on Lord Edwin the same way as it had attached itself to all of the humans on board the ship.

Edwin smiled sadly. His eyes were bloodshot and black circles made them look sunken and small. He was even paler than usual, disheveled and surprisingly frail-seeming, and though the room was warm and humid from the tap water, he had a blanket wrapped around his shivering, feverish body.

Malcolm's master considered him for a long moment before speaking. He mumbled almost as if he were delusional. "My friend,

I'm still waiting for the 'ever after' that never came." He glanced down at the water wistfully. "The life I will never have. A very human thing to do." He chuckled at that. The sound broke in his chest into a chunky cough.

Malcolm, suddenly concerned, shifted back to human, grabbing a bathrobe hanging on the wall so he could cover his nakedness. "My Lord," he said softly when he had a human mouth to do so. He looked him over with concern. "Edwin. You're not well. I can take you to safety. I can—"

Edwin held up a hand to halt him. Malcolm respectfully stopped speaking. Nodding, Edwin narrowed his eyes with determination. "I do need your help, my war dog, but not with that. Not with escape."

A sinking feeling gripped Malcolm then and he felt his stomach fall. He glanced at the water and shook his head. "My Lord…Edwin…no…"

"I need your help, mate," Edwin confirmed, interrupting him. "I need you to help me. I can't do this on my own."

Dread made Malcolm speechless for a good thirty seconds. And then: "I will do anything for you, my Lord. But…I will not do…that."

"Mate, I can't help my family or my ship in this human body." Letting out his breath in a phlegm rattle, he added, "Dr. Hans told Eliza I may be able to reclaim my old body with a shock. Something that could stimulate my real body awake—"

"You're weak," Malcolm protested. "You could also die the final death and never return."

"I'm dying now, my friend." Edwin's voice trembled with desperation. "I can feel this body failing around me."

"No!" Malcolm cried, clenching his big fists. "No. I will not. It's…it's not in me to harm my master."

Edwin smiled. "I understand. If things go the way you think, and I never wake up, Eliza will blame you. She'll say you were the cause, and that you cannot live with."

Malcolm blinked at him, stunned by how well his master knew him.

"I know it isn't about loyalty to me but to her. I don't mind, you know. It's bloody perfect, in fact. You'll do anything for Eliza, and that's what I want. But she can't defend the whole ship. Malcolm..." Edwin grew very serious then. "...I need my body back. I don't have a choice any longer."

The tub had finished filling. Edwin switched off the tap. When Malcolm made no move toward him, Edwin pulled off the blanket. His body was battered and bruised, blackened by battle, with long gashes in his flesh. He struggled to get down into the tub in his pajama bottoms without irritating his terrible wounds, but Malcolm couldn't make himself help him.

The water sat at the level of Edwin's shoulders. He gripped the edges of the tub and gave Malcolm a pleading look. "I can't do this, my friend. I'm not strong enough."

Malcolm slowly shook his head. "There are other ways. My Lord, I could bite you..."

"Mate, I told you: I'm not strong enough." Edwin sighed wearily. "I wouldn't survive it anyway. I *need* my vampire body back! Malcolm, as a father, surely you understand sacrifice?"

"I do, my Lord."

If he thought about it too much, he knew he would never do it. As a result, Malcolm moved so quickly that Edwin never finished his next argument. He was suddenly at the side of the tub, leaning over it, palming Edwin's face as he pushed him under.

At first, Edwin, his head resting at the bottom of the tub, lay peacefully, even happily. But soon enough, he began to thrash.

* * *

Their clicking noises escalated into a single, primal scream as the horde of ice vampires fast-crawled down the corridor and toward their little group. Eliza felt her mind separate at the sight. She was not afraid. She didn't have time for fear—not when these two babies' lives were dependent on her. She grabbed Ollie and Ariel and crushed them against her, then looked to Cesar, who gave her a reassuring nod.

Cesar, for his own part, took up a position in the center of the living room, an undead buffer, his posture alert and ready. His eyes scanned the room, and when he spotted the wrap sofa, he moved toward it, grabbed it as if it was a toy, and tossed it at the door of the flat. It blocked the bottom half of the door, but the ice vamps—blackened and crawling spiderlike along the floor and even the walls—just went over it as they skittered into the room.

"Hide," he said in an eerily calm voice. He crouched down, his wings fully extended and his posture predatory. "I'll hold them off as long as I can."

Nodding, gripping both children's hands tight, Eliza retreated to the farthest bedroom in the flat. Meanwhile, she heard the ice vamps chittering...and then the screaming began as they were wetly torn asunder by the vampire defending them. Bodies, and bits of bodies, slammed into the walls. An ice vamp shrieking its last was the last thing she heard as she kicked the door closed, cutting off the sight of the massacre. Ariel began to cry.

"It's okay, sweetheart," Eliza said, though she never paused as she eyed the room for potential weapons, an escape, or anything at all that might be useful. She spotted a heavy tallboy and headed for it. She started shoving it across the room, the bulky furniture squealing as she forced it to screek across the hardwood floor. A wordless Oliver got in beside her and helped her push it until it was up against the door.

"Thank you, baby," she told him. Just beyond, the wailing continued.

Oliver lurched back and glared at the barricaded door.

"Uncle Cesar will be okay," she assured him, not knowing at all if that was true as she pulled him against her. Rubbing his hair, she leaned down to kiss it, reveling in his sweet little boy smell, and told him. "I need you to take care of Ariel while I look for a weapon. Can you do that, sweet pea?"

Oliver nodded before moving to stand protectively over Ariel, who was sitting and sniffling on a throw rug on the floor. The sight of them made Eliza's heart hurt. Sometimes, she was so scared for what Oliver would become. And then, at other times, she was reminded of how much Oliver cared about his friends—how like Edwin he was, wanting to be the hero.

Sniffing, she went about the task of tearing the room apart, looking for a weapon. Unfortunately, there was nothing here she could use. Ariel's parents didn't even have an iron bed that she could potentially break apart into a weapon. The closet. She'd look there.

Eliza slid back the mirrored door—and immediately, something leaped out at her. She screamed in surprise as the small ice vamp—undoubtedly one of Ariel's siblings—landed on top of her, knocking her flat on her back and making her breath cough out. It was black and gangly, sexless, but full of bright white teeth and crazed eyes. It snapped at her like a rabid dog. Only the fact that Eliza had thrown her arm up in defense kept it from biting her face.

Instead, it got her forearm. Eliza screamed again as its jagged teeth cut like knives through the fabric of her sleeve and sliced into her flesh. She flailed in anger and pain, kicking at it, but it was small and gangly and she couldn't get her legs under it properly to throw it off. It growled and foamed around her forearm, now deftly lodged in its mouth, and soon her face was covered in its stinking black blood and droplets of her own red. Ollie leaped forward but Eliza screamed for him to get back.

He slid back a step, unsure as to what to do. But before he could react again, Eliza got her other, unharmed arm up and started beating at the creature's head. Her strength, better than a human's, caused it to squeal and let her arm go. Hurt and confused, it slipped a ways down her body and, at that point, Eliza got her knee under it and kicked it across the room.

It hit the closet doors hard enough to spider-crack the mirrors, but that didn't seem to even faze it much. It dropped to the floor but then immediately got up on its hands and weirdly backward-facing legs like a giant spider and lunged at her again.

Groaning, Eliza forced herself to sit up. Her mind was buzzing and her body filling with agony, but she only had one thought, one imperative, one reason for her whole existence: *She had to save the children from this thing.*

With no obvious weapons, she simply scrambled around on the floor, her fingers falling upon a large photo frame that had fallen to the floor—one of those family collages—and as the thing sprang at her again, she swung the collage at it, hitting it square in the face and knocking it back against the mirrors.

Oliver turned his attention on the creature and, reacting to the violence, bared his teeth at it. She saw the flash of his fanged eye-teeth, longer than any vampire's had any right to be. She saw his eyes go all blackity-black. "No!" she screamed at him, hoping he would understand. She did not want her boy turning into that thing!

Throwing aside the new bent frame, Eliza turned to the ice vamp shaking its head as it attempted to stand back up and screamed, "Me...come at me!" while waving her arms at it.

It swung its glowy white eyes at her and dropped its jaw, its teeth flashing at her as it let out that horrid clicketing of hunger. The sound of its jaws clacking together seemed to vibrate in the closeness of the room.

Eliza felt her body respond to the feral sound in some alien way she didn't expect. She anticipated fear. Instead, her anger skyrocketed and seemed to fill her. It felt like a physical force inside of her, swirling beating-heart red through the byways of her body until that force reached her head and limbs and all the outer parts of her body. Her vision went dark and then brightly lit in a way that was hauntingly familiar to her—like something she had experienced in a dream or nightmare.

She realized she had felt this once before, but, somehow, she had forgotten about it. Yes...the night Summersfield summoned her to the ballroom where he was killing Edwin. This was like that. At first, she couldn't see. And then she saw too much. She saw everything! She could even see through the walls and the humans' bodies to the blood inside of them. After that, her mouth ached like her teeth were too large and her jaws couldn't contain them. When she dared to touch her lips, her fingers came away bloodied by her gnashing, raggedly sharp teeth.

Even Oliver, so willing to jump in to save his mother, paused and took a step back at the sight of her.

Finally, when she felt her wings ripping painfully through the back of her jacket, she knew at last what had happened to her. From the corner of her eye, she spotted a figure standing in the corner of the room—one that was hauntingly familiar. A nightmare that had never quite let her go.

Tall and shadowy, he nodded to her, his lips drawn back over a bloody, victorious smile full of teeth.

"The Walking Man," she said, her voice strained and hissing out of her chest and through her savage grin of teeth.

When the juvenile ice vamp started moving away from her and toward an easier target, toward the children, she never even hesitated. She lunged at it, teeth and fingernails fully extended and her body humming with pain and power. Then, like last time, all went black.

***

"There has to be a way of getting the network back up," Narissa said from the captain's chair. She was mostly talking to herself, seeing how Tommy was stationed at the door of the bridge, shooting at anything that moved.

He was keeping his aim steady and his rifle set to its lowest sonic setting so he wouldn't blast the walls or ceiling. The whole level had already suffered too much damage, and rubble lay everywhere, as well as several dead ice vampires crumpled up and looked like giant insects. Live wires swung above Narissa's head, spitting electricity like angry eels, and each small sound in the grated ceiling above made her flinch as she anticipated another attack. But she continued to man the gyro as best she could. Edwin had given her the responsibility to keep this pile floating, and she had no intention of letting him down.

Three times a signal had come in from an approaching craft. It was still fifty miles out but closing in fast. She knew what it was, but without the network up, she couldn't receive messages, confirm who it was, or even get the docking gates open. That was going to prove an issue—a big one.

Turning to Tommy, she cried, "Can you cover me? I need to get to the Old Navigational Deck!"

Tommy swung around, the ponderous gun in his hands, and looked her a silent question.

"If I don't get the gates open, Violet will never be able to dock."

He nodded. "Do you think the old network is even still functional?"

"We didn't trash it or anything. And it's on a different circuit system. It's worth trying to boot."

He grunted and swiveled around, aiming the gun down the hallway. "Stay in my shadow. Let me do the work. No heroics!"

Narissa grabbed a laptop to use as an interface and got behind Tommy, who started down the hallway to the old bridge. She kept a hand on the knife in a sheath on her belt but concentrated on keeping the laptop safe from falling debris. She was going to have to let Tommy do all the heavy lifting—which was hard. As a soldier, she was used to taking charge of situations, but, in this case, and with her injury leaving her at a disadvantage, her most important task was getting to the old bridge and getting those damned bay doors open.

She heard the now familiar chattering before she saw the next collection of ice vamps crawling toward them from around the bend in the corridor ahead. They moved on hands and knees, their body twisting unnaturally. She angled her head to better see what was happening, keeping her blindside to the wall.

Narissa's sensitive ears pricked. One vamp was creeping up behind them on near-silent feet but even before she could say anything to Tommy, he swiveled slightly and nicked it efficiently with the boomer before swinging back to face the horde now moving in. Aiming once more, he took out the closest one clean, causing it to ping into its fellows. That caused the others to chitter in excitement as they turned on their own, attracted to its blood and entails.

"Jesus, they're cannibals," she breathed.

"We can use that." Tommy, a pinhole shot, cleanly blasted a vamp further down the hallway near the door of the old navigational deck. The ones not chewing on their fallen fellow turned to descend on the wounded one at the back. It cleared a temporary path for them. Narissa picked up quickly on what he was doing.

"I got it. I'm going through," she said, pushing in front of him.

"Wait...Narissa!" Tommy stated, but she couldn't. She had to get to the old deck.

She was ten feet down the corridor when she picked up on a faint rumble in the floor. She stopped, confused, before she could reach the door of the deck. She sucked in a sharp breath when she saw a towering figure turn the corner, the ice vamps moving aside for him.

The Jotunn Gorm stood blocking the corridor, glaring down at Narissa. She couldn't understand how he'd gotten out of cold storage—not that it mattered now. But, at least, the ship's infection made sense. He wore his cold harness across his burly chest, as well as a faint smile on his dark blue face. Slowly but steadily, the ice vamps turned away from their bloodied feasts and gathered around his legs, fawning like children. A few pawed at him. Gorm reached down to absently pet one blackened head. Narissa watched with quickly escalating horror as the ice vampire purred happily.

"Do you like my pets?" Gorm asked.

Narissa dropped the laptop and absently touch her missing eye. Inside of her, she felt that dangerous rumbling of rage—the same rage that had dogged her for her entire life. It started the day the Vampire Lord who bought her like some exotic pet raped her as a child, and it continued to grow from there. Even though Lord Edwin had taken her in, given her a purpose, no part of it had abated. It had simply been dormant.

With a sudden shriek, Narissa launched herself at Gorm, her knife at the ready.

***

Deep within the Hydraulic Protection Compartment located in another part of the ship, Edwin McGillicuddy, the sitting Lord of the *Queen's Gambit*, finally opened his eyes.

| xxvii |

"Narissa...stop!" Tommy insisted, raising his sonic rifle.

But of course she didn't listen. She didn't stay behind him as he had asked her to. And now, he couldn't get a bearing on the Jotunn without hitting her. His friend and fellow crewmember, her face twisted into a bestial mask and her wings fully extended, had thrown herself at their enemy and somehow gotten herself thoroughly anchored to Gorm. She had one arm wrapped around his shoulder and was plunging her knife into the side of his neck while he grunted and twisted this way and that, trying to dislodge her.

It was an impressive display of Fae ferocity. Unfortunately for Narissa, she didn't seem to understand that her small knife wasn't sharp enough to penetrate the giant's thick, armor-like skin. It only sank in shallowly, enough to make Gorm grunt and shake his head, but not deep enough to hit an artery and wound him. She kept screaming and stabbing him, anyway.

Finally, Gorm reached up with one gigantic hand and grabbed Narissa by the back of the neck, ripping her off his shoulder and flinging her down the hallway like she was a rag doll. She roared in anger even as she smashed into the wall at the end and then fell down crookedly, her head nodding into an odd angle.

Tommy turned to face the Ice Pirate, growling, "That was my friend!"

Gorm looked on him emotionlessly. "Don't care. Out of my way, metal man. This ship is mine."

"No!" Tommy would sooner blow the ship up than give it to the likes of Gorm. He lifted his boomer, centering it on the trunk of Gorm's body, certain he could do a fatal amount of damage. "You will go no further. Turn yourself in and face trial and I won't kill you."

Gorm laughed at that and several of the ice vamps gathered around him chittered in response. "You sound like a cop."

"I was a DEA agent."

Looking him up and down, Gorm snorted. "Was that before they turned you into a pile of scrap metal?"

"Last warning."

Gorm grinned. "One gun. Many of us!"

He was right. Tommy hadn't really thought this through. So, he raised the rifle, aimed it at the ceiling, and squeezed the trigger. The burst of sonic energy ripped through the panels in a bright blue burst, pulling them and the circuitry grates and wires above their heads down upon them all. The last thing Tommy saw before he was buried alive was Gorm's surprised O-face.

He snortled. It was bloody fantastic.

***

After unlocking the HPC from the inside, Edwin crawled out of the compartment and onto the floor of Eliza's guest bedroom. He fell like a block of concrete onto his back and simply lay there for a long moment, listening to his clockwork heart ticking along in its slow, determined, mechanical way. It sounded like war drums in his ears.

War...his entire ship was at war. War with those *things*.

He forced himself up, grabbing at whatever furniture was within reach to haul himself upright. He felt stiff and queasy.

Hungry. Aye, the hunger was upon him in a way it rarely ever was these days. Edwin drank the wretched blood substitute almost constantly; he was rarely entirely satisfied, but neither did he ever really hunger.

He was finally able to stand upright, held onto the room's dresser, and looked into the mirror. He looked gaunt and waxen pale. His eyes were an utter glistening black, and his lips, slightly parted, were drawn back and framed his saber-like eyeteeth. He looked savage. It surprised him, though he wondered why it should. He'd heard that vamps coming out of hibernation were some of the most dangerous creatures to encounter. Even loved ones were not safe.

"You need to pull your shite together, mate," he told his reflection.

It took enormous will, but after a few minutes of deep breathing, he was able to stuff the hunger down into a private spot in his being. He thought about hunting out some nourishment but then decided against it. He wanted the edge. He wanted the energy granted to him by his baser nature.

Then his bloodlink with Eliza hit his system, and it nearly crippled him. He went down on one knee, groaning under the weight of it. Ah. So, it wasn't all his hunger he was feeling after all. It was hers as well. And, via their link, he knew exactly where she was, too. Pulling himself back to his feet, he made his slow way out of his wife's quarters and into the corridor.

By then, he was getting tunnel vision. The corridor was crawling with ice vamps, most of them fully turned and chittering as they slunk along the floor and even the walls. They moved toward him as one, drawn to whatever life essence he had, but Edwin didn't even feel concerned. His brain and senses were in hyperdrive. As a result, they seemed to be moving exceedingly slowly to his mind's eye.

Long before the first one reached him, he grabbed it by the back of its neck and snapped the vamp into eternal sleep. By then, they were closing in, making a circle around him. One grabbed his ankle and tried to bite through the leather of his boot. Edwin casually lifted his foot and smashed its skull to pieces. When another leaped at him, he met it halfway, grabbed it by the throat, and flung it so hard against a nearby wall that it shattered like black glass.

The lift lay just ahead. He could not afford to lose any more time. He could feel Eliza's hunger and terror as if it was his own. It dragged him forward like he was on invisible wires. As the vamps came at him, he knocked them away, punching or slamming them to pieces around him. The journey down to the employer's quarters seemed to take forever, and he was out of the lift even before it was fully open.

The corridor ahead was littered with debris and vamps. He started out dodging them deftly as he followed Eliza's psychic thread, but when the vamps became too numerous and started to slow him down, he gave into instinct, loosened his wings, which split his jacket down his back, and took to the air. He'd never been much of a flyer, but in his present almost dreamlike state, he felt no fear as he launched himself down the corridor, pinging off the walls and, in some instances, the ceiling, to avoid the vamps.

In minutes, he reached the apartment where he felt her presence the strongest.

Cesar was here, looking on him in delighted surprise. The bodies of ice vamps littered the whole apartment where he had torn them apart.

"Eliza? Eliza, it's me," Edwin said as he casually shoved some heavy furniture aside and stepped into a bedroom at the back of the apartment. When he stepped inside, he found something he never expected to see. Or, perhaps he had but had never really accepted it until this moment.

Oliver and his little friend stood clutching each other near the wall. His wife was stationed in front of him on her knees, bent over a crumpled shape that Edwin took a moment to recognize as an ice vamp. The creature had only recently turned; it was still, to some extent, human, and it had contained human blood. Eliza, covered in that blood—dark and unnatural but still blood—was tearing into the remnants of the body, seeking more of the substance, her face wetly roughed in the stuff, her hands, hooked into claws, slathered in a way that made it seem she was wearing crimson gloves.

He stood and gaped down at her, his heart breaking apart at the sight. "Eliza? Lovey?"

She glanced up—and then snarled at him like an animal unwilling to share its kill, showing off her long, blood-yellowed teeth. Her eyes were as black as his, as black as a moonless night with no stars. He feared she might leap upon him and tear his heart out, but her face suddenly blanked of all emotion.

Getting slowly to her feet, she swayed a moment before speaking. "Lord Edwin," she said, and her voice was not her own. "You little upstart…you're pathetic. What did your master ever see in you?"

* * *

The rubble was heavy, but Tommy was strong. For once, he was grateful for his Colossus body and its ability to shift thousands of pounds of debris. Wriggling, he was able to slide first one shoulder loose, then the other. What followed was just a case of just shimmying loose from the hole he was in and climbing to the top of the pile. He didn't have the gun any longer, but that was fine. He only needed to do a military crawl over the debris to the doorway of the old bridge.

Halfway there, something lunged at him from behind, wrapping its burly arm around his neck. He knew it was Gorm by the way the Jotunn was wheezing through his injuries, and his unnaturally powerful grip only confirmed it.

"Let...go, wanker!" Tommy roared as he twisted this way and that, servos grinding and working to loosen the creature's hold. He could feel Gorm trying to do that trick to him again, to freeze him up, but he must have been severely injured and didn't have much energy to put into it. The cold trickled along Tommy's nerve endings but then quickly receded. Still, even without his cold powers, Gorm was strong and determined as he dragged Tommy back into the rubble.

Twisted metal exploded around them both. "You go nowhere!" Gorm growled in Tommy's ear. He even bit down on the side of Tommy's neck, though it didn't hurt and Gorm only wound up just growling in frustration when he got nowhere doing that. So, instead, he threw his other arm around Tommy's chest, his fingers trying to dig through the metal breastplate across Tommy's chest and presumably damage his sensitive nerve endings beneath.

Tommy, meanwhile, had been desperately scraping at the rubble around him, trying to tear himself out of the hole that Gorm was dragging him down into. He knew that once they were buried together, he was finished. He wouldn't be able to move and Gorm could take him apart slowly and at his leisure.

Above Tommy's head swung a light fixture on its wire, spitting with raw electrical power. Tommy let go of the debris and made one valiant effort to jump, his fingers just closing over the fixture.

The shock of power rolled through both his organic and synthetic system like someone was punching him from both above and below at the same time. It stiffened him and he gasped. A part of him even prayed this was the end. If he could take Gorm with him, it would be worth it.

Gorm screamed and shuddered as the current flowed through Tommy and into him. Tommy could tell it hurt Gorm even more than it did him.

Tommy mule-kicked the ice pirate in the groin area, more reflexively than with any real intention, and Gorm let him go with a cough of breath, falling backward into the rubble, his whole body crackling with flames. The whole corridor spat with electricity and went dark except for Gorm, whose hair was on fire. Although intense pain was radiating all through his body, Tommy hadn't blacked out. And, as far as he was aware, his body hadn't shut down as he had both hoped and feared it would.

Heaving himself upward, he climbed to the top of the debris and glanced behind him. Gorm lay at the bottom of the weirdly manmade open grave of debris, blackened and burning fitfully, his body twitching. After a few seconds, he lay perfectly still.

Tommy let out his breath. Was the wanker dead? He certainly looked it.

Crawling carefully over the ridges of debris, Tommy soon made it to a slope where the ceiling had crashed down. He slid carefully into the old bridge and stood up, trying to be gentle on his synthetic body. A quick scan told him the electrical shock had taken out his left arm and one of the servos in his leg was badly damaged, but the rest of him seemed to be functional.

He limped across the bridge to where the old equipment was located in a heap. Thankfully, some time ago, Narissa had shown him what went where in case they ever needed to hook the obsolete things back up. Come to think of it, he and Narissa had become good mates over the years. While he was reconnecting the old router, he stopped to think about Narissa, her body out there under the rubble, and his heart felt unaccountably heavy. Of all of the crew on board the *Queen's Gambit*, she, better than anyone, knew what it felt like to be an outsider.

He grunted out an apology to her. He wished he had been able to do more...

He didn't have a tablet or laptop, so he was forced to hook the router to his own circuitry through a plug in his side usually reserved for upgrades. The bulky device, so long quiet, scrambled to life, and he toggled a few switches to get the old network that NEWTON had replaced back online.

After a few seconds, a screen came to life in front of him. The old system worked differently. It didn't have the upgraded voice or mental commands that NEWTON had. One had to punch in codes and respond with keystrokes.

A message had come in about ten minutes ago—a docking request from the craft *Motoko Kusanagi*. It was accompanied by a note from his friend Violet. That meant the Mechi-people from the Oublies were here!

He wasted no time putting the request through. "The cavalry has finally arrived," he said to himself in the moments before he felt a familiar constriction as Gorm slung his burly arm around his neck and breathed a gruff "No!" in his ear.

It unbalanced him badly and he couldn't recover with his bad leg. The two of them wheeled backward, with the weakened Gorm cursing as they smashed into the opposite wall where a large pile of equipment was stacked up. Gorm's arm immediately fell away and Tommy swung around, taking a limping step backward that eventually sent him crashing to the floor on his arse.

Gorm, singed and ragged, tried to grab at him but found he couldn't move. He was hanging against the wall, a piloting gearshift sticking out of the center of his chest. He looked down at it and at the torrents of dark, bluish blood pouring from the wound, the expression on his face comically surprised. Shuddering, he lifted his head and eyed Tommy savagely. "She...will avenge me," he told Tommy.

Tommy assumed he meant his queen. "I don't think so, mate. When I checked the scanner, the Sky Shark was long gone. Yrsa left you to die." He felt bad about saying that—even to Gorm. So, getting slowly to his feet, Tommy limped forward. As much as he hated what Gorm had done to his ship and his people, he wasn't a man to leave a soldier to die alone. "I'm sorry, mate."

The Jotunn made a groaning noise of disappointment and blue blood bubbled out of the corner of his mouth. The light quickly faded from his eyes and his chin fell upon his chest, leaving him hanging there, eyes wide open, in a way that made Tommy feel almost sorry for him.

* * *

Violet never asked to be a leader. It was never her ambition. However, she had heard that sometimes you did not seek a calling. Sometimes, it sought you. And this seemed to be the case.

After Fuyuko went to her final death, the other Mechi-people were thrown into low-key chaos. Duties continued on board the Vault, of course, but no one was being particularly organized about it. Her people became confused and argumentative. It was not that they recognized Fuyuko as their queen, exactly. It was only that of all of them, Fuyuko was the most decisive. She was a thinker and strategist. She made the decisions the others couldn't—or wouldn't —make. Once she was gone, the Mechi-people found their whole world upside down. Even Lord Wincott—the Warden, a title he had held in name only—was gone. There was no one to lead her people.

Who would fill the role of queen now? No one wanted to step up. And the corporation was no help. The humans who had created them long ago were no longer involved in their day-to-day minutiae. Since the Mechi were efficient and unsentimental, the humans had turned the operation of the Oublies over to them entirely. They no longer looked in on operations. They didn't even create future generations of Mechi. The Mechi did that, a kind of synthetic reproduction, if you will.

That was how Violet had come to be. Once, she had been human—a brilliant computer hacker. She'd been quite skilled at cybercrime, but her friends had betrayed her, and she was tried and sent to the Oublies for a sentence of 120 years. She was fifteen at the time, and she had served a mere handful of her sentence when she became aware that if she did not get out of her cell, she would simply die or go mad. As a result, she had opted to become a Mechi-person herself.

Did she regret it? Was it horrible? She couldn't answer that question because she had very few memories of her life prior to her transformation and no details of the actual surgery. She did know that, unlike the others, she wasn't what they called "an empty." Maybe that was because she was a new, upgraded model. The older Mechi only had the emotions or ambitions programmed into them. Violet, however, could still think about things if she wanted to, and sometimes she felt emotions, too. Sometimes, she felt phantom pain in the body that no longer existed within her metal exoskeleton.

In many ways, it set her apart from the others. And maybe that was the reason she had connected so strongly with Lady Eliza. Eliza was a Poppet, but one that could think and make her own decisions. She felt Eliza, too, understood what it was like to be different from your own kind. Violet felt a kind of kinship with her.

So, when her husband, Lord Edwin, pleaded for help from the Mechi-people, Violet, who was monitoring incoming messages due to her good attention to detail, immediately responded. Since the Oublies technically belonged to Lord Edwin now, she knew it was their duty to go to him and help their new Warden. But, secretly, she just wanted to see Eliza again.

"We must send a party to aid our Warden," she told her co-worker, a Mechi named Reuben. "Will you put together a capable squad? I will act as the staff sergeant of the group."

Reuben looked at her oddly before stating, "Should I be taking orders from you, Violet? You're new."

"I am new," she admitted. In her mind, she frowned deeply as she considered her actions and their consequences. Finally, she said, "But I am asking you to do this thing."

"Fuyuko was our leader," Reuben mused. "Does that mean that now, you're our leader, Violet?"

She gave him a long look. "Do you want me to be your leader, Reuben?"

He thought about that for a long second before answering, "You're capable. Yes. I think I do."

"All right. I will be your leader. Please put a squad together and set a course for the *Queen's Gambit*. We will use the *Motoko Kusanagi*."

Reuben nodded. "Yes, Commander-in-Chief Violet."

She liked the way he had addressed her. She felt it suited her. And just like that, she had been promoted to leader.

In less than a half hour, Violet had her squad and her ship and they were off. It would take a while, approximately four hours, to intercept the *Queen's Gambit* in its current orbit, but she planned on doing the best she could for Lady Eliza.

She told the pilot Rahul to hurry. Rahul looked at her and, after a moment, said, "It will be done, Commander-in-Chief."

Again, Violet absorbed the way her fellows were addressing her. She enjoyed their respect. It filled the empty within her. It made her feel confident that what she was doing was good and just.

When they arrived at their destination, Rahul requested a boarding pass from the *Queen's Gambit*. Tommy, another Mechi (though not Corporation-made), appeared on the screen. "Docking pass granted. Please hurry, Violet. The whole gyro is under attack by ice vampires. We can't hold out much longer."

Violet, feeling quite confident at that point, snorted. "These ice vampires will be no match for the Mechi-people, Tommy." Whatever infection was spreading across Lord Edwin's ship would have no ill effect on her squad. The Mechi-people were impervious to human diseases, and they were even stronger than most of the Supes. She had total faith in her people to contain and neutralize the threat, and she told him that.

As soon as she and her squad disembarked the shuttle, she spotted the people in the bay, both humans and Supes, seeking a way off the *Gambit*. Thankfully, the *Motoko Kusanagi* was large enough to transport them all. And even if it was not, she could have her underlings pilot the other shuttles for their escape.

Her first order of business was to get the humans to safety. The next was to sterilize the ship. After giving her soldiers their marching orders, she turned to Rahul and Reuben, who had accompanied her as her Seconds, and told them, "You two are with me. We have a special mission to find and protect our Warden, Lord Edwin, and his wife, Lady Eliza. Then we must sterilize the ship. Do you understand?"

"Yes, Commander-in-Chief Violet," they said as one.

Using a heat-signature scanner, they tracked a small group of survivors to a room on the employer's floor. The signature suggested there were three vampires (cold signatures), one human (warm signature), and one indeterminate signature. The rest of the signatures were below freezing, which meant ice vampires.

"The floor is crawling with ice vamps. Be alert," Violet said as they came up the stairwell.

Using modified boomer rifles that were twice as large as the regular ones, Violet and her two companions started picking off the vamps as they lunged at them—something she knew the other Mechi were doing on other floors or anywhere the ice vamps might be hiding. The blackened, twisted creatures came at them across the floor, the walls, and even dropped down out of holes in the ceiling, but she and her cohorts had sighted guns and quick reflexes, and each carefully placed shot found its mark.

When Violet arrived at the door of the flat where the heat signatures were radiating the strongest, she found it was guarded by a blond male vampire who flew at her, his wings and hands extended.

Violet, whose reflexes were faster than even those of a vamp, caught it and tossed it to the floor on its back. It grunted as it fell. Before it could jump lickety-split to its feet, she stepped on its stomach and aimed her gun at its head. "Surrender."

It immediately held up its hands. "Don't shoot. I thought you were one of those things!"

"Obviously not." Glancing around, Violet stated, "Lord Edwin and Lady Eliza. Where are they?"

The vampire indicated the back room, which is where Violet ultimately found them.

* * *

Eliza's words jolted Edwin to a halt. That was something Summersfield said to him years ago during their titanic fight for this very ship. He went absolutely still and glared at her—or, rather, at the thing inside of her. "Michael. How did you worm your way out of hell, mate?"

Michael grinned at him through the use of his wife's mouth—an act that made Edwin want to kill him all over again, if that were even possible. "I never left, upstart." Still smiling, he added. "I'll take them, you know. I'll take them both. My Heirs..."

Edwin couldn't help himself. He jumped upon Michael, grabbing him by the chin so he could look into his enemy's eyes. "And I will defeat you again and again, if need be. Because I'm alive and you're but some shadow...some dead thing clinging to the living like a parasite. Nothing more than that..."

Michael giggled in response. His eyes blinked and then quickly lightened to Eliza's more familiar shade of blue. Edwin felt the shadow slip away even as the darkness left Eliza's body and she slumped back into his arms. Like the last time this had occurred, her vampirism seemed temporary, and her teeth shrank in her mouth and her wings flaked away beneath her.

Seconds later, the Mechi army smashed their way into the room. But, by then, the battle was already over.

| xxviii |

The fleet of Ice Pirates, sensing defeat, made a quiet retreat into the night sky.

All of the infected humans, including Dr. Veronica Vu, were destroyed in the Mechi-people's initial purge. But thanks to Violet and her people's assistance, most of the Supes and many of the humans aboard the ship survived the plague. Violet had Edwin's people transported to his new rig, the Oublies, where they received top-notch medical treatment from the Mech doctors and surgeons. Most survived, but most also decided not to return to work aboard the *Queen's Gambit*. So, in that way, Lord Trasch succeeded in his plan to shake the humans' confidence in Edwin's Congress.

During the initial infection, the Poppets, who were well-versed in critical situations due to the abuse they had received at Summersfield's hands, had quickly locked down their floor and were thankfully spared the violence of the attack. Because of their special anatomy, none of them were infected.

Ariel and the children barricaded in the Learning Center also survived. She and the rest were quickly airlifted to a nearby hospital on Earth, and, after a period of isolation, were found to not be carrying the virus—one bright spot in an otherwise terrible mess. Oliver asked to see Ariel, and, once at the hospital, he refused to leave her side, sitting next to her bed and holding her hand the entire time.

Eliza, who had accompanied her son to the hospital, was both proud of him and terrified for him. She had no idea if and when he might revert to his krsnik form. And if he did, what would she do then? No doctor on Earth (or above it) could help him.

Anjou made the difficult decision to leave Malcolm and the *Queen's Gambit*, taking Malcolm's children with her. She cited a need to keep her children safe and away from Edwin's Congress, which was becoming increasingly dangerous ground to live on, but Eliza secretly knew it was at least partly her fault she was leaving Malcolm's pack, and she didn't know what to do about that.

As for that night—that terrible night of her blackout—well, Edwin was very cagey about it. He said she had been injured in her fight with the ice vamp, had hit her head, and passed out, but she could find no injuries on herself. Still, no matter how she pressed Edwin for details, he stuck to his story.

Edwin, Tommy, and Cesar stayed on board the gyro with Violet and her people so they could clean up the last of the ice vamps. And although Violet, as the new leader of the Mechi-people, was obligated to return to the Oublies and take control of operations, she assigned her two soldiers Reuben and Rahul to the *Queen's Gambit* as an extra layer of bodyguard protection for Edwin, who was now, incidentally, the Vampire Lord of two vast gyros, a gigantic Congress that included the Mechi-people, and also the second wealthiest vampire on Earth (after Foxley, of course). He accepted Violet's gift in the spirit it was given because he knew that from now on, he was walking around with a giant target on his back.

After the last ice vampire fell, Edwin visited the gyro's non-denominational chapel and knelt to pray before the simple altar and the stained glass window of Mary holding the crucified Jesus in her arms. A devout Catholic in life and unlife, he hoped some pearls of wisdom or direction would fall from heaven and into his lap. But, for the first time, he heard no voices in his head at all. God, he decided, had finally abandoned him.

As for Foxley, following the battle aboard the Oublies, he disappeared mysteriously. Edwin even put a call into Mr. Stephen to see if the old boy had turned up on the *Gypsy Queen*, but Mr. Stephens confirmed that after Foxley left his gyro to help Edwin with his little problem (as he called it), he had not been seen since. Off to another little adventure, Edwin assumed. Because there was no way something like Foxley, even wounded as he was, was dead.

A few days after the incident aboard the ship, Edwin went down to the brig where Cesar was being held once more. After the ship was locked down and "sterilized" (as the Mechi-people called it), he'd politely asked Cesar to return to his cell and wait for him, which he had.

His Heir was sitting against the wall, paging through a novel he'd gotten off the library cart when Edwin arrived, but he quickly set it down and stood up, eagerly approaching the bars. "Edwin! Are you here to spring me finally?"

Edwin stopped and looked at the vampire behind the bars—the one he had made long ago. The one that was his. His Heir. He felt his heart tick slowly and dreadfully in his chest as if a weight were upon it.

"Edwin?"

It took him a moment to speak. "We need to talk."

Cesar looked unsure. "All right."

Using his keycard, Edwin unlocked the cell and stepped inside. The two drifted to the bunk at the back and Edwin sat down, indicating that Cesar follow suit.

"What's wrong?" Cesar asked, suddenly hunched over in worry. "If it's about Foxley, I already know. I heard the guards talk that he's up and vanished." A slow smile spread across his boyish face. "I figured since the old guy's gone, maybe I can stay with you a little while longer and we can have some time together."

When Edwin didn't answer immediately, he added, "I've missed you, my Lord." He reached out to touch Edwin's face, but Edwin caught his hand and stayed it.

"This isn't about Foxley," Edwin told him sternly. "And you can't stay."

Cesar suddenly looked crestfallen. "What?"

Edwin had to swallow down the emotions cutting off his voice and making it hard to speak. "I deeply appreciate what you did to protect my family. For that, I can't thank you enough. But I also heard what happened. What you did."

Cesar shook his head. "Then you didn't hear it all. I didn't do anything!" he insisted, referring to his assault charge. "That bartender just overreacted!"

"The bartender you assaulted was an ex-Poppet and reported you," Edwin told him. It was hard to say the next words but he forced it out. "We have a strict policy aboard this gyro. No Poppet may be touched or proposed without their consent. And we don't tolerate assault. Eliza wrote that rule."

Cesar snorted in frustration. "Let me talk to Eliza. Let me explain!"

"There were witnesses, Cesar. You broke the rules and, as the sitting Lord, it's my job to sentence you. My duty, in fact."

Cesar stared at him for a long, hard moment before sitting back and folding his arms. "Okay. So, what are you saying?"

"I have to follow the rules, too. That's how this Congress works. And since you broke the rules, you need to leave."

"All right. For how long?"

"For good. You cannot be allowed back aboard."

His beautiful young Heir blinked at him as if he were speaking a foreign language. "Do you mean ever? I can't ever come aboard the *Queen's Gambit*?"

Edwin swallowed hard. "That's correct. Your welcome pass aboard this ship has been rescinded for all time. You'll be escorted off the *Queen's Gambit* by one of my Court Guards and left on Earth with a warning to not return."

Cesar simply gaped at him. "But..."

Edwin stood up. Belatedly, he realized Cesar was grasping his hand. He pulled it away but looked down tenderly and with enormous regret on his Heir. "I'm sorry. It has to be like this. I love you. I will always love you. But if I don't enforce the rules, someone may challenge me. And if I don't keep my people safe, I will lose their respect."

"I...Edwin!" Cesar sounded on the edge of tears.

Stealing himself against his own emotions, Edwin turned and stepped out of the cell, closing it behind him. He left Cesar sitting there, gaping after him. His Heir. His hard-headed, impetuous Heir. He was certain their paths would cross again in the not-so-distant future. He just had no idea if, during their next encounter, they would be greeting each other as friends or foes.

***

One week later

Despite everything he had experienced as both a man and a vampire, Edwin had never considered himself a particularly vengeful person. He'd had his moments of bad temperament, of course, the way any living creature might, but overall, he considered his even, easygoing nature to be one of his best features. He didn't grapple with many regrets, and he didn't make revenge a part of his lifestyle. But he also had his limits.

And in the last few days, those limits had been reached.

As he carried his wife to the bed in his personal quarters and set her down, he felt her hand clutch his arm tight. She was looking up at him sweetly...sexily, her lips faintly parted. The white stripe in her very black hair made her even more beautiful than when he first laid eyes on her.

"Edwin. Edwin, look at me."

He did even as he joined her on the mattress.

Eliza felt it. She could feel it through their bloodlink. She could also see it in his face and body, the hard set of his jaw, the way he chewed his tongue when he was thinking about what happened with Yrsa. One would need to be blind not to notice his ongoing agitation. His barely contained rage.

Her hand tightened on his arm, her fingers digging in. "Are you all right? I wish you would talk to me."

He smiled down at her, picking his words carefully. "The painting in the ballroom."

It took her a moment to react. "The Andy Warhol?"

Nodding, he said, "I've decided to have it removed. It's bloody ugly anyway." He hesitated a moment before continuing. "I would like to do a family portrait—you, me, and Oliver. I even have an artist in mind. Not very famous, but she's very good. I know it seems old-fashioned, but do you think you'd like that?"

Eliza considered that before answering. "I think that would be amazing. But, Edwin, what I was saying—"

He interrupted. "Trasch killed her," he whispered hoarsely. "I know she wrecked my ship and caused you all of these problems, but it was him. It was always him. He preyed on her. Used her." He added, almost reluctantly, "He used her feelings for me." He didn't mention the other threats that Trasch had made, the ones where he promised to come for his family next.

Most of the Supes and some of the humans had agreed to return to their stations aboard the gyro. But many more of their friends were gone. Captain Enzo, Narissa, and Dr. Vu, to name just a few. They had buried them only the day before. The Mechi-people had agreed to fill in for his lost crew, but, honestly, nothing would ever be the same. Trasch had irretrievably damaged his Congress in a way it might never recover from.

Eliza nodded. "I understand." Frowning, she considered his words before saying softly, "We could still run away. We don't have to engage him or the High Courts."

He thought about that, turned it over in his mind, and then said, "Perhaps" even though he knew he wouldn't walk away. That he couldn't. He kissed her, touched her, and spent the next few hours loving on her gently until she had fallen asleep.

Eliza lay very still beside him, resting soundly, her hand in his. Edwin lay there in the dark, wide awake, staring up at the ceiling, his mind churning with mostly darkness and the blood-red things he wanted to do to his many enemies. The things very old vampires full of years and vengeance were wont to think about as they planned their next move.

He was becoming more like them than he would ever want to admit, and he would never say it aloud to Eliza, but what had happened to his Congress would not go unanswered.

ABOUT THE AUTHOR

K.H. Koehler is the bestselling author of various novels and novellas in the genres of horror, SF, dark fantasy, steampunk, and young and new adult. She is the owner of KH Koehler Books and KH Koehler Design, which specializes in graphic design and professional copyediting. Her books are widely available at all major online distributors and her covers have appeared on numerous books in many different genres. Her short work has appeared in various anthologies, and her novel series include *The Kaiju Hunter*, *A Clockwork Vampire*, *Planet of Dinosaurs*, *The Nick Englebrecht Mysteries*, and *The Archaeologists*. She is the author of multiple Amazon bestsellers and was one of the founders and chief editors of KHP Publishers, which published genre fiction from 2001 to 2015. She has over fifteen years of experience in the publishing industry as a writer, ghostwriter, copyeditor, commercial book cover designer, formatter, and marketer. Visit her website at https://khkoehler.net.

www.ingramcontent.com/pod-product-compliance
Lightning Source LLC
LaVergne TN
LVHW031608060526
838201LV00065B/4780